REDLINING

DAVID SETCHFIELD

The Book Guild Ltd

First published in Great Britain in 2024 by
The Book Guild Ltd
Unit E2 Airfield Business Park,
Harrison Road, Market Harborough,
Leicestershire. LE16 7UL
Tel: 0116 2792299
www.bookguild.co.uk
Email: info@bookguild.co.uk
X: @bookguild

Copyright © 2024 David Setchfield

The right of David Setchfield to be identified as the author of this
work has been asserted by them in accordance with the
Copyright, Design and Patents Act 1988.

All rights reserved. No part of this publication may be
reproduced, transmitted, or stored in a retrieval system, in any form or by any means,
without permission in writing from the publisher, nor be otherwise circulated in
any form of binding or cover other than that in which it is published and without
a similar condition being imposed on the subsequent purchaser.

This work is entirely fictitious and bears no resemblance to any persons living or dead.

Typeset in 11pt Minion Pro

Printed on FSC accredited paper
Printed and bound in Great Britain by 4edge Limited

ISBN 978 1835740 040

British Library Cataloguing in Publication Data.
A catalogue record for this book is available from the British Library.

For Mum and Dad

PROLOGUE

The sound of the shot seemed to echo endlessly around the small room, intensified by its bare walls. Jassim felt himself twitch fleetingly and knew he was still alive, despite the blackness that surrounded him. He didn't see the body of the woman as it slid from the hard wooden chair onto the stone floor but sensed the man was close to him now, his silent approach deepening his fear. In an instant the blindfold was ripped off and he found himself blinking as his eyes struggled to adjust to the brightness. Then he saw her, a rictal smile etched on her face as strands of her long black hair, now flecked crimson, danced in the cooling air of the four-pronged ceiling fan. An expanding rivulet of blood snaked down her cheek from the wound in her temple.

"Amira, Amira," Jassim whispered as he gazed numbly at her unseeing eyes. He leant forward, wanting to caress her, but the rope that bound him to the back of the chair was unyielding. He sobbed, his body convulsing at the horror before him. Then he became aware of a darkening shadow and a moment later, a gun barrel, still warm, was rammed against his head.

"Well, champ, are you ready to talk?" asked the gunman, his penetrating blue eyes demanding a response.

"My wife, she was innocent," said the Iraqi.

There was an impatience in the other man's voice. "Your house was a shelter for terrorists coming to Baghdad. Our troops found evidence of bomb-making equipment and forged documents." He paused for a second, his face just inches from that of his captive. "I want names, where they're from, who's funding them and likely targets. And I want it now!"

Tiny balls of sweat rolled down Jassim's face and neck, dampening the collar of his faded blue shirt. "We had no choice; we were forced to help them or we would die," he said.

"I figure your prospects don't seem to have gotten a whole lot better," retorted the interrogator. "Now, start talking."

Despite the heat, Jassim shivered. His mouth was dry. "There were three of them. They came one day and made us prisoners in our own home. They told us nothing and we were too scared to ask."

There was a renewed menace in the questioner's tone. "I'm not hearing what I want to hear and you need to understand that. The terrorists came to your area because people like you support them and they know they can have refuge."

Jassim sighed heavily, his shoulders sagging as he looked dolefully at the body of his wife.

"Tell me – where are they from and who's backing them?"

Slowly, the prisoner raised his head to stare at his tormentor. "If I had names, I would tell you. If I knew who sent them, I would tell you. But I don't have the information you want. I'm an Iraqi and proud of it – but I'm not a terrorist." His wrists were numb and he tried to move them but the rope that bound him only tightened as he struggled.

"I'll be the judge of that," said the tall American, a lithe and muscular man, whose fair hair seemed to accentuate his tanned features. He put the Browning nine-millimetre pistol on a small table behind the captive and started to loosen the rope that bound him.

Jassim was unnerved; his right foot began an involuntary but rhythmic tapping of the floor. "What are you doing?" he asked.

"I'm giving you the chance to escape," smirked his captor. "Just like the others." He slackened the rope sufficiently for the prisoner to pull himself free, picked up his weapon and moved a few steps away.

The Iraqi, no longer bound, rubbed his arms vigorously to ease their numbness. Then he knelt beside the body of his wife and stroked her hair. "Amira, my dear," he murmured and gently closed her eyelids before kissing her cheek.

"So, what's it to be?" snapped the interrogator. "Are you going to make a run for it?"

Jassim looked up at him scornfully. "You have taken away what was most precious to me. You cannot do anything to me that is worse." Still on his knees, he turned again towards his wife and clasped her hands.

The American started to raise his pistol. "I can't leave a witness to what's happened here today. We both know that."

Jassim, still clutching his wife's hands, prayed. "Allahu Akbar. Allahu Akbar."

The sound of the shot startled the birds. Wings flapping, they wheeled away, their fluttering shadows receding from the sun-washed building and climbing high into the afternoon sky.

ONE

Wisps of sea mist drifted sporadically across the track as a dozen racing cars, propelled by howling three-litre V10 engines, shattered the normally peaceful area of the Antipodes. As the sun pierced the clouds above his home circuit, New Zealander Pete Maitland knew he had something to prove. He darted right then left at the chicane and accelerated onto the long straight that hugged the shoreline of Tasman Bay. With fingertip control, he moved seamlessly through the gears up to seventh, and a glance at his computer display confirmed the engine was revving at close to its limit of 19,000 rpm.

The veteran driver had not achieved his full potential despite ten years competing in FS – Formula Super – the sport's ultimate test. Now, in the first event of the new season, he was determined to put his team – the American-owned Akron Racing – on the podium. The thirty-four-year-old had recorded the first victory of his career at the three-and-a-half-mile race track, north-west of Nelson on South Island. Maitland, Akron's number one driver, had cursed the poor qualifying session that put him at the back of the grid, but he had fought his way through the field and was lying fourth with just one lap of the sixty remaining. At 180 miles per hour, he was reeling in his target, the young Russian, Yuri Petrenko. As in the previous lap, the Kiwi slipstreamed the rookie driver for two-thirds of the straight – but this time, he told himself, he would make it count.

Watching the duel unfold on the small screen on the pit wall, Viktor Makarov sniffed through bad-tempered nostrils. The faded two-inch scar on the back of his right hand was still visible as he reached for the transmit button on the garage-to-car radio. "Don't let him pass!" was the terse command. The Russian driver, fully aware of the threat from his pursuer, gave the briefest acknowledgment to his team owner.

Maitland was now less than a car's length away. He ripped the final protective strip off his helmet visor and, at full throttle, feigned to pass on the right. The rookie, whose eyes were seemingly glued to his wing mirrors, immediately responded and edged across to block him. Anticipating the move, the New Zealander swung his steering wheel to the left and seaward side of the track and pulled alongside the car displaying the garish purple and orange colours of Makarov Racing. Overhead advertising hoardings flashed by in a blur of lost letters and symbols as the cars raced wheel-to-wheel at 195 miles per hour.

Almost imperceptibly to the thousands of cheering spectators in the grandstand opposite the shoreline, the Akron started to inch ahead. Its driver knew he had to overtake before both cars reached the braking point for the corner that turned right and away from the sea at the end of the straight. But Maitland was confident he could outpace the Russian as his car set-up sacrificed some downforce grip in the corners for straight-line speed. Now that braking point was just 600 metres and seconds away, with his car's engine screaming at maximum revs, the veteran driver began to gain on his inexperienced rival. The Akron's rear wheels drew level with Petrenko's cockpit as the New Zealander, in an adrenaline-pumping surge, sought to put daylight between them. His concentration was intense but he allowed himself the briefest image of a P3 podium celebration.

Maitland could see the braking point for the right-hander looming but by now he was almost clear. Then, without warning, Petrenko veered to the left and rammed the Akron, shattering its offside rear wheel and catapulting the car high into the air. It headed seaward, a broken, twisting projectile, scaling the tyre wall and catch fencing seventy feet away, and flying over boulders close to the shoreline. Securely strapped into the cockpit, Maitland vowed to confront the Russian after the race. Instinctively he continued to wrestle the steering wheel whilst airborne but was powerless as his car, parts of the rear suspension still falling off, somersaulted over Tasman Bay. The New Zealander braced himself as he plunged towards the sea but the Akron landed upside down in two feet of water and its occupant, concussed by the force of the impact, was trapped under the surface.

It took several minutes for three race marshals, wading through waves whipped up by a strengthening south-westerly wind, to reach the partly-submerged vehicle. The mounting swell hampered their frenzied efforts to right the car but eventually they succeeded. As they freed the driver's helmet and pulled it off, a torrent of water cascaded from it. His fireproof balaclava was then removed. Maitland was motionless, his arms hanging limply and eyes closed, but the rescuers could see his face was unmarked apart from an expanding bruise on his jaw. More crucial time elapsed as they struggled against the choppy water to release the tightly fastened belts that harnessed the stricken driver in the cockpit. Twelve minutes after Pete Maitland first entered the water, he was carried to the foreshore, where the FS medical director, Dr Rick Manvers, was waiting. The forty-six-year-old South African and two paramedics worked frantically to save his life, applying all the resuscitation techniques to try to stimulate a response – but there was none. After half an hour the driver was strapped gently into a helicopter and airlifted to hospital, but those standing close to the sea, watching as the rotating blades lifted the craft upwards and in the direction of Nelson, knew it was too late. The luck that had helped the New Zealander survive a decade of driving on the edge had finally run out.

Back on the track, Petrenko's car had lost its nose cone and the front suspension was damaged in the impact but he was still able to complete the final lap, although lost two places. Horrified spectators who had witnessed the Russian driver's ruthless manoeuvre jeered as his car limped across the finish line in P5. Confirmation of the fatality cast a widespread gloom over the paddock. Despite intense rivalry between teams and drivers, they knew they had lost one of their most respected and popular competitors. The racing community was stunned by the tragedy, made worse because of the circumstances surrounding it and that a driver had died in front of his home crowd and in the inaugural event of the season.

As a tribute to the memory of the dead racer, the chief steward, Floyd Collins, decided to scrap the traditional podium presentation ceremony and instead, trophies were handed over behind closed doors after thousands of fans, many distressed at what they had seen, had left the circuit. But victory was a hollow one for the aristocratic Spaniard with a playboy lifestyle who had led the race from start to finish. Count Rafael Luis Rodriguez had qualified on pole and set a new lap record for the circuit in his drive for the El Oro racing team. He was closely followed by the Englishman Nick Stallard, in the final year of a three-year contract with Gorton Racing. The Frenchman Philippe Guiscard of Drogan Racing came third.

Anger was seared on the face of Lucas Tait. His grey eyes moved restlessly across pictures depicting motor races from an earlier age hanging from a wall in his palatial motor home. The fifty-two-year-old American boss of FS had summoned the owner of Makarov Racing to explain his driver's actions that preceded the fatal crash. Immediately after confirmation of Maitland's death, the race stewards met to consider the incident. After viewing video replays of the moments before the high-speed impact and interviewing Petrenko, they disqualified the rookie driver and annulled the two points he scored. Tait's mood was not improved as Makarov had at first been reluctant to co-operate with the stewards' inquiry and only grudgingly agreed to meet him to discuss the incident.

"We lost one of our best racers today, a guy who gave a lot to this sport. Now he's gone and one of your drivers shunted him off the track." Tait looked across his desk at Makarov, his unflinching gaze demanding a response.

The Russian team owner shrugged his shoulders, triggering a slight movement of the snake-embossed pendant dangling from his neck. "What do you want me to do about it?" he answered sourly.

"I was hoping you might have expressed some regret for what happened."

"The drivers know the risks."

"They know the risks alright, but they don't expect to be sent hurtling to their death in the sea."

"Isn't that what you call a racing accident?"

"Accident? Accident?" repeated Tait in disbelief. "The stewards found your man guilty of dangerous driving and that's why he was disqualified and stripped of his points."

Makarov still bristled at the stewards' reaction. "Petrenko just moved across a little to hold the line before the corner. It was a normal racing manoeuvre."

The fingers of Tait's left hand drummed impatiently on the desk. "That excuse was rejected by the stewards. I've seen the video and it clearly shows Maitland had almost pulled clear when your driver deliberately rammed him. Petrenko has been told that if there's any repetition, he'll face severe punishment. And the same goes for you!"

Makarov stood up slowly and stared through sullen brown eyes at Tait. "Nobody tells me how to run my team – not even you! You may own FS but you don't own me. I'm warning you – I want a bigger cut of the profits and I'm not the only one. I have influence in the paddock and without us, you don't have a business." Limping slightly, the owner of Makarov Racing walked to the door and opened it before turning back to the FS boss. "You'd do well to remember that."

"And there's something you should remember," said

Tait acidly. "This is where the big lions piss – and in this game, you're still wet behind the ears."

Makarov spat angrily on the floor and slammed the door behind him.

Soon after the Russian reached his team's quarters, his mobile burbled into life. "Makarov," he identified himself peevishly.

"We need to move soon," said the caller urgently. "The judge has completed his investigation and is due to pass his report to the minister next week."

"Are you sure?" questioned the team owner.

"Yes, our informer has just confirmed it."

"Then you know what to do," said Makarov with a quiet menace, and ended the call.

TWO

A solitary powerful street light stabbed the darkness that surrounded the dacha. A chill wind scattered the occasional flurry of snowflakes in the direction of the small forest of pine trees that marked the boundary of the country house at Rublyovka on the south-west outskirts of Moscow. A lamp, encased in its glass and metallic cage, hung from a slender cord attached to a narrow wooden ledge above the front door. It swung aimlessly, creating its own transient shafts of flickering brightness. The half-timber, half-brick building stood in two acres of snow-covered grounds and was bordered by neatly-trimmed hedges that screened it on one side from the street, and on the others from neighbouring properties.

Inside, Leonid Andreev was working in his wood-panelled study on the ground floor. A slim, avuncular man, with befriending blue eyes, he sat at an antique mahogany roll-top desk decorated with an oval-shaped intarsia depicting a rural scene. Book cases lined three walls of the room, each filled with faded leather-backed volumes detailing the Russian legal system. A meticulously-angled desktop lamp cast sufficient light as the sixty-three-year-old judge leant forward, his ebony-coloured fountain pen moving purposefully across the paper. Occasionally he stopped to adjust his spectacles and to run a hand through his thinning grey hair. The desktop was relatively unadorned apart from a solid silver paperweight in the shape of a miniature samovar, a framed photograph of his late wife, Svetlana, and a blotting pad.

By any standards, Andreev had triumphed in his chosen career. A graduate of the Moscow State Institute of International Relations, where he obtained a diploma in International Law, he had risen effortlessly through the ranks of the Russian judiciary. Now a senior federal judge, he had recently been directed to head a commission set up with the aim of raising the professional standards of judges and administrators in the Courts of General Jurisdiction. He checked his watch and paused to sip from a glass of his favourite Stolichnaya vodka.

In the street outside, a black Range Rover eased quietly to a halt, its engine cut at the same time as its lights were extinguished. The driver remained in the vehicle as two other men emerged and moved silently towards the dacha. The shadowy figures swiftly reached the entrance gate, opened it and padded down the drive, their footprints disturbing the freshly fallen snow.

The judge's manservant of eighteen years was in the kitchen preparing supper for his employer when the doorbell rang. Nikolai Kamensky had the refined bearing of someone who had spent his working life in domestic service. A tall, upright man in his late forties, he paused in his preparations and considered who might be calling to see the judge. No one was expected this evening and it was unusual for visitors to arrive without warning. Nikolai wiped his hands and methodically replaced the towel on its brass hook at the side of the store room. He strode into the corridor, which led to the large central hallway with its luxuriant patterned red and gold carpet. A series of prints made from wood-cut engravings of nineteenth-century European capitals hung from the walls.

He ensured the safety chain was in place then reached for the door handle and slowly pulled it open. It was his last conscious act. The chain had barely travelled its full length of six inches when a nine-millimetre bullet ripped into the left side of his temple. Immediately, a second tore apart his windpipe. The manservant was dead before he hit the floor. The Beretta pistol that killed him had been fitted with a silencer. Inside, the judge was unaware of the drama unfolding on his doorstep. One of the gunmen used bolt-cutters to sever the door chain and they were inside. Two corridors led from the square-shaped hallway, one to the kitchen and the manservant's accommodation, the other to the judge's living quarters.

"Take that one," said the big Serb to his accomplice, pointing to the corridor to the right. "I'll go this way." He flung open the door to the first room he came to but it was in darkness. It was the same with the second. At the far end of the corridor, he could see a light coming from a partly open door. He inched towards it, manoeuvring his bulky six-foot-three frame with a sinister silence.

In his study, Judge Andreev momentarily stopped writing and looked up, perhaps alerted by a sixth sense. But he heard nothing and resumed his work. The intruder was now at the door. A furtive glance inside the room told him he had found his target. He pushed the door fully open and stepped inside, brandishing his pistol. The judge glanced up with a quizzical look on his face. He was about to speak when two bullets hit him in the chest. He slumped onto the desk, still clutching his pen. The gunman moved forward and at point-blank range fired at Andreev's head. A thick red mist sprayed over the report the judge had been working on and blood trickled down one side of the desk, channelled along its ornate carving pattern. The second gunman, holding a can of petrol, entered the room. He drenched the study and the corridor leading to the hallway. Both men stepped over the body of the manservant and from the doorway, one of them threw a lighted match inside. Within seconds the ground floor of the dacha became an inferno with flames shooting up the walls and spreading rapidly towards the study. The gunmen ran towards the Range Rover, which had its engine revving and lights switched on. Once inside, the vehicle accelerated fast and disappeared in a gathering snowstorm.

Twenty miles across Moscow, in the luxury penthouse suite of a city centre hotel, Valya Doletskaya was anticipating a busier night than usual. The capital was hosting a week-long international trade conference and a number of delegates were expected to enjoy some of the more sensual attractions on offer in a major city. But whatever the demand, the tall, elegant blonde knew she could cope because the variety of expensive services her team provided were by appointment only. She studied her client list, a veritable roll call of the glitterati of Russian society. Government ministers, senior military officers, bankers, lawyers and foreign diplomats were frequent visitors. They paid for, and demanded, utter confidentiality and that was what they got. Valya prided herself on the efficiency with which she managed the business. She had personally recruited many of her 'girls', as she liked to call them. They were all attractive, some slim, others full-bodied, mostly in their twenties and thirties, but she had astutely employed some in their forties and fifties because she suspected certain clients had a predilection for the more mature woman. She insisted on regular medical screening for all her staff due to concern for their wellbeing, but also because their clients found such health checks reassuring.

As she looked around at her sumptuous surroundings, Valya pondered what her parents would think if they knew of her current lifestyle. The twenty-nine-year-old had had a rural upbringing about 70 miles from Moscow. Her parents, like most in the village, were poor. Her father, Sergei, kept a few goats and chickens, and her mother, Yelena, earned a little extra money as a seamstress. The youngest of four children, Valya was a bright, pretty girl who loved animals and was devoted to her pet rabbit, Igor. Her parents idolised their only daughter and when she was sixteen, they had saved enough to send her on a school trip to the capital. It was to prove a life-changing experience.

During a visit to Red Square one hot summer, the smiling, vivacious teenager was spotted by the owner of a children's advertising agency who thought she had potential as a model and wanted to employ her. But first, he told Valya, he would need her parents' consent. As she swivelled gently on the red leather chair in her office, waiting for the imminent arrival of the night's first client – a former high-ranking Army officer – Valya recalled how her parents had initially been reluctant to allow her to enrol with the agency. She had never been away from home before and they found the prospect of her moving to Moscow a daunting one. But she was strong-willed and when they saw how determined she was they relented, on condition their daughter lived with an aunt in the capital. Within days of a successful photo test, the teenager had left home and her tearful parents, and found herself in the heart of a city that excited her. She found the agency owner, Boris Petrovin, a kindly and patient middle-aged man who treated and paid her well.

At first she modelled clothes and headwear for clients of the agency who were targeting the teenage market. It was almost a year after she started work when her boss told Valya that a lingerie manufacturer had asked him to provide a model to display their latest underwear. A leading photographic agency had been commissioned by the company to produce the colour pictures to be used in the marketing campaign. Boris had seemed a little embarrassed when asking her to accept the job but he stressed it was a lucrative contract and she would be well rewarded. She laughed inwardly now as she remembered how she had agreed without hesitation to do the work because she was proud and confident of her body. At seventeen, Valya was well-developed and she knew her bulbous breasts and long, alluring legs were assets she could exploit. She found the photographer, Anatoly Tarasov, to be a perfectionist in his work and the sessions at his studio were intense. He was exacting of himself and his subject in terms of diversity of pose, and a wide range of lingerie necessitated frequent changes for her. The nature of the product also called for a variety of props, including a large sofa that converted into a double bed.

A tall, lean man with dark collar-length hair, Tarasov was talented and ambitious. The thirty-two-year-old combined flair with a sedulous approach to every assignment and this one was no different. Valya was intrigued by him – although he wasn't handsome in the conventional sense, he exuded a certain charm and she liked that. They worked together for nearly a week but the memory of what happened one afternoon still made her catch her breath. It had been a sweltering July day; the two rectangular windows of the first-floor room were fully open and a cooling fan hummed soothingly on a table. She had been reclining on the bed clad only in a cerise-coloured bra and panties that were trimmed with lace. As she sipped a glass of water, Tarasov stood over her and kissed her lightly on the cheek.

"My work takes everything," he had said. "I have to give so much but I have to demand so much of you as well."

"Have you noticed me protesting?" Valya smiled as she put the glass on a bedside cabinet.

"I wasn't sure how you would react. For all its glamour, this is a tough business and you are still so young."

"I know, it's hard sometimes but it's what I want."

"Posing for the camera, constantly being on show, having to create the right look, requires a special discipline and not everyone has it."

"So, what's the verdict then? Do I have what it takes?"

He paused for a moment then sat down on the bed. "I think you know the answer to that."

He leant across and, placing his lips gently on hers, ran his hand slowly through her shoulder-length hair. Valya trembled for a moment then pulled him closer as she felt a sense of arousal. She didn't resist as he unclipped her bra and her heaving breasts were unbounded. She helped him pull off his shirt and within seconds both were naked. She gasped as his lips explored her and a desire she had never known before coursed through her body. Despite his passion, he touched her with a tenderness she had not imagined possible and she responded with an ardour that matched his. Valya had closed her eyes and quivered as Tarasov surged within her, and anticipation turned to fulfilment.

"Good evening, my dear." Valya recognised the voice instantly and she swung around on her chair. Standing at her open office door was the familiar figure of Vladimir Morozov, General-Colonel of the Russian Federation. Now in his late sixties, he tried to retain the military bearing of a man who had devoted his professional life to the service of his country. But time and extravagant living had taken their toll and the balding former government adviser on the armed forces had started to stoop and looked overweight in a brown serge suit. Dull grey eyes were deep-set into a gnarled face and a stern-looking mouth hinted at a lack of compassion.

"Good evening, General. We've been expecting you," answered Valya as she rose from her chair to greet him. She turned her head as he tried to kiss her but he was insistent.

"I like to feel welcome when I come here. The motherland gives me a good pension but what you provide is not cheap."

"You are always welcome, General, and you know that what you get here is the best."

"I'm not so sure," Morozov retorted. He stared intently into Valya's lustrous blue eyes. "Why are *you* never available?"

A scintilla of a blush crossed her face. "Now, General,

you know the rules as well as anyone. And as a soldier, you also know they have to be obeyed."

"That's right, but sometimes we had to make new rules."

"That may well have been true when you were in command, but here I'm in charge!" Valya laughed then took his arm and led him towards one of several bedrooms at the far end of the suite. "I know you wanted a change so tonight the lovely Anna will be your hostess. She hasn't been with us long but she is very affectionate and I'm sure you'll be well looked after."

Valya stepped into the lavishly furnished bedroom. The object of the General's protracted gaze was in a tight-fitting and revealing lime-coloured dress and lying on a chaise-longue. "Anna, this is General-Colonel Morozov. He is your guest tonight."

The dark-haired, curvaceous woman in her mid-thirties stood up at once. "Good evening, General."

Morozov nodded in her direction then quickly surveyed the room. The king-size bed with black silken sheets caught his eye first. He observed that the sheets matched the colour of the long velvet curtains, which were fully drawn. Suspended from the high ceiling was an ornate chandelier, its lights dimmed, and to the side of the bed was a table on which rested a bottle of Mumm Grand Cru champagne and two crystal flute glasses. At a corner of the bedroom was a door that led to an en-suite bathroom.

"You'll have a drink, General?" smiled Anna as she filled both glasses and handed him one.

Valya prepared to leave the room. "The General is a special client, Anna. He's a war hero and served his country with distinction. I know you'll do whatever's needed to help him relax." She smiled at both of them then closed the door and returned to her office. Once inside she locked herself in and walked a few paces to where an oil painting depicting a Siberian landscape was hanging. She activated a remote control and the section of wall holding the picture moved silently to one side to reveal a safe. She tapped in the code and opened the large reinforced metal container that held thousands of rouble notes. The business generated substantial profits and her boss had ruled that all clients, without exception, must pay for services in advance and in cash. It made for simpler accounting, the patrons didn't object and, Valya reasoned, it kept the tax authorities at bay and facilitated a high degree of money laundering. She seized a pile of notes, locked the safe, re-positioned the picture and strode to the desk, where she placed the money in her handbag. A hurried glance at the appointments list told her the next client, a leading lawyer, was due in a little over fifteen minutes.

THREE

A gentle Mediterranean swell lapped against the big yacht, the hawsers tying it to the quayside creaking sporadically as the vessel rode the tide. With an overall length of forty-two metres, the FS – registered at Nassau in the Bahamas – occupied one of the larger berths on Quay Zero at Puerto Banús on Spain's Costa del Sol. The 1100-ton, diesel-powered, twin-screw ship had a maximum speed of over 30 knots, with a range of more than 600 miles when cruising. With ten guest berths and a crew of eight, the yacht was lavishly furnished throughout. Forty-inch plasma televisions and hi-fi surround systems were installed in the living rooms and, for the more adventurous, two jet skis were stowed in the stern garage.

The salty tang of the sea wafted on a stiffening northerly breeze blowing towards La Concha Mountain, the spectacular backdrop to the port and to Marbella, six kilometres to the east. Passers-by, strolling along Muelle de Benabola, ogled the larger luxury yachts and a handful of brightly coloured, high-performance sports cars parked in reserved spaces on the dockside. Across the road stood the circular edifice housing the port's administration offices, its light-brown stone structure and brown painted windows in stark contrast to the gleaming white boats at their moorings. The fronds of the palm trees at the front of the building swayed in harmony with the breeze and close by, an ancient black cannon pointed impotently towards the sea-going leviathans.

Just yards away, at the southernmost tip of the quay, the monument to Don Juan stood sentinel-like at the harbour entrance. Scores of smaller boats, including charter craft for fishing trips, shifted lazily at their berths at the eastern end of the marina. Nearby, expensively clothed women marched doggedly between the stores of the leading fashion houses in search of eye-catching dresses and the latest range of designer shoes, handbags and jewellery. Tourists sat idly at waterfront bars and restaurants, looking up at the yacht masts and watching the flags flailing at the sky. A light aircraft droned steadily overhead, a banner billowing behind it advertising a disco party at one of the area's numerous nightclubs.

Aboard the FS, Lucas Tait went to the bar and poured himself a chilled beer and one for his visitor who had arrived minutes before. They were alone in the main saloon; the aft sliding door – made of stainless steel and safety glass – was closed as the host wanted total privacy for the meeting of the two men. They were seated on separate black leather sofas, a glass-topped coffee table squatted between them. A deep pile aquamarine carpet partly covered the floor and the mahogany and marble interior added to the sense of opulence. Tait eyed his compatriot keenly, the hum of the air-conditioning unit barely audible.

"Mr Wyatt, I guess you're wondering why I had you flown across the Atlantic to the coast of southern Spain."

"Well, it had kinda crossed my mind," said the fair-haired Californian slowly. "I figure it's a long way to come just to get a free beer, even if it is by private jet."

A glimmer of a smile crossed Tait's face but it quickly vanished. "I'm not in the business of wasting my time or that of other people. I never have and I'm not about to start now." He paused to sip his drink. "I have a certain problem that needs fixing and I'm told you're one of the best at what you do. I know—"

"I *am* the best," Wyatt interrupted. "Your contacts should know that. My record speaks for itself."

"I've done my research – if I hadn't, you wouldn't be here. I'm aware you haven't been active lately but I was assured you were available."

"You may be surprised to hear this from a man in my profession, but I don't take every job I'm offered."

"I thought a man for hire was exactly that," said Tait coolly.

"It's not always about money, although when I take an assignment the fee has to reflect the degree of difficulty involved. No, what's more important to me is that society in general will benefit from what I do – but if I feel a contract is not justified, I won't take it."

"How can a man in your line of business have those sorts of scruples? It doesn't add up."

Wyatt's piercing blue eyes flashed angrily. "Don't question my motives or the way I operate. We all have choices to make whatever we do – and I'm no different. Maybe it's my way of justifying what I do."

Tait, his dark hair receding at the front, fixed the American with a steely look. "Wyatt, let's get one thing straight. I have a serious proposition to put to you but if you turn it down that's the end of the matter. You don't breathe a word to anyone. Got it?"

"That's just how I like it and don't forget, it cuts both ways."

Tait got up and went to his desk and from one of the drawers pulled out a manila envelope. He handed it to Wyatt. "This is my problem."

The back of the car twitched and threatened to break away as it exited the 140-miles-per-hour left-hander but a deft correction of the steering wheel brought it back under control. Kate Lockhart swore silently. It had been a near-perfect lap until that point but she knew the error would cost her two-tenths of a second on the lap time. The test session at the track in southern Germany had already lasted ninety minutes but she radioed the Gorton Racing engineers in the pits to say she would try another lap. The team was working to improve the balance of the car before the next race at Kowloon, Hong Kong. After the first three rounds of the FS championship, Gorton's number one driver, Nick Stallard, was joint leader but there was concern about the performance of the number two, Luigi Corazza. He had yet to score a point and the Italian had been at fault in the second race when he spun off the track, badly damaging the car's front suspension, and failed to finish.

Lockhart flattened the throttle as she approached the start-finish line and was determined to record her fastest time of the morning. One minute and twenty-three point six seconds later she had done exactly that. Another lap to slow down and the twenty-four-year-old from Chicago pointed the test car, in the team's distinctive black and green livery, down the pit lane. Mechanics manoeuvred the vehicle into the garage and unfastened the restraining belts and Lockhart pulled her five-foot-seven-inch figure out of the cockpit. She removed her helmet, flame-proof balaclava and neck brace, and her sweat-drenched raven hair tumbled to her shoulders. She spent the next hour with the engineers, analysing the telemetry data from the session. Although the American had adjusted the balance of the car while driving, she had been unable to achieve equal grip between the front and rear tyres.

"Kate, the boss wants to see you when you've finished the debrief," shouted a mechanic from the garage entrance.

Ten minutes later she walked the thirty metres to the motor home of the team owner. Joe Gorton was a no-nonsense, self-made man from the north of England who had built up a fortune by shrewdly acquiring unused land in run-down areas that he calculated had development potential. And so it proved. When state-funded regional regeneration schemes were implemented, his foresight paid off and he commercially exploited his growing land bank. His millions allowed him to indulge his passion for motor sport and, following an abortive joint venture, he had formed his own race team.

Lockhart reached the door, pushed it open and went inside. Gorton's burly figure was resting on the edge of his desk when the driver entered.

"Good to see you, Kate. That was some test session." He walked across and embraced her.

"Not bad," she answered, "but I'm still not entirely happy with the car's set-up."

The owner gestured towards two armchairs in the

corner of the room. "The chief engineer tells me your lap time was just three-tenths off the record for this circuit – and you hadn't driven here before this week."

"I'm a quick learner but I know I can go even faster once the car is properly balanced."

Gorton, in his late fifties, casually pushed a lock of light-brown hair back from his forehead. "I've been impressed with the way you've performed as our test driver. Car reliability is key in this business and you've put in the miles and given valuable feedback."

"It's all part of the job description and it's what I signed up for."

"I know, but I've decided you deserve your big chance – I'm going to give you a drive in the next race." Lockhart took a sharp intake of breath as the team owner continued. "I'm very disappointed with Luigi's efforts so far this season. He's not been competitive despite being in a good car and he's a bit accident-prone. So I've told him you'll be replacing him as the number two driver."

The American's hazel eyes lit up at the prospect of what lay ahead. "Oh, Joe, I can't believe it – it's such an opportunity for me."

"You're a feisty woman but you need to be – this is a tough environment in which to make it, but for a woman it's even harder. You'll be the first to compete at this level in a male-dominated sport but I believe you can cope with the pressure."

"I really appreciate your faith in me. I won't let you down."

"I know you won't." He looked thoughtfully at her then went on. "I want you to know that, whatever our personal situation, you are here on merit and nothing else."

Lockhart, still in her racing overalls, nodded. "As long as we're both comfortable with it and can handle it, it's not an issue."

"I think we should celebrate your promotion, Kate. While you get a shower I'll prepare the champagne." She gave him a knowing smile and headed for the en-suite bathroom. Shortly after, she emerged with just a large towel draped around her and joined Gorton in the bedroom.

Wyatt reached inside the envelope and found a seven-by-five-inch colour photo. Tait pre-empted the obvious question. "He's a Russian, by the name of Makarov... Viktor Makarov. He's forty-two and he's ruthless. He's trying to muscle in on my business – and I don't like it!"

"I've done my research, too, and found you're running quite an enterprise."

"I inherited a family-run karting company that had two tracks in upstate New York and I expanded it across the States. Then I turned it into what it is today: a global motor sport empire where the world's best drivers compete against each other. I'm the commercial rights holder and I ain't gonna stand by and let an outsider cash in at my expense."

Wyatt studied the photo. "What's his background?"

"Ostensibly he runs Makarov Racing, the first Russian outfit to challenge in FS, but it seems to be a front for his other less savoury business dealings. I've done some digging and discovered he has links to organised crime in Moscow and one outlet for the money laundering is through the funding of the racing team. This is an expensive sport and with technological advances, costs can spiral out of control. This led to one of our smaller independent teams struggling not only to remain competitive on the track but to stay in business, and eventually it had to pull out. That left a vacancy and such was the interest generated, I had more than a dozen applications to fill the position, including one from Makarov." Tait sipped his beer. "I had wanted to expand FS and broaden its appeal for some time and taking on a Russian entry would do just that and facilitate the first race to be staged in Moscow. Makarov met all the financial criteria and I awarded him a place on the grid – but it was a bad call on my part."

"How come?"

"Last season, his first in the championship, the team was banned for two races after the stewards discovered they were cheating by installing a second fuel tank. It was a little one, admittedly, but the smallest margins can be crucial in gaining an edge over the opposition in a sport like ours."

"So who dishes out the punishment around here?" asked Wyatt.

"My chief steward, Floyd Collins, deserves the credit for nailing Makarov Racing on that breach of the regulations – he needed to be tenacious and he was. Make no mistake, I control FS with an iron fist, but Floyd is my right-hand man. We've worked together for some years and I trust him completely to deal with the stewardship role and administer any discipline that's needed."

"But you say Makarov is ruthless."

"He is. Last month his leading driver, Petrenko, caused the death of one of our veteran racers, Pete Maitland, at a coastal circuit in New Zealand. The young Russian, who's in his rookie season with us, has immense potential but he also has a callous streak in him. He forced Maitland off the track at high speed and his car became airborne and landed in Tasman Bay. By the time the marshals got to him he'd drowned." Tait's eyes tightened as he recalled the fatality. "While Petrenko caused the crash, I'm sure he's under orders from Makarov to do whatever it takes to win the championship – and if that includes putting other drivers at risk, tough shit! Now, that's shocking enough but I reckon his main motivation is financial. He knows FS is high-profile with a major following across the world and he's very aware of what that means in terms of merchandising and sponsorship. Makarov has already said he wants a bigger piece of the action and I don't want him inciting unrest amongst the other team owners."

"Is that a real threat?"

"Not this season as the contracts have been agreed and signed but I want to avoid any complications next year. What I'm trying to say is," Tait waited a second or two as if to give his words greater effect, "I want the Russian taken out of the picture."

Wyatt eased himself into an upright posture on the sofa. "I guess that's why you called me," he said impassively.

"I'll pay you half a million US dollars – half to be paid upfront, the balance on completion. Your cover is that you've got a record as a successful entrepreneur but now you're employed as a freelance troubleshooter. I've hired you to examine the operational structure of this business, its finances, and race safety issues. I'll instruct the team owners to co-operate fully with you and to ensure you get the access you need. Now, are you interested?"

The Californian appeared deep in thought. "What's the timescale?"

"There's just one condition then it's up to you. The race in Moscow later this year is the penultimate one in the FS calendar and will be the first to be staged there. It's taken a lot of high-level negotiation behind the scenes to clinch it. I don't want it jeopardised by a hit before the event as I don't know how the city authorities would react. Afterwards we move on to Morocco for the final race in the series and then the timing is your decision. I'll leave it to you but there has to be no trail back to me – that's crucial. Do we have a deal?"

Wyatt's face remained expressionless as he listened to the warning tone of a ship's horn in the distance. "Not on those terms. I'll take the assignment but at twice the fee – that's half-a-million bucks upfront and the rest," he paused a moment, "on delivery."

Tait stood up, sauntered across the room and peered out of a porthole.

"Otherwise I walk away," Wyatt added.

The FS boss turned to face the American. "I don't intend to haggle with you, Wyatt. We'll go ahead on that basis but no one must ever know of this deal. There'll be nothing in writing – we have to trust each other."

Wyatt allowed himself the faintest of smiles as he got to his feet. "In this business I only trust myself." The two men shook hands. "By the way, Tait, you can call me Jack if you want."

FOUR

Laser beams lacerated the night sky, their intense columns of light arcing across the skyscrapers standing as monuments to the commercial prosperity of one of the world's leading cities. Cruise ships packed with tourists and flat-bottomed Chinese junks with large squarish sails were briefly illuminated as the roving lights, in a synchronised display, criss-crossed the darkness. From his lofty hotel balcony at the southern tip of Kowloon, Nick Stallard's pale blue eyes gazed out over the Tsim Sha Tsui waterfront and across Victoria Harbour towards the stunning skyline of Hong Kong Island. He savoured the pleasantly pungent aromas drifting on the East Asian air, and from a distance came myriad voices from the bustling open-air street markets.

As he tried to relax on the eve of the fourth race, the twenty-nine-year-old fair-haired, clean-cut Englishman wondered whether the season ahead might finally bring him the driver's crown he had coveted for so long. After three rounds, he and Raffa Rodriguez, with a win each, were jointly leading the FS championship on fifteen points, followed by Philippe Guiscard on eleven and Yuri Petrenko a further three points adrift. Stallard regarded the

Spaniard as his main rival but the talented Russian, with one podium finish so far, had already fatally demonstrated an aptitude for ruthlessness and was also a threat. After almost a decade competing at the top level, and driving for two of the leading teams for the last five years, the Briton had twice been runner-up but the main prize had eluded him. The closest he had come to lifting the victor's trophy was last season, when he finished just a point behind the champion, an Italian, who then retired.

Stallard ruefully considered the 'Gentleman Nick' tag that had seemingly bedevilled his career. The product of an English public-school education, his early racing career was funded by his father, a wealthy City banker who had bought him a seat at one of the smaller teams competing in FS. The young driver was rated an honourable man both on and off the track but his critics – while accepting he was technically competent, with a solid record – pointed to a lack of killer instinct when racing. On the last lap of the previous season's title decider, he had slipstreamed his opponent for 200 metres as they approached the final bend, the last chance to overtake. Stallard had tried to delay his braking fractionally as both men slowed their cars from 175 to 80 miles per hour in less than two seconds, in an attempt to give him a slight edge going into the right-hander. But the Italian had also braked late and with their wheels nearly touching, Stallard knew that if he tried the move both drivers could be out of the race. He backed off; his rival maintained his slender lead and seconds later took the chequered flag and with it, the championship.

So, despite coming second overall, another year had ended in relative disappointment for the Englishman and his team owner had accused him of lacking the passion needed to clinch the title. As Stallard viewed the light show above the harbour, he struggled to reconcile the inner conflict between his easygoing temperament and the need to be aggressive, even ruthless, on the track. Although outwardly confident, he was a shy man with insecurities and he recognised they were becoming more pronounced with his failure to win the highest accolade in the sport. The racer questioned whether his internal strife might make him reckless when competing and, for the first time in his career, provoke him into taking risks not normally in his nature. His thoughts were disrupted by the intermittent ringing of the phone in his room. He left the balcony and went inside.

"Stallard here."

"Good evening, sir," sounded a cordial East Asian voice. "It's the hotel switchboard. There's someone on the line for you, but he won't give his name. Will you accept the call?"

The driver hesitated for a moment. It was the night before the race and he regretted not giving instructions that he wasn't to be disturbed. "Alright," he said eventually.

A couple of seconds elapsed. "Stallard, are you there?" questioned the caller, in what the Englishman surmised was an eastern European accent.

"Who's calling?" he said curtly.

"That's not important. All you need to know is that I represent a client who wishes to make you an offer… an extremely generous one."

"I'm not open to offers, I'm already under contract," said the racer, who was starting to become tetchy.

"I think you might be interested in this one," the caller persisted. "My client is willing to match your annual fee but he requires that you—"

"Requires what?" Stallard interrupted angrily.

"You have to make sure you don't win the drivers' championship. If you agree I will contact you again to make arrangements for a first payment."

Stallard was becoming incensed. "You've chosen the wrong guy to buy off. You can tell your client the one thing I want most is to win the title – and I won't be party to a dirty underhand deal."

"But Mr Stallard, it's easy money for you."

"Go to hell!" he retorted and rammed the phone down. Then he did what he should have done several hours earlier: he rang reception and told them not to put any calls through.

The twenty-six-year-old Spanish nobleman eased his tall muscular physique into the snug cockpit of the racing car that now occupied pole position on the starting grid. Rafael Luis Rodriguez, the twelfth Count of Algaidas in the province of Cordoba, had put in a blistering qualifying lap around the two-and-three-quarter-mile southern Kowloon street circuit. He had been runner-up in the previous race in the rarefied atmosphere of Mexico City but a mistake had cost him a win and he was determined to stamp his authority on the south-east Asia event.

Born into a life of wealth and privilege, he had been captivated by speed at an early age. The family home, set in a thousand acres and with distant views of the thirty-kilometre-long lake at Iznajar, had provided an ideal setting for the youngster to indulge his obsession. An accomplished horse-rider by the age of twelve, he turned to four wheels to go faster and drove a specially-modified car around an improvised track running through the olive groves. Spurred on by a competitive nature, the teenager raced against the clock in an effort to improve his lap times on the makeshift circuit, and there first displayed the daredevil attitude that would later manifest itself when racing cars and power boats. But at seventeen he lost the man closest to him and the one who had actively encouraged his sporting flair. His father, an outstanding horseman and equestrian competitor, was killed in a freak riding accident and the youthful aristocrat inherited the title and the estate. In a simple ritual that preceded the start of every race, the Spaniard kissed the ring, bearing the family crest and previously worn by his father, that now sat on the little finger of his right hand.

"Good luck, Raffa," shouted his race engineer before leaving the grid. The handsome dark-haired driver – frequently seen in the company of beautiful women – signalled his acknowledgment, squeezed his hands into his gloves and pulled his helmet visor down over his deep brown eyes. His car, in the gold and blue colours of El Oro Racing, was a length ahead of that of the Russian, Petrenko. Behind them on row two was Stallard, who qualified third, and the dashing young Frenchman, Guiscard, of Drogan Racing. The promising Indian driver, Dev Pavani, was in the second El Oro car in P5, and alongside him was Dan Seton in the all-green colours of Seton Racing, the English-based team owned by his father and former world champion, Tom Seton. The Russian, Alexandr Orlovsky, was at the wheel of the second car entered by Makarov Racing in P7, just ahead of the Chinese driver, Wang Hu, in another Seton. The American, Kate Lockhart, who had performed well in qualifying and was making her FS debut for Gorton Racing, was in P9, with the Brazilian, Ricardo Gonzalez, of Akron Racing, next to her. On the sixth row were the German, Otto Werner, in the second Drogan car, and the American, Al Boyd, the Akron test driver promoted after the death of Pete Maitland in the opening race.

The protective blankets covering the tyres of each car were removed just before the engines were fired up electronically, to minimise the time for pressure to drop. Then, at varying intervals, twelve mighty V10 engines roared into life with a collective guttural ferocity and the cars set out on the warm-up lap around the circuit, swerving from side to side as the drivers tried to put some heat into their tyres to improve grip on the track. Behind them, mechanics from all the teams broke into a trot as they wheeled away the grid trolleys carrying the computerised car-starting equipment. Each racer knew they were about to compete in one of the most physically demanding events in the FS calendar, with the air temperature in the mid-thirties degrees Celsius and humidity at over seventy percent.

As thousands of cheering spectators looked on from their seats in the specially built grandstand along the pit straight in Salisbury Road, the Spaniard placed his car at the front of the grid and the remainder of the pack found their respective slots behind him. A dozen pairs of eyes were riveted on the two-foot square light suspended from a steel wire stretching across the track thirty feet above the start-finish line. Rodriguez hand-operated a lever on the steering wheel to engage the clutch, selected first gear, sucked in water through the tube in his helmet and steeled himself for the huge overhead starting light to change from red to green. He knew his reactions were fast but he was realistic enough to accept that some of those around him were equally quick, and with a short sprint to the first corner, a clean getaway was crucial.

Alongside him, the Russian, Petrenko, found time to contemplate a season that so far had led to a disqualification, a podium spot, and a P4 finish in the last race. He was now lying fourth in the drivers' standings – a striking performance for a rookie, but it wasn't enough for him. A karting star from boyhood, the twenty-one-year-old stockily built driver from one of the poorer suburbs on the outskirts of St Petersburg had the arrogance of youth and immense self-belief that he could win the title at his first attempt. He took in a deep breath, flexed his gloved fingers for a final time before gripping the steering wheel again, looked imperturbably at the track ahead and waited.

On the second row of the grid, Nick Stallard stared intently at the back of the two cars in front of him and tried to visualise the initial stampede when the race began. The drivers knew that opportunities for overtaking on the street circuit were limited but the 400 metres leading to the first corner, a sharp right-hander, provided a chance to gain a place if a rival failed to get away quickly. Positioned directly behind the pole-setter and on the right-hand side of the grid, the Englishman was on the racing line, which had much more grip, whereas the Russian, slightly ahead and to the left of him, would have to negotiate the dirty side of the track. As he tried to maintain the right engine revs with the race start imminent, Stallard was confident he could beat Petrenko to the ninety-degree turn at the end of the straight.

The official starter, standing on the rostrum, took a final look at the cars lined up on the grid and checked that every driver was ready, his finger poised over the button that would activate the starting process, which was controlled by computer. Each competitor was well aware that sensors embedded in the track would detect the slightest movement of any car before the go-ahead was given, and any infringement of the regulations would incur a penalty later in the race. After an intensity of watching and waiting, the bright red light was replaced by one of glowing green… and engines started to scream.

Rodriguez got off the line well but the Russian, on the inferior side of the track, struggled for grip and found himself losing ground. Behind them, Stallard had a near-perfect start. He floored the throttle and rocketed away, carving through the gap left by the faltering Petrenko. Halfway to the corner he had drawn level with the Spaniard as their cars reached 155 miles per hour, while Pavani was challenging Guiscard for P4. The Englishman braked at the last possible moment and reached the turn into Canton Road a car nose ahead. He swung the wheel to the right and led into the tight corner but with his brakes and tyres not yet up to temperature, his extra speed forced him to run wide. He berated himself for his carelessness as the Spaniard and Russian moved up on the inside and regained their positions as they exited the bend and accelerated hard along the short straight leading to another sharp right-hander into Haiphong Road. This was followed by a left-hander for a fast burst along Nathan Road that led to a heavy braking zone for a right into Kimberley Road but again, Stallard found a lack of grip from his tyres. His car was sliding and bouncing on the variable surface as the trio headed for a chicane that led onto Observatory Road before a right-left flick into Granville Road. A short sprint led to a ninety-degree right onto Science Museum Road followed by a sweeping right-hander back onto Salisbury Road to attack the fastest part of the circuit flat out in seventh gear for three-quarters of a mile close to the waterfront.

The Englishman's teammate, Kate Lockhart, had made an impressive start, overtaking Wang and Orlovsky to gain two places and move to P7 by the first corner. Seated on the pit wall, Joe Gorton clenched his fists in delight as he watched the American's calmly executed manoeuvre. "That's my girl," he shouted, and slapped the back of her race engineer who was sitting alongside him in front of a row of monitors. "I think we've got something special here."

His colleague nodded agreement. "She's got more balls than Luigi, that's for sure." He resumed his analysis of the telemetry data appearing on the screen.

In the Makarov Racing camp, the atmosphere was icy. The team owner's eyes blazed with fury as he saw his number two driver outpaced in the opening moments of the race and he radioed the hapless Orlovsky. "That's not good enough. I pay you to be competitive and that's what I expect – start racing!" The ill-tempered Makarov did not expect a reply and there wasn't one. But his driver had got the message.

After a brilliant start, Stallard found himself back in P3 and chasing his major rivals. His early mistake had left him three car lengths behind Petrenko, who had recovered from his poor getaway due to wheel spin on the dirty side of the grid and was now hunting down Rodriguez. Despite the setback the Englishman remained confident; he prided himself on his performance on street circuits as they offered a different kind of challenge. They were used as public roads for the rest of the year so practice on them was restricted to just the two days before the event and they provided a rigorous test of drivers' concentration levels as, with limited run-off areas, the slightest error could pitch a car into a concrete wall and out of the race.

A hurried glance in his wing mirrors confirmed that Guiscard, who had twice locked up his front tyres in braking, sending blue smoke pouring from them, was now a second and a half behind him. The Frenchman had managed to keep Pavani at bay during the first ten laps but both were pressing hard and remained a danger. Stallard allowed himself the briefest of thoughts about how his colleague was faring on her debut but his team had said nothing and he could only concentrate on his own race. He had plenty to think about. Although his tyres had now heated up, he found he was getting understeer because when he pointed the nose of the car into a corner there was a tendency to go straight on, leading to front-end breakaway and running wide. That meant he had to wait to get on the throttle as he exited the turn and was losing time to the two cars ahead of him. He attempted to adjust the balance of the car from the cockpit and radioed his race engineer, who said the team would bring him in earlier than planned to put on fresh tyres.

The first to pit was Seton's number one driver, in P6, who was constantly being harassed by Lockhart in the Gorton. Dan Seton had always known he would be a racing driver but was finding it hard to live up to expectations as the son of a former world champion in the same sport. The twenty-six-year-old had struggled early in his racing career and found it tough to deal with accusations that he had only landed a 'drive' because his father owned the team. The gossip-mongers in the paddock pointed to a lack of significant results and claimed there were more competitive drivers who could replace him. In the current season he had finished in P4 in the first race in New Zealand, failed to score in the second at Delhi and managed a P5 in Mexico City. Seton was called in on lap nineteen for a pit stop that was to prove anything but straightforward. He turned off the track into the pit lane and pressed his speed-limiter button, located at the top right-hand side of the steering wheel, just before he crossed the white line marking the entry point. He stopped with a practised precision, his wheels inches from the legs of the front jack man, who raised the car hydraulically while the man at the rear used a manual jack. Standing close to the nose of the car was the chief mechanic who held down the lollipop sign that had three words in large print on it: 'No Throttle. Brakes.' The pit crew, waiting in their allotted positions, went instantly into action, changing the tyres and refuelling with no sign of the drama to come.

The time he was stationary seemed an eternity to the driver, who was conscious of the threat posed by the American woman who had been all over the back of his car for most of the race. His visor was cleaned and then, with the pit stop having lasted a little under six seconds, he saw the lollipop man move to reverse the sign to read: '1st Gear. Throttle.' In a reflex action, and before the pole had been lifted, the impetuous Seton tapped the throttle pedal lightly and his car moved forward, taking the refuelling hose with it. The chief mechanic and two others, including the refueller, fell to the ground and the delivery nozzle was ripped out of the fuel tank, spilling some of its contents onto the car's red-hot exhaust system. Flames shot three feet into the air as the car travelled twice its own length before coming to a halt and an alert mechanic smothered the fire with an extinguisher. The embarrassed driver's relief at seeing the mechanics scramble to their feet was mixed with anger at his own mistake, which had cost him precious time.

From his seat on the pit wall, the tall lean figure of Tom Seton watched his son head down the pit lane to resume the race but his face belied the intense disappointment he felt. The error wasn't the first this season and could have had a devastating outcome. After two years of solid engineering development in the company factory and extensive track testing, he felt he had provided a competitive car whilst acknowledging it still fell short of the performance of their Gorton and El Oro rivals. Makarov Racing, meanwhile, was something of an unknown quantity, although its leading driver seemed to be exceptionally talented and focused. The Seton boss sighed as he reflected on his own achievement of winning the world championship more than thirty years before. He had raced in a totally different era when car and track safety were not considered major issues and drivers appeared almost nonchalant as they jumped into their high-speed machines with helmets their only protection. It had been the culture of the day but it had taken a heavy human toll, with fatalities occurring at regular intervals during the season, and he had lost some good friends along the way.

He rarely talked about his championship success as he felt his son had enough pressure to deal with but he found himself increasingly questioning whether Dan had the mental toughness that was crucial to progress in the sport. His teammate, the Chinese driver Wang, was in his first season with the team but already there were signs of the talent that the Seton owner had first spotted in the young man from Beijing when he was competing at a junior level on the Far Eastern and Asian circuits. Whilst still adjusting to the faster pace at the top level, Wang had demonstrated a capacity to learn quickly and stay calm under stress and Seton Senior had identified a maturity of approach surprising in one so young.

As for his son, the scale of the error became evident once the first round of pit stops had been completed as he found himself trailing Lockhart by nine seconds and relegated to P7. As he set about chasing the American, Seton was told that Orlovsky in P8 had found more speed and was gaining on him by almost half a second each tour of the circuit. Spurred into action by the stinging rebuke of his team owner, the young Russian had even set the third fastest lap time of the race and by lap 27 had closed to within a car's length and was trying to slipstream the Briton on the long straight past the pits. Seton held his line into the first corner and managed to fend off his pursuer but at the next turn, another tight right-hander, Orlovsky made a more ambitious attempt to pass. This time the back end of his car swung out and it spun off the track, striking a safety barrier with some force. Wang in the second Seton and Gonzalez in one of the Akrons went by, but the Russian kept his engine running and was able to rejoin the race in P10, ahead of Werner in a Drogan and Boyd in the other Akron.

Orlovsky's race engineer watched the telemetry read-out with a growing unease as there appeared to be some rear-wing damage following the accident but the driver's request to be pitted as a safety precaution to check the car was forcibly overruled by the team owner. "Tell him to race on," muttered Makarov with an air of hostility. "He's lost three places already and we're not wasting any more time. He can wait for the next scheduled pit stop." The race engineer duly radioed the order and Orlovsky pressed on, knowing that any effort to compel a change of mind was futile, but his suspicion that something serious was amiss remained. The Russian realised the sensible course of action was to try to maintain his position until the next stop but the hardline message from his boss left no doubt about what was expected of him. Despite his better judgment, Orlovsky flung his car around the circuit and for the next lap and a half his aggression was starting to pay off. When he emerged from the long right-hander into Salisbury Road on lap twenty-nine, he could see the Akron driven by Gonzales about a third of the way down the straight and knew he was gaining on him. Orlovsky pressed the gear upshift button several times and thrust his throttle pedal to the floor and the advanced electronics of the semi-automatic gearbox launched the car from 75 to 180 miles per hour in under two seconds.

With his engine screaming and rev counter needle oscillating in the higher range, the Russian was now halfway along the straight. Still uncertain as to the extent of any damage that might have resulted from spinning off, he was alert for the slightest lateral movement that could indicate a problem with the handling of the car. Despite his vigilance, he had no warning when the cumulative stresses caused by the earlier incident finally proved overwhelming. The rear wing fractured at 185 miles per hour, causing complete loss of control. Orlovsky was helpless as the car ploughed head-on into a wall on the pit side of the straight, the huge impact tearing off the front wheels and sending them flying into the air. The car rebounded, rolled over then hurtled back across the track and slammed into a barrier. Pieces of bodywork flew off as the wreckage slid on its side for ninety feet before coming to a standstill. There was no sign of movement from the driver.

Trackside marshals immediately double-waved yellow flags to warn other racers of immediate danger, instructing them not to overtake and to slow down, and the safety car was called out. The crash happened in full view of the main grandstand close to the pits and Dr Manvers and his back-up team were quickly on the scene. He found Orlovsky unconscious but still breathing and after immediate emergency treatment, the driver was slowly removed from his wrecked car and taken to the medical centre nearby. Standing in the pits, Viktor Makarov had watched impassively as his driver's race ended in spectacular style in front of thousands of spectators. He sent an assistant to check on Orlovsky's condition but appeared to be relatively unconcerned. He then turned his attention to the progress of his leading racer, who was having an outstanding drive in P2 and was relentless in his pursuit of the Spaniard. When the race leader came into the pits, Petrenko still had enough fuel to go three more laps and took full advantage of a lighter car to set the fastest time on consecutive laps before pitting. When both men had completed their stops, the Russian was three-tenths of a second behind and pursuing Rodriguez like an Exocet missile tracking its target.

As Makarov's eyes flitted across two banks of data-spewing monitors on the pit wall, a hundred metres away a pair of powerful binoculars brought into focus his thickset figure. A slight tweak of the zoom adjustment lever produced a sharper image of the Russian's head and close-cropped dark hair. The unseen observer studied the pockmarked face and looked for any mannerisms with a professional attention to detail and made a mental note for future reference. The clandestine surveillance continued for several minutes and ended only when its target headed for his motor home. It was there the team owner was handed a bulletin from the medical centre stating Orlovsky had regained consciousness but an early diagnosis indicated serious back and leg injuries and he had been transferred to an intensive care unit in hospital.

On the track, Stallard found the Gorton's handling had improved with a new set of tyres, although he was still struggling to keep in touch with the front-runners who were sustaining a blistering pace, but now he faced a new problem. With the temperature in the cockpit climbing to over fifty degrees Celsius, he pressed the drink supply button to take in water but was startled to find it was malfunctioning. A steady flow of cold water at the beginning of the race had turned into an irregular trickle and what little water was available was now becoming hot. With less than half of the seventy-two laps completed, the Englishman – acknowledged as one of a new breed of super-fit drivers – was starting to suffer from the onset of dehydration. He had drunk several litres of water before the start but in the extreme heat he would lose about five litres in body fluid over the full race distance. He radioed the pits about his predicament but knew it was likely to worsen and could have debilitating physical implications for the latter stages.

By lap 44, Guiscard, who had slightly increased his lead over Pavani, was told over the team radio that he was also gaining on Stallard in P3 and there was a chance of a podium place. But as the Frenchman negotiated the fast chicane leading to Observatory Road, his nearside front tyre punctured without warning. He fought to keep the car on the road and cut its speed before the next turn but the tread started delaminating and a two-foot length of it was pounding the front wing, bodywork and suspension. The car limped back to the pits where a detailed inspection confirmed that Guiscard, who had been attacking the kerbs throughout the race, had locked up the tyre in braking. This had created a flat spot that led to a loss of grip and the resulting vibration had weakened the tyre and caused the puncture. The delay in reaching the pits and the unscheduled stop meant the French driver lost places to Pavani, Lockhart, Seton, Wang and Gonzalez. When he rejoined the race, Guiscard found himself in P9, just ahead of the back-markers, Werner and Boyd.

As Kate Lockhart in P5 ripped another protective strip off her visor she was in no doubt as to her immediate strategy. Seemingly glued to the back of Pavani's El Oro car, she had already planned her next overtaking move, although such opportunities were few on the street circuit. The single-minded American had coolly observed the Indian driver for several laps and noticed that his car appeared to be lacking an initial burst of speed when exiting corners. She calculated he had some kind of lower gear selection problem and was determined to exploit what she saw as an opening. On lap 59, as Pavani turned his car into the sharp right leading to Science Museum Road, Lockhart was just inches behind. The Gorton was forced to go on the dirty racing line but its driver gambled she would be able to get on the throttle earlier than her rival and reach the long right-hander leading onto the straight before him. A roar from the mechanics in her garage confirmed the manoeuvre had worked. The American was having an inspired drive.

Two laps later, with new tyres on his Drogan, Guiscard was flying and he quickly reeled in three of the drivers who had taken advantage of his puncture, regaining his place from Gonzalez, Wang and Seton to go P6 behind Pavani. At the front the battle for supremacy was unrelenting with Petrenko's brilliant drive giving the Spaniard a severe test in the sweltering conditions. The Russian, who was displaying a skill beyond his years, had closed the gap to Rodriguez to just two-tenths of a second but the rookie's tenacity in pursuit was having an adverse effect on his own car.

The radio message from his team was blunt. "Yuri, your engine is starting to overheat. It's taking in all the hot air that has already passed through the engine and exhaust of the car in front. You must overtake soon or back off to get a cooler airflow."

"I hear you," was the brief reply. Backing off was not in the Russian's nature but although he continued to harass Rodriguez for the next two laps, he knew he couldn't postpone a decision much longer. He was aware there was very little difference in straight-line speed between their cars and overtaking on the street circuit had already proved difficult.

"Yuri, you must cool your engine," repeated his race engineer with renewed urgency. "Do you read me?"

The question went unanswered as Petrenko turned left out of Haiphong Road and accelerated rapidly along the straight leading to the right-hander into Kimberley Road, closing to within inches of the Spaniard's car. The race leader, who had been driving under constant pressure from the rookie for most of the race, was determined to stay ahead with only eight laps remaining. But the strain was taking its toll and he was just about to make his first, and last, mistake. Rodriguez allowed himself a brief glance in the wing mirror but the split-second action meant he missed the braking point for the corner. The El Oro car approached the 70 miles per hour turn carrying far too much speed and it spun off the track, striking a wall and badly damaging the front suspension. The Spaniard knew at once his race was over and as he climbed out of his car he cursed the single error that had gifted the Russian a likely win.

By now, in the furnace that was the cockpit of the Gorton, Stallard was sweating badly and fighting to maintain his concentration. His water supply had dried up completely and he had been forced to drive for more than half the race without any fluid intake. As the Englishman passed the Spaniard's broken car, his relief at finding his leading rival out of a race he seemed certain to win was tempered by his growing physical discomfort as he became increasingly dehydrated.

"You're now P2, Nick – that's P2," radioed Jim Crowley, his race engineer. "Give it everything you've got and there may be a win at the end of this one."

Stallard's immediate reaction – *I'll be bloody lucky to hang on to P2 the way I'm feeling* – he kept to himself. His tyres, his third set, were well past their optimum performance level in the scorching temperature and he was struggling to stay fully alert. "I need water and the tyres are losing grip," he responded. "It's not looking good."

Crowley tried to sound encouraging. "Nick, just stick

in there. Not long to go now. If you can keep chasing Petrenko he might make a mistake."

Crowley cancelled the radio transmit button and turned to his boss, standing next to him on the pit wall. "Joe, I'm worried about him. He's getting dehydrated and then fatigue sets in. The concentration level starts to drop and that's when mistakes happen."

Gorton was forthright in his response. "There's no way we can fix it at this stage of the race. He's got this far; he just has to dig in and keep going but he's fit enough."

The English driver had cut the deficit at the last pit stop but was still nearly three seconds behind the Russian and doubted he had the energy or enough laps remaining to make a serious challenge. As he tracked the race leader, Stallard was becoming increasingly aware of a potential attack from behind and was surprised to find his female teammate closing on him. He tried to comprehend how she had gone from P9 on the grid to P3 and wondered why no one had told him about her progress, but now was not the time for speculation.

As Stallard battled the fatigue that threatened to envelop him, he was informed he was starting to narrow the gap to Petrenko but the American was gaining on him by three-tenths of a second a lap. He assumed she was acting as rear gunner to protect him from Pavani and Guiscard, who had found some extra pace since their last pit stops. But with less than two laps to go, Gorton Racing's number one driver was astonished to find Lockhart slipstreaming him along the pit straight and looking to overtake.

"What's she playing at?" he radioed his team. "Tell her to back off!" There was no response so he repeated the question. "What the hell's going on?"

After a pause he heard the voice of his race engineer. "The boss says there are no team orders – it's got to be sorted on the track."

Stallard found what he was hearing hard to believe but did not prolong the exchange, knowing he needed all his concentration to maintain position in P2. He weaved across the track in an attempt to disrupt his pursuer and was first to reach the turn into Canton Road with a burst of acceleration leading to another ninety-degree right-hander into Haiphong Road. The Gorton team cars were now just feet apart as they exited the left-hand corner into Nathan Road and both drivers floored the throttle along the straight, urged on by screaming spectators. Stallard had been trying to preserve his tyres but he knew that was no longer an option with Lockhart hunting him down. His energy sapped by a combination of the humidity and lack of water, the Englishman sped into the turn leading to Kimberley Road but felt his car begin to slide on the uneven surface. He was almost through the corner when the rear end broke away and the Gorton spun twice across the track, narrowly missing a concrete wall, before coming to a stop facing oncoming cars. Stallard swore in frustration as Lockhart, who had reacted instantly to avoid a collision, flashed by and into P2. The joint championship leader was able to avoid stalling his engine but as he started to position his car to rejoin the race, he found himself relegated to P5 as the cars of Pavani and Guiscard swept past. "The bitch!" he muttered angrily as he contemplated the loss of precious points in the title race.

For her part, Lockhart was ecstatic as one lap later she followed the Russian across the finish line and took the chequered flag. As her car slowed down, she punched the air with both fists and acknowledged the cheers of her mechanics, who had run from their garage to assemble on the wall overlooking the track.

"Brilliant race, Kate," shouted her team owner over the car radio. "Fantastic effort!"

"Oh, Joe, I'm on the podium," shrieked his driver. "It's unbelievable!"

"P2 on your FS debut, what a drive! Well done!"

"Its amazing… and thanks to all the guys, they did a great job."

A stern-looking Stallard was waiting when the euphoric owner and number two driver returned to the garage after the podium presentation ceremony. "Bad luck, Nick," said Gorton, patting him on the shoulder, "but you're still leading the championship and you're now two points clear of Raffa."

"I would have scored more points today if…" he gestured towards Lockhart, "…she was more of a team player."

"Kate had a great race. I know you were suffering from the heat and lack of water and your car spun near the end, but you finished in P5 and got two points."

"My car didn't spin because I was dehydrated," said Stallard tetchily. He stared hard at his colleague. "She was all over the back of me while I was chasing Petrenko. Instead of hounding me, she should have settled for P3 and the team would have had more points."

Lockhart took a step forward, using a small towel to wipe her long black hair, which was wet and glistening from the champagne sprayed on the podium. "Look, Nick, I know you're heading the championship but I race because I want to win. We both do, that's why we're in the sport. There are no team orders and it's a fight between ourselves."

"That's right," said Gorton, "I've always run things that way. It keeps the drivers, the engineers and mechanics on their toes. Competition is healthy, especially within a team. There's only one exception – if later in the season a driver has a good chance of winning the title, then we all have to unite behind…" he paused for a moment, "…that driver."

Stallard remained stony-faced. "I don't think you saw it that way when Corazza was driving as my number two. I had the distinct impression that most of the focus and effort was on me to win the title, but it seems the situation has changed."

"Luigi wasn't up to it," said the team boss, "but now we've got a second driver who is. That's obvious from what happened today and we should all be celebrating and then trying to improve again for the next race."

"OK, so the rules have been altered," said Stallard. "That's a new ball game and I can play it differently too."

"What are you suggesting?"

"I don't like what Kate did this afternoon but if that's the way it's going to be from now on, then the gloves are off."

Gorton's eyes hardened and his words came slowly. "I think you need to remember something, Nick. You're in the last phase of a three-year contract but, as you know, in this sport it's sometimes difficult to give any guarantees about renewal."

Stallard glowered at his boss then strode out of the garage.

Floyd Collins eased his well-built frame into one of three leather-backed chairs in the motor home that also doubled as the stewards' office. Flanked by two colleagues, the forty-seven-year-old sandy-haired Canadian chief steward eyed the man sitting opposite him across the oblong table.

"Mr Makarov, you've been summoned here to answer a charge that you endangered the life of your driver, Alexandr Orlovsky, during the race here in Kowloon. It's alleged that after his car struck a barrier, you ordered him to carry on without first calling him into the pits to inspect the vehicle for any damage. A subsequent investigation by the stewards has revealed that a broken rear wing later caused a major crash and your driver suffered serious injuries as a result. What have you got to say in response to the accusation?"

The boss of Makarov Racing had been scribbling idly on a notepad. He stopped and looked up at the three officials, a scowl on his face. "I don't understand why you called me here today. What happened was an internal matter and if there are any lessons to be learnt they will be, but I don't believe the stewards need to get involved."

"Don't be in any doubt, Mr Makarov," said the chief steward firmly, "it *is* our business and we intend to proceed on that basis. Now, why didn't you bring the car in to check for any possible damage after the initial spin into the safety barrier?"

"Our initial assessment was that there wasn't a major problem and we would examine the car at the next pit stop."

"But the telemetry read-out we've seen confirms there was some damage to the rear wing and you must have been aware of that evidence. Orlovsky had already pitted on lap

22 and the next scheduled stop wasn't due for some time, so weren't you taking a calculated risk that something might go wrong before the car was inspected?"

The team boss paused for a moment as he eyed each of the three men facing him. "I may be mistaken, but I thought motor racing does involve an element of risk," he said with more than a touch of sarcasm.

Floyd Collins ran a finger across his moustache as he surveyed the Russian but chose to ignore the gibe. "Your driver has been badly injured and I gather he's likely to remain in hospital for some time, and may well be out of action for the rest of the season. Do you accept that if you had acted responsibly the crash would probably have been averted and Orlovsky would have been spared the subsequent trauma?"

Makarov was uncompromising. "Mr Collins, you have a job to do. I have mine. You need to understand that I run my team my way. My drivers have confidence in me and they respect my decisions. Sometimes I get it right, sometimes not, but they know I make the call and they accept that."

The chief steward fixed Makarov with an austere stare. "I would remind you that an important aspect of our role is driver safety and we never shirk our responsibility in that respect. You would do well to remember that. Have you anything more to say before we adjourn to consider our decision?"

The team owner shook his head and the hearing ended.

The next day Viktor Makarov was notified that the FS stewards had found him guilty as charged. He was fined 100,000 US dollars and given a warning as to his future conduct.

FIVE

Valya Doletskaya allowed herself a faint smile of satisfaction as she studied the income statement for the previous month. Sitting at her desk in the penthouse suite of the hotel in the centre of Moscow, she flicked through the various pages documenting the list of appointments and was heartened to note that a recent hike in fees had not led to a drop in revenue. There had even been a slight increase in the number of clients – but then, she mused, she was working in an industry driven by carnal compulsions and that was insulated from the vagaries of market forces.

A light tap on the half-opened office door caught Valya's attention and she looked up to see the willowy figure of the receptionist. "What is it, Natasha?"

"It's Olga, she's phoned to say she's not well and won't be in this evening. She had just one client tonight and he's due here in just over an hour."

"Who is it?"

"The German diplomat."

Valya sighed. She knew some clients liked to enjoy the company of the same woman every visit and they could become irascible when their preferred choice wasn't available. And Ralf Hartmann was no exception. "Can someone take Olga's place?"

"There are four girls on duty tonight but they're all fully booked. Irina was on stand-by but she's had to take a couple of late appointments."

"Natasha, would you…" Valya paused as she looked at the auburn-haired receptionist, contemplating a thought that had recurred in recent weeks. She had wondered whether the twenty-five-year-old with the svelte figure would consider becoming a hostess with the incentive of a significant boost in earnings. But with a client inclined to ill-tempered outbursts due to arrive shortly, perhaps now was not the appropriate time to raise the issue. "Natasha, would you contact Herr Hartmann to tell him Olga is indisposed this evening and suggest he might wish to arrange another appointment when she is available. Do it now and we might reach him before he leaves the Embassy."

Valya's assistant acknowledged the request and returned to her office in the reception area.

Fleeting puffs of smoke spiralled upwards through the evening drizzle as the landing wheels of the Boeing 767 jet hit the tarmac at Moscow's Domodedovo International Airport. Precisely thirty-nine minutes after British Airways flight 874 from London touched down, a tall, wiry figure in a light-grey raincoat and carrying a briefcase stepped from the arrivals hall. He gave the impression of a practised familiarity with his surroundings but still looked intently around him before starting to move away from the terminal building. He had taken less than twenty paces when the large limousine slowed to a halt at the kerbside and the rear nearside door was flung open.

"You're bang on, Jack," drawled a voice from the far passenger seat. "Get yourself aboard and we'll be outta here." The chauffeur-driven car was soon outside the airport boundary and heading north towards the city centre more than 30 miles away, the rain falling heavier now. "You ain't changed a whole lot," said the dapper, middle-aged man, turning in his leather seat to look keenly at his compatriot. "I reckon it's gotta be at least five years."

"All of that," said the thirty-seven-year-old as he returned an equally penetrating gaze. He paused then added, almost as an afterthought, "It was a difficult mission."

George Ainsworth nodded assent as he looked through a darkened side window, watching the rain hammering down and sending torrents of spray dancing along deserted pavements. "I've had some challenging assignments in my time but that was a tough one and we lost some good men along the way." He broke off for a few moments then resumed sombrely. "But I didn't think it would end like that for you."

The other man waited awhile before responding. "I didn't want it to be that way. Sure, there were some things I did I'm not proud of, but at the time I didn't see it like that."

"There was a line, Jack, and you crossed it," said Ainsworth without a trace of emotion.

"When you're fighting in the shadows you have to survive, and that's what I did."

"I saw your file and knew the background. You were regarded as something of a maverick but you built up an impressive track record. In fact, I considered you to be one of our best field officers but…" His voice tailed off. "I felt you were always driven by what happened to Lucy."

Even the fading light of the car interior could not conceal the anguished look that fleetingly crossed the face of Ainsworth's companion. The memory of what happened more than a decade ago was still seared into the distant recesses of his mind and occasionally, like now, the mere mention of her name rekindled some of the mental pain he had strived for so long to erase. But however hard he tried, the stark, immutable details of that day would never go away. It was all meant to be so different, but those events had haunted him ever since.

He had been on the undergraduate class studying International Relations at Stanford University when his younger sister had gone with friends to a nightclub in downtown Los Angeles to celebrate her eighteenth birthday. Five young people – happy, vibrant, expectant and demanding of what life had to offer. Five among many, talking, laughing, drinking, dancing. But in their midst on that summer Saturday evening moved one who detested them and their country. The darting disco lights had created their own ephemeral patterns against the darkened ceiling and walls, like wayward searchlights straining to stay synchronised to the tempo of pulsating music. Breathless, Lucy and her friend Todd Latham, a year older, left the dance floor and rejoined their companions at one of a dozen circular tables lining the sides of the club. The couple had gone through high school together as classmates and had recently confided to others that their long-standing friendship had blossomed and they planned to become engaged the following year. After sipping from their drinks to cool themselves, they were soon in animated conversation, their feet tapping subconsciously to the rhythm of the beat.

Like the scores of other visitors to the club, they scarcely noticed the young man sitting alone on a stool by the bar, his fingers impatiently caressing the tall glass containing the one soft drink he'd ordered in the half-hour since his arrival. The barman, the only person subsequently able to give any kind of a description, saw the black-haired, olive-skinned man, of average height but with a rounded figure, finish his drink then close his eyes briefly as his lips appeared to silently mouth a short verse. Then the man rose slowly from his stool and began to walk between the tables and towards the crowded dance area. He moved without hurry, almost methodically, as if ruthlessly stating the power that was his but which, for just a few seconds more, was known only to himself. For a moment his dark, deep-set eyes caught those of Lucy, who happened to glance up from her chair, which backed against the wall, and allowed her to look across the room. But his eyes pulled away as if he was afraid he might somehow betray his terrible secret.

He moved on, closer to the dance floor now but still only yards from Lucy's table. A triangular-shaped chrome-plated clock, glistening in the glare of the flashing strobe lights, told those who cared to look that midnight was still twenty-seven minutes away. A quizzical look appeared on the face of one of the dancers, a woman in her early twenties, as she watched the man approach the shiny marble floor. He stopped two feet away from her, his face expressionless. The woman, feeling intimidated by the invasion of her space, took a step back. The man seemed to hesitate for a moment then his right hand started to reach inside his unbuttoned jacket. The woman looked uneasily across at her dance partner and was about to suggest they return to their table but her words would never be uttered. By then it was too late. For her, for Lucy, for Todd, and for everyone whose only mistake that night was to be within deadly range of a brooding stranger.

A grotesque horror unleashed itself in the blackness. For many, the end was instant, from the blast and from the speeding sharp-pointed missiles from the nail bomb that flew on their random mission of death. Broken, bleeding limbs were strewn across the room as bodies were ripped apart. Then, after the frenzy of noise, it was the stillness that was loudest, pierced only by the occasional moaning of the badly injured, some of whom were trapped under piles of rubble. The barman, although partly shielded by a protruding section of the bar, had been hurled to the floor. Dazed by the blast, he suddenly became aware of an acute pain and when he tried to get to his feet he found his left arm hanging limp and broken by his side. But he and several others who happened to be furthest away when the packed explosives belt was detonated had been the lucky ones. So many weren't.

The younger man looked out of the window, lost in his thoughts as the car sped through the darkness along Kashirskoye Shosse en route to Moscow. "Lucy and the others, they had everything to live for. What right did a suicide bomber have to go into that club that night and play God with their lives?" He was angry now. "And for what? All in the name of a so-called anti-American jihad!"

Ainsworth intervened gently. "They believed their cause was justified by what we did in Iraq, and one worth dying for."

"But there's no way the slaughter in that club could be justified."

"Of course not, but in war senseless things happen, you know that."

"I paid a heavy price, George."

"I know, and it ended a promising career. To the authorities it seemed you had become obsessed by revenge for your sister's death. They could understand it but they couldn't sanction it. You were fortunate they wanted to keep a lid on things; that's why they didn't prosecute you. They figured it was better to avoid the adverse publicity of a trial and kick you out of the service instead."

"I know you pitched in on my side when a prosecution was being considered. I'm grateful for that."

"It was the least I could do after what happened in Afghanistan. You saved my life, Jack – I don't forget stuff like that." He paused. "And there's something else I haven't forgotten. It was a long time ago but I remember you telling me that Lucy was a committed Christian who had great compassion and believed in forgiveness." Ainsworth looked hard at his companion. "She wouldn't have wanted you to kill in her name."

Wyatt tried but failed to stop the emotion registering on his face. "You know, George, it's something I have to live with most days. She could forgive but I can't and I guess it'll always be that way."

For the first time in a while, both men fell silent as their car headed towards the capital and looked out on sporadic clusters of pine trees, standing sentinel in the damp night sky.

The phone call to the Embassy had been several minutes too late and now Valya Doletskaya found herself confronted by an irate foreign diplomat, a predicament she had hoped to avoid. The tall German had reacted impatiently on his arrival at the penthouse suite when informed by Natasha that his regular hostess was not available. He swept past the receptionist, strode into Valya's office and glowered at her.

"I'm sorry, Herr Hartmann, but we tried to contact you before you left the Embassy. Of course, we couldn't leave a message with your secretary because you've instructed us not to." She studied the man who had forged a successful career as a skilled negotiator but who seemed, she felt, to contrive to antagonise her every time they met. She was not about to be disappointed.

"This is not the first time this has happened to me. I have to run my department efficiently and I expect others to do the same."

"But Olga has been taken ill and that's why she's not here for you tonight. She's human, these things happen."

"I like Olga, she is very good at her job. That's why I get annoyed when she is not available."

"I understand," said Valya, trying to sound sympathetic. "That's why we wanted to reach you so another appointment could be made." Her conciliatory tone in an attempt to appease the German did not appear to be working.

"Who else is available?" he said brusquely.

"I'm afraid there is no one else. All the ladies on duty this evening have their own clients and are fully booked."

"Considering your charges, you should have the resources to provide a full service regardless," he retorted.

Valya glanced at her assistant who was hovering at the door. For a moment an earlier thought came back to her but she decided now was not a suitable time to suggest that Natasha might be interested in placating the man. The diplomat, whose tousled brown hair and trim figure belied the fact he was in his late fifties, moved towards Valya. She saw a determination in his hard, grey eyes and guessed what was on his mind.

"I have a suggestion to resolve this matter. I think you, my dear, would be an excellent replacement for Olga, if I may say so. And I…"

"You know the house rules," Valya interrupted curtly. "You know I'm not available, and that applies to you as well."

"Is that so, Miss Doletskaya? I had the distinct impression that…"

"Herr Hartmann, please! We should talk in private."

Aware that her assistant was still in earshot, she asked Natasha to shut the office door and return to reception. A stern-faced Valya motioned her visitor towards one of two armchairs upholstered with Moroccan leather and she sat behind her desk. "Now, I don't know what you've been told but a man in your position must know that discretion is everything in a business like this. I have instructed my staff to operate on that basis and I expect our clients to reciprocate."

"I was just making the point that I felt there was another option to deal with the situation and that option involved you."

"Herr Hartmann, if you wish to make any insinuating remarks about me, I would hope you would ensure my personal assistant is not present at the time."

His face registered a chastened look that suggested he felt he'd been justifiably admonished. "Miss Doletskaya, I do apologise if I have caused you any embarrassment. That was not my intention when I came here tonight. I was upset when I discovered Olga had gone sick and there was no one to take her place."

Valya contemplated the German sitting opposite her. She disliked the irascibility of the man but he was a frequent client who provided a regular income and, although she was reluctant to admit it, she did find him physically attractive. He accepted her offer of a drink and she poured him an Armagnac while she settled for a vodka and lemonade and moved to the second armchair.

"Herr Hartmann, tell me, what made you choose a career in the diplomatic service?"

He seemed a little taken aback at the unexpected nature of the query but after a short pause he pulled himself up in his chair. "Interesting question," he observed with a wry smile, "and one I'm not sure I've ever fully answered. I suppose it was a combination of something of a family tradition – my father was a career diplomat – and I also had a rather vague notion that by serving my country I could somehow be a force for good in the world. But it's not for me to make that call, it's something for others to judge."

Valya continued to probe. "I suppose a posting to Moscow is one of the more difficult jobs in your line of work."

"I think I know what you're driving at. It's certainly one of the more challenging diplomatic assignments, especially dealing with the fall-out from the break-up of the old Soviet Union. As an experienced Kremlin watcher, one learns to discern the nuances of the decisions of the governing elite within its walls. That's our job: to try to maintain cordial relations between our countries. We may not always achieve it but that's what we strive for."

"Spoken like a true Embassy official," laughed Valya as she ran a hand through her blonde hair, the movement accentuating the firm outline of her breasts beneath her semi-diaphanous crimson-coloured blouse. "But do you feel you can make a real difference, that you can improve the quality of the lives of ordinary people?"

The second-ranking official at the German Embassy in the Russian capital pondered the point for a moment. "That's a difficult one. I suppose at a senior level, it's hard to quantify directly the impact of skilled diplomacy on a population. But it's all to do with a nation's standing in the world and creating a general feeling of wellbeing. There's obviously a trickle-down effect from negotiating beneficial trade treaties and other measures to stimulate industry in one's own country, which eventually helps people feel good. But it's not easy to point to a definite link."

He looked keenly at Valya and a sliver of a smile passed his lips before he continued. "And you, my dear, how would you respond if I was to pose the same question to you?"

The woman who managed the most exclusive vice establishment in Moscow showed no hesitation in her reply. "Oh yes, we make a real difference, there's no doubt about that." Her eyes twinkled. "You can see it in the faces of our clients every time they leave here."

"But ordinary lives, can you improve those?" the German persisted.

"Not those of the working man, that's not our function," she said sharply. "They have other options for their needs. We cater for a specialised clientele that's very much up-market and…" she paused, "…our fees reflect that, as you know."

"I'm well aware of my fees for Olga and it's money well spent. I have no complaints on that score," he added hastily.

"I'm glad to hear it," smiled Valya. "After all, she is one of our more experienced and mature ladies."

"I appreciate her undoubted charms, of course, but…" He was thoughtful for a moment. "When a man sees the prospect of forbidden fruit before him, Miss Doletskaya, that can be an intoxicating potion."

"Forbidden fruit means exactly that, Herr Hartmann. It's forbidden."

"But that's what makes it so tantalising. When something is just out of reach it becomes alluring."

"But still forbidden!" Valya was insistent. Her eyes roved across the diplomat, seeming to taunt him, but they also registered unease. "A little earlier you made an allegation about me. Am I right in assuming that someone has been, shall we say, a little indiscreet?"

"I did not intend to cause you any offence and I accept I was wrong to raise the matter. I have duly apologised but I think it is not for me to divulge the source of my information."

"That's so very diplomatic of you," she sighed. Valya considered whether to remove his name from the client list but that would only provoke questions from her boss about why she had taken such action and she would rather avoid that. The second option was to make herself available for the German but make him pay for the privilege. "You are a long-standing client and I regret that tonight your regular hostess is unable to be here. It's also unfortunate there are no vacancies amongst our other ladies."

The diplomat shifted uncomfortably in his chair as Valya went on. "Occasionally, Herr Hartmann, forbidden fruit can become available – but at a price. If you wish to proceed, my fee is double that of Olga's."

A sharp intake of breath was swiftly followed by a nervous-looking smile from the German.

"Those are my terms. Are you interested?"

He paused then spoke quietly. "I think we have a deal."

She rose from her chair and walked towards the door. "There's a spare room at the end of the corridor. Come with me and I'll order the drinks."

He followed her down the passageway and felt himself sinking into the deep pile turquoise-coloured carpet that covered the entire floor of the suite. His mouth tightened as Valya's close-fitting black skirt highlighted the tautness of her body.

At reception she turned to her assistant who was seated at her desk, flicking idly through the pages of a fashion and beauty magazine. "Natasha, I have a guest this evening and we'd like some champagne. Can you arrange it, please?"

The assistant glanced up, a look of surprise on her face. "I thought Herr Hartmann would be making an appointment with Olga for another time."

"He will at some point but when it's convenient for him. Now, I'd appreciate it if you would order the drinks. Also, make sure I'm not disturbed for the next hour."

"I will." She hesitated as she looked at her boss. "But I thought you weren't…" Her words trailed away.

"Natasha, I suggest you do your job and let me manage this establishment." Valya stared stonily at her aide then turned on her heel and escorted the waiting diplomat to the vacant room. Natasha, meanwhile, reached for the phone and placed an order for the champagne.

The rain was still falling as the car approached Moscow city centre, its dipped headlights reflecting like shimmering spheres off the wet tarmac. Traffic was still heavy for late evening, and just visible through the murk were the distinctive red-brick high outer walls and towers of the Kremlin. Less than a mile away, and to the south-west of the headquarters of the Russian Federation's political leadership, the chauffeur manoeuvred the vehicle into a turning off Gogolevskiy Boulevard. It travelled a short distance, stopping at a large pair of electronically operated black iron gates, which slowly swung open. The car swept into a dimly lit courtyard, beyond which stood a three-storey stone-coloured building, the sides of which were in the shape of circular towers surmounted by a parapet linking both.

"Gotta hand it to you, George, you've built up quite an empire for yourself."

Ainsworth looked slightly amused. "To be honest, I've never seen it that way. At the end of the day, it's only a job title. Nothing more, nothing less."

"Bureau chief is some title. I reckon it's one hell of a job."

"It does have its moments," he conceded. "And what keeps you out of trouble these days?"

"With my record I don't have much choice – I have to freelance," he laughed. "I run an international consultancy, security issues mainly. My clients include major companies, a couple of governments in Africa, and some high-profile individuals who would prefer to stay anonymous and alive!"

The other man nodded. "Not bad for someone who was nearly court-martialled. Mind you, freelancers always did make more dough!" Then he raised the issue that had been intriguing him for a while. "I guess you haven't come all this way just to pay your respects at the Kremlin."

A half-smile crossed the face of the younger man but it soon faded. "After what happened in Afghanistan, you said you owed me big-time. Now I need to call in the favour."

"What d'you want, Jack?"

"What does the name Viktor Makarov mean to you?"

Ainsworth's facial expression didn't change but his companion sensed there had been an immediate recognition. "If you don't count the guy in the Kremlin, you're talking about probably the most powerful man in Russia."

"As big as that?"

"They don't come much bigger." By this time the car had come to a halt and the chauffeur had opened the rear doors. "Look, Jack, it's getting late and you need to settle in for the night. Let's start on this tomorrow."

George Ainsworth had been at work for more than an hour when his secretary showed Jack Wyatt into his office the following morning.

"Hi Jack, I wondered when you were going to show."

"It's reassuring to know that while the rest of the world sleeps, those on Uncle Sam's payroll are dutifully earning their dollar."

"I don't think any of us are in this game for the money." He gestured his visitor towards a chair in the middle of the room then reached into a drawer and pulled out a thickish red-coloured file and placed it on his desk. "As you can see, we have a considerable amount of background material on our friend, Mr Makarov. But first I want to know what brings you here to find out more about him."

"I thought you might be curious about my motives," smiled Wyatt. "A month ago I was approached by an intermediary who represents a syndicate from the Middle East that's looking to invest in Moscow. I'll level with you. I'm told this group of businessmen has criminal connections and their so-called investment reflects that. It involves plans to open a network of strip clubs and massage parlours that will be a cover for prostitution, and they'll be staffed by a constant supply of young women who'll be trafficked across eastern Europe."

"Another trail leading to the Russian capital that'll end in misery and exploitation," said Ainsworth bleakly. "But it won't be easy for them to set up their stall here because there's already a well-established criminal structure in this city."

"That's precisely why I'm here. I've been hired to find out what sort of competition the syndicate will be up against, and that brings us to Makarov. I know he has links to organised crime but I need to know more about the scale of his involvement, bearing in mind your remark last night."

"I guess that's where I come in," said the bureau chief as he leant back in his chair. "But don't you have any misgivings about working for people connected to the underworld?"

"A contract is a contract, George."

"So it's all about the bottom line."

"Not always. I don't take every one I'm offered. Anyway, what can you tell me about Makarov?"

"We've been aware of his activities for some time; in fact, it would be difficult not to be. To say he has links to organised crime is a massive understatement – he's the *boss* of the Russian mafia!" Wyatt's eyes displayed a trace of surprise but he said nothing and Ainsworth continued. "He's a psychopathic killer who made his fortune from protection rackets, drug-trafficking, gambling and prostitution. And we've recently discovered he's financing a gun-running operation to terrorists seeking to destabilise parts of the old Soviet empire. Our concern is that such activity will worsen tensions between those regions and Moscow and lead to a crackdown by the Russian government."

"So is the guy pushing some kind of political agenda?"

"It's possible… we're not sure. He's been greasing the palms of dishonest officials for years and yet the authorities say they want to tackle corruption, so if he can do anything to embarrass them, he will. You've got to remember that a much-respected judge who spent more than a year investigating mafia activities in this city was assassinated a few months ago, just days before his report was due to be submitted to the Interior Minister. I'm pretty certain that was Makarov's way of warning off those with similar intentions."

"Not much doubt then about the message he was sending," said Wyatt, who had a penchant for understatement. "I'm intrigued as to how he made it to the top job."

"He had a tough upbringing as a child, coming as he did from a broken home in one of the most deprived suburbs of Moscow, and, like so many, got sucked into the gang culture. But he showed he could compete with the toughest and soon become leader of one of the most powerful gangs, and had killed a rival before he was twenty. And so it went on – he built up a reputation for violence and being ruthless in enforcing a strict disciplinary code. Of course, he made enemies along the way and was the target of a shooting, but survived, although the incident left him with a slight limp. Then, while still in his late twenties, he came to the notice of the city's mafia and gradually established a power base there that was later to prove crucial in forcing his way up the hierarchy."

"He's clearly a high-flier in terms of organised crime. So what drives him?"

Ainsworth smiled. "That's the easy bit. Power and money. Power because he likes to be in control of people and events, and money that gives him the freedom to pursue a lifestyle that's in stark contrast to the poverty of his youth. One of his passions is speed and he created his own motor racing team. He poured millions of roubles into the venture to buy in the most modern technology and expertise and it's the first Russian team competing at the highest level in FS."

"I suppose it's one way of money laundering," said Wyatt noncommittally. "What about the women in Makarov's life? Who lights his fire?"

"He's not short of female company, that's for sure, but there's one woman who plays a more prominent role in his life. Her name is Valya Doletskaya, a very attractive former model who met Makarov at one of his casinos and now runs his vice empire from one of the city's leading hotels, which he owns. From what we've uncovered, she has day-to-day control of the business but is also his mistress."

"Sounds like you've had her watched."

"You could say that. One of our guys drew the short straw for the assignment and naturally we had to give him a bogus ID just so he could get accepted as a client. It's only a whorehouse, but a high-class one. The mafia boss trusts her to run it but he won't allow her to sleep with any of the customers. It seems he's imposed a strict 'only for Makarov' policy on their relationship – but we've discovered she does occasionally break that rule, unknown to him, of course."

"Am I heading in the right direction on the source of this intelligence?"

"Probably, but it cost. It took some inducement, but our man was able to adopt the pillow-talk approach in an attempt to find out what he could about her boss – but his expenses claim for so-called work in the line of duty was eye-watering!"

"I hope she was worth it," said Wyatt with more than a touch of envy.

Ainsworth laughed. "Well, I've had no complaints, but at least it demonstrates there's still a role for the human element in our intelligence gathering, despite major advances in surveillance technology."

"Did he come up with anything new?"

"She wasn't exactly an open book and that's not surprising, considering her position. But she said enough to confirm what we already suspected: that Makarov is a control freak who tramples over anyone who gets in his way."

"That probably explains why he is where he is," Wyatt responded drily.

"No doubt. But the woman hinted he's paranoid about being overthrown by an internal coup and runs the organisation with an iron fist, ruling by fear."

"Have you got a handle on who does his dirty work?"

"The main 'heavy' is a Serb called Vuk Jovanovic. He's aptly named. Vuk is short for Vukasin, which means wolf, and that sums up the guy. He's been a loyal member of Makarov's inner circle for some time and gained his trust to such an extent that he's now seen as his confidant. He's as hard as granite with an explosive temper, and someone his boss relies on to take care of the grubby jobs without asking too many questions." Ainsworth reached across his desk and touched the solid-looking file that bore the imprint of the circular CIA logo on the cover. "I think you'll find all you want in here. This document is classified and cannot be taken out of the building, so you'll have to read it here in my office." He stood up, handed the file over and headed for the door before turning to face his former colleague. "Remember, this is payback time. It's a one-off but now we're quits."

Wyatt glanced at the report and was intrigued by its title. "Why Operation Serpent?"

The bureau chief was nearly out of the room. "When you go into a snake-pit you usually find snakes. Be careful, Jack."

SIX

"There's only time for one more flying lap. It must be maximum assault. Give it everything you've got!"

Philippe Guiscard nodded his helmet in assent but otherwise didn't respond to the bidding of Alain Gaudet, his race engineer. There was no need to. They were both well aware that with much of the qualifying session disrupted by a number of niggling technical problems, time was running out to produce a fast lap at the central Australian circuit. The twenty-three-year-old Frenchman, currently lying fourth in the drivers' championship, stared at the figures flashing up on the display screen attached to his car. They gave a visual reinforcement, if any was needed, of the extent of the task ahead. He studied the individual sector and overall timings of the other drivers and observed his main rivals had already set a challenging pace in the battle for pole position ahead of the sixth race of the season. Stallard's Gorton was the car to beat, the Englishman having shaved two-hundredths of a second off the lap record around the circuit located amid the sun-baked plains of the Northern Territory.

The front-end mechanic strapped the driver into the

car while another disconnected the monitor and carried it to the rear of the Drogan Racing garage. Increasingly exasperated by the earlier delays, Guiscard's gloved hand impatiently brushed aside some of the desert flies endemic to the area. He pulled his visor down, eased the car into the pit lane and headed for the track. The debonair racer knew he had just the out-lap to put some heat into his tyres before attacking the circuit to nail down a quick time and elevate himself from the back of the grid. Gaudet, a man with a rigorous attention to detail, had made the fuel load calculations based on the minimum amount needed for the out-lap, one flying lap and the return to the pits, and the car had been fuelled accordingly. The circuit, regarded by some of the teams as not providing the toughest test on the FS tour, was still exacting and required total concentration as ever. Essentially flat due to the nature of the surrounding area, it consisted of two long parallel straights with three curves comprising a virtual U-shape at one end and a series of fast bends, separated by a hairpin, at the other. A left-right chicane, some distance down the start-finish straight, could be taken in fifth gear in a well-balanced car. The track, a little over 2.5 miles in length, was bounded by scrubland and sometimes the wind dumped grains of red clay on the road surface, creating an additional hazard. When that happened the continuous lapping of the cars forged a racing line, but the drivers knew the slightest deviation from it could pitch them off the circuit.

As he started the out-lap, Guiscard tried to suppress the slight unease he felt at a lack of familiarity with his surroundings. He had missed the previous year's race due to a neck injury and qualifying this time had been beset by a number of minor but persistent complications linked to the car's set-up. His team, like its rivals, had ensured the relevant track details had been fed into a computer to recreate its topography and before arriving in Australia he had spent hours in the simulator acquainting himself with the layout of the circuit. And while that had been of some benefit, he knew there was no substitute for putting in the laps along the straights and through the bends. Despite the pressure of having just one lap in which to determine his car's position on the grid, the Frenchman's mood was lifted by the knowledge that being last to qualify would at least give him one advantage. Competitors who went out first would suffer from a relative lack of grip due to dirt and debris on the track, resulting in slower lap times. But as the session wore on, rubber from their tyres would be laid down on the road surface and grip levels would increase, so drivers who left their qualifying late could record times up to a second a lap faster.

Guiscard came across two other cars on his out-lap but their drivers were slowing down and when they spotted him rapidly approaching in their rear-view mirrors, they moved aside and he passed them without incident. He exited the last bend before the pit straight, a tight right-hander, and moved up through the gears knowing he had less than ten seconds to begin his flying lap before the clock ran down. It was not an unfamiliar situation for the Frenchman, or indeed, any of his rivals. In a profession demanding total commitment and where the difference between success and failure is calibrated in fractions of a second, its practitioners have trained to deal with such pressures. He felt the adrenaline kick in as the Drogan flashed over the start-finish line, its three-litre V10 engine shrieking as the driver buried the throttle. Spectators in the tiered seats of the half-full grandstand watched as Guiscard accelerated past the elevated structure but he was oblivious of them as his eyes focused further down the main straight and the looming high-speed chicane. He knew he had to drive aggressively through it to have any chance of setting a quick lap time but precision and a skilful change of direction were also vital. Two hundred metres before the chicane he selected fifth gear and positioned the car for the left-right manoeuvre at 145 miles per hour. Then he was on it, a flick of the steering wheel to the left followed almost immediately by a reverse movement, the tyres generating sufficient grip as the car attacked the kerbs.

The Drogan came out of the chicane almost as fast as it had entered and Guiscard capitalised on a decent exit, changing up to sixth then seventh gear and approaching top speed for a flat-out burst along another section of straight leading to the three curves at the northern end of the circuit. He instinctively jabbed the brake pedal and the car slowed from 195 miles per hour to just over 90, and a firm touch of his finger found third gear for the first of the sequence of corners, a moderate right-hander. Alert to the need to not over-cook his tyres early in the lap, the driver put the nose of the car exactly where he wanted it, the right front and rear wheels clipping the apex of the bend and hurling a cloud of dust into the air. Then he was through it and having to grapple with the next two corners: a tight turn to the left followed by a fast right, which led to a high-speed section down the long back straight.

Due to the elongated nature of the track, and with nearly two-thirds of the lap spent at full power, the team had decided to run the car with as little downforce as possible. This sacrificed some grip through the corners but boosted performance on the straights, and Guiscard, a figure of utter concentration, was intent on exploiting this element of the car's set-up. Carrying a substantial amount of speed through the last corner, he up-shifted to top gear and set out on the run down to the bottom of the circuit. Aided by a prevailing northerly tail wind, the car, displaying the red and green colours of Drogan Racing, sped along the deserted straight. For all the intensity of thought and dexterity needed to drive at high speed and under pressure to record a quick lap time, the Frenchman remained composed. Cocooned in his cockpit he felt at ease with his car, an empathy that racers are always seeking but that, he told himself, can be strangely elusive. And still the rev counter needle continued to climb, the car hurtling along at more than 200 miles per hour. He steadied himself for the next corner, a sweeping right-hander that dared a driver to stay on the throttle for as long as possible before the laws of physics started to exert their inevitable influence on the car's ability to stick to the track.

Guiscard relished the challenge and kept his foot to the floor as the bend rushed towards him. A slight touch of the steering wheel induced a marginal change of direction without any discernible loss of speed. As the Drogan advanced deeper into the corner, its driver waited for the moment when he sensed the front wheels were close to the limit of adhesion. When it came, he forced his car into a controlled sideways slide and the resultant scrubbing effect and lateral loads on the tyres acted as a brake. With his speed cut to 170 miles per hour, the Gallic driver dropped down a gear to sixth and skilfully brought the car out of the slide as he found the shortest route through the corner. Then it was back on the power for a short section of straight before some heavy braking and into second gear for a downhill right-hand hairpin. The track fell away slightly on the exit but the tarmac offered a firm grip and Guiscard accelerated rapidly towards the penultimate corner, a wide left-hander that took him onto a tight right that gradually unwound itself and led to the home straight. As he rounded the last turn and the grandstand came into view, the audio receiver in his helmet activated and Gaudet's animated voice was brief and to the point. "Pole is in your grasp. Go, Philippe, go!"

The driver needed no such exhortation from his engineer. He was already flooring the throttle but the message confirmed what he already knew: that his flying lap had been error-free, with much of it driven at close to the limit. The car devoured the remaining 300 metres with the voracity of a shoal of piranha and streaked across the start-finish line. Almost immediately, the qualifying time – a new lap record – flashed up on the many small screens located on the pit wall and in the various team garages. The Drogan mechanics punched the air in celebration and Gaudet was jubilant. "Great drive, Philippe! Fantastic effort to get pole! Well done!"

Guiscard was matter-of-fact in his response. "It was a team effort. Thanks to everyone, but the hard part is yet to come."

Although outwardly wanting to play down his prospects, he was quietly confident about achieving a second race win following his victory in the third event of the FS calendar in Mexico City. He reduced his speed but as the car headed along the back straight on the return lap, its engine began to stutter. It briefly regained power but then cut out completely and Guiscard parked at the side of the track. He smiled wryly and radioed his engineer with just the slightest trace of irony. "Congratulations, Alain, you did a brilliant job. I've run out of fuel but there was enough to do the flying lap and that's what counts. Just make sure there's enough in the tank so I can go a bit further tomorrow!" The driver released himself from the cockpit, removed his helmet and fire-proof balaclava and started the long walk back to the pits. As Guiscard took out his earplugs, he heard the discordant laughing call of a kookaburra, the Australian kingfisher, in the distance. He couldn't be certain if it was a song of praise or just mocking him.

The meeting had been called at short notice. Two hours after the qualifying session had ended and as the early evening shadows from the lofty kurkara trees began to lengthen, five team owners filed into the air-conditioned motor home occupied by Makarov Racing. The Russian, who was sitting on the front of his desk, said nothing as they entered but motioned towards two sofas displaying his team's colours and featuring its logo. His rivals, all multi-millionaires and high achievers in their respective fields, had something else in common – they were self-made men who epitomised an unwavering determination to succeed, a characteristic also reflected in their host.

Joe Gorton had pondered long and hard over his invitation to the meeting. The Gorton Racing boss always tried to stay on amicable terms with his fellow owners but had taken an instant dislike to the Russian when he joined FS. He found him irascible and domineering in debate, a man who tried to impose his views on others with greater knowledge of the sport. Also present was the second Englishman, Tom Seton, a former world motor racing champion and the founder and chairman of Seton Racing; Olivier Maigny, an airline owner and principal of the French-based Drogan Racing; Ramon Lorenzo Torres, a media tycoon and head of the Spanish team El Oro; and the American, Gus Johnson, a steel magnate and the boss of US-based Akron Racing.

Viktor Makarov waited for them to settle before he spoke. "Gentlemen, I'm grateful you could find the time to come here. I know it's the night before the race and there is still much work to be done but I hope you'll agree that what I have to say is relevant to all of us. I'll come straight to the point and make my position clear so there can be no misunderstanding. I don't like the financial structure in which we operate and which has been imposed on us by Lucas Tait. Take this season's contract – it's yet another example of how the teams were sidelined by FS in the negotiations over international marketing deals and broadcasting rights." A couple of his competitors shifted a little uneasily and raised eyebrows were exchanged as the Russian warmed to his theme. "We had no role in the discussions; we weren't even consulted. We were presented with a percentage figure and told we had to accept it as our share of the revenue. Yes, it was an increase on what we had last year and that was to be expected, but it's still well short of what we should be getting. FS is raking in huge profits from across the globe but we, the team owners, are effectively in a commercial strait-jacket and being screwed financially by Tait. From what I can see, it's been going on long enough. I don't like being ripped-off and I imagine you don't either, so I want us to do something about it."

"So what exactly have you got in mind?" asked Gorton, who found it difficult to conceal an element of sarcasm in his voice.

"We need to show him we're not prepared to put up with this situation any longer and that we mean business," answered Makarov as he raised himself from his desk. "And we hold the power because without us he has nothing. FS is about racing but if there are no cars then Tait has no show."

"Are you suggesting…" Maigny's voice tailed off as he realised he knew the likely answer before he had finished the question.

"What I'm saying is all the teams should boycott tomorrow's race to force his hand. We'll give Tait an ultimatum – we'll only take part if we have an assurance of meaningful talks to follow soon after at which this issue can be properly debated."

"So you want us to withdraw our cars from the race with less than twenty-four hours' notice?" queried Johnson.

"I do," confirmed Makarov. "That should concentrate his mind and show we are serious."

"In effect, you intend to blackmail Tait with the threat of strike action," retorted the American.

"Blackmail is an emotive word, my friend. I prefer to think of it as putting forward an action plan that seeks to achieve what is rightfully ours."

"You can look at it whatever way you like," said Gorton dismissively, "but what you are proposing is holding him to ransom until he pays up. In my book, that's blackmail!"

The Russian shrugged his shoulders. "OK, if that's your view – but you should remember that all the teams are losing out here, including yours. Each of us is being exploited and if we're going to put a stop to it, we have to act. But I think it's obvious to everyone here that if we're to win this fight we must be united in any action we take."

Torres looked thoughtful as he ran a hand through his shiny collar-length black hair. "I don't think I need to remind you, Mr Makarov, that we've all signed an agreement with FS for this season and if we go on strike we'll be in breach of contract."

"We should also remember the teams have contractual obligations to their respective sponsors and any refusal to race would contravene those commitments," added Maigny in an attempt to dissuade the Russian.

Makarov's eyes betrayed an underlying impatience but he persisted. "Sometimes contracts are signed for the wrong reasons by people who fear the consequences of not signing. Instead of having the guts to stand up for what they believe to be fair, they are railroaded into a deal because they prefer to have something rather than nothing. As a result, those contracts aren't worth the paper they're printed on."

"If you just want to tear them up, why did you sign yours?" demanded Gorton.

"As you know, I'm a comparative newcomer to this game. This is only the second year that my team is competing in FS and, to use one of your quaint English expressions, I didn't want to upset the apple cart as soon as I joined. The teams have a pivotal role in this worldwide circus but it has become increasingly clear to me that we don't have the financial recognition we deserve."

"Have you confronted Tait with your claim?"

The Russian averted his eyes from Gorton's unblinking gaze. "We had a brief discussion at the end of the race in

New Zealand but as I recall he didn't seem to be in the mood for negotiation. In fact, I got the distinct impression the subject was a no-go area." Makarov was aware that one man in the room had so far stayed silent. He turned towards Seton. "You've heard the initial reaction of your fellow owners to my proposal. I would be interested to know where you stand."

The lanky Englishman leant forward slightly in his seat. "I've been listening with interest to what's been said. I've felt for some time the teams have been at a disadvantage in the way the commercial cake is sliced but I don't think we're being ripped off by Tait, as you allege. He's had to take risks along the way but he's established FS as the pinnacle of motor sport. He deserves credit for that and he's entitled to reap the entrepreneurial rewards that result – but my gut feeling is that we're an integral part of this circus, as you call it, and we're entitled to more than we're getting."

A flicker of a smile passed across the face of the Russian. "Thank you for your support. I think your views should be treated with respect, coming as they do from a former world champion in this sport, and your colleagues would do well to note them."

But Seton wasn't finished. "Whilst I consider the teams have a genuine grievance, I don't think strike action at such short notice is the answer, apart from all the legal ramifications that would ensue. I believe we have a case, and a strong one, and we should apply pressure if we have to but we shouldn't box Tait into a corner. There might be an argument for a strike at some point down the line but first I think we need to adopt a reasonable approach in the hope of encouraging a positive response."

"I assume you have something in mind," said Torres.

"First, and most importantly, we have to prove our claim is a valid one. And that means producing the evidence to back it up based on our revenue figures in recent years. If we can convince Tait that our share of the income from marketing and broadcasting sources has declined in relative terms compared to that of FS, then he has to listen. And second, we have to demonstrate our determination to seek even-handed treatment and that we are prepared, if necessary, to consider all possible action to achieve our objective."

"But we need to apply pressure now," insisted Makarov, "otherwise there's no incentive for Tait to take us seriously."

"No, I disagree," countered Seton. "I've known him for many years and if we start acting like a bunch of British Leyland shop stewards from the 1970s and make all sorts of threatening noises, he'll refuse to negotiate. I'm convinced that if we can put forward a justifiable case, cogently argued, that'll be our best chance of winning him over."

"I think you're right," said Gorton, "but timing is crucial. I'm not sure that raising the issue halfway through the season would be to our benefit; in fact, it could backfire on us. My suggestion is that instead of taking hasty action we might come to regret, we should be thorough in preparing a water-tight case and submitting it to Tait ahead of the annual negotiations for next season. That should significantly increase our bargaining power in the new round of contract talks."

"I reckon I could go along with that," drawled Johnson. "It seems the logical step to take and could well lead to the result we're looking for."

Maigny threw a glance in Makarov's direction. "I know our Russian colleague is straining at the leash to make a challenge but I think we should be patient for a little longer. Most of us know from our own business perspective of the need for good industrial relations and FS is no exception. I founded and expanded an airline that is now one of the most efficient operators in Europe and much of that success is due to developing a culture of teamwork amongst the workforce." The Frenchman went on, "That ethos of team spirit is a powerful one and it's something I would like to see fostered even in such a competitive sport as ours. We're rivals but we're all performers on a roving international stage. We put on a display, the crowds come to see the cars and the drivers, and the ringmaster should recognise that. I think he will but if he doesn't," he paused as he surveyed the other team owners, "that will be the time to find another way to influence him."

Makarov found Maigny's comments much too conciliatory for his liking. "You make it sound as though we're all members of a cosy club and any disputes will be settled amicably by gentlemen acting in an honourable way. But we know the reality is not like that. We're in a cut-throat business where split-seconds can mean the difference between success and failure and the loss of millions in sponsorship. In our sport, car and engine development costs can quickly spiral out of control and team budgets regularly become stretched to the point that we're always looking for new backers. We can't afford to wait any longer; we should act now." The owner of Makarov Racing studied the faces of the men ranged in front of him as though seeking some visible sign of support, but their expressions remained impassive. He decided to persevere. "I don't understand why you can't see the urgency of this situation. Why aren't you convinced of the merit of our case and the pressing need for us to do something about it?"

After a brief pause the American was first to respond. "It's clear from what's been said here today that there is some support for your argument. But it's equally obvious that most of us are opposed to rushing in and taking industrial action without first giving Tait the chance to negotiate. I think our colleague, Joe, has just about gotten his finger on the right button when he advocates we should take our time and prepare the strongest case we can."

"You're just scared of Tait. You're all scared of him," said the Russian accusingly. "He seems to have a hold over the teams and you dance to his tune."

"Look, Makarov," said Gorton, failing to control his annoyance, "I think it's about time you remembered your place in the pecking order. You've been a competitor in FS for less than two years but you're acting like it's your personal fiefdom. Some of us have been here a long time and we don't like it when an upstart comes through the door and starts throwing his weight around."

Makarov glared at the Englishman. "You can call me what you like but perhaps you've been here too long and got too comfortable. It's time for change but you can't see it or don't want it."

"Don't lecture me," said Gorton. "When you've been in this business as long as I have, I might listen to you. But until then I suggest you keep your opinions to yourself."

"Whatever you say, change will come to FS, it's inevitable," said the Russian. "Without change, a business dies. That's true of any organisation and it's the way I run mine."

Gus Johnson heaved his ample frame from the larger of the two sofas and took a step towards the man hosting the meeting. "So what exactly is your business, Mr Makarov? What kinda outfit do you run out of Moscow?"

A scowl appeared on the Russian's face. "What I do in my country is not your concern, nor that of your colleagues. All you need to know is that I head a number of companies and each makes a profit."

"I'm sure we're all suitably impressed but from what I've heard some of your commercial interests are, to put it mildly, dipping their toes in illegal waters."

"You should watch your mouth, Johnson. My advice is to be very careful what you say. Insinuation is one thing, proof is another."

"Well, if we're throwing advice around pal, let me give you a dose. I don't care how you operate in Russia but I get angry when my senior driver is forced off the track and killed by a man who competes under your colours. That was the most unscrupulous racing manoeuvre I've ever seen and it cost me dearly, but you, as owner, set the tone for your team. I consider you were just as responsible for Pete Maitland's death as your driver, Petrenko, and nothing will ever change my view."

"If that's your judgment, you have to live with it. All I can say is the incident was investigated by the stewards and disciplinary action taken against my team and my driver. But that does not mean we set out to kill Maitland – that's a ludicrous idea!"

The American eyed the other team principals and said curtly, "I've heard enough. I'm outta here," and headed for the door. The others followed. It was an austere-looking Gorton, the last to leave, who turned to face the Russian.

"We didn't take a vote but there was no point. It would have been five to one against your call for immediate strike action. You have to accept the democratic will, but with your background that might be difficult."

"You're wrong there, Gorton. I don't have to accept anything."

"That's your call," said the Englishman coldly. "The rest of us will try it our way but there's nothing to stop you withdrawing your team from tomorrow's race if you want to put pressure on Tait."

Makarov sneered. "Yeah, sure, and give your guy Stallard a free ride for the championship? No chance! We want the title and we'll do everything we can to get it. Don't say I haven't warned you!"

Gorton said nothing more. He turned on his heel and left.

There was a certain incongruity about proceedings at the nearby hotel on the eve of the race. The melodic sounds of one of the great romantic concertos could be heard drifting on the desert night air. Inside the main lounge, the driver who had seized pole position in the dying seconds of qualifying with an electrifying display of car control was giving an equally virtuoso performance at a grand piano. An audience of his racing peers listened intently as the accomplished Guiscard demonstrated his musical talent by playing Brahms' Piano Concerto No 1 in D minor. The recital, for such it was by a gifted pianist, had become the central feature of the entertainment enjoyed by the drivers as they tried to relax on the night before each race. It had started as an impromptu sing-along the previous season when the charismatic Frenchman with sparkling grey-green eyes and fine features had provided the accompaniment. But one evening he revealed part of his classical repertoire to his spellbound rivals, who had since insisted he perform on a regular basis.

Guiscard had shown a versatility of promise early in life. The son of a senior politician and his lawyer wife, he was academically bright and exhibited a sporting flair as a schoolboy as well as a musical talent. His parents hoped their only child would use his linguistic skills to carve out a career in the diplomatic service but he had other ideas. An afternoon spent watching a road race for classic cars on the outskirts of his home city of Paris triggered a passion for motor sport in an eight-year-old enthralled by the spectacle. Once smitten, the youngster persuaded his father to take him to see races at a local track and eventually to buy him a kart so he could compete in junior events. Success followed but at the cost of domestic disharmony. Whilst initially supportive of their son's competitive activity, Guiscard's parents became increasingly disillusioned when he announced on his fifteenth birthday that his career choice was that of a professional racing driver. All subsequent efforts to dissuade him failed, although they clung to the hope that he might consider other options when he passed his final school examinations with distinction. But for the teenager there was no going back. He turned down a university place and instead set his mind to achieving his goal.

His karting skills had been spotted by a talent scout for Drogan Racing, who immediately recognised a raw but exciting racing aptitude. Guiscard was offered a two-year probationary contract to compete in junior series events with the option of a further two-year term with the senior team, conditional on results. His record in the formative series had been impressive, winning the drivers' title in his second year, and Drogan had no hesitation in activating the contract option. He was promoted to the number two slot in the team's FS line-up, replacing an Austrian whose performances at the senior level had been inconsistent. Guiscard soon established himself at the sport's top level and in his rookie year achieved three podium finishes in a car that experienced more than its share of technical problems. The Frenchman demonstrated an ability to learn quickly and in the current season, as Drogan's leading driver, was lying fourth in the title standings after five races, having won in Mexico City and gained another podium place in New Zealand. His teammate, the thirty-one-year-old German Otto Werner, was in joint eighth position in the championship challenge with just a single scoring finish – P4 at Mumbai.

As he played the concluding notes of the concerto, the work of the nineteenth-century German-born composer, Guiscard reflected on the major decision of his life. He had no cause for regrets even though it had provoked considerable angst in his parents at the time. But they gradually recognised his steely resolve to pursue his chosen course and became reconciled to it. Since then, he mused, they had taken a great deal of pride in his exploits, although his mother stopped watching him race after he was badly injured when a broken rear suspension flung his car into a wall at more than 140 miles per hour. It proved just a temporary setback and he was behind the wheel again within two months. Now, at almost the halfway point on the FS calendar, he was enjoying his most competitive season in a reliable car and, he reasoned, was well placed for a tilt at the title.

As the sound of the final note faded away, a spontaneous mix of applause and cheering erupted. The popular Frenchman, still seated, ran a hand through his dark wavy hair then turned and smiled at his fellow drivers, modestly acknowledging their ovation. "Bravo, Philippe, bravo," shouted the Spaniard, Rodriguez, currently heading the championship table. For all the intense and sometimes bitter rivalry between them in a sport where winning was everything, there were times, thought Guiscard, when the ferocity of the hunting pack could be subdued and it rediscovered its soul.

SEVEN

The Northern Territory sun beat down, its searing heat unrelenting as an errant cloud scudded across the cobalt-blue sky. Smoke wafted across the circuit, carried by a stiffening breeze as many fans watched the event on huge TV screens in a special compound while loading steaks and snags onto dozens of charcoal-fired barbecues. The low-pitched resonant sounds of a lone Aboriginal didgeridoo could be heard echoing intermittently against a backdrop of snarling racing engines. Guiscard had exploited pole position with an outstanding start, and with a clear track in front of him his Drogan had built up a lead of more than four seconds over his closest rival, Stallard, after twenty-two laps. The Englishman was nearly two seconds ahead of El Oro's Rodriguez, who was being pressed by the Russian, Petrenko, in P4.

The American, Lockhart, was next. She had made an exceptional start from P6 on the grid and had overtaken Pavani in the second El Oro car at the first corner, the Indian having made a relatively sluggish getaway. Seton followed with his teammate Wang and the Brazilian, Gonzalez, in the Akron, close behind. Makarov Racing's number two, the Russian Dmitry Baikov – the team's former test driver who replaced his colleague, Orlovsky, badly injured in the crash at Kowloon – was having his second outing in FS and was in P10. The remaining two racers – Boyd in an Akron and Werner in the second Drogan – were beginning to lose touch with the rest of the field. Werner was paying the price for a poor qualifying session, his car spinning into a wall, and the German had started from the back of the grid.

Guiscard was intent on enhancing his position in the championship based on a scoring system that rewards the first six drivers to finish, with six points for a win reducing to one point for P6. On sixteen points, he was three behind Petrenko, four adrift of Stallard and five off the current leader, Rodriguez. After the first round of pit stops, the Frenchman had substantially increased his lead. He had just set the fastest lap time and was now over six seconds ahead of the Spaniard, who had displaced Stallard in P2. The Englishman's mechanics had struggled to remove the refuelling hose from the Gorton's tank, losing valuable time, and Rodriguez had taken advantage. Stallard, meanwhile, was battling to hang on to P3 as he came under mounting pressure from Petrenko, whose car was quicker through the corners but couldn't match its rival on the straights. The threat was highlighted on lap 29 as the pair sped down the long back straight, the Gorton's faster pace allowing it to slightly extend its lead in the high-speed sector of the circuit before the Russian started to claw back the gap during a series of bends. The Englishman was less than a car's length ahead as he approached the downhill hairpin, braking heavily and selecting first gear to negotiate the tight right-hander at a speed of 45 miles per hour.

He controlled the racing line into the corner but the inferior grip from the Gorton's tyres was exposed as his adversary moved alongside. It was a manoeuvre the Russian had tried on previous laps when Stallard had been able to defend his position but this time he had a sixth sense that Petrenko was about to up the ante. His intuition was spot-on. As both drivers fought for supremacy, Stallard felt a nudge to the side of his car. Despite its relatively low speed, it spun violently through 360 degrees, although the driver was able to keep the engine running. But he was furious at himself for giving his rival a sniff of an opening as the car bearing the purple and orange colours of Makarov Racing was the first to reach the exit of the corner. A look of dismay spread across the face of the Englishman's race engineer who had watched a replay of the incident on one of the small screens on the pit wall.

The garage-to-car radio burst into life as Jim Crowley pressed the transmit button. "Get after him, Nick, you've got more speed on the straights."

"But he's got better grip through the corners. He glanced me as he came by – probably deliberate but hard to prove."

"Yeah, I guess the stewards will look at it but I expect the Russian will claim it's just a racing incident. Get your own back in the only way that counts – take him on the track."

Stallard didn't need any such urging as he began the chase. He had already mentally computed the circuit layout and while he could get close on the pit straight, he knew his best chance of overtaking would be on the long back straight. But his immediate task was to cut the two-second gap that separated him from his quarry. Within six laps the deficit had been reduced to half a second and by lap 38, as the two cars exited the fast right leading to the high-speed section down the back straight, the Gorton trailed by just two-tenths. Angered by the manner in which he had lost his advantage, Stallard continued to gain on the rookie. At the halfway point on the straight and accelerating in seventh gear, he was close enough to follow in his slipstream with both cars eating up the track as they approached 190 miles per hour. By now the breeze had strengthened and as random gusts deposited grains of red clay from nearby scrubland on the track, a racing line of rubbered-in grip started to develop. The Englishman was confident he had the extra speed he needed but also knew he had to risk going off the racing line, where the limited amount of grip made overtaking difficult.

A quick flick of the eyes to check the wing mirrors, then he pulled out from behind the Russian's car and got an immediate response from the three-litre V10 engine as he floored the throttle. Aware of the rookie's tendency to resort to forceful defensive tactics when under threat, Stallard swung across to the dirty side of the track as he attempted to pass. With its engine screaming and rev counter nearing its limit of 19,000 rpm, the Gorton quickly drew level then surged ahead as Petrenko tried too late to block the move.

The radio crackled once more, conveying Crowley's familiar tones. "Great move, Nick. You're five seconds behind Rodriguez but you've got the faster car and we're only just over halfway." In response to his driver's query, the engineer added, "Guiscard's right out in front – the guy's having a blinder today."

Finding himself in clear air, Stallard exploited his car's extra pace as it swallowed the track at over 200 miles per hour. Having regained P3 and intent on retaining it, he set about hunting down the Spaniard.

Floyd Collins took the call in the office of Race Control, where FS officials were monitoring the event via a raised bank of screens taking a feed from the circuit cameras. The chief steward tapped his pen on the notepad in front of him as he listened intently. "So what's your best guess? Is it likely to be a hazard at any point?" he asked. He started to frown. "If it gets any worse, be ready to flag it. Make sure you keep us informed." He abruptly ended the conversation. He replaced the phone and swivelled his chair to face his two colleagues, who by now had an inkling that something was amiss. "That was the marshals' post at the northern end of the circuit. It was an early warning. They're reporting some smoke drifting across the track close to one of the corners, the fast right-hander. It's not much at the moment but the wind's getting up and it could be a problem."

"Smoke?" queried one of the stewards. "What's causing that?"

"It seems to be coming from the nearby compound. There's a hell of a lot of fans in there and many have got their barbies going."

"Maybe it's something we should think about for next year," said the second steward.

"I'm more concerned with this year's race," snapped Collins. "I just hope we get a change of wind direction before long. Give the guys at Connellan Airport a bell and get a weather update so at least we know what to expect."

The chief steward swung his chair around with a mechanical ease and his eyes swept across the screens, searching for a visual corroboration of the marshal's report. Dozens of trackside cameras relayed pictures of the racing action and others displayed the sometimes frenetic activity of the mechanics in the pits. Despite the comprehensive coverage there was no sign of any smoke, but Collins remained uneasy. He was accustomed to being in charge of events and planning accordingly but factors outside his control posed a threat, and suddenly the odds of a trouble-free race had appeared to lengthen. As he continued to stare at the screens, the stark images of an incident more than two decades before played unbearably at the back of his mind. It still haunted him. As a team manager he had been instrumental in developing the career of a young Canadian driver who had shown great potential and was tipped as a future champion. Although just eighteen, Brent Warner had already displayed a tigerish temperament on the track and achieved a number of podium places. Collins recalled with sadness the last time he'd spoken to his protege, shortly before the start of a trans-Americas formula race at a circuit in New Mexico, when the youngster had talked with a passion about the sport he loved.

A typically bold getaway had seen him gain a couple of places from his mid-grid position and after seven laps he was challenging for the lead. The teenager in P3 emerged from a fast corner, a sweeping left-hander, and approached an incline that led to a straight. Even now, many years later, Collins still shuddered at the memory of what happened next. Two men carrying placards with wooden poles had decided to highlight the plight of unemployed Mexican immigrants to the US and picked that moment to make their protest. Warner, by now accelerating at close to 140 miles per hour, was hidden in the dip before the brow. Cresting the slope, he was confronted by the men running across the track but had no time to react. The car struck the protestors, killing them instantly, but one of the poles they were carrying smashed into the driver's helmet. The young racer who promised so much was already dead as his car flew out of control down the straight before slamming into a tyre wall. *An act of sheer lunacy and an appalling waste of life,* thought the chief steward, *the epitome of the needless racing tragedy.* It was a recollection he chose not to share with his two associates.

Crowley's description of the race leader was well merited as Guiscard was giving an exhibition of consummate driving skill. Such was his pace that by lap 45 he had extended the gap over his nearest pursuer, Rodriguez, to fifteen seconds and the French team were confident that, barring mechanical failure, their leading driver was on course for his second win of the season. The technical data from the telemetry read-outs was impressive and bolstered the feeling of optimism in the Drogan garage. But that was tempered by concern about the performance of the marque's second driver, Werner, who was in P12 and last position and in imminent danger of being lapped by his teammate. The point was reinforced by the leader's race engineer, Alain Gaudet, who told his man, "At the rate you're catching Otto, you'll be on him soon. It won't look good for him but you know what you have to do."

The driver didn't answer immediately but his response when it came was measured. "I guess it's part of racing but the team comes first. Let's hope there are no hard feelings."

"C'est la vie," was Gaudet's answer. "There's something else you should know, Philippe. A marshal's reported smoke across the track towards the northern end of the circuit. Could be a hazard so be careful."

"That's a new one but thanks for the warning," replied the French ace as he headed down the long back straight.

The team's other driver had also been alerted to the danger. Although driving another Drogan, Otto Werner's race had been in stark contrast to that of his colleague. Starting from the back of the grid after failing to record a qualifying time, his overriding aim had been one of damage limitation. As the race developed, he was involved in a thrilling clash with the American Al Boyd, in an Akron, as both men found themselves trailing the rest of the field. Werner cursed the crash early in qualifying that stopped him from putting in laps around the circuit and creating the optimum set-up for his car. The German was a man under pressure. His season had been indifferent so far, the only points coming from P4 in the second race at Mumbai, and he was currently joint eighth in the championship standings. After seven years at the top level, including stints with two other teams, he had failed to fulfil the potential displayed in the various junior categories of the sport. Now in the final year of his contract with the Paris-based outfit, he was acutely aware that another term's mediocre performance would probably spell the end of his FS career. Whilst not the oldest racer on the circuit, Werner knew that competition to secure a drive with any of the teams was fierce, with a steady stream of talented young hopefuls waiting to be plucked from the ranks of the feeder formulas.

Those thoughts were uppermost in his mind as he continued his duel with Boyd, the former Akron test driver who had found the transition to FS a difficult one since replacing the New Zealander Pete Maitland, killed in the opening race of the season. The American had often struggled in qualifying, finishing as a backmarker in several races, but pride was now a major motivating factor and he was determined to keep the German behind him. Both drivers, separated by less than a car's length, negotiated the tight right-hander that led to the pit straight to complete lap 49 and headed north. The fervour of the fans in the packed grandstand signalled they were becoming as much enthralled with the battle unfolding at the back of the grid as with the rivalry for places at the front. The two tail-enders approached the high-speed chicane, down-shifting to fifth, their cars seemingly glued together. Then they were through it and accelerating along the flat-out section leading to the series of bends at the top end of the circuit. Both had acknowledged the alert about a potential smoke threat but they were irresistibly caught up in a conflict demanding all their energy and attention. Werner, almost involuntarily, had pushed the warning to the back of his mind as he concentrated on the one imperative that dominated his thoughts – overtaking Boyd.

Meanwhile, the senior marshal who had raised the alarm after spotting the first wisps of smoke wafting between the tall kurkaras bordering a section of track wondered if he had over-reacted. An experienced observer, Jim Harkin could only recall one previous incident of a similar kind at another Northern Territory circuit but that race had not been adversely affected. He tried to convince himself he had imagined it but the appearance of a second pall of smoke quickly brought him back to reality. He could smell it now as it lingered in the air for a moment before being propelled on a gust of desert wind. Then the realisation that the strengthening wind had suddenly changed direction left him with a sense of foreboding. It was blowing the smoke directly towards the track at the last of the three corners on his sector. Jolted into action, Harkin pulled out his mobile phone to alert the nearest flag marshals and then started to sprint back to his post. He fervently hoped there was still time to warn the drivers.

Boyd, with Werner in his slipstream, was now approaching the first of those bends, a right-hander, at 190 miles per hour. His eyes sought and found the braking point. Down to third gear and with his speed more than halved, the American cajoled his car through the turn. Just inches behind, Werner knew there was little to choose between them for straight-line speed and that his best chance of getting past was at a corner. He steeled himself to strike as the pair raced towards the next two curves leading to the back straight.

Trackside, as Harkin's stocky, panting frame came into view, the two flag men were working non-stop. Each was vigorously waving a yellow pennant, the signal for drivers to slow down, prepare to take evasive action and stop if necessary. The flag marshals in the preceding post, located 300 metres before the series of bends, had also been told of the danger and immediately started waving their own yellows. Despite their prompt response it was now too late. The American and German racers, engrossed in their private feud at the back of the field, had streaked past them seconds before.

The phone rang again in the office of Race Control. The chief steward instantly recognised Harkin's voice but this time it was breathless and agitated. "It's the marshals' post in the northern sector. That smoke I told you about, it's getting worse. We're yellow flagging up here. You need to do the same across the circuit."

"How bad is it?" asked Collins.

"As far as I can tell, it seems to be affecting the area close to the fast right that leads to the back straight. You're going to have to put those fans with the barbies further back from the track in future. It's got out of hand this time."

"I'm well aware what's causing this problem but the priority is to deal with what's happening now. Have the leaders gone by yet?"

Harkin continued to gasp for breath. "I haven't seen them but they can't be far away."

"Stay on the line." Collins paused as one of his colleagues had an urgent word with him. Then his grip tightened on the phone as he pressed it close to his mouth. "Because of the way the race is developing, it seems the two backmarkers will be in the danger area first. For God's sake, make sure they see the flags in time!"

The chief steward hung up, the anxiety he felt clearly projected on his face, and once more scrutinised the bank of screens before him.

On the track, Boyd and Werner had slowed sufficiently to take the tight left, the second of the sequence of corners. Then both were hard on the throttle for a fast burst along a short straight rimmed by kurkaras leading to the sweeping right that could be taken at close to 145 miles per hour.

There was barely any daylight between the cars as they neared the bend, with Boyd's focus alternating between keeping his eyes on the road ahead and watching hawk-like in his wing mirrors for any sign of an attempt to overtake by his pursuer. As the American sped into the corner, the protective strip on his helmet visor suddenly misted up. He swore and one hand reached up to tear it off but in a split-second he was confronted by every racing driver's worst nightmare – a total and unexpected loss of vision. As his car clipped the apex of the turn it was enveloped in a sheet of smoke. Temporarily blinded, Boyd instinctively started to brake, but the German, immediately behind and in stubborn pursuit, was still on the power. His right-front wheel struck the rear of the Akron, which acted as a launching ramp and shot the Drogan twenty feet into the air. It struck a tree, uprooting it, then flew across to the other side of the track and landed upside down in a cloud of dust on a grass verge.

Seconds after the impact, a stunned Werner realised he was still conscious. With his body facing the ground, he tried to move but couldn't unclip the metal buckles that fastened the car's restraining belts. Then he smelt it – the first hint of the horror to come. A fuel pipe had fractured in the crash and there was a brief flare-up of flame, which soon subsided, but ominously, smoke started to enter the cockpit. By now the other drivers had seen the waved yellow flags and cut their speed as they approached the danger area. The first to reach the scene was the race leader who was dismayed to glimpse the crumpled wreckage of his teammate's car. Without a moment's hesitation, Guiscard pulled over to the side, braking hard, and skidded to a stop. He scrambled out of his machine and ran back to the spot where his trapped colleague was shouting for help. Despite a sudden flicker of bright reddish-yellow flame, the Frenchman seized one of the upturned wheels and, straining every muscle in his body, tried to push the car over. But his repeated attempts proved futile. Frustrated by his failure, he looked around and saw two marshals watching him from across the track. He ran towards them, raising his visor. He grabbed the arm of one, imploring them to assist. "You've got to help me! There's a driver in there. We've got to turn the car over and get him out."

There was no response. Both men seemed paralysed, the fear they felt showing in their eyes, unable to force themselves to approach the Drogan. Inexplicably, thought Guiscard, neither marshal was wearing fireproof clothing, but now wasn't the time to interrogate them. One was holding a fire extinguisher. The Frenchman snatched it from him and returned to the smoking car, where the distressed Werner was still pleading for help.

"We're going to get you out of there, Otto. Just hang on a bit longer, help is on the way," said Guiscard, anxious to reassure his teammate. He tried to operate the extinguisher but it lacked sufficient pressure and what foam had been in the container oozed agonisingly slowly from the aperture on its top before trickling down the side. He flung the white-coloured cylinder violently onto the track and, gripping another of the upturned wheels, renewed his efforts to right the vehicle. The Frenchman felt as if every sinew was at breaking point, his head pounded and the veins on his temple stood out like strips of rope. Again and again, he tried to force the car upright but it barely shifted. Raging at his impotence, he vented his fury at the watching marshals. "Is that all you cowards can do – stand and stare?

There's a driver who could be burnt to death in there and you won't help him. You're both gutless!"

A crackling noise caught his attention. As he turned back to the Drogan, the fire flared up again and black smoke, thicker now, curled high into the air and Guiscard was forced to take a few steps back. Then he heard a distant siren and immediately recognised the distinctive sound of a fire truck. He whirled around expectantly but the vehicle was still some way from the scene of the accident. Cars were continuing to pass by although at a reduced speed under the yellow flags. *What the hell's going on?* thought the Frenchman. *Why aren't they waving the red flags to stop the race so the fire truck can get here quicker?* He tried to move closer to the burning car and called out repeatedly to his teammate but this time there was no response. The German had fallen silent, his anguished cries now just a piercing memory for the distraught Guiscard.

The full extent of the tragedy unfolding on the track was not yet apparent to those in the office of Race Control. One of the trackside cameras had captured the image of the crashed car but those viewing the pictures could see a driver nearby and initially concluded he had escaped from the wreckage. But their relief was quickly followed by a sense of puzzlement when the camera focused on two marshals venturing closer to the Drogan, resulting in seemingly angry exchanges between them and the driver. When the officials tried to lead him away from the scene, he shook them off, pointed at the car and lashed out with his foot at the fire extinguisher lying on the ground.

"That's Guiscard, the race leader," asserted Floyd Collins, identifying the Frenchman by the Gallic-inspired colours on his crash helmet. "But I thought the backmarkers were…" His voice faltered and a second later the inference of his words hit home. "Oh shit, that's not his car! It's a Drogan alright but it's got to be Werner's."

At that moment, as if to confirm the chief steward's mounting anxiety, a troubled Harkin had put in another call. "You've got to stop the race. There's a driver trapped in a burning car but we can't get near him."

"Where on earth are the fire-fighters?"

"Don't ask! It seems the nearest marshals had just one extinguisher between them and that was worse than useless. The fire truck's on the way but it's having to make a detour to get here because the race is still on. And we're going to need a doctor."

Collins glowered into the phone. "I'll have the race stopped at once," he bristled, "but afterwards I'll want to know what went wrong – and you'd better come up with some answers!"

The air of uncertainty that had temporarily descended on Race Control vanished abruptly. The flag controller was in immediate radio contact with the marshals' posts and ordered red flags to be displayed around the circuit. The drivers slowed down and headed for the start-finish line to come to a halt on the grid in the positions they held when the race was stopped. Precisely five minutes and twenty-three seconds after Werner's car plunged to the ground, the driver of the fire truck manoeuvred his vehicle close to the scene of the crash. Two fire-fighters, clad in orange-coloured flameproof overalls, were standing next to two large extinguishers with hose reels mounted in the back of the pick-up. From a range of twelve feet, one fired short bursts of dry powder at the burning Drogan. More powder was directed and the flames began to subside. The other then activated the second extinguisher, spraying foam onto the smouldering car. A little over a minute after the arrival of the fire truck, the blaze was out.

The three-man crew leapt from the truck and joined Guiscard as he tried again to right the upturned car. The two track marshals started to move closer but the Frenchman, who had now removed his helmet and fire-proof balaclava, was still seething at their earlier refusal to assist him in the rescue attempt. "You're too late, you arseholes," he yelled at them, "five minutes too late! You had your chance but you didn't have the balls. You're a disgrace to the sport!" Stung by the criticism, the pair retreated and one bent down to pick up the discarded white cylinder lying on the track, provoking a parting shot from the driver. "And next time, if you're ever allowed near a race track again, make damn sure your equipment's working!"

Guiscard rejoined the others who were straining to push the Drogan over onto its wheels. All four men were impelled by the thought that so much time had already been wasted in a situation when speed of reaction was crucial but each clung to the fervent hope that somehow the trapped driver would survive. Grunting and clammy in the heat, they gave a concerted massive shove and the burnt, battered racing car finally toppled over, shuddering as its tyres hit the ground.

Werner, in stained fire-resistant overalls, was unmoving. Still firmly strapped in his seat, his head rested at a slight angle on his chest. With no sign of the circuit's mobile medical unit, one of the fire crew supported the driver's neck to prevent it twisting while Guiscard hurriedly undid the chin strap of the helmet and eased it off, together with the balaclava. The Frenchman noted his colleague's eyes were open but appeared to be unseeing. Bending down, he called out his name several times but there was no response. Drogan's leading driver looked around forlornly.

"Where the hell is the medical back-up?" he yelled at the fire-fighters. "What sort of clowns are running this race?" He removed his gloves, turned back to his teammate in the smoke-blackened cockpit and pinched the skin on his face. Again there was no reaction. He tugged off one of Werner's gloves, feeling his wrist for any sign of a pulse, and thought he detected the faintest trace when the clanging sound of a two-tone klaxon heralded the arrival of medical assistance. A specially equipped estate car carrying Rick Manvers and a couple of paramedics, followed by an ambulance, pulled alongside.

Guiscard and the fire crew stepped back to allow the emergency team access to Werner. After an initial assessment it was decided to remove him from the car and he was laid gently on the track, a folded blanket under his head. The medical director ensured the German's airway was clear and the paramedics began an intensive session of cardio-pulmonary resuscitation, one giving mouth-to-mouth breaths followed by the other with chest compressions. After several minutes they paused to check for evidence of breathing but there were no visible signs. Manvers administered oxygen and the paramedics redoubled their efforts, but it was becoming increasingly apparent to Guiscard that they were simply going through the motions and the fight to save his colleague had been lost in the critical moments immediately after the crash.

Eventually, those trying to force life into the lifeless Werner yielded to the inevitable. The doctor's final tests confirmed the driver was dead and he summoned the stretcher crew from the ambulance to convey the body to the circuit's medical centre before it was airlifted to the nearest hospital for a post-mortem examination. As the physician picked up his medical bag and started to walk to his car, he felt a hand on his arm and turned to find himself facing a disconsolate Guiscard.

"He shouldn't have died, doc. He survived the crash, he was alive. I could hear him shouting for help but I couldn't reach him."

"Don't blame yourself, Philippe. It's sad but sometimes these things happen in motor sport."

"But this was avoidable. Otto wasn't badly injured – he was asphyxiated by smoke inhalation. That's what killed him! If only the marshals had helped me, we could have got the car the right way up and released him in time. But they were more concerned about not putting themselves in danger."

Manvers looked sympathetically at the Frenchman. "I know you've lost a teammate and I understand what that means, but it's too early to give the cause of death. There'll have to be an autopsy and then we'll know."

The normally imperturbable Guiscard was starting to lose patience. "Yeah, sure, the pathologist will state the exact cause, the formalities will be completed and the FS circus will move on to the next circuit. But we fucked-up, doc, and you know it! We let a driver die when there was no need. A good man, a professional racer, has gone and we could have saved him."

"Look, Philippe, you guys know the risks every time you drive out of the garage, it's part of racing. You can't torment yourself every time there's a fatality or you would never get in a car again."

"Of course we accept the risks, but what happened here today was totally unacceptable! Two marshals failed to perform their duties. They weren't wearing fireproof clothing – they were in shorts, for heaven's sake – and their equipment was grossly inadequate. They had just one fire extinguisher between them and even that didn't work!"

The medical director started to move towards his car. "I'm sure the organisers will have to answer some searching questions from Race Control but that's for later. Now I'm going back to the medical centre – I have to supervise the arrangements for transferring Werner's body to hospital. And you need to return to the grid before the race is re-started."

"Let me tell you something, doc. When the other drivers find out about this, they'll be asking some probing questions themselves. We've got to improve track safety and I'm damned if any of us are going to put up with a repetition of this sort of shambles!"

The despondent French driver walked slowly to his car parked at the side of the track and found two members of his pit crew waiting for him. They had been authorised to access the circuit to assist the former pace-setter, who would have to re-start at the back of the grid following his heroic but futile attempt to save his teammate. Guiscard climbed in, replaced his balaclava and helmet, and the mechanics strapped him into the safety harness, tightening his lap and shoulder belts before firing up the engine. A thumbs-up from the driver and the Drogan headed down the long back straight towards the series of bends that led to the start-finish line. As he swerved his car from side to side in an attempt to put some heat back into the tyres the Frenchman knew the time to grieve for a lost colleague would come later. His predominant feeling was one of rage as he slotted into position at the rear of the pack but he was also enough of a professional to realise an angry driver can easily make a mistake.

It was a thought that had not escaped his race engineer. "I can only guess how you must be feeling Philippe," radioed Gaudet, "but you must put what's happened to one side. You have to channel all that resentment into your driving, make it work for you. For now, there's only one objective – go from the back of the grid and gain as many places as possible."

Guiscard's reply was nothing if not laconic. "This one's for Otto!"

His immediate focus was on the rear of the two cars just ahead of him, Boyd's Akron and the second Makarov with Baikov aboard. Then his eyes lifted and settled on the large steel-encased light suspended thirty feet above the track. He engaged the clutch, selected first gear and waited. An anticipatory hush descended over the thousands of fans filling the grandstand. The tannoy announcer had told them a car had crashed at the northern end of the circuit and they had watched the television pictures on the big screen but were unaware of the fatality as it was decided to withhold details until the race was over. They weren't alone. Of the eleven racers lining up for the re-start, only Guiscard knew of the grievous tragedy that had befallen his fellow driver. But he was intent on pushing it to the back of his mind, at least until he crossed the finishing line.

A wholly contrasting feeling – one of relief – was coursing through the Spanish nobleman, who unexpectedly found himself at the front of the grid. Before the crash he had been in P2, fifteen seconds behind Guiscard and struggling to prevent the gap widening. Now his car, in El Oro's gold and blue colours, sat just ahead of Stallard's black and green Gorton and Petrenko's purple and orange Makarov. Rodriguez, currently leading the championship by one point, knew he had to capitalise on his stroke of good fortune, whatever the circumstances that triggered it. Like the others, he stared incessantly at the elevated light, impatient that it still showed red. "Come on," he muttered to himself, "get us out of here! The engines are starting to overheat and we're losing temperature from the tyres."

Five rows back on the grid, Guiscard was concentrating on holding his engine at the right amount of revs and stopping his car inching forward, aware of the ultra-sensitive track sensors that would detect any movement. He steadied himself, poised like a cheetah that has just spotted its prey. Then red turned to green and his pent-up fury and frustration were unleashed in a masterly display of racing skills. The Drogan swiftly arrowed between the Akron and the Makarov, catching Boyd and Baikov unawares. Each had been expecting an attacking move to come from the outside of the track but both were wrong-footed and in less than 150 metres they found themselves trailing the Frenchman.

At the front, Rodriguez had started badly. Eager to press home his unexpected advantage, he had spun his front wheels and was slow getting off the line. Stallard seized his chance and raced into the lead with twenty-two of the seventy-five laps remaining. Petrenko in P3 also tried to cash in on the opening but the Spaniard moved across the track, forcing the Russian to run wide. Side by side, they chased after the Gorton driver who was heading for the high-speed chicane nearly two-thirds of the way along the main straight. The Englishman negotiated the left-right turns at 145 miles per hour closely followed by his pursuers, with Rodriguez just having the edge on Petrenko. Both would have to ease off the throttle and the Spaniard gambled that as he was on the racing line, it would be the Russian who would lift first. But the rookie refused to give way and kept his foot down and the cars touched. Rodriguez struggled to keep control; he maintained his angle of approach and avoided the kerbs but his rival hurtled across the gravel trap, spinning twice before coming to a halt. Petrenko managed to keep his engine running and, finding some grip, steered the Makarov towards the track but lost two places as Lockhart and Pavani went by.

Despite the incident at the chicane, the fans were soon galvanised by the drama that was unfolding behind the front-runners. As the race entered its closing stages, Guiscard displayed the unrivalled flair he had shown earlier. After his explosive start from the back of the grid, he moved steadily through the field, passing Gonzalez, Wang and Seton on consecutive laps to claim P6. Having cleared the midfield traffic, the Frenchman powered around the circuit, beating his own lap record set an hour earlier. Ahead of him, Petrenko had regained P3 after Lockhart and Pavani ran into trouble. The American driver experienced an intermittent gearbox problem and the Indian was forced to make an extra pit stop to replace a flat-spotted tyre caused by repeatedly locking his brakes. Now they were next in the sights of the Frenchman who was racing with a belief borne out of an ardent desire to avenge the death of his teammate. He quickly closed on Pavani, who had just exited the pit lane, and overtook him before the chicane. Then he hunted down Lockhart who was holding on to P4 despite the occasional loss of fourth and fifth gears. She kept him at bay for as long as she could but the Gorton's lack of mid-range pace was no match for the Drogan, which sprinted past shortly after emerging onto the back straight following the series of bends at the northern end of the circuit.

The crowd enthused over Guiscard's stellar racing performance and roared for more as he hunted down the three drivers in front of him, but with less than five laps to go he was aware time was starting to run out. He was gaining on Petrenko at a rate of two-tenths of a second a lap and with the Russian leading by just over a second, the Drogan driver knew that if he could get close enough to put real pressure on the rookie it might force a crucial error. Spurred on by the increasingly vocal urging of his race engineer, he remorselessly reeled in his younger opponent like a pack of hounds scenting blood, closing on its quarry.

By now Petrenko was mindful of the threat looming in his rear-view mirrors. So too was the hectoring Russian owner, who commandeered the team radio and left his driver in no doubt as to what was expected of him. "You have to keep that French car behind you at all costs! And no mistakes – don't forget, you are P3 in the championship and fighting to win it." Makarov's protege needed no such reminder. With Stallard and Rodriguez – the other main contenders for the title – now leading him by several seconds and almost certain to finish the race in P1 and P2, Petrenko knew there was no room for error.

As the pair started out on the long back straight for the last time, the Drogan closed to within slipstreaming distance and got a tow from the Makarov as it punctured the air in front. Petrenko nailed his throttle in an effort to extract the last ounce of power from the engine to preserve his slender lead. The experienced Frenchman knew he would have to deal with the turbulence caused by running in the dirty air expelled from the car ahead, which made overtaking more difficult, but he hadn't reckoned on a freakish quirk of fate. As the Russian tore the last strip off his visor it flew directly into the Drogan's air intake, partly blocking it and restricting the air flow needed to cool the ten-cylinder engine. Guiscard's peripheral vision had detected the merest blur as the visor cover was sucked violently into the duct above and behind his head but he feared the worst. As both cars swallowed the track at speeds approaching 200 miles per hour, the Frenchman swung out from behind and tried to pull alongside his rival. His car inched closer to the Makarov and at one point the cockpits were level, but the Drogan engine, with its cooling system impaired, was starting to overheat and lacking the extra pace to move ahead. Guiscard knew his opportunity had gone and the Russian stayed in front, preserving his lead through the series of fast bends, separated by a hairpin, at the southern end of the circuit.

As the pair emerged onto the home-straight with barely any daylight between them, the screaming fans in the grandstand leapt to their feet, hoping the Frenchman could produce an even more sensational climax in the remaining 300 metres. It was not to be. Petrenko, benefitting from his opponent's misfortune, narrowly staved off the challenge and crossed the start-finish line to claim the last spot on the podium. Guiscard completed his slow-down lap, parked his car in the area reserved for scrutineering and walked wearily back to the garage. He raised a hand as the crowd, which had just been informed of Werner's death, yelled their admiration for a gutsy display by a driver who had put loyalty to a stricken colleague before his own title aspirations.

Despite the Frenchman's exceptional race, it was a subdued Drogan team that met for dinner in the hotel that evening. Mourning their dead driver, the atmosphere was not improved when they heard the circuit's owners had issued a statement implying that Werner had died in the impact. But the following day the official post-mortem report confirmed what Guiscard already knew – the German had been alive and uninjured but died of asphyxiation. The French-based outfit lodged a formal complaint against the race organisers, claiming gross negligence in their safety procedures, and threatened court action. The circuit's director of racing was ordered to appear before a specially convened disciplinary panel of FS stewards and asked to account for the actions of the two marshals allegedly implicated in Werner's death. Drogan's leading driver was also called to give evidence.

The stewards' findings, released twenty-four hours later, left no room for doubt as to the gravity with which they viewed the circumstances surrounding the fatality. The organisers were ordered to pay a fine of one million Australian dollars and informed that the Northern Territory circuit would be dropped from the FS calendar for the following season. They were also warned that any future application to stage a race would be subject to a rigorous inspection of track safety and marshalling standards. A brief sentence at the end of the statement dealt with a protest by the Russian team owner, who alleged Petrenko had been deliberately impeded by Rodriguez and forced to run wide during the re-start. Makarov's call for his driver to be awarded the P2 spot on the podium instead of the Spaniard was rejected by the stewards, who argued the action had been defensive and a legitimate racing manoeuvre.

Later that day Floyd Collins made a point of calling at the motor home of the Drogan principal to convey his sympathy over the loss of the team's number two driver. The chief steward found Olivier Maigny and Guiscard in a sombre mood in one of the ground-floor offices. The two men had minutes earlier returned to the paddock from the hospital mortuary, where they had viewed the corpse of their erstwhile colleague.

"I just wanted you to know the rest of us are feeling some pain as well," said Collins. "Whenever we lose anyone in a sport like ours it casts a long shadow."

"We appreciate you taking the time to come over, Floyd." Maigny looked at his driver. "I know we're supposed to be hardened to this kind of thing but…" his voice faltered, "it still hurts. And the way it happened only makes it worse."

Collins glanced up at a photo of a smiling Werner in racing overalls that adorned one of the walls. "The organisers failed your guy, no doubt about that. They screwed up big-time but they're not getting away with it. We've imposed a heavy fine; we're switching to an alternative circuit for next year's race; and they know they'll have to up their game substantially if they want to be reinstated."

Guiscard had been staring out of a window watching the huge Seton Racing transporter. Capable of storing forty tons of equipment, including enough spares to build a car from scratch, the articulated leviathan was driven slowly out of the paddock.

"Reinstated?" he asked rhetorically. The Frenchman turned to face the chief steward. "After what we've been through this weekend?"

"There'll be a major shake-up," said Collins. "I can promise you that."

"Not before time. The people who run this circuit must be fired and those who replace them have to demonstrate their competence to do the job. Driver confidence has to be restored, it's a vital issue for us."

"I understand how you feel and I—"

"I doubt if you can," interrupted Guiscard. "This afternoon Olivier and I were at the mortuary. We were shown into a darkened side room. The blinds were drawn and the only light came from a small table lamp. A plain wooden coffin rested on a central platform covered in purple velvet with gold edging and the lid was raised. I guess we each had our own expectations in that moment but you can never be fully prepared for it. If ever there was a condemnation of the failings of our sport, it was lying right there. Otto looked serene, not a mark on his face, not a broken bone in his body. He died from smoke inhalation, his brain starved of oxygen. But we all know what the real cause of death was!" He looked intently into the eyes of the chief steward. "He was killed by incompetence and neglect. He died because of the failure of those responsible for his safety to carry out their duties properly. And that's a disgrace!"

Collins took a step forward and gently put an arm around the Frenchman's shoulders. "Philippe, it may not be much consolation to you but I can only say we're all hurting. It should never have happened, we know that. It's too late for Otto but we owe it to him to work like hell to prevent a similar tragedy in the future."

"In my country," said the Drogan driver, "we have an old saying – *aux grands maux les grands remedes*: to desperate evils, desperate remedies. If that's what it takes to make this place safe, you must act. There can be no excuses now."

"Floyd knows that," said Maigny, trying to reassure his racer. "This has been an appalling episode for our team but you must not allow yourself to be distracted, Philippe – you still have a job to do. After six races and midway through the season, you are fourth in the championship and only seven points behind the joint leaders. You have to re-focus and maintain your challenge for the title."

Guiscard turned to face his boss, the airline owner who had taken him from kart racing and provided the chance to compete at the top level of motor sport. "There's no need to worry on that score. Otto's death and the way he died has given me all the motivation I want."

The cranking sound of winching equipment outside caught his attention and he spun around to see Werner's car slowly being hoisted onto one of the team's race trucks. The sight of the battered monocoque that had entombed his colleague re-ignited in Guiscard a feeling of utter futility at the needless waste of a life. As the wreck was ratcheted upwards, it seemed that each turn of the creaking, winding mechanism was inflicting yet more psychological pain on him.

EIGHT

It stared at him with malign intent, its baleful eyes unblinking. Its forked tongue darted in and out of its mouth as it basked in the thirty-three-degree-Celsius heat that radiated from the four spotlights and ceramic heating elements of the wood and acrylic glass enclosure. Its skin, displaying a variegated light brown and black pattern, was lustrous in the brightness. Although virtually motionless, the twelve-foot-long Burmese python, weighing 140 pounds, exuded a muted menace. Viktor Makarov stared back with equal resolve as he waited for his chief henchman to arrive. It was a routine he always observed when at his office in central Moscow. The large and powerful snake, which had been specially transported from south-east Asia, both fascinated and amused him, particularly at feeding time. It only required food once every ten to fourteen days and the importers had stressed the need to serve it a diet of pre-killed prey. But the mafia boss derived a perverted gratification from seeing live animals placed in the reptile's cage and the ensuing but inevitable outcome.

He had witnessed a rat put up a desperate fight for life, inflicting several bites on the python, before succumbing.

When the constrictor was ready for its next meal, a fully grown rabbit was duly put in the enclosure. The petrified creature sat seemingly paralysed as the predator moved towards it, slithering slowly over the layer of aspen wood shavings and paper bedding that covered the floor of the enclosure. At the last second, the animal's instinct for survival overcame the terror that had rooted it to the spot and it tried to evade its deadly pursuer – but it was too late. Makarov had watched mesmerised as the python struck with an open mouth, its sharp backward-pointing teeth firmly gripping the animal, while throwing loops of its body around its quarry. Tightening its coils, the snake crushed its prey, which ceased struggling and quickly suffocated. The python then unwound itself before starting to devour its victim, using the elongated ligaments in its jaws to swallow the rabbit whole. In his warped satisfaction, the Russian wasn't quite sure whether he preferred to be a spectator to a grossly unequal struggle to the death or to admire the masterly technique of one of the world's most efficient killing machines.

As he pondered the point, a rap on the door signalled that his call had been answered. Despite having regular access to his employer, the shaven-headed Serb knew his place and waited for the summons to enter the room. "Get yourself in here, Vuk. Come and have a look at this baby." For a big man, Vukasin Jovanovic moved with feral agility, striding across the large office to join Makarov, who gestured in front of him. The Slav slightly arched his six-foot-three frame but his coal-black eyes, focusing downwards on the creeping occupant of the well-lit enclosure, did not betray his secret. The man of violence who never hesitated to obey his master's orders had just one phobia – and now he was looking straight at it.

He had told himself a hundred times his fear was irrational but, however hard he tried, a shadowy recess of his mind always induced the recollection of an incident that cemented the resentment he felt about his childhood. His father, an agricultural worker in central Serbia, deserted the family before his son was born. His poverty-stricken mother, struggling to cope with three other children, abandoned him in a neighbouring village soon after and he was taken to an orphanage in the city of Smederevo about 40 miles south-east of the capital, Belgrade. It was a tough upbringing made worse by the staff using a bullying culture to encourage discipline, and the youngsters also had to endure a meagre diet. Vuk's pugnacious nature flourished in such conditions and at fifteen he nearly killed another boy in a fight over a girl and was himself badly scarred on his right cheek, a physical legacy he still bore. The brawl, one of a series of such incidents and coming after several warnings about his behaviour, prompted his expulsion from the orphanage and he was left to fend for himself.

Forced to sleep rough in farm outbuildings, he found food hard to come by and stole whatever he could to survive. After several days without eating, the teenager had stopped close to a stream to rest during the early afternoon heat when he became aware of the slightest movement in the stunted undergrowth nearby. Squatting on a patch of weed-covered grass he instinctively recoiled when the reptile came into view. Greyish-green in colour and over a metre long, the non-venomous dice snake slid along the ground for twice its full length before stopping, its chemical receptors alerting the creature to the whiff of danger. Vuk's initial desire to flee the scene was swiftly displaced by the debilitating pangs of hunger that were starting to overwhelm him. Searching nervously for a makeshift weapon, his eyes alighted on a stone the size of a man's fist. The youngster's mouth was dry and his pulse quickened as he rose from his haunches and picked it up. Holding it aloft, he warily approached the motionless snake from behind.

Vuk was closer now, standing over his target as though transfixed. A second later the rock came down in a deadly arc but the potency of the strike was diminished as the serpent had begun to move. It sustained a glancing blow to its head and, although stunned, tried to slither away. Its assailant, sweat pouring from his temples and driven by fear and starvation, launched a savage attack. The snake lay writhing on the ground, its dark-red blood staining the grass, its body twisting and jerking as the stone rained down in a repetitive frenzy. A final, contorted spasm and then its death-throes were ended. Gasping for breath, Vuk sank to his knees. Turning the snake over with a stick he was surprised to see its belly was coloured a vivid yellow with black spots.

Pulling a small knife from his pocket and gritting his teeth, he severed the reptile's battered head, tossing it into the undergrowth. More frantic slicing and the salivating Serb removed the skin from a six-inch length of the snake's body before raising it to his lips. Tightening his eyes against the sun, and his mind against the abnormality of the moment, he hesitated. Then, biting ferociously, he started to devour the disconnected flesh. He ate with gusto, swallowing quickly as if to mask what he was ramming into his mouth. The knife blade glinted again in the bright sunlight and another slice was in his hand. Impatient, thrusting fingers forced the snake meat towards eager jaws as the youngster sated his appetite with a fervour known only to the starving. He continued to gorge like a vulture feasting on carrion until he could feed no more.

Still on his knees, Vuk had raised his head and looked about him but there was no one in sight. The silence was palpable, punctuated only by sporadic birdsong. As his eyes drifted down to the remains of the snake, the first wave of nausea swept over him. He hoped it would pass but the feeling persisted and grew stronger. Sour juices filled his mouth and he began to retch. Seconds later, stomach heaving, the vomiting started. His body jerked forward each time he threw up, ridding itself of every vestige of its last meal. Eventually it ended and he could spew no more. He had no idea how long it lasted. Rolling wearily onto his back, he lay exhausted on the ground. Closing his eyes to the sun, he let its warmth invade him. In the intervening years the Serb tried to erase the incident from his memory but it had left an indelible mark and a pathological hatred of snakes. The long-felt aversion was rekindled as he stared intently at the Burmese python, which was gliding sinuously over the floor in the direction of the large tub of fresh water located to one side of the enclosure.

"A fine specimen, eh Vuk?" Makarov continued.

Jovanovic merely nodded and seemed unimpressed as his boss became effusive in its praise.

"The way it moves, the way it looks, the way it kills. It excites me and I like that." He turned to face his right-hand man, who was gazing impassively at the reptile. "The way I see it, in its natural environment this creature dominates in order to survive. It has to, and it's the same with us. We're in a different kind of jungle but the same law still applies."

He waited a second: "I may be wrong but I get the feeling this is not exactly your kind of pet."

The Serb swallowed hard before replying. "It's just a snake, boss, it's something I can deal with."

"Not any old snake, Vuk, this one's a beauty. The python has inspired myths and legends throughout the ages and is one of the most feared of its species. Don't ever forget that."

The Russian stepped away from the enclosure and moved towards the large, rectangular carved oak desk with a black leather top in the centre of the room. As he sat down, he motioned the Serb to a nearby chair. Makarov pulled on a drawer handle, took out a well-worn file and removed a single page, which had a black and white passport-size photograph pinned to it. "I have a problem that requires your attention. The monthly takings from one of our drug-pushers are falling below what's expected. No one else is reporting a shortfall and that's how it should be. We're running a major supply chain in this city and those involved need to be reminded that we set financial targets for a reason. This individual must be shown that such behaviour is – how can I put it?" He paused. "Not acceptable."

Jovanovic uncrossed his legs and leant forward slightly. "I understand. Which dealer is it?"

"Turov. Yevgeny Turov." Makarov handed the page to his subordinate. "As you can see, he's been working for us for two years and hasn't given us any trouble before."

"And we don't want any now," said the Serb darkly, his thick eyebrows, as black as ebony, curving as one.

"I'm told there's been a change in his spending habits recently. Young Turov seems to have acquired a taste for fast cars and expensive jewellery and I have to ask myself how he's funding it. I think that's a question you ought to put to him, Vuk," said Makarov meaningfully. "You can pick him up easily enough – he trades in an area in the northern suburbs, east of Mira Prospekt. I don't care how you do it but we need to set an example and send a message to the others. I want them to know we operate under certain rules."

"Leave it with me, boss."

Jack Wyatt turned off Kutuzovskiy Prospekt and walked down the fountain-lined road that led to Victory Park, located to the west of Moscow city centre. A glance at the face of his bejewelled Breitling told him he was a few minutes early and he instinctively shortened his stride. In the distance on Poklonnaya Hill, towering into the sky, stood the Nike Monument bearing a bronze statue of the mythical Greek goddess of victory. As he entered the park, built to commemorate the Soviet defeat of Nazi Germany in World War Two and to honour the millions of Red Army soldiers and civilians who died in the conflict, the American was aware that many Russians considered it hallowed ground. The climbing mid-morning sun was starting to glint on the dome of the Central Museum of the Great Patriotic War as a couple in their twenties jogged along one of the broad avenues that carved its way between the brightly coloured gardens with the dark purple flowers of the lilac trees prominent.

Ainsworth had facilitated the clandestine encounter and his briefing, as ever, had been short and to the point. "It was a tricky meeting to set up and, to be honest, we didn't want to get involved again. We had to use the same man as intermediary and we can't afford to have him compromised. This is your project and you've got to keep it that way."

No need for the reminder, reflected Wyatt, as he headed towards the rendezvous. He knew secrecy was imperative, not least to ensure the safety of what he hoped would be a fruitful informant. As the sound of speeding roller-blades grew closer, he wheeled around to see three teenagers approaching from behind, zig-zagging along the path. He hastily stepped aside but the youths, as they had done many times before, effortlessly adopted a single-file formation and moved swiftly on their way. Wyatt had memorised the written directions handed to him by Ainsworth and identified a number of landmarks, including two sculptures of Soviet heroes, that told him he was on course and not far from the meeting point. He walked towards a junction and turned left, following the path, which had narrowed slightly and was now bordered on one side by birch trees. This area of the park was relatively quiet with several elderly Muscovites enjoying a leisurely stroll and a young mother sitting on the grass playing ball games with an excited toddler. Wyatt's eyes were drawn further along the path and focused on the sole occupant of the second bench beyond a section of wild garden. Even from a distance of thirty metres, he recognised the description he'd been given and quickened his step. When he was a dozen feet away, she turned in his direction and eyed him with seeming indifference. Moving closer until he was almost level with her, he observed she was as attractive and well-proportioned as her photo had suggested.

"May I ask, what is your favourite flower?" The unlikely question hung in the air for a while but the American thought he discerned a hint of recognition in the facial expression of the tall blonde.

"There can be only one," she eventually responded. "The rose." The look of detachment that had previously been evident appeared to soften a little and she motioned to him to join her. He became aware of the faintest trace of expensive perfume as he sat down.

"Out of all the benches in the park I guess I've hit the right one."

She nodded but said nothing.

"I appreciate you being here today, Valya. It can't have been easy, not knowing who's gonna turn up."

"I was assured I would not be in danger."

"Sometimes you have to learn to trust people."

"You do, but it can be a painful lesson if you get it wrong."

A light breeze pushed her hair onto one side of her face and her hand reached up to pull it back. "I agreed to meet you but I have a business to run and I work to a tight schedule."

"I understand and I'll get to the point. My name's Jack Wyatt and—"

"I know that," she interrupted. "They didn't tell me much but I needed to know who I was dealing with."

"That's my rule, too, and I try not to break it," he smiled. He glanced up as a balding, middle-aged man with a bulging belly jogged slowly by, gasping for breath and using a faded red cloth to wipe the sweat pouring down his face. "I'm told you have a high-powered job and you do it efficiently."

"Who told you?" she snapped.

Wyatt adopted the nonchalant expression of a man

accustomed to parrying such questions. "I have my sources, but in my business, as in yours, it pays to be discreet."

"There's discretion and sometimes there's need. I want to know," she said with an obdurate tone to her voice.

"All I can tell you is that my contact is reliable and has no axe to grind. I needed a go-between to reach you and this guy could do it."

Valya, stylish in a floral-patterned cotton dress and a taupe-coloured corduroy jacket, gazed intently at the American. "You seem to have gone out of your way to track me down. What do you want from me?"

He fixed her with an equally resolute look. "I believe I have something of interest to you. Let's call it a new career opportunity…" he paused, "but at twice what you're getting now."

"You have no idea what I'm paid," she retorted testily. "My earnings are confidential and known only to me and my employer."

"It doesn't matter what money you're on. The people I represent want you to work for them and they'll pay double."

"They don't know me! Who are they?"

"Businessmen from the Middle East. They're looking for a piece of the action in what they call the leisure and entertainment industry in this city, but you and I know it as something else. The syndicate wants to exploit your expertise and they're willing to pay for it."

"What do I have to give in return?"

"Transfer your skills and experience to them. You're an effective operator and they want to cash in on that."

Valya looked uneasily around her, checking she wasn't being watched. "And if I don't want to work for them?"

"You should be aware the syndicate would prefer not to take no for an answer."

"What does that mean?"

"What I said. I don't think I need spell it out, but these guys have their own way of problem-solving."

"Is that some kind of threat?"

Wyatt shook his head. "Just a statement of fact." He waited a few seconds as he wanted his words to have the utmost impact. "Is your boss aware that you sometimes boost your income with substantial bonus payments?"

Valya's eyes flashed angrily. "I don't know what you're talking about."

"I think you do."

"You have no proof."

"I don't need any, but we both know it's true."

"So that's the end-game, that's why you're here. You want to blackmail me!"

"Whoa, steady girl, you've misread the runes. I've no intention of forcing you to do anything."

"Why did you mention the bonuses?"

Wyatt looked benignly at her. "Let's cut to the chase, Valya. We know how Makarov operates – he cuts no slack to anyone in the organisation, including you. So when you get the chance to make some extra, you take it. But if a new opening shows up you should grab it."

The blonde tetchily brushed away an insect that had landed on her lap. "You don't understand, it's not like that. It's not just a job, it's more than that…" She paused. "I'm also his mistress."

"How long has it been that way?"

"More than two years. I was working as a fashion model when I met him in one of his casinos. We became lovers soon after and he installed me in a luxury apartment in central Moscow. Then he asked me to manage the high-class brothel that operates from the penthouse suite of the hotel he owns. Since I've been in charge I've put my stamp on it and we've seen a steady growth in profits."

"Is he based at the hotel?"

"When he's in town. He has his own office and suite there and it's the registered headquarters of all his companies."

"How many has he got?"

"Nine or ten at the last count."

"I assume they're just a front for money laundering from the various criminal enterprises he's running?"

"You can make whatever assumptions you want, Mr Wyatt."

"I guess he's also got a dacha somewhere."

"He has but doesn't use it much."

"What's his security like?"

"He's paranoid about being toppled in a palace revolution so he surrounds himself with those he knows he can trust, and that's not many. There's a tight-knit group that acts as his eyes and ears and reports back, but there's one individual who's closest to him."

"Who's that?" said Wyatt, with more than an inkling of who it might be.

Valya was about to answer but stopped. She was beginning to look edgy. "Why are you asking all these questions? You don't know Viktor. If he knew I was talking to a total stranger like this I could be…" Her voice faltered.

The American was blunt in his response. "In danger?"

"Yes. He can be moody and violent and would react badly if he found out about our meeting today."

Wyatt placed a hand lightly on her arm in an attempt to reassure her. "He isn't going to hear anything from me and no one else is going to tell him."

"But you can't be sure of that. Even if he doesn't find out, I wouldn't be able to leave as I know too much about the business and I don't think he's in the habit of writing references. I feel trapped."

"That's not a good place to be, Valya, and you need to get outta there." He could see she was becoming restless. "I know you can't stay here long but maybe there's something else you can help with. Earlier this year there was extensive media coverage when a judge was murdered in this city shortly before his report on mafia activities was to be handed to the government. Did Makarov ever talk about the killing?"

Wyatt tried to look into Valya's face but she turned away. Her answer simply confirmed what he expected to hear. "I don't think Viktor would want to discuss such things with me."

"Not even in his more relaxed moments – pillow talk, perhaps?"

"I think I've said enough already."

"I don't think Makarov deserves your loyalty."

"What d'you mean?"

"He doesn't show you much. You must know he sleeps around." For the first time Wyatt glimpsed an emotional vulnerability in the Russian's face.

"You don't need to tell me. I suppose it comes with the territory." She glanced at her watch. "I must go now. I have to get on with the job I've got."

Valya rose to her feet, straightening her dress. The American got up too, easing his six-foot-one-inch frame off the bench. He detected a trace of resignation in her voice.

"You must know I don't have a choice. I'm working for someone who's given me money and a certain status, but on the downside, he has power over me and that's scary. You'll have to tell your syndicate to look elsewhere."

"I admire your guts, I'll say that."

"It's not guts, I'm being realistic." She cast an anxious glance in both directions along the path as if to satisfy herself she hadn't been followed. "I think it's better if we leave the park separately and I'd appreciate it if you could give me a head-start."

Wyatt nodded. "I'll wait a couple of minutes." He pulled a small embossed card from an inside pocket of his jacket. "If you change your mind, this is where I'm staying."

"Perhaps you overestimate your powers of persuasion, Mr Wyatt."

A half-smile surfaced on his features. "Maybe I do. Anyway, have it as a keepsake, a souvenir of our meeting."

She hesitated for a moment then took the card from his grasp. "You're persistent, if nothing else."

"I'm not sure we're gonna meet again, so look after yourself," said the American.

Valya fixed him with steely blue eyes. "Do you care?" Without waiting for an answer, she turned abruptly and strode off. Wyatt sat on the bench again and watched her until she reached the point where the path met the junction and her lissom figure was obscured by the trees. As he did so, he found himself wrestling with a nagging thought: he did care, but somehow wished he didn't.

Five minutes after taking the call, Yevgeny Turov locked the door to his apartment, hurried down two flights of stairs and let himself out of the main entrance to the unimposing four-storey block. Clutching a package in his hand, the twenty-four-year-old walked a short distance along the pavement before activating the remote control that gave him access to the Honda sports car parked nearby. Stowing the small parcel under the passenger seat, he pressed the engine start button and the scarlet-coloured hardtop sped off. As he drove through the grey, bleak suburbs of northern Moscow, the spindly built Russian reflected on his recent change of fortune. A product of a dysfunctional family, his early life had been defined by his father's prolonged spells of unemployment and his mother's alcoholism. An only child, the lack of parental stimulus at home had a predictable consequence at school. Although brighter than average, he was lazy and disruptive in the classroom and left with a sub-standard education.

Turov's experience in the labour market had not provided much fulfilment either. Jobs had been sporadic and low-paid and several ended amid accusations he was work-shy. He preferred not to dwell on the two that had been terminated for more sinister reasons. Even now he felt a sense of injustice following his dismissal from the petrol station for taking fuel for his own use without paying for it. Staff had long considered it an incidental benefit to supplement inadequate wages but he was convinced he was made a scapegoat to deter others.

He also brooded on the circumstances surrounding his forced departure from a security guard position at a gated residential community 30 miles to the east of the capital. A succession of uneventful night shifts led to him routinely snatching a couple of hours' sleep in a chair while on duty in the gatehouse. But one night the community administrator, a burly man with a penchant for precision in the management of his domain, decided to monitor the competence of his latest recruit. Appalled to find him slumbering instead of patrolling the grounds, the bureaucrat seized the dozing guard with both hands and, cursing loudly, slapped him repeatedly around the head. Turov recalled how, disoriented by the violent awakening, he had tried to defend himself against the stronger man but had become overwhelmed. In an attempt to break free, his outstretched hand picked up a heavy torch lying on a nearby table and he lashed out, the improvised weapon striking his attacker on the side of the head. Stunned, the administrator released his grip and when a second blow landed on his temple, he slumped to the floor unconscious.

Fearing the man was dead, Turov panicked and fled the scene. Desperate to avoid detection, he returned to Moscow and kept a low profile for several weeks, staying with a drug-addict friend who had a spare room. But the pressing need for money combined with poor job prospects drew the young Russian into the criminal arena and, although a small-scale user of drugs, he soon grasped the financial benefits of being a supplier. Scornful of his peers, he always considered himself a cut above them and had no qualms about pushing misery and degradation on to countless addicts.

It was the first job, he mused, he was good at. So good, in fact, he was approached by two strangers and offered the chance to move up to what they called the 'big league' and work for a syndicate that controlled much of the drugs industry in the capital. They highlighted the earnings potential but warned a strict disciplinary code was enforced. Turov had been quick to accept the offer, regarding it somewhat quirkily as belated compensation for surviving a difficult adolescence and knowing it would facilitate the materialistic lifestyle he yearned for. Although recollection of the gatehouse incident always rekindled some anxiety that one day justice would catch up with him, he savoured the irony that it had been the aftermath of the confrontation that had kickstarted what he hoped would prove to be a lucrative career.

Turov had something else on his mind as he headed towards the appointed venue for the handover, the call for which had come unexpectedly but that he presumed was due to a problem with the regular dealer for that area. He was seeing Yelena tonight and the thought filled him with a warming sense of anticipation as the memory of their previous meeting still lingered. She was in her mid-forties but that wasn't a drawback as he preferred older women. His experience had taught him they were seasoned performers and tended to be more innovative than their younger counterparts. He smiled as he recalled how the busty brunette, who was divorced and worked for a property rental company, had amply confirmed his theory. They had met in a bar a week earlier and the physical attraction was immediate. Seemingly oblivious to the amplified output of a local rock band reverberating around them, the pair indulged in a drinking session before she invited him back to her apartment.

There had been no discussion about what should happen next. There was no need to speak as their lust was tacit. She had clasped his hand and led him to the bedroom, where they had kissed and undressed with equal urgency. Yelena pulled him onto the bed and his lips devoured her with a roving hunger. When he paused for breath, she laughed and gently pushed him away as if teasing before rolling over and sitting astride him. Then, taut and unyielding, he found her and she moved up and down on him with an animal-like fervency, her pendulous breasts swaying from side to side. The smile had gone. Instead, her face reflected the exertions of her brutish love-making. Yelena started to moan and her eyes closed. The moaning grew louder, reached a crescendo and then slowly faded. Turov arced his arms around her lower back and drew her down to him. Now it was his turn. He worked her easily at first but his movements became hurried, frantic. She sensed it was close and tightened on him. A final thrust and he erupted, filling her. To Turov it seemed like a torrent before the passion subsided. After a while Yelena slid off and lay by his side, running a finger gently through the sweat on his temple. Both were silent, no words needed. Gratification had its own language.

But thoughts of sexual indulgence and the expectation they engendered would have to be deferred. He had a more pressing issue to focus on as he negotiated the heavy late afternoon traffic. He had not recognised the voice at the other end of the phone but the caller had given the correct password. Turov worked to a co-ordinator, a man who organised his supplies and to whom he handed over the cash from his sales. It had always been that way. The hierarchical nature of the organisation meant that he and dealers like him had just one point of contact and therefore no knowledge of others on the payroll or those who controlled them. Such a system was in place to minimise damage to the syndicate if the authorities ever succeeded in penetrating any part of it. The call had taken Turov by surprise. It was the first time his handler had not issued instructions directly and it left him puzzled.

The feeling continued to gnaw at him as he passed block after humdrum block of grey-coloured tenements exhibiting a uniformity of drabness that was probably only matched by the dreary existence of their occupants. The poor sods, struggling to survive amidst the angst and tedium of empty lives. How much better his life was, he told himself. He had stepped off the treadmill of routine drudgery that afflicted so many of his fellow Muscovites and for the first time could afford the material possessions he craved. He gave himself credit for turning his situation around, and if he sometimes found it hard to suppress the feeling the world owed him a living, so what?

The caller had sounded aloof and the message was terse. He had a buyer and Turov was ordered to bring a bag of cocaine. Details of the appointed meeting place were given together with a warning not to be late, then the line went dead.

The Honda's driver cut its speed and it left the main highway linking the estate, turning down a side road leading to a strip of wasteland. Beyond it were a number of hulking buildings, now derelict but once bustling factories targeted by apparatchiks in their drive for economic expansion in the Soviet era. Turov drove across an area of broken concrete where weeds protruded like rampant green tentacles and brought the S2000 to a halt behind a stationary black Mercedes S-Class with dark-tinted windows.

He retrieved the package, pulled himself out of the low-slung sports car and walked towards the vehicle in front. At the same time two men, whom he guessed were in their thirties but he didn't recognise, emerged from the limousine.

"I have the merchandise. Who's closing the deal?" enquired Turov. Neither man uttered a word, their faces expressionless. "I work hand-to-hand, it's the way I operate – direct delivery for direct payment," he continued. "So, who's going to close this one?"

Again there was no response, the two strangers just stared at him. Turov shifted uncomfortably, unable to disguise the first hint of unease.

The shorter and bulkier of the two took a step forward. "We're not dealing, bag man."

The supplier looked perplexed. "But you set up this meeting. You wanted the stuff and that's what I've got." He emphasised his words by holding up the pouch containing the drugs.

"I don't think you heard the man," said his associate, a figure of unkempt appearance with sullen, implacable eyes. "We ain't buying today. We've got some other business to look after."

Turov swallowed hard and tried to resist a growing sense of foreboding. "I don't know what you guys want but I'm not sure I can help."

The taller man moved closer. "Oh, I think you can." He grinned sardonically. "We've got some questions and we need answers."

Turov stood his ground although the man had advanced to within touching distance, his yellowish uneven teeth clearly visible. "There must be some mistake, you've got the wrong person."

"There's no mistake."

"Who are you?"

Both men ignored the query. Then, without warning, the nearest one pulled a hand out of his jacket pocket and Turov found himself staring down the barrel of a Beretta. "Move," ordered the gunman, "that way." He pointed the semi-automatic in the direction of one of the dilapidated buildings. "Act normal and don't do anything stupid."

"What the hell are you doing?" gasped a startled Turov as the pistol was jabbed into his chest.

"You heard me. Move!" The tone was strident, coercive.

The supplier looked around in despair, seeking help, but the area was deserted. He was forced towards a grimy-looking side door of what had once been a bonded warehouse. The door's time-worn metal hinges creaked in protest and flakes of faded brown paint fell away as one of the men pushed it open. Sandwiched between the two, with the gunman behind him, Turov found himself propelled along a narrow dimly lit corridor, its high-sided walls stained damp from a leaking skylight in the roof high above. Amid the mustiness and the gloom a rat scurried by, its shadowy outline briefly illuminated by light spearing through a gap under a bulky wooden door ahead of them. The trio came to a halt and the man in front tapped the entry code on the security control panel. The door opened slowly and Turov, prodded in the back with the Beretta, was shoved forward.

He was assailed by the glare from powerful arc lamps suspended from overhead wires and it took a few seconds for his eyes to adjust. They swept across what had once been a factory where workers toiled under relentless pressure, driven by the production targets handed down by the commissars of Gosplan, the former Soviet state economic planning committee. Little tangible evidence of the manufacturing process remained, most of the heavy plant long gone, although rusted brackets that had supported machinery still hung, some precariously, from the walls. Deep gouge marks and ancient oil stains on the floor bore testimony to years of laborious activity by those forced to respond to the economic diktat of the ruling elite.

"I'm so glad you could make it, comrade Turov."

The captive swung around to see a tall, shaven-headed figure emerge from the shadows at one side of the building and move towards him.

"I've been hoping you would join us."

"I don't seem to have had much choice."

"I suppose we could have sent you an official invite but I doubt you would have accepted."

He was closer now and Turov could see he had a prominent scar on his right cheek. "Who the hell are you and why have you brought me here?"

"You'll find out soon enough." The man took another step forward. "You won't be needing this." He seized the bag of drugs the supplier was still holding.

Despite the stress he was under, Turov persisted. "But what do you want?" he pleaded.

"You need to understand you are here to answer questions and not to ask them. It would be preferable if you co-operate with us. If you don't..." he paused as if to emphasise the menace underlying his words, "...we shall have no option but to adopt other methods of persuasion." He clicked his fingers. Immediately his two henchmen, standing behind the dealer, stepped forward and dragged him towards a large chair, where he was forced down onto the seat and his wrists bound by rope to its wooden arms.

The hapless Turov felt a chill run through his body. He looked up to see the big man standing over him. "That's a nice watch you're wearing, comrade, very stylish – a Rolex, if I'm not mistaken. They don't come cheap, must have set you back hundreds of thousand of roubles for that one, eh? And that sports car of yours – a new one, judging by the registration plates." He turned towards his accomplices. "Young Turov seems to be doing very well for himself and at such an early age, too. How d'you think he does it?"

Both men sniggered and moved closer to the chair. One said mockingly, "We don't know, boss. How *do you* think he does it?"

"I don't know either but I think it's about time we found out. Well, comrade, are you going to tell us?"

The shackled man looked impassively at his interrogator before muttering, "Who are you?"

The speed of the arm movement caught Turov unawares, not that he could take evasive action, and a fist crashed into his stomach. It took the winded man a while to regain his breath and when he raised his head again, he found himself staring into the coal-black eyes of his assailant.

"You're not listening to me, friend – I *ask* the questions, you *answer*! When you grasp that we should get on a lot better."

Turov struggled against the cords that restrained him, his fear made worse by the impotence he felt.

"Now," the man resumed, "let's try once more. Don't underestimate us. We know the street prices and in recent months your takings have fallen sharply. But it's no secret you've developed an extravagant lifestyle and we've got our own views about how you're funding it."

"Listen to me," said the captive earnestly, "it's not what you think. I know my returns have been down but I can explain it. Dealing is not so easy these days, there's more competition out there and it's—" Turov's words ended in mid-sentence with a stinging slap across his face.

"You lying bastard," yelled the questioner. "You expect me to believe that when the syndicate has an iron grip on most of the supply in this city? We set financial targets but you're the only one failing to meet them." He leant down until his face was just inches away from that of the confined man. "You're proving to be a big problem for us, comrade. We don't have this trouble with the others."

"Look, I don't know who you are but you've got to trust me," implored Turov. "I hustle long hours and try to get the best price but that's not always possible. Sometimes it's better to hook them at a lower rate and raise it the next time. Some guys push shorts and keep the profit but I don't work that way." His temple started to glisten as balls of sweat trickled down from his hairline and a note of desperation sounded in his voice. "For God's sake, I'm just trying to earn a living. What's wrong with that? I'm not cheating anyone and that's the truth – you've got to believe me!"

His interrogator took a couple of steps back. "You seem to be having some difficulty understanding this process." He gestured at one of his henchmen. "Ivan, I think our friend needs a little help to loosen his tongue."

The shorter and bulkier man nodded eagerly, picked up a sledgehammer lying on a nearby table and advanced towards the terrified dealer. Heart thumping, Turov squirmed against the ropes that pinioned him but knew his efforts were futile. He saw the man wielding the long-handled weapon with both hands half-turn his torso before swinging back at him. The fettered man screamed as the solid flat metal head of the sledgehammer slammed into his right knee-cap, instantly fracturing the triangular bone at the front of the joint. A second later the heavy-duty instrument thudded violently against the other knee-cap, also breaking it. Turov shrieked in agony as pain racked his body, his head moving from side to side in an involuntary reaction to the deep aching of his wounds.

The assailant, a smirk playing on his lips, drew back on a shouted instruction. The interrogator moved closer to the chair. "Comrade, perhaps that has helped restore your memory. Now I think it's time you admitted your crime, don't you?"

The writhing Turov, traumatised by the assault, gripped the arms of the chair as if somehow trying to dull his suffering. Eventually, with beseeching eyes and in an undertone, he found himself begging for mercy. "Please, whoever you are, don't kill me. I'll say whatever you want but let me go. You must get me to hospital, I need treatment urgently."

His tormentor stood directly in front of him. "You disappoint me, Turov. I thought you had enough sense to realise your options were limited. We gave you a chance to confess but you didn't take it. You've been stealing the syndicate's money and that's something we won't tolerate."

"I'll pay it back, whatever it is. Just tell me what I owe, give me time and I'll repay every rouble, I promise!"

"You're right, comrade, we are expecting repayment – but in your case there's a difference."

"What d'you mean?"

"When you joined the organisation you were told a strict code of conduct was in force and any breach of discipline would be dealt with severely. You were given a clear warning but you chose to ignore it. Now you have to pick up the tab."

"But you've already punished me. I've done wrong, I know that, but I won't do it again."

"You know something, Turov, I believe you. I don't think you will," he sneered. "The problem we have is that you may have learnt your lesson but we need to send a strong signal to others who may be tempted to rip us off. But if it's any consolation, my friend, you still have a role to play in helping us do that."

As the injured man groaned from the excruciating pain, the inquisitor turned to look at his cohorts. "I may be mistaken but young Turov is looking a little pale. I think it's about time we put the colour back into his cheeks. You know what to do."

Acknowledging the order, they approached their victim and untied the ropes binding him to the chair. Ignoring his howls of anguish, the men pulled the dealer to his feet then dragged him across the factory floor to the side of the building. He looked on as one seized the rim of a tarpaulin draped over what appeared to resemble a large sofa and tugged it. As the faded green canvas cover was yanked away, Turov, clinging to the second man to stop himself falling, stared at the apparatus in front of him. It took a few seconds before his mind, addled by the throbbing soreness of his injuries, recognised the nature of the device. But it took a little longer for his brain to grasp the sinister implications associated with it.

Indifferent to his suffering, the men tore off Turov's black leather jacket and white and blue check shirt then callously pushed him onto his back on the sunbed. He screamed from the agonising pain as his shoes, socks and blood-stained denim trousers were pulled off, followed by his boxer shorts. Then his wrists and ankles were tied by rope passing under and over the padded bench he was lying on. His eyes roved fearfully across the curved canopy with its array of fluorescent lamps above his head. Stripped naked and whimpering like an animal snared in a trap, the dealer became aware of the shaven-headed man standing over him.

"Relax, comrade, there's no point in struggling. But you won't be needing this." He leant forward and removed Turov's diamond-studded watch. "Once we switch this machine on, you'll be able to lie back and enjoy the heat. It won't be long before you develop the sort of all-over tan that many Muscovites would envy."

Turov grimaced as the inference struck home. "I'm sorry, I really am. I'll do whatever you want, sign anything, I'll work for you for nothing."

"It's too late for that now."

"Please, don't do it. Let me go!" he begged.

"Shut up, I've heard enough," scowled the big man as he turned to the second of his henchmen. "Mikhail, it's time to practise your cookery skills. I reckon this piece of meat needs a high-set oven."

"You're right, boss. It does look a bit on the tough side, so I guess we ought to start at full blast." He adjusted the power control then extended both hands and pulled the canopy down to enclose Turov's body. The shackled man started yelling as the lamps began to glow.

"It's no use," said the interrogator, "no one will hear your cries. You're a long way from the street."

"Where are you going? You can't leave me like this. My God, I'm going to die!" he whined.

"If you're lucky, you will. Goodbye, Turov."

Ivan picked up the dealer's clothes and shoes, shoved them in a plastic bag and headed for the exit, followed by the other two. Extinguishing the overhead arc lamps and locking the big wooden door behind them, they retraced their steps along the corridor. By the time they reached the side entrance to the old warehouse they could no longer hear the screams.

NINE

He hunted her down as an animal pursues its quarry. The intensity of the chase was fired by a barely suppressed rancour emanating from an earlier race. Stallard was still resentful of his teammate's conduct at Kowloon where, despite battling against dehydration for much of the event, he had seemed assured of a P2 finish. Then Lockhart had exerted sustained pressure, causing him to spin off the track, instead of trying to maximise points for the team. And what made it worse, the Gorton owner had condoned the tactics that relegated Stallard to P5, citing the absence of team orders. Fearing his position as leading driver was being undermined, the Englishman found himself empathising with a former world champion-turned-pundit whom, recounting his own long and chequered career, had controversially advised the current crop of racers never to trust a teammate. Fuelled by a combination of skill, animosity and sheer bloody-mindedness, Stallard was also motivated by the knowledge he had yet to win his home grand prix.

The London race – the seventh in the calendar – always attracted huge crowds and this year's event was no exception. Specially erected grandstands lined the street circuit that stretched for a little over 4 miles through the centre of the capital, taking the drivers past some of its most evocative landmarks and crossing and re-crossing the River Thames. From the start-finish line on Piccadilly, with the pit lane and paddock located alongside in Green Park, the cars headed north-east on the long straight towards Eros at Piccadilly Circus then turned right into Haymarket before taking a left into Pall Mall East, a short burst to Trafalgar Square, around Nelson's Column and along the Strand before a right took the drivers past Somerset House and over the Thames on Waterloo Bridge.

Another right into York Road and they were close to the London Eye, located on the South Bank and – standing at over 400 feet – the second-tallest Ferris wheel in Europe. The track led to three bends in a U-shape, a left and two rights in quick succession, before the cars re-crossed the river over Westminster Bridge. Then past Big Ben and the Houses of Parliament, skirting the Treasury in Great George Street, and onto Birdcage Walk with the Home Office and Wellington Barracks to the left and St James's Park on the right. The racers floored the throttle on this lengthy section before braking hard for the ninety-degree right-hander in front of Buckingham Palace, followed by a left around the Victoria Memorial. Up through the gears, accelerating along Constitution Hill then slowing to navigate Hyde Park Corner before exiting onto Piccadilly, picking up the revs again and crossing the start-finish line.

Despite initial opposition, the English capital had proved a popular venue and the race had become one of the high spots of the FS calendar. Fears it would cause major civil and economic disruption had been unfounded.

Admittedly, a significant area of central London had to be sealed off for four days each year to secure the circuit, and road closures were necessary in the run-up to the event to move bollards. Bus routes had to be redrawn to accommodate traffic restrictions and the use of parking bays in the vicinity of the track suspended. In addition to a substantial fee demanded by FS to bring the race to the capital, major outgoings in establishing an infrastructure and policing were also incurred. But the Greater London Authority was convinced the high-profile event would showcase the city to a global television audience, attract tourists and boost income. And so it had proved, with revenue outstripping costs and civic leaders basking in the kudos of staging such a prestigious contest.

Intending to build on the impetus of his victory in the previous race in Australia, Stallard's championship challenge had been dented by a troubled qualifying session. He reported a lack of front-end grip when cornering and lost vital time as his engineers worked to rectify the problem. With the clock running down, he took the car back onto the circuit but was only halfway through his out-lap when the session ended. His place on the grid was determined by an earlier qualifying time and he slotted in at P9. With his car better balanced, a spirited drive saw the Englishman move steadily through the field and with thirty of the fifty laps completed, he was in P5 and closing fast on Lockhart. At times, just inches separated the two cars in the black and green livery of the Gorton outfit, as if they were linked by an invisible cord.

Stallard realised the American was a match for him on the straights but was slower out of the corners and he speculated that she was being hampered by tyre degradation or had a problem in the lower gears. Two more laps went by and he could see his prospects of a podium finish being thwarted by what he felt were Lockhart's blocking manoeuvres every time he attempted to overtake. Finally, he vented his frustration. He radioed his race engineer.

"She's slowing me down. I'm all over the back of her but she won't move out of the way."

Jim Crowley's response was swift but sounded a warning note. "Be careful, Nick. One mistake and you could both be out of the race. Stay close and your chance will come."

"I couldn't be much closer," retorted the driver tetchily. "This is costing me. I need to get down the road."

Both cars neared the end of the start-finish straight, flashing past the 300-metre marker board prior to Piccadilly Circus, braking from over 170 miles per hour to eighty-five before changing down again and sweeping by the statue of Eros, then through the Circus and the right-hander into Haymarket beckoned. Again, the leading Gorton faltered slightly on exiting the corner and Stallard cursed as he was forced to hit the brake pedal to avoid a collision. Then up through the gears for the short sprint that led to the ninety-degree left onto Pall Mall East. Lockhart had the inside line but went defensive when the Englishman pulled onto the outside of the bend. He cut back inside but was checked again and the American retained her narrow lead as the pair sped towards Trafalgar Square. Both slowed for the tight right opposite the National Gallery, on the north side of the Square, then speeded up for the short dash to an equally sharp left that would take them past Nelson's Column.

Despite his growing exasperation, Stallard knew he had to stay focused. Impatient to overtake his female teammate, he was acutely aware the slightest error could shunt them both off the track, possibly out of the race, and incur the wrath of an owner who for some reason now seemed predisposed to favouring the less experienced driver. The towering monument, standing almost 170 feet high and commemorating the death of the naval hero at the Battle of Trafalgar, came into view. The sound of the screaming V10 engines scattered dozens of pigeons resting on the four bronze lions standing proud on their granite plinths and facing outwards at the base of the Column.

As the Gortons approached the tight left-hander, Stallard delayed braking until as late as he dared in the hope of gaining an advantage. Mindful of Lockhart's blatant obstruction at the previous corner, this time he feigned to go outside but almost immediately cut back and put his car on the inside line, and resolved to hold position whatever tactic the American adopted. In second gear and with their speed reduced to a shade over 60 miles per hour, both drivers were unyielding as they launched themselves at the apex of the bend – and the inevitable collision. To those spectators closest to the action, it appeared the Englishman's car was marginally in front when it was struck by its rival but the impact sent the Gorton number two racer spinning across the track and slamming into a tyre wall. The car sustained only slight damage but the engine stalled and Lockhart's race was over. Stallard pressed on, hoping it had just been a glancing blow to his machine with no adverse effects on his prospects for a competitive drive.

He got on the radio once more. "She's been asking for it. I had the faster car but she wouldn't move over."

Crowley's reply was supportive but carried a hint that his man might have to answer for what had happened.

"You have a job to do and you're doing it. Let's hope the boss sees it that way."

His driver did not drag out the conversation. Not wanting to be distracted, he knew that now was not the time to debate the issue. Sitting on the pit wall, watching a video replay of the incident on one of the bank of monitors angled above his head, the reaction of the team owner confirmed that Stallard's race engineer had been more than a touch perceptive in his comments. Joe Gorton clenched the sheaf of papers containing telemetry data that he was holding and swore.

With his immediate path clear, the team's number one driver set off in pursuit of the three men ahead of him – Guiscard, Rodriguez and Petrenko. The current joint leader of the championship race with the Spaniard at the season's midway point, Stallard needed no reminder that a win would keep him at the head of the standings and put daylight between him and his main rivals. Released from the impasse with Lockhart, which had cost him precious time, and with just seventeen laps remaining, the Englishman's first task was to chase the Frenchman who was two and a half seconds ahead of him. The message from the pits was that Guiscard's recent lap times were inconsistent, which might indicate the Drogan had a technical problem or else its driver had made a mistake somewhere on the circuit.

By lap 37 Stallard had cut the deficit to such an extent that as he raced along the Strand, he caught sight of the red and green car braking for the sharp right that led to Waterloo Bridge. Two laps later and he was on the tail of the French entry as it braked at the same spot for the ninety-degree turn into Lancaster Place. As both drivers accelerated out of the corner, speeding past the neoclassical building, Somerset House, the Gorton racer narrowed the gap further and at the point the cars were passing above the Victoria Embankment he had drawn level. The sun's reflection shimmered on the placid waters of the Thames below as higher gears were engaged and two mighty engines revved up on the bridge – at eighty feet across and over 1200 feet in length, the longest in London. Buoyed by the relative ease with which he had wound in his rival, Stallard was fractionally quicker on the power as the pair headed towards the southern end of the bridge, thundering across it at more than 140 miles per hour. Gradually, almost imperceptibly, the Gorton started to move ahead. Then it was hard on the brakes as the cars swallowed up the track and by the turning-in point for the right-hander into York Road, the Englishman had captured the racing line and was first through the corner.

Having seized the initiative, he pulled clear of the Drogan and set his sights on the two drivers locked in their own battle for P1. His two-way radio burst into life again. "Great move, Nick. The two in front are almost three seconds ahead of you but they're fighting each other so there's always a chance. Don't let up!"

Stallard's focus was so intense he did not acknowledge his race engineer but no such prompting was needed. In stark contrast to the lack of grip that blighted his qualifying session, driver and car were now in total harmony. The balance of the Gorton was much improved and its response when turning into a bend was precise and consistent, giving Stallard renewed confidence when attacking the curves. His tyre management skills had also paid off, limiting the amount of degradation, although he knew that could change as he mounted an all-out assault on the leaders. His car was flying but with ten laps to go, he knew time was not on his side.

The two men tussling for supremacy at the front were absorbed in their own duel and Stallard was not yet on their radar. Petrenko had held a comfortable lead for much of the race, followed by Rodriguez, but a slipshod pit stop involving the Makarov Racing mechanics had allowed the Spaniard, who refuelled at the same time, to emerge from the pit lane only half a second behind. Now closer still, he was constantly harassing the Russian in an attempt to force an error but the rookie racer, displaying a maturity beyond his years, was resisting the challenge. Both were impelled by different motives. Petrenko had already exhibited a naked ambition to be the first driver to take the world title in an inaugural year of FS competition, while Rodriguez, a previous runner-up, was determined to go one better and claim the top prize.

Stallard, too, had something to prove. Not only to himself but as a riposte to his team owner, whose assertion that he lacked the passion to be a champion made at the end of the previous season still rankled. He had upped the aggression in his driving, prepared to take greater risks when overtaking yet feeling more comfortable with the strategy. But gnawing at the back of his mind was a growing uncertainty about his future with Gorton Racing and the possibility that next season, if forced to seek a drive with another team, he might be handling a less competitive car. His overriding thought was that the current campaign might just provide his best chance yet to stake a claim for the title. Bit by bit, Stallard began to reel in the leaders and by lap 46 the alarm bells were starting to ring for the Makarov Racing and El Oro race engineers on the pit wall.

Gaining on his rivals by a third of a second on each tour of the circuit, the Gorton driver had narrowed the gap to just under a second, and assuming he could maintain that pace, it would put him right on the back of Rodriguez at the end of the penultimate lap. Warnings of the impending threat were radioed to the front-runners by their respective teams but the drivers, engrossed in their own head-to-head clash, did not respond.

Their lead over the Englishman was pared down even more when they came across two backmarkers fighting to avoid finishing last – Dmitry Baikov in a car bearing the colours of Makarov Racing and Janos Varady in a Drogan. The Russian Baikov, in his mid-twenties, had been promoted from test driver to replace the team's number two racer, Orlovsky, who was still recovering from injuries sustained in the fourth event around the streets of southern Kowloon. The Hungarian Varady, just nineteen but said to be an upcoming talent, had been drafted into his first grand prix at short notice to replace Werner following the German's fatal crash in Australia in the previous race.

Petrenko was confident that Baikov, in last place, would move over as he would have been told to give way with the minimum of delay as his colleague prepared to lap him. But the race leader was less certain about Varady's likely response to being lapped on his debut as he knew nothing about the teenager's temperament. Petrenko – with Rodriguez pressing him – closed on the tail-enders at the end of the straight on Birdcage Walk but had to brake hard for the ninety-degree right-hander in front of Buckingham Palace. Then a quick burst and it was on the brakes again for the left around the Victoria Memorial.

As the straight along Constitution Hill opened up, Baikov predictably pulled over to allow both pace-setters through but Varady, although in P11, seemed determined to carve out a reputation for himself at the start of his FS career. A glance in his mirrors showed Petrenko and Rodriguez closing fast but the young Drogan driver stayed calm and moved over to defend his position. The Russian tried to attack again from the other side but was baulked for a second time. He shook his fist at the Hungarian but by now all three drivers had reached the braking zone for Hyde Park Corner. Varady had the racing line for the long sweeping turn and was through first but when he exited on to Piccadilly he saw a track marshal waving a blue flag at him and immediately recognised the signal ordering him to yield to the men trying to lap him. He reluctantly pulled over to let them pass and consoled himself in the knowledge they had quicker cars and would have overtaken him anyway on the long straight leading to Piccadilly Circus.

Petrenko swore and raised a gloved fist in the teenager's direction as he went by, acutely aware the Hungarian's tactics had cost him valuable time and allowed Stallard to whittle down the deficit even further. The Englishman had seen the leaders delayed by traffic and needed no extra spur in his efforts to catch them. More blue flags were waved on Piccadilly and he too was swiftly past Baikov and Varady. With under two laps remaining, the Gorton was now just metres from the back of the gold and blue El Oro of Rodriguez, which itself was virtually clinging to the exhaust pipes of Petrenko's machine. The thousands of yelling spectators lining the main straight in the grandstand, and thousands more watching the action on giant screens from other vantage points around the circuit, were suddenly galvanised by the prospect of an epic finish.

The leading trio crossed and re-crossed the Thames, skirted around the Palace and Victoria Memorial again, swept through Hyde Park Corner with their tyres barely sticking to the tarmac and flashed over the start-finish line for the final time. Stallard's black and green Gorton inched ever closer to his rivals but the mounting pressure he had exerted on the men ahead of him had not forced a mistake. Convinced he had the faster car, the Englishman also knew time was running out and he had to make his move but was well aware the two drivers ahead of him would be anticipating such a manoeuvre and would do everything in their power to resist. Urged on by shrieking British fans, Stallard was relentless in hounding the Spaniard and the Russian as their cars devoured the tarmac. They crossed Westminster Bridge for the last time, emerged from the shadow of Big Ben and accelerated towards the second-longest straight on the circuit. Birdcage Walk stretched ahead, shadowed by a seemingly endless dark green canopy of foliage from dozens of horse-chestnut trees lining the track. Petrenko appeared to be spending almost as much time peering in his mirrors as looking ahead as he braced himself for a last-gasp challenge from behind.

Approaching the midway point of the straight, it was Rodriguez who attacked first. Slipstreaming the Russian, he closed to within a matter of inches at nearly 180 miles per hour then pulled to the right, to the side nearest St James's Park, and started to gain ground on the leader. But Petrenko was alert to the ploy and moved swiftly across to cover it. Seeing the Spaniard go on the offensive and anticipating the likely outcome, Stallard seized the moment. He steered his car slightly to the left, flattened the throttle and aimed for the gap that had opened up. The Russian, preoccupied by his blocking manoeuvre on Rodriguez, was out of position and unable to defend. Revs racing, the Englishman surged past but, mindful of Petrenko's tendency to resort to aggressive measures when under threat, Stallard knew his concentration had to stay rock-solid to retain his slender lead.

With its rev counter needle hovering around the 19,000 mark, the Gorton streaked past the first of the marker boards heralding the arrival of the tight right in front of the Palace. Then it was hard on the brakes, downshift, brush the apex, exit the corner and back on the power. A spurt to the Memorial before a dab on the brakes for the left-hander then up through the gears to sixth for the stretch along Constitution Hill. With the Russian swarming all over the back of him, Stallard knew it was crucial to avoid any contact as they neared the final bend. He braked, found second gear and had the racing line as his car, seemingly glued to the track, sped around Hyde Park Corner. Turning onto the home-straight on Piccadilly, Stallard was instantly on the throttle, accelerating towards the start-finish line 600 metres away.

Just feet behind, Petrenko strained to extract the last ounce of thrust from his car in an attempt to re-claim P1 but was increasingly distracted by the challenge of Rodriguez, who found himself relegated to P3 after appearing to have at least secured the runner-up spot on the podium. From their commanding viewpoint in the main grandstand, the riveting high-speed battle being played out below them electrified the spectators, many waving the Union flag, as they cheered the Briton who was intent on ending a dismal sequence of failing to record a win in his home grand prix. He was pressing so hard on the throttle pedal it felt as though his foot was about to force a hole in the car floor.

Stallard could see the marshal 200 metres down the track, poised with the chequered flag, standing on a raised platform overlooking the start-finish line, but another glance in his mirrors confirmed that easing up was not an option. He was convinced that if Petrenko could get his car within touching distance, the Russian would try to take him out of the race, even at this late stage. But the Gorton driver was in no mood to relinquish what, after a problematic qualifying session, had seemed an unlikely win. One hundred metres. Fifty metres. The crowd roared its favourite home. The chequered flag waved – and Stallard knew victory was his. It was only after crossing the line and lifting off the power that he became aware of the numbness of his fingers, such had been his vice-like grip on the steering wheel. But he was determined to acknowledge his supporters and as he slowed down he punched the air with both hands in a euphoric gesture.

The audio receiver in Stallard's helmet burst into life as his race engineer voiced the feelings of the team. "Great drive, Nick – brilliant! And back-to-back wins! This has got to be your year!"

"Thanks, Jim, and to all the crew. I owe you for this one. What a race – unbelievable! Wow!"

On impulse the winner slowly toured the circuit, responding to the rapturous applause, shouts of encouragement and flag-waving of thousands of motor racing fans who had witnessed a popular driver finally fulfil a long-awaited ambition. The emotion was no less tangible when he finally parked the car at parc fermé, the area reserved for the mandatory round of post-race technical checks by FS scrutineers. The Englishman released himself from his machine and ran across to greet his ecstatic mechanics, who had already started celebrating.

A minute later, after stepping onto the scales to verify that he and his car had not been underweight and clutching a partly-consumed bottle of mineral water, the victor led Petrenko and Rodriguez up the steps and onto the podium. But something struck him as odd. He was delighted to see his race engineer on the platform to represent the constructor but surprised to find the owner – who invariably carried out that role as he relished basking in the reflected glory of his drivers – was absent. But Stallard put the thought to the back of his mind as the band struck up with *God Save The King*. As the Union Jack was hauled ceremonially skywards, he gazed down at the smiling faces of his elated team members and the hundreds of fans beyond, determined to enjoy the moment. For a second or two he even allowed himself to wonder whether this would indeed be his year to seize the drivers' title and thus administer the ultimate put-down to his critics. But a glance at the two men sharing the podium with him quickly brought a reality check. Both personified in different ways a major threat to his aspirations and he had no doubt both would pursue their own cause with a passion and tenacity rivalling his own.

The national anthem ended and he was presented with a cut-glass trophy in the shape of the London Eye by the city's mayor. Presentations to Petrenko and Rodriguez followed, then the civic dignitaries made a dash for the exit as the three drivers unleashed a barrage of expensive champagne in the ritualistic revelry. The victorious racer targeted Jim Crowley who, despite the drenching, displayed a beaming smile and raised Stallard's arm aloft in triumph. It was an ebullient Englishman who appeared before journalists representing the broadcast, print and online media shortly afterwards. The gritty nature of his win, after starting from near the back of the grid, elicited praise from his questioners but they demanded to know his view of the collision that put his teammate out of the race.

"Kate was slow out of the corners, possibly because she had an issue with gear selection or tyres. Whatever, she was holding me up and I needed to get past."

"Was it worth the risk of taking a colleague out?"

"These things happen when you're racing, it's part of the sport."

The reporter pursued the point. "Were there any team orders?"

"No." The Gorton driver looked thoughtful as he towelled away the sweat running down his face then added, "Maybe that was a situation where team orders would have been helpful and the crash could have been averted."

"Are you saying your guys got their strategy wrong?"

"I've said what I've said. I know you're looking for a story but I'm just telling it from a driver's standpoint."

"What does Lockhart think about what happened?"

"Why don't you ask her?" he answered curtly.

Soon after the news conference ended, it was announced the FS stewards had conducted their own investigation into the crash and both drivers were cleared of any blame as it was deemed a racing incident. But Stallard had a hunch the internal inquest might be a more protracted matter and he wasn't surprised when, during the debrief with his engineers, he was summoned to the motor home of the team's owner. The racer found a sullen-faced Joe Gorton sitting at his desk and immediately sensed the man's irritability before he had uttered a word.

"Well, you got the result you wanted but you won't find any corks popping here."

"You surprise me, Joe – I always thought winning was a reason to celebrate."

"Most times it is but victory can sometimes be a two-edged sword – and you proved it today."

"I won the race after starting from P9. What's the problem with that?"

"I'll tell you what's wrong. You put Kate out of the race and stopped her and the team getting more points."

"She was holding me up, you must have seen that. Her car had clearly got some kind of problem and she should have moved over to let me through."

"I shouldn't have to remind you, but one of the cardinal rules in this sport is that teammates don't take each other out."

Stallard took a couple of steps towards the desk and made eye contact with the Gorton owner, his voice rising a notch. "Perhaps you should have spelt that out to your number two driver. Do you have a short memory or have you conveniently forgotten what happened in Kowloon when she cost me a podium spot?"

"You made a mistake and you paid for it. That's motor racing."

"That's not the way I saw it. My tyres were going off but I was holding on to P2 with just a couple of laps to go.

What I didn't need was Lockhart all over the back of me. If she had stayed where she was the team would have had both drivers in the top three and scored more points in the constructors' championship."

"Kowloon was different. Kate had fought her way through the field and you were in trouble when she caught you. Besides, she had every right to overtake. I don't allow team orders, as you know, so I don't need you telling the media we might have got our strategy wrong."

The driver leant forward, putting his hands on the desk. "The stewards found I did nothing wrong but you're sending out a clear message that says there's one rule for Lockhart and another for me. Every time there's a dispute between us you come down on her side and that's no way to run a race team."

Gorton swivelled his chair and stood up, the veins on his neck standing out like strips of cable. "What exactly are you insinuating?"

"You must be aware of the gossip in the paddock. And it didn't start yesterday!"

"What the hell are you talking about?"

"Look, I don't care what you do in private but if it's going to affect my career prospects, that's different."

"Be careful, Stallard. You may be heading the championship but that doesn't give you the right to make such an allegation. I don't need to remind you that your contract runs out at the end of the season."

"Is that some kind of threat?"

"It's a statement of fact."

The racer was in no mood to be intimidated. "As the leading driver I'm entitled to more support than I'm getting. I'm the one who's got the best chance of winning the title and that's where the focus should be, but I feel most of the effort is going into Lockhart's side of the garage and you're more concerned with her performance."

"If you're accusing me of favouritism, you're way off-beam. Maybe you can't handle it because Kate is the first woman competing at this level and she's a genuine rival."

"That's absurd and you know it. She's sixth in the drivers' standings on eight points while I've got three times as many."

"Perhaps you just don't like to admit she's made a good start in her rookie season."

"I don't have a problem with Lockhart, but…" He hesitated.

Gorton stepped around the desk and towards his driver until they were just inches apart. "But you have one with me, is that it? Am I your problem?"

"If you're not prepared to back me one hundred percent I need to know."

"All you need to know is you're hired by me and your job is to race. My job is to run the team. Don't concern yourself with anything else!"

The racer glared at the owner then headed for the door.

"There's something else you should remember, Stallard."

The driver turned to face the proprietor.

"It's taken a lot of my time and money to build this outfit to where it is now. I don't have to justify the way I run it, least of all to you!"

For the brothers it was the best time of the day. Kicking a ball on wasteland in a run-down northern suburb of the Russian capital compensated for long hours in the classroom. This day had been no different. Fyodor, aged ten, and Sergei, two years younger, had hurried home, pulled on their well-worn and faded red and white replica shirts and run outside, where they tried to imitate the skills of their FC Spartak Moscow idols. Light rain had started to fall but the boys' enthusiasm was undimmed as they practised spot kicks against a wall that marked the perimeter of what they liked to call their pitch but was today the scene of a penalty shoot-out in the Champions League final.

White chalk lines on the five-foot-high wall marked the goalposts and Fyodor could feel the tension of the capacity crowd at the San Siro stadium in Milan as he placed the plastic ball on a makeshift penalty spot. Leading FC Barcelona four-three, glory beckoned for his beloved Spartak if the youngster could outwit the Spanish goalkeeper and score. Fyodor took a long look at his brother masquerading as the goalie, inhaled deeply then ran forward and booted the ball. But in his excitement he misjudged the angle of contact and instead of heading towards its target, the yellow and black sphere soared into the air and disappeared over the wall.

"Call yourself a penalty-taker!" shouted Sergei at his crestfallen sibling. "The coach will keep you on the bench for the next match. Anyway, it's your turn to get the ball."

As the boys had often done before, Fyodor trudged twenty feet to the point where the wall had partly crumbled and climbed over. Behind the stone barrier, in an area of fractured paving slabs, a jungle of weeds had proliferated over the years, accentuating the air of neglect that pervaded the district. The detritus of urban living was much in evidence: sodden cardboard boxes, smashed liquor bottles, decaying slats of timber fencing, the corroding shell of a fridge-freezer, tyres and plastic containers long since discarded, all interspersed with the rusting skeletons of abandoned cars.

The brightly coloured ball, resting incongruously in the cheerless landscape, was quickly spotted by Fyodor. He walked towards it, surprised at how far it had travelled, and chided himself again for the lack of precision when aiming his kick. The boy had become accustomed to the accumulated debris that littered the area and tended to not pay much heed to it but this time was aware of something that he was certain wasn't there a couple of days earlier. He noticed a piece of old carpet, grimy and frayed at the edges, that had been dumped amongst the weeds but was angled against a rotting tree stump. Whether it was a sixth sense or curiosity just got the better of him the youngster wasn't sure, but he made a slight detour.

"Come on, Fyodor! Where's the ball?" shouted Sergei from the other side of the wall.

"I'm coming now," answered his brother. By this time he had reached the carpet. Leaning over, he grasped one end and slowly pulled it back. He stared hard for several seconds, not comprehending what he was seeing. Then the full horror of what lay before him slowly permeated his consciousness. He gaped at the charred corpse, bewildered by what his eyes were showing him. Fyodor's mouth was open but he was incapable of uttering any sound. It was the first dead person he had seen but he wasn't to know that few have to endure the experience in such a nauseating manner. His fingers released the strip of carpet and it fell back, concealing yet again its grisly secret, but too late to obliterate from the senses what should never have been witnessed by one so young.

"What are you doing, Fyodor?" yelled Sergei, a growing impatience clearly evident in his voice. "I'm getting bored."

There was no response from his elder brother, who by now was running back to the wall. Impelled by the nightmare image playing in his mind, he scrambled over and grabbed Sergei by the hand. "We must get out of here. Don't ask me why. Come on, run."

The two boys scurried home, Fyodor ignoring Sergei's grumbling at the curtailing of their football practice. Their mother – a woman long resident in the area and inured to incidents involving criminal elements – at first found it hard to believe her son's story and insisted on seeing the body before calling the police. All they could tell her was that pending the result of the autopsy they were treating the death as suspicious, but they would have to check their lists of missing people. It would be another ten days before the badly burnt remains were identified as those of Yevgeny Turov.

TEN

Jack Wyatt looked out across a Moscow skyline painted red by the dying sun. The fifth-floor balcony outside his hotel suite, overlooking the Moskva River, provided striking views of the Kremlin, Red Square and the multi-coloured twisting onion domes of St Basil's Cathedral. He was momentarily distracted by the distant sound of voices and laughter, enlivened by alcohol, emanating from the river below. He glanced down to see one of the double-decker boats – this one festooned with balloons – that regularly carried tourists on sightseeing cruises through the heart of the city and presumed it had been chartered for a special celebration.

As the American's gaze reverted to the familiar landmarks of the Russian capital, he pondered the phone call he had taken in his room forty minutes earlier. The hotel switchboard operator had apologised because the person on the other end of the line would not give their name and Wyatt was asked if he would accept the call. When he was connected the voice was instantly recognisable. The contact had been unexpected and the conversation brief, but it left him puzzled. Had there been a change of heart? If so, what was the motivation? Or could it be something more personal? As he turned the questions over in his mind the door buzzer sounded. He turned away from the balcony railings and walked inside. A glance through the glass spyhole – its fish-eye lens allowing him a 180 degree view – identified his visitor and he slid back the security chain before opening the door.

They looked at each other for a few moments before Wyatt broke the silence. "I can't say I had you down on my guest list for today."

The merest hint of a smile flitted across the woman's face. "There's always someone who tries to gatecrash." She paused, her stiletto heels creating transient indentations on the thick pile beige-coloured carpet in the corridor as her weight shifted from one foot to the other. "Is this a convention for men only?"

The American grinned. "Sorry. Come right in, Valya." He stepped aside and as she entered the room, Wyatt was suddenly and agreeably aware of the scented fragrance redolent of their encounter in Victory Park.

The Russian noted the spacious layout of the accommodation, which included an olive-coloured three-piece suite and an oak desk and chair with a slimline, rectangular wall-mounted television above. A large potted palm stood near the window leading to the balcony. She peered out then turned to face the American. "Nice lodgings you've got here, and the views aren't bad either."

Wyatt was pulling open the door of the mini-bar. "I had noticed. I'm gonna have a drink. What's your poison?"

Valya sat down on the well-sprung sofa. "Any wine? I could murder a glass of red."

"There's a couple of half-bottles of Chilean merlot in here."

"That'll do."

Wyatt poured two glasses, handed her one, then eased himself into an armchair. "It didn't take you long to get here."

"The Metro runs on time these days and it's only a ten-minute walk from Novokuznetskaya Station." Valya sipped her drink then looked up. "You sounded surprised when I called."

"I didn't think you'd change your mind."

"What makes you think I have?"

"Why else would you be here?"

"Perhaps I'm curious."

"About what?"

"About you, Mr Wyatt."

The American looked thoughtful as he gently twirled the contents of his glass. "You ought to remember that old proverb, Valya – it was curiosity that killed the cat."

"What d'you mean?"

"You told me Makarov runs everyone on a tight leash and you could be in danger if he found out about our meeting in the park. But this time you came looking for me and put yourself at risk."

The supple blonde, in a cherry-red blouse and black skirt with black tights, crossed one leg over the other with a practised elegance. "I guess I'm making a statement by coming here today."

"What sort of statement?"

"About myself. I feel a need to show I've got a will of my own and that I'm not going to be intimidated by him."

"I can't fault you for that but you need to be careful. From what I've learnt about your boss…" Wyatt paused. "Let's not kid ourselves – we both know what he's capable of."

"That's why I can't leave my job. He would never let me work for anyone else, he'd kill me first, but he also has power over me and I don't like it. I can't go on this way. I must have some normality in my life."

"No one would argue against that."

"The easiest option is to do nothing but there's a price for that – and I'm not prepared to pay it."

"But your other choices are not exactly risk-free," he cautioned.

"I'm well aware of that but the feeling of being trapped is worse than the danger involved in defying Viktor."

Valya was drinking quickly so Wyatt downed the remnants of his glass then refilled both.

"Thanks." She gestured towards the seat next to her. "Why don't you join me? You should be safe, I've been house-trained!"

Looking down, he smiled at her benignly. "Never doubted it for a moment." The tall American eased himself onto the sofa. "I guess you're in defiance mode tonight and that's why you're here."

"Partly that, but I also try to make some space for myself, although it's hard at times. But you intrigue me, Mr Wyatt, and I wanted to find out more."

"It could be a dangerous strategy. Makarov could have had you followed to the hotel."

"You forget, I'm well used to covering my tracks. I know I need to take care but I have to live as well. If I don't, he wins."

"I like your attitude. You must have a rebellious streak running through your DNA."

Valya smiled. "I was brought up to speak my mind. My parents were poor and from a rural background but they prided themselves on their independence of spirit. I've never forgotten that so when I found myself with a man who wants to control every aspect of my life, my first instinct was to rebel. Let's just say I've learnt to deal with the situation but I've had to develop a certain amount of cunning along the way."

"Lesson number one, Valya – never underestimate the power of feminine guile."

"Lesson number two, Mr Wyatt – beware the stranger in the park who makes a tempting job offer."

"But not so beware you can't come knocking on my door. I think you know I'm not a threat." He sipped his wine. "Anyway, spare me the formalities – you can call me Jack, if you want."

"Maybe I should get to know you better."

"That may not be such a great idea."

"Why is that?"

"I might be hard to get to know."

"Are you always this defensive when you meet someone?"

Wyatt stared intently at the glass he was holding then turned towards the Russian. "Over the years I've become self-sufficient, I've had to, and that's made me selfish. That ain't a good recipe for sharing anything."

"It wouldn't help in a marriage."

"You're damn right!"

"Sounds like you've had personal experience."

"Hey, what *is* this? I could do without the third degree!"

"Sorry, I didn't mean to pry."

"No point raking up the past. It's been a while and I've moved on."

Valya ran her fingers through her lustrous, shoulder-length hair. "OK, I get the message – your personal life is off-limits. But there is something I've been curious about since we met in the park. What's your connection with the Middle East?"

Wyatt drew a lengthy breath before answering. "I guess it's only natural you should want to know about my involvement. I had service in the military and now I work in the security business as a consultant. My work takes me to various countries and I've built up a sizable network of contacts in the process. It was one of those contacts, acting as intermediary for a syndicate from one of the Gulf States, who approached me."

"To do what exactly?"

"I was coming to that. It was made clear to me that a major financial investment in Moscow is on the cards but, as in any calculated business venture, the syndicate wants to find out the likely strength of the competition before committing itself."

"And that's where you come in?"

"You got it."

The blonde nodded knowingly. "So that's why you set up the meeting between us."

"You were a significant part of my research but, as I explained at the time, the syndicate was also hoping to recruit you."

"That was never going to be an option for me."

"I can see why but that ain't a place you want to be, Valya."

"You might as well save your breath, it's not going to change anything. I am where I am and have to deal with it." She looked down at her empty glass then turned appealingly to the American. "This seems to be hitting the right spot. Did you have any plans for that other bottle?"

"Nope, but I guess I do now!" He poured them each another drink. "Have you eaten?"

"It's been a while."

"Same here. Let's check out the menu and call room service."

An hour later they had finished their meal and were standing outside on the balcony. The capital's lights grew brighter as twilight turned to night but the air was still warm.

"I love this city, Jack," sighed Valya. "It's always excited me and I never want to leave it."

"You're gonna stay then, despite everything?"

"I have to. I can't let him win."

"It seems Makarov acts like he owns you."

"I'm not sure how to explain it. Sometimes it feels like I'm in a cage and constantly pushing at the door but somehow I can never force it fully open."

The description hung in the air for a time as the couple stood silent, watching a seemingly endless procession of car headlights in the distance. Wyatt was first to speak. "If he wasn't unfaithful would you feel different?"

"That's a hard one. I'd like to think I would but it's not just that. When I became his mistress I had to buy into the whole sordid package and that created its own problems." She paused, the night breeze catching her hair, before looking into Wyatt's eyes. "If you're wondering, I don't owe him much in the loyalty stakes."

"I kinda guessed that."

Valya took a step forward and kissed the American softly on the mouth. "Maybe defiance is good for the soul."

"Don't ever stop pushing at that cage door."

The Russian smiled. "As if I would."

Wyatt pulled her closer and found her lips again and she responded with a new fervency. As her fingers hastily undid the remaining buttons on his shirt, he kissed her neck and ran his hands down her thighs, the firmness of her flesh accentuating his desire. "I want you, Jack," she murmured as she clutched his hand and led him from the balcony into the lounge.

One of the two doors at the far end of the room was open and although the interior was dimly lit, Valya could see the outline of a queen-size bed. She swiftly took off her blouse and unzipped her skirt, discarding both on a goatskin rug on the floor, before sitting on the side of the bed. Wyatt, now stripped to his boxer shorts, helped ease the tights off her long willowy legs and she lay on the bed, clad only in magenta-coloured bra and panties, a look of expectancy playing on her face. "I'm leaving the rest to you," she laughed. The American took off her panties with one hand while deftly unfastening the clasp of her bra with the other, liberating her bulging breasts. She pulled his head downwards and his eager mouth found her hardening nipples.

"It's about time these came off," Valya whispered, and he grudgingly came away from her chest as she helped remove his underpants. Her hand reached out at his groin and began working him, slowly at first, then quickening her pace. Abruptly, she released her hold and guided his fingers towards her crotch, directing, exhorting. He rubbed her, kneaded her. Then she was ready. Frantic, insistent, she pulled him closer. Valya had an urgency, a carnal craving that would not be denied. Wyatt found her core and moved rhythmically, the tempo escalating with every thrust of his body. Culmination when it came was as intense as it was inevitable. As both panted in the afterglow, the euphony of lust was palpable. Valya sighed deeply and, holding her in his arms, the American once again sensed a vulnerability he had first detected during their encounter in the park. They were briefly aware of faraway late-night sounds of revelry drifting up from the river before sleep overcame them.

More than 1500 miles away, an early evening sun shone down on another capital and another river. The three men occasionally looked up to take in the impressive views from the private roof terrace of the penthouse overlooking the Thames, St Paul's Cathedral and Southwark Bridge, but each was focused on the issue under discussion. The meeting – hosted by FS supremo Lucas Tait two days after the London race – followed an urgent request from the owner of Akron Racing.

"I think you have a right to know Makarov was threatening strike action less than twenty-four hours before the cars lined up for the start in Australia and he wanted the rest of us to join him," said an animated Gus Johnson. "You gotta hand it to him – the guy's got balls!"

Tait exchanged glances with his chief steward before responding. "D'you think he was serious in what he was proposing?"

"No doubt about it. If he could have gotten our support, he'd have gone to you with an ultimatum – either promise talks on an improved financial deal for the teams or no cars on the grid. That's what he was looking to put on the table."

"I heard nothing so I guess there weren't any takers," said Tait drily.

"Not at that point. It seemed he was trying to blackmail you into submission at short notice but the rest of us decided we didn't want to go that route."

Floyd Collins cleared his throat. "Look, Gus, we appreciate you tipping us off about the Russian and we can't say it's a big surprise, knowing his track record. We're also aware it was a meeting of the team owners so we're not asking you to divulge any secrets, but it would be useful," he glanced at Tait, "if you could give us some kind of steer as to the general tone of the discussion."

"I don't think I'm…" The American steel magnate stopped mid-sentence as a Metropolitan Police helicopter flew close above them, the sound of the twin-engined Eurocopter EC145 drowning him out. He watched as the high-tech aircraft headed across the river, the sun's rays reflecting off the fast-rotating blades, before resuming. "I don't think I'm talking out of turn when I say the majority view was against rushing headlong into the sort of action put forward by Makarov. As I said, we got the impression he wanted to hold you to ransom to force a concession, but more moderate voices made themselves heard. Although, if I'm honest, I got a definite sense the teams will be looking for a better deal next time."

"And what's your personal take on all this?" enquired Tait.

The Akron Racing boss shifted a little uneasily in his chair before answering. "I gotta say, my hat's in the ring with the other guys. I know you staked everything to get FS to where it is today and no one begrudges you the rewards associated with that, but there's a growing feeling on the pit wall that we're coming off second-best."

"How d'you work that one out?"

"Well, take our share of the revenue from global marketing deals and broadcasting rights. We know the percentages are gonna be in your favour, we accept that, but we reckon our cut has failed to keep pace and it seems the slippage gets worse each year."

The FS principal struggled to contain his irascibility. "Look, Gus, I don't have to remind you, but I'm the commercial rights holder and that's because I've built this business into what it is today."

"I know that and it would be churlish to deny it but—"

"No, wait a minute. I want you to hear me out on this one. You and the other team owners also need to remember I've helped grow your businesses, too. I've organised the teams in such a way as to represent their best interests by negotiating en bloc with the circuit owners for improved entry fees and prize money. And I've created an end product that's much in demand by a worldwide television audience, which has grown exponentially in recent years. And, yes, maybe I've had to act like a despot at times to do it, but without me you wouldn't be where you are now!"

"But where would you be without us?" Johnson persisted. "Whichever way you look at it, the teams are the pivotal part of your empire and there's no way of ducking it."

"That's not in dispute but a contract's a contract and you would all be in breach if you refused to race."

"That point was made and we know the repercussions of going on strike."

"And that's not all. You have obligations to your respective corporate multi-national sponsors. They would go ape-shit if their agreements were flouted en masse."

"No need to give me the legals, we've got our own lawyers."

The fingers of Tait's left hand tapped fretfully on the arm-rest of his chair. "Look at it this way, Gus. Every circus needs a ringmaster, someone who pulls the strings, runs the show and makes everything work. It's got to be that way. If you guys – the team owners – were in charge, it would be chaotic. The in-fighting would make it impossible to reach agreement on anything and crucial decisions would be deferred. It would be a recipe for disaster."

"Take it easy, Lucas, we're not talking about a palace revolution here. No one wants to usurp your role as head of FS, that's not what this is about. Let's take your analogy of the circus. The crowds go to see the lion tamer crack his whip and watch the big cats prowl around the ring. But they also pay the admission price because they know there's a whiff of danger in the air and that excites them. And it's no different with us. Drivers put themselves at risk every time they climb in the cockpit and the fans know that – it's part of why they watch races. They don't set out hoping to see a racer killed or maimed, but they know the law of averages dictates that every now and then it will happen. It's hard-wired into the human psyche and you can't escape it. The teams, and especially the drivers, are the excitement magnet for the spectators and we just want our fair reward for that."

Tait stood up and walked slowly towards the chrome-plated iron railings marking the boundary of the roof terrace and looked down as a barge, laden with a cargo of timber, made its way up river. Then he turned to face the team owner. "There's something I need to know. Is strike action a real possibility or just a negotiating ploy?"

"I can only go on what was said at the meeting of the owners in the Northern Territory and I've given you my views on that."

"Don't be evasive," snapped the questioner. "Give it to me straight!"

"Alright, Lucas, I'll level with you. The way I read it, if you force the teams into a corner, my gut feeling is we would refuse to race. But I reckon we would do so reluctantly and only after a complete breakdown of talks. I have no doubt, and I guess this goes for most of my colleagues, that we would much prefer to negotiate an agreement."

"Except Makarov," said Collins.

"You got it."

Johnson levered himself out of his chair. "I need to make tracks, gentlemen. Thanks for your time but I've got some other business to take care of whilst I'm in London."

"Gus, before you go," said Tait, "did you ever get any kind of apology from the Russian following the death of your guy, Maitland?"

"Like hell I did!" The steel magnate's contorted face was as expressive as his words. "There's more chance of me pissing on the moon than getting Makarov to say sorry."

"Can't say you surprise me."

"To be honest, I didn't expect any sympathy, but what upset the team most of all was his total lack of compassion towards Pete's widow. There wasn't even a letter or a phone call. The guy sucks."

"You ain't the only one around here who feels that way. He angered everyone in the paddock that day."

"I know we operate in a highly competitive arena – some would even call it cut-throat – where there's little margin for error, but what happened to Pete was beyond the pale. But for neither Makarov nor his driver to show the slightest remorse afterwards was the ultimate insult."

Tait sent a reassuring look in Collins' direction. "At least the stewards registered the disapproval that was widely felt both on and off the track. I know the video evidence was overwhelming but official condemnation was needed and they provided it."

Johnson chose his words carefully. "We all know Makarov's driver was disqualified and his race points taken off him, but I felt the stewards should have gone further and put down a marker to express the racing community's utter contempt of what happened."

The chief steward stared quizzically at the team owner. "What exactly did you have in mind?"

"It's easy to be critical in retrospect, and there's no point having recriminations this long after the event, but I thought a two-race ban would have sent the right message. To be candid with you, a disqualification and loss of points just seemed like a slap on the wrist in the circumstances."

Tait grimaced. "You need to tread carefully here, Gus. We're not in the business of re-writing history and nothing we say or do is going to bring back Pete Maitland."

"Floyd asked the question but he ain't gonna like my answer."

"You should have realised by now that I have full confidence in the way he and his colleagues administer discipline in FS. It's a thankless task and they have to take difficult decisions sometimes, but it's to their credit they've been able to gain the respect of those they regulate. I don't want to stir the embers of what was a distressing episode for all of us, but if you felt the punishment wasn't severe enough you could have said so at the time."

Johnson was unable to conceal the fleeting facial expression that vented the emotional pain he still felt at the loss of his leading driver. "Lucas, it's hard to put into words what I felt and still feel at the way Pete was taken from us. The anguish is still there; it never leaves me. To say I was overcome by grief and anger is not overstating it, and I'll admit, it put me out of kilter for a time. But the guy's been gone a while now and whatever my views about the way the stewards handled the aftermath, they ain't gonna change anything. I know that and have to live with it."

Collins turned uncomfortably in his chair. "We called it as we saw it, Gus. We were mindful of the fact it was Petrenko's first race in his rookie season and we—"

"You don't have to justify it to me now," Johnson butted in, looking down at the chief steward. "You and your colleagues came to a judgment and ruled accordingly. What I'm saying is that, in my opinion, you got it wrong. You found him guilty of dangerous driving but that wasn't reflected in the sentence handed down."

"I understand why you still feel resentful and I'm sympathetic to it but you're coming at this from a specific standpoint. Our investigation into the incident had to be unbiased and we needed to examine all the relevant facts before reaching a decision."

"I don't need your sympathy, Floyd. It's too late for that. Frankly, this is not what I came to discuss and I'm outta here." Johnson moved briskly from the terrace, stepped inside the penthouse lounge and headed for the main door, closely followed by Tait.

"Wait, Gus. I want you to know I appreciate you coming here today to give us the low-down on Makarov's strike-call and where the other teams stand on the issue. It can't have been easy."

The Akron boss turned to face his countryman. "It

wasn't. But don't get the wrong idea – I'm no Judas, although I'm starting to feel like one!"

"Don't worry. Our meeting was confidential."

"Make sure it stays that way."

After Johnson had gone Tait rejoined the chief steward, who was leaning against the terrace railings and looking down on the Thames, its greyish-black waters beginning to ripple under the influence of a strengthening south-westerly breeze.

"He's still sore and nothing we say is going to change that," said Collins.

The FS supremo nodded agreement. "It's hard for any team when it loses its number one driver. We can never stamp out the danger in this sport but when it happens that way, it's tough to deal with."

"And it doesn't help when you've got an owner who's hell-bent on winning at all costs."

"I had noticed."

"I'm all for competition – hell, that's the business we're in – but when you have a guy like Makarov who clearly has no scruples in breaking the rules, maybe it's time for a mid-term assessment."

Tait eyed his colleague keenly. "What exactly have you got in mind?"

"He's got a three-year contract, right? It expires at the end of next season. Well, let's say I wouldn't be overly disappointed if it wasn't renewed – and I guess there are others on the pit wall who would probably agree with me."

"I can name at least a couple."

"We won't have any difficulty finding a replacement. There was no shortage of applicants the last time we had a team vacancy."

"That's never a problem. You can guarantee there'll be a bunch of multi-millionaires queuing up for a slice of the action. They're awash with bucks but they're greedy and want to make more. But it doesn't always pan out that way as a number of once-famous marques can testify. This circus can be brutal at times in the way some of its own self-destruct."

"There's one option Makarov might consider," said Collins thoughtfully.

"Go on."

"You could make a generous offer to buy him out of his contract."

"I'm not sure I'd want to put more money his way even if he was willing to go."

"He could be open to inducement."

"No doubt, but he knows he's got a box-seat in this sport and I suspect he wants to be here for the duration."

"Yeah, you're probably right."

"Besides," said Tait, as he stared long and hard at some of the well-known landmarks dotting the horizon, "anything could happen between now and then."

Collins appeared puzzled. "What d'you mean?"

Tait waited until a pack of swooping, screeching gulls had passed overhead. "Life has a habit of throwing up the unexpected and this game is no exception."

ELEVEN

To the protestors it was anything but heaven and earth. But the repetitious chanting of the small group of placard-wielding demonstrators had long since been drowned out by the sounds of high-revving engines that shattered the tranquillity of the upper Hemel en Aarde Valley in the Western Cape. The Afrikaans name for it was well merited. The physical backdrop to the circuit staging the inaugural race on the African continent was impressive by any standards. Nestling in the shadow of the towering mountain ranges of the Overberg region east of Cape Town, and with the Atlantic Ocean to the south, the valley boasted stunning views, bountiful vineyards and fruit orchards.

Environmentalists were quick to mount a campaign of opposition when plans to build the circuit were mooted but their efforts were undermined by a landowner who was persuaded to sell his extensive vineyard at a price far above the prevailing commercial rate. Local hostility to the scheme was partly assuaged when hundreds of unemployed labourers were hired to assist the contractors' own workforce and the project was completed on schedule in eighteen months. But an underlying feeling of resentment still lingered in the community despite a further boost to the region's economy with the construction of a five-star hotel and executive-style chalets nearby, and a resultant influx of tourists.

The track – one of the longest in the FS calendar at a little over 4 miles – carved its way through a landscape of undulating hills covered with fynbos, the natural vegetation as soft and smooth as velvet, its variety of proteas, ericas and grasses swaying gently in a cool sea breeze. It climbed gradually, in line with the contours of its surroundings, during the early stages of the lap but a counter-balancing fast downhill section leading to a tricky hairpin bend made its own demands, accentuated by a capricious circuit designer. Spectators at the most elevated part of the circuit could look south to Hermanus and the rocky coastline beyond, where every year the southern right whales migrate from the sub-Antarctic to calve in the sheltered, warmer waters of Walker Bay. But for the drivers and the groups of engineers whose eyes were glued to the banks of monitors on the pit wall, there was no time to admire the spectacular scenery. The young Russian, Petrenko, who had put in a superb late effort in qualifying to claim pole position, had never been headed, and with three laps to go was on course for his second win of the season. Setting a series of fastest laps, he had built up a commanding lead over his nearest challenger, Guiscard, who was closely followed by Rodriguez and Stallard.

Viktor Makarov's curmudgeonly instincts rarely allowed him to hand out plaudits to those who earned them, but as he watched his rookie driver – who had been on the podium five times in seven races and was lying third in the championship – he acknowledged he had found a special talent and a potential world-beater. The owner's eyes glinted at the prospect of his man being crowned champion in his first season at the top level, and the ensuing commercial spin-offs to the team brand. Even better, he told himself, it would ensure he had a potent bargaining tool in the next round of negotiations with Tait, when the teams would be seeking to increase their share of the income from international marketing contracts and broadcasting rights.

On the track, Petrenko, who was forced to make a pit stop two laps early to change a tyre that was losing pressure, was not easing off the throttle despite a nineteen-second gap between himself and the Frenchman. The Russian's car was about two-thirds of the way down the longest straight on the circuit, its engine screaming and revving at near its limit of 19,000 rpm. Ahead was a backmarker, the American Al Boyd, who had already seen a marshal waving a blue flag, instructing him to move over and allow the race leader to lap him. The Akron duly pulled away from the racing line and the car displaying the purple and orange colours of Makarov Racing flashed by at over 185 miles per hour.

The Russian continued to accelerate until he approached the end of the straight and passed the marker board indicating 300 metres to a right-hand bend. Back on the pit wall, his race engineer, Igor Smirnov, was starting to become uneasy as he monitored the flow of technical data on the car's performance. His finger found the transmit button on the garage-to-car radio. "Yuri, you're well clear of P2. You've been pressing hard all race. You can ease off a little now." The rookie understood the message but did not respond, preferring to maintain his intense concentration. Smirnov waited thirty seconds then radioed again, this time a greater urgency in his voice. "You're revving too high. I want you to short-shift between the gears and lower the revs."

The driver's reply was terse. "Almost there."

The engineer's tone was becoming shrill. "Your fuel's running low and you need to save the engine. Turn it down!"

But Smirnov was wasting his breath – and he knew it. Their working relationship was far from harmonious. Although an experienced professional, he had found the twenty-one-year-old difficult to manage from the outset. Whilst admiring Petrenko's undoubted talent, he disliked his know-it-all attitude and an arrogance that seemed to grow with each race. Smirnov was also mindful that the rookie was the protege of the team's owner and if the youngster felt like breaking the rules, he would probably get away with it, which added to the engineer's frustration.

Confident that victory would soon be in his grasp, the rookie was about to begin the penultimate lap. The gap to Guiscard had been extended to twenty seconds, the Frenchman having to settle for the runner-up spot, with Rodriguez and Stallard fighting it out for the remaining place on the podium. Then came an inkling that something might be amiss. As Petrenko's car approached the main grandstand opposite the pits, a wisp of smoke could be seen coming from its rear. A few seconds later there was a plume, this time clearly coming from the right-hand side of the V10 power unit.

Watching the race coverage on the television monitor, Smirnov swung around in his seat on the pit wall to look directly at the racer, apprehensive at the first sign of trouble. The team owner, sitting next to him, cursed. In the suffocating heat of the cockpit, the driver felt a vibration behind him, slight at first and then a rumbling. In a reflex action he lifted his foot from the throttle but it was too late. A wall of smoke billowed out from the back of the car and flames licked the air as the three-litre engine blew up. Oil spurted on to the track, creating a potentially deadly stream for those following behind. Petrenko hammered a gloved fist on the steering wheel in anger at the sudden loss of power but retained sufficient awareness of the situation to guide his car on to the grassed run-off area, where it gradually rolled to a stop, leaving a greyish-white haze in its wake.

The course marshals responded quickly to the drama unfolding before them. Two reached the vehicle as the driver was clambering out and used their extinguishers to douse the flames still shooting upwards from the rear. Meanwhile, their colleagues were frantically waving yellow flags to warn the new race leader and his rivals to slow down, be prepared to take evasive action and stop if necessary. Guiscard had seen the smoke in the distance as he entered the straight but his first reaction was to maintain his speed as Rodriguez and Stallard were pressing him hard. It was only when he glimpsed the flag-waving marshals that he started to brake and then spotted oil on the track. The Frenchman swerved at the last moment and managed to avoid most of the spillage and the other two, close behind, took similar evasive action.

An exasperated Petrenko, his helmet and fireproof balaclava in his hands, leant against a fence and could only watch as his rivals sped by at the start of the final lap. Race

Control decided not to call out the safety car and instead directed the marshals to continue warning the drivers of the hazard. Guiscard, jubilant at the surprise nature of his victory, took the chequered flag and the Spanish driver just managed to hold off the Englishman in the battle for P2. A spirited drive by the American, Kate Lockhart, was rewarded with P4. She was followed home by the Indian, Pavani, and the Chinese racer, Wang, finished in P6. The Frenchman's win put him joint third with Petrenko in the championship on twenty-eight points. Stallard remained at the top of the standings on thirty-six, with Rodriguez on thirty-five. The four had put daylight between them and the next two contenders, Pavani with fifteen points and Lockhart with eleven.

As a sweaty but elated Guiscard stood atop the podium savouring the melodic strains of *La Marseillaise*, an enraged Makarov confronted Smirnov in the team's motor home. It wasn't the first time Petrenko's engineer had been summoned after a race to appear before an owner notorious for short-tempered outbursts when events on the track had gone against him, but this time Smirnov, although fearing the worst, was determined to stand his corner.

"What the hell happened out there?"

"We were unlucky. He was almost there when the engine let go. Another two laps and he'd have got the win."

"Unlucky? That's not what I want to hear!" sneered Makarov. "Luck. Chance. Fate. What good are they to me? I've always had to create my own destiny."

"The engine was the same one used in the previous race in London. Yuri was pushing it to its limits and it couldn't take any more."

"So you're blaming the driver now."

"I tried to warn him. The V10 was taking a lot of punishment and I told him to ease off but he…" Smirnov's voice tailed away.

The owner took an intimidating step towards the engineer. "But what, Igor?"

"I don't think he was interested in taking my advice."

"What d'you mean?"

"OK, I'll spell it out. Yuri is a talented driver but he has a problem. He's only been in this game five minutes but he thinks he knows it all. For a rookie, he's had a sensational start to his FS career, but that's made it worse because it's all come too easy for him. Eventually he'll learn but he'll have to do it the hard way like the rest of them."

"Are you sure you've finished?" The team owner paused to let his words sink in. "You got one thing right. We have a young driver who's quick, very quick. I think he's capable of winning the title in his first season but to do it he needs an engine he can rely on."

"It's the first failure we've had."

"It's one too many!"

"But these things happen in motor racing."

"Don't lecture me, Smirnov. Our guy qualifies on pole, has a brilliant race and is heading for a certain win but then his engine blows and he ends up with no points. I've ploughed millions into this team and that sort of performance is not acceptable. If it happens again…" His words trailed away but the unspoken threat was not lost on the engineer.

Yet he refused to be cowed. "We're not the only ones, other teams have had similar—"

"What sort of excuse is that? I don't give a fuck about the opposition. These engines are designed to last for two races plus practice and qualifying."

"But the problem seems to develop soon after a pit stop when a car has been stationary in the pit lane for seven or eight seconds. Don't forget, Yuri pitted for fuel shortly before he lost power." The owner remained unimpressed. "I've ordered a full investigation. All the telemetry readouts and data are fed back to the team base in Moscow, where they're being closely examined. We've got to establish the cause of this failure."

Makarov moved across the room and stood before a wallchart. "This has also given us another problem." He gestured to Smirnov. "I want you to look at this. It's just been updated and shows the latest drivers' standings. If Yuri had won today he would be joint second with Rodriguez and only one point behind Stallard. But instead, he's now joint third with Guiscard and the gap to the leaders has widened."

The engineer tried to placate his boss. "There are four races to go. There's still time for Yuri to force his way back into contention. Sometimes the leaders are so preoccupied with fighting each other they don't see the next guy coming and they're vulnerable to a pass."

"But he's lost ground when he should have been in a position to put real pressure on the front men. That's when drivers make mistakes, when they know the slightest error can be exploited by a rival." The owner appeared deep in thought. "But now there's another threat on the radar."

"What's that?"

"The Frenchman. He could be a dangerous outsider in the run-in to the championship."

"But our man is showing great form and can still influence what happens. Don't write him off just yet. It hasn't got to the point where it's out of his hands."

"Not yet – but another fiasco like the one today and it will be. Perhaps it's time for a change of strategy."

Smirnov looked surprised. "Sounds like you've got something in mind."

Makarov smiled thinly but remained evasive. "I like to keep all options open. You need to remember something, Smirnov – a rookie only ever has one opportunity to win the championship in his first year and it's never been done. If he can achieve it, Petrenko will become a legend, and this team will go down in history, too."

As dusk fell, the sounds of revelry emanated from the swimming pool area of the luxury hotel. Located high on a plateau in the upper Hemel en Aarde Valley, it overlooked the race circuit and in the distance could be seen the lights of Hermanus on the southern coast. The mood of those relaxing on the poolside loungers was of undisguised celebration. The unexpected win hours earlier by their number one driver and the subsequent boost to his FS title hopes had raised spirits in the Drogan camp following the untimely death of their German teammate, Otto Werner, in the Australian round of the championship.

Whilst a number of his mechanics were playing a water-based variant of handball in the pool, Guiscard – in a cotton T-shirt and shorts and with a glass of champagne in his hand – was in animated conversation with the team owner, Olivier Maigny, and race engineer, Alain Gaudet. "I got lucky today," said the driver in his typically understated way. "The Russian set a blistering pace from the start and maintained it throughout the race. He was still pulling away from the rest of us when his engine blew. He deserved to win."

The owner smiled in an avuncular way. "Philippe, don't play down your part in what happened. You had a good race and were in the right place to cash in when Petrenko broke down. You have to make your own luck sometimes."

Gaudet nodded. "I agree. You were in a dogfight with Rodriguez and Stallard for much of the afternoon but when it mattered you were able to take advantage of the opening that came your way. All credit to you."

"Thanks, guys, but I still think the rookie was hard done by."

"Another day it'll be different and fortune will favour him," said Maigny. "You did your job – now bank the points and focus on the next race."

The owner pulled several sheets of paper from his briefcase and handed them to the driver. "This is what excites me – take a look. Our design team is already working on next year's car and these printouts show how it's taking shape on the computer screen."

Guiscard studied the images. "Looks impressive, even at this early stage."

"I know sometimes it's just a tweak here and there or a minor modification, but this time I've asked our chief designer to come up with something special for the new season. Each of the project leaders responsible for the chassis, the aerodynamics, the transmission and so on has been fully briefed and knows what's required."

"Has it got as far as the wind tunnel yet?"

"A scale model of the new car has been built," said Gaudet, "and testing started last week. As you know, we can replicate a variety of aerodynamic conditions in the tunnel and the early signs are promising, although there is still much research to be done."

Maigny re-filled three glasses from the bottle of Bollinger standing in an ice bucket on a nearby table. After a profitable early career buying and selling aircraft parts, he had founded an airline and turned it into one of Europe's most successful carriers, and had a personal reputation for being hands-on as the business expanded. And his approach to owning a motor racing team was no different. Whilst delegating certain managerial functions, he insisted on retaining a supervisory role in the decision-making process and took a keen interest in the technical aspects of competing in such a high-powered environment.

"In some races this season we've run the cars with minimum downforce in order to maximise our speed on the straights. That resulted in a relative loss of grip through some corners and we paid the price at a number of tracks."

"It's a matter of trying to create the optimum balance in a range of areas," said Gaudet defensively. "Finding the best set-up is not easy."

"I'm aware of the difficulties, Alain, and what I'm saying is not intended as a criticism. Any form of set-up on a car has to be a compromise, we all know that. But we operate in a very competitive arena and if we can develop a car that corners well and still has sufficient speed down the straights, we should be able to gain an edge on our rivals. And at the end of the day that's the only thing that counts."

"I think we're all agreed on that," added the race engineer.

Guiscard's grey-green eyes sparkled and he grinned. "You guys give me the tools and I'll finish the job."

The owner looked up at the darkening sky and a crescent moon seemingly suspended by some invisible celestial thread and appeared lost in thought. Eventually he spoke. "I don't think this team will ever come to terms with the tragedy in Australia. Every driver who races knows that death can hitch a lift at any time and accepts the risk. But the way Otto went, it was all so needless."

The other two were silent for a while then Guiscard was the first to respond. "For a day or two I felt like quitting. I kept it to myself as I knew it had to be my decision but I got very close to walking away from this sport."

"I can understand why," said Maigny, "and would have respected your decision. But I'm relieved you decided to stay."

"I did so because of Otto. His death was such a waste and I felt I owed it to his memory to fight on."

"He would have wanted that," said Gaudet. "You did everything you could to save him. There was nothing more you could have done."

"It doesn't make it any easier."

"Of course not," said the owner. "It's hard to put an incident like that to one side and get back in the car, but after Otto died you came from the rear of the grid at the re-start and finished P4. In fact, you were desperately unlucky not to get on the podium that day. Then you followed that up with another P4 in London and today you won here. That says a lot about your consistency on the track and your strength of character."

"Otto's loss has given me motivation, if I needed any."

"I don't think that was ever in doubt," said Gaudet.

Maigny looked his driver squarely in the eye. "With two-thirds of the races completed, any of four drivers can win the title this year and you're one of them, Philippe.

You have the talent but you have to want it more than the others. It's all about desire and belief."

Guiscard sipped his drink. "No pressure then."

"Not much," laughed Maigny. "For now, just know you're in a good place. Relax and enjoy the win."

"I don't need any incentive to do that, Olivier."

The three men watched as the mechanics, their improvised game at an end, pulled themselves out of the pool. In high spirits following their driver's victory, they towelled themselves dry before downing their half-finished cans of beer. Then, still laughing and joking, they walked towards the hotel's side entrance to return to their rooms ahead of the Drogan team's celebratory meal that evening.

Maigny swallowed what was left of his drink then rose to his feet. "I think I'll head to my room to freshen up before dinner."

Gaudet also stood up. "I need to do the same. Are you coming, Philippe?"

The driver twirled the stem of his empty glass to and fro. "I'll just have another one of these then I may have a dip in the pool to cool off. I won't be long. I'll join you later."

Guiscard watched as his two colleagues disappeared in the direction of the hotel. The Berg wind that blows hot, dry air down from the mountains towards the coastal regions ruffled his dark wavy hair, and two large candles resting on a wall at each end of the pool flickered in unison. The twenty-three-year-old sipped his champagne and, alone for the first time in a remarkable day, reflected on the stroke of fortune that had boosted his prospects of winning the drivers' title.

His thoughts also turned to the vivacious young woman he had met in London several weeks before.

Amelie Dubois had been a guest of Drogan's marketing division at a reception to mark the signing of a major sponsorship contract prior to the race in the English capital. A photographer with a French motoring magazine, she had at once captivated the driver with her charm, bubbly personality and insightful knowledge of the racing scene. Their encounter had come at the right time for Guiscard as he and his former companion had recently ended a long-term relationship. Now the debonair Frenchman was looking forward to seeing the new woman in his life and the flight to Paris had been booked for the following day.

He emptied the contents of his glass before placing it carefully by the side of the lounger, removed his T-shirt, shorts and underpants, strolled to the edge of the pool and dived in. A strong swimmer, Guiscard completed half a dozen twenty-five-metre lengths, alternating between the crawl and butterfly strokes, then hauled himself out. Surveying the now deserted pool area, he pulled a freshly laundered towel from its rack and began to dry himself. To one side stood a couple of palm trees, their crowns of fan-shaped leaves swaying in the light wind, and a line of shrubs that screened a large hot tub from the poolside area and hotel.

On impulse, the driver walked over, placed his towel on one of the pegs fixed to the exterior steel panelling of the structure and climbed the three steps leading to the whirlpool. He lowered himself into the heated water and settled into a seat with an illuminated headrest. Immersed up to his chest, he leant across to a control panel and pressed the button that activated a dozen power jets. In an instant the water started churning and convulsing around him and Guiscard experienced a gentle pummelling effect as the jets directed their contents onto the back and sides of his body. At the same time underwater bulbs had become energised and cast a rippling, translucent glow from the depths of the circular bath. A handful of small candle-shaped lights attached to the palm trees about six feet off the ground struggled to radiate any degree of brightness in the darkness. Invigorated by the pulsating water, the driver listened to the constant chorus of chirping cicadas in the undergrowth, the only other sound to disturb the night. He closed his eyes and somehow the song of the raucous insects seemed amplified. Ten minutes in the tub, the Frenchman told himself, and then he would return to the hotel and enjoy the camaraderie of his colleagues. For the first time since the race ended, he started to relax and could feel the tension in his muscles melting away.

A second later he was fighting for every breath, his legs flailing in the water. A body conditioned to the rigorous physical demands of race driving found itself struggling to resist an unknown but remorseless threat. Gasping for air and eyes now wide open, his hands went to his neck in a desperate attempt to stop the choking. His fingers reached frantically for the ever-tightening ligature but, for once, Guiscard's strength and razor-sharp reflexes could not help him. The sustained force exerted on his windpipe was relentless. His gurgling grew less and his arms fell back limply as slowly, mercilessly, the life was squeezed out of him. His final battle lasted a little over fifteen seconds, when he lost consciousness, but it was another minute before the deadly pressure eased and a length of rope was pulled away. The lifeless body of the Drogan driver was pushed under the water. The singing of the cicadas continued unabated.

TWELVE

Standing at one of the hotel's bars, the owner of Drogan Racing listened to the exuberant voices and surveyed the joyful faces around him. The scene cemented his belief that an FS race victory did more to boost morale and bond team members than anything else. Winning created an aura of unity and sustained its participants in the notion that trophies and titles were realistic goals. Maigny took pride in that he had assembled the essential building blocks and fostered an environment of communal effort, but was quick to recognise that success could hinge on one moment of individual brilliance by the man strapped in the cockpit.

The airline tycoon noted his leading driver had not yet appeared for a pre-dinner drink but was not overly concerned. He was aware of Guiscard's new romantic attachment and guessed he might be involved in a long-distance call to the French capital. There were other possibilities, too. He could have lingered by the pool for a little longer to collect his thoughts and reflect on what had been a momentous day for him and the team. Or he might have been spotted by one of several journalists staying at the hotel and agreed to an impromptu interview before returning to his room.

Another twenty minutes passed and Maigny observed some members of his group becoming restive at the prolonged absence of their star driver. It was an edginess he shared although he tried not to show it. He had worked with Guiscard for four years since the youngster started racing in the team's colours in junior series events and had never known him miss a testing session or fail to turn up for an off-track meeting with sponsors or the media. His non-appearance was out of character. The call to dinner had already come from the banqueting manager who had then been discreetly persuaded to delay the start of the function.

The owner glanced up to see the driver's race engineer hurrying towards him. Gaudet was looking increasingly agitated. "There's no sign of Philippe. I've tried his mobile and knocked on his door but had no response. And no one's seen him."

"It's very odd."

"It's not like him to disappear into thin air."

"That's just what I was thinking," said Maigny. "We need to find out what's going on. Can you explain our concern to the hotel duty manager and ask him to enter Philippe's room so we can check it out?"

"Yes, I'll do it now." The engineer turned on his heel and headed in the direction of the main reception desk.

The owner strode over to the Drogan mechanics standing by the bar. "Guys, I need some help. Our man still hasn't appeared. We're having his room opened up but I think we should look outside."

"What d'you think has happened, Monsieur Maigny?" responded one of the group. "I don't know, Gilles. It's possible he's had an accident but we need to find him – and quickly." The men needed no further bidding and immediately put down their drinks. "Can one of you get hold of a torch from the concierge?" he added. "We may need it. The rest of you follow me."

The makeshift search party exited the hotel through the revolving doors at the front of the building. The owner directed three of his men to scour the extensive gardens, including a conservatory housing exotic plants, then set off with the others towards the swimming pool. Then they heard it. Through the hanging humid night air came a yell. Maigny was the first to react. He started running towards the source of the sound, his heart pounding. He soon reached the pool but there was no one in sight and all appeared normal. Suddenly, from behind the screen of shrubs rushed a man visibly distressed, his face contorted by fear. Confronted by strangers, he stopped, unsure of his next move. The Drogan boss saw he was wearing the distinctive garb of the hotel's maintenance staff. "What happened?" he demanded.

The man hesitated for a moment then turned to point at the palm trees and shrubs. "Behind there, in the hot tub, that's... that's where I found him."

Fearing the worst, Maigny stepped forward and looked into the spa bath, the power jets still functioning. There, face down in the swirling water, Guiscard's body moved in a gentle, ghastly gyration of death. "We've got to get him out," barked the owner, discarding his jacket as he climbed into the whirlpool followed by two mechanics. "Turn off the power," he shouted at the hotel worker, at the same time reaching for the corpse and pulling it to the side. The three men lifted the driver from the water and, with all the solemnity they could muster in the circumstances, carried him gingerly down the steps and laid him gently on the sky-blue mosaic tiles encompassing the tub. They stared down in disbelief, unable to comprehend what had happened. Hardened to fatality on the track, this was different. So shocking. So needless.

Maigny looked into Guiscard's unseeing eyes and wondered what they had last focused on. On closer inspection he noted something that both puzzled and disturbed him. There was an area of redness and significant bruising on the skin around the dead man's neck. The team owner glanced at his mechanics. "I don't know what's gone on here and I'm not a doctor but this doesn't look like an accident. I want you to stay with Philippe while I alert the hotel management and the police." He walked over to where the maintenance man, who appeared to be traumatised, was sitting on a lounger. "I want you to wait here," he ordered. "When the detectives arrive they will want to talk to you as a key witness." The hotel employee nodded but said nothing. Then Maigny, his eyes moist and overwhelmed by a feeling of sheer emptiness, picked up his jacket and turned away.

Numb with shock at the loss of their leading driver and anxious to inform his family before the news broke, Drogan Racing managed to delay the announcement of his death until just after midnight. But the following day the media pack was out in force. Television and radio reporters and their newspaper colleagues descended in a swarm on the police station at Hermanus, where a briefing had been scheduled for midday. A number of satellite news-gathering outside broadcast vans were parked close to the building on Main Road on the outskirts of the town and engineers carried out last-minute technical checks. Whilst some correspondents consulted their editors about the content and projected duration of live inserts into television news programmes, others passed the time chatting in groups as they waited for the press conference to begin.

Captain Pieter Steyn, of the South African Police Service, had acquired a reputation for being punctilious throughout his twenty-five-year career. A tall, well-built man in his late forties, he had encountered the worst excesses of the criminal classes during his service but dogged attention to detail in his investigations and an unflappable temperament had enabled him to rise steadily through the ranks. He exuded a commanding physical presence and those who crossed his path found the most striking characteristic to be his huge hands, an aspect reflected in a vice-like grip. That had served him well in close-quarter combat and many an offender had realised too late the futility of struggling to break free from his grasp.

Over the years the senior detective had dealt with a number of high-profile cases but none had evoked such international interest as this one. A conference room at the station – one used for training presentations and containing a video projector and interactive whiteboard – had been set aside and additional chairs provided to accommodate the waiting press corps. Seated at a desk at one end of the room, under a picture of former President Nelson Mandela and facing the members of the media, the officer was flanked by the owner of Drogan Racing, Olivier

Maigny, and the FS supremo, Lucas Tait. Each had a glass and bottle of mineral water within easy reach. At the far end of the room, standing with his back next to an open window and behind the rows of reporters, Jack Wyatt went virtually unnoticed.

Captain Steyn, in an open-neck bright blue shirt and black leather jacket, eased the belt holster containing the standard issue Z88 nine-millimetre pistol resting on his left hip. Brown eyes deep-set over a twice-broken nose, he studied his watch for a full ten seconds. Then at noon precisely, in an accent that bore testimony to his Afrikaans upbringing, he called the assembled journalists to order. "Good afternoon, ladies and gentlemen. Thank you for coming here today. I won't beat about the bush as we all have work to do. I am here to update you on developments following the sudden death in the upper Hemel en Aarde Valley last night of the French racing driver, Philippe Guiscard. I propose to make a short statement then we," he paused, turning to the men sitting either side of him, "Monsieur Maigny of Drogan Racing, Mr Tait of FS and myself, will attempt to answer your questions."

The high-ranking officer looked at the phalanx of expectant faces and battery of cameras and microphones ranged before him then started reading from a prepared statement. "The duty constable at Hermanus police station was alerted at eight forty-five yesterday evening about an incident at the Coastal International hotel. Two uniformed officers were sent to that location and then directed to the area of the swimming pool and a hot tub nearby. There they were shown the body of Monsieur Giscard, which had been taken from the whirlpool and placed on the decking surrounding it. The officers immediately cordoned off the area and secured the scene. Statements were taken from a number of people, including a hotel maintenance worker who discovered the body in the water."

The captain paused to look up from his file of papers before resuming. "A forensic pathologist conducted a post-mortem on the deceased at Hermanus Provincial Hospital early this morning and the result of that examination has now been passed to me. The cause of death was given as asphyxia due to strangulation by some form of ligature. It was not – I repeat, *not* – due to drowning. We are still awaiting the results of toxicology tests that were also carried out to determine whether Monsieur Guiscard had any traces of alcohol or drugs in his body. I can now confirm the police are treating his death as murder and the detective branch has taken over responsibility for the investigation."

The senior detective looked up at the reporters again, using his right hand to push back the locks of light-brown wavy hair that had fallen across his forehead. "We will now take questions but I must stress that some may be off-limits for operational reasons and we would appreciate your co-operation in that respect. Anyway, let's get underway." He pointed towards a familiar face, that of the Cape Town-based correspondent of the South African Broadcasting Corporation. "Max, would you like to kick-off?"

"Thanks, Captain. I know the inquiry is at an early stage but from what you've learnt so far, are you treating this killing as opportunistic or premeditated? And do you have any firm leads to follow?"

"To take your first point – you're right, we're at the beginning of our investigation and there's a long way to go. All I can say at this time is that we're keeping an open mind on the evidence before us and nothing has been ruled out. We're pursuing every line that's relevant to this case and I want to give a public assurance that I have all the resources I need for such an operation."

The officer gestured at another reporter he recognised, this time from the daily, Cape Argus. "Tom, what's your question?"

"Can we assume it's premature for you to have a suspect at this point in the investigation?"

"I'm not sure you should assume anything at the moment."

"What does that mean? Do you have a suspect?"

"Clearly there is no one in custody or I would have said so. All I'm saying is that it's preferable not to make any assumptions when we're dealing with a crime that, inevitably, is making headlines across the world."

The reporter persisted. "Is the fact that the murder victim was a famous racing driver going to make it harder for you to solve this case?"

"I don't think so. The police approach in trying to solve this killing will be the same as for any other. Of course, we will need the assistance of those close to Monsieur Guiscard in the Drogan Racing team and FS, and I'm sure that will be forthcoming." He turned to the men sitting either side of him as if seeking reassurance. Both nodded their confirmation.

Many arms were raised by those eager to ask questions. Captain Steyn motioned to a young woman sitting in the third row from the back and she stood up. "I represent The Mercury, published in Durban, and would like to know if the scene-of-crime officers found the ligature that was used to strangle the driver?"

"There has been no sign of it so far but an extensive search of the hotel grounds using tracker dogs is continuing."

"Do you have any idea what type of ligature it was?"

"We believe a length of cable or rope, or something similar, was used by the killer."

A reporter from The Star, published in Johannesburg, caught the attention of the senior police officer. "You referred to the body being found by a hotel maintenance worker. Has that person been eliminated as a suspect?"

"All I can say at this stage is that he has given us a statement."

"But is he central to your investigation?"

"He is a key witness in that he found the body, so in that sense he is important to our inquiries. And, like others, he may well be questioned again. But I repeat to all the members of the press gathered here today, I suggest you exercise caution in the way you report this story."

A reporter from the French news agency, Agence France-Presse, was next in line. "I would like to direct my question to the boss of Drogan Racing, Monsieur Maigny. As far as you know, did your driver, Philippe Guiscard, have any enemies?"

The team owner shook his head emphatically. "Before I answer I would just like to put on record that yesterday was the blackest day in the history of this team. The murder of this dashing young man has shocked the motor racing world but it is also a personal tragedy for Philippe's family and friends and for those of us who were privileged to know him through his chosen sport. He was a true professional and utterly reliable in his work. And his courage was never in doubt, as evidenced by his valiant but ultimately futile efforts to save his colleague, Otto Werner, whilst sacrificing an almost certain win during the race in Australia. As to your question, Philippe had no enemies that we know of. On the contrary, he was a popular figure and well-liked, not just in this team but throughout the paddock. That's why what's happened is so mystifying."

"I understand what you're saying but you must have given some thought as to a possible motive for the killing."

"Of course. It's something I've been asking myself ever since we found Philippe but I cannot imagine why anyone would want to commit such an evil act." The Drogan Racing principal eyed the serried ranks in front of him and issued a warning. "I think it would be wise to avoid any speculation about a motive so early in the police investigation and I would urge you to be circumspect in your coverage."

The AFP reporter managed to squeeze in another question. "Because of the year you've had, team morale must now be at rock bottom. You're going to have to write off this season, aren't you?"

The stress caused by the latest catastrophe to afflict his team was evident in Maigny's face but he was determined to appear positive. "Drogan Racing has lost both its drivers in under two months. It's been a nightmare for us but we won't be down for long. This team has the capacity to fight back. We replaced Otto with the young Hungarian driver, Janos Varady, and we'll have to find a replacement for Philippe. I know he would want us to do that to demonstrate our determination to compete again. We don't want to be seen acting in undue haste so soon after this tragedy but I can reveal we'll be talking to our test driver, the South African, Phil Scolton. He's been a loyal member of our team for three years and deserves his chance, even though it's come in such dreadful circumstances. I accept it will be tough for us for the remainder of this season but we intend to be a force again in FS."

The captain backed the Frenchman's cautionary words, then, looking at his watch, apologised but said there was time for only one more question. It came from the BBC's Southern Africa correspondent. "I would like to ask Lucas Tait as the head of FS – the commercial rights holder who runs motor sport at the highest level – if you feel its image has been badly tarnished by this incident?"

"It's certainly not helpful but that's not my main concern at the moment. My thoughts right now, and those of everyone at FS, are with Philippe's family and the Drogan team who have suffered an appalling loss in the most unexpected and brutal manner. We are all stunned by the events of the last twenty-four hours and want time to come to terms with what's happened."

The correspondent was still on his feet. "Do you believe the key to solving this murder lies somewhere within the motor racing fraternity?"

The American tugged at one of the pockets of his mohair jacket as he considered the question. "You need to understand we operate in a highly competitive sport where the slightest margins can be critical and make the difference between winning and losing. We accept that fatalities sometimes happen on the track, but to lose one of our own in this gruesome fashion has sickened everyone. Philippe was an extremely promising driver and had already demonstrated his skill and commitment by winning two races this season, and was currently joint third in the championship. And, as Olivier has just observed, Philippe's bravery was never in question. We've lost a major talent in the sport and, I believe, a future champion."

The journalist was determined to ram home his point. "With all due respect, you've not answered the question. I ask again – have you considered whether anyone involved in FS would have had a motive to kill Guiscard?"

Tait struggled to suppress a growing irritation. "I would remind you that the investigation into this crime is in its early stages and I think it would be unwise of me to speculate at this time. I am confident the police operation will be conducted in a way that will leave no stone unturned and I can only hope that whoever is responsible for this outrage is brought to justice as quickly as possible." But pressed again, the American replied curtly. "I have my own thoughts on the matter but I'm not prepared to say any more."

Steyn turned to face Tait. "You have my assurance that this inquiry will be conducted with the utmost rigour and tenacity. This is one of the most disturbing cases I've had to deal with and we'll do all we can to solve it."

As he thanked the FS boss for his comments and started to announce the end of the press conference, Maigny indicated he wanted to speak again. His words came slowly, his voice laced with emotion. "I would like to appeal to anyone out there who can help the police in any way to come forward immediately. This is a shocking crime and the slightest detail, however insignificant it may appear on the surface, could be crucial in tracking down the killer. That's the least we can do for Philippe's loved ones."

The police chief endorsed the words of the Drogan Racing owner then addressed the reporters. "Ladies and gentlemen, I think that's an appropriate note on which to finish. We shall, of course, keep you informed as the investigation proceeds and if there are any major developments to report we will call you back here for another briefing. Thanks for your time."

The next day, the two Americans took lunch on the hotel's lower terrace, which provided a spectacular panorama of Hermanus and the coast. They had chosen the dining area not for the view but because it was less congested, and a table in the corner ensured the privacy they wanted. Shielded from the sun by a parasol, Lucas Tait paused the conversation until the waiter had poured each of them a glass of locally produced chardonnay, placed the bottle in an ice bucket and wandered off to the kitchen with their food order.

"Are you sure?"

"Yeah, totally. Makarov was outta here soon after the race ended. A taxi took him to Cape Town International for a flight to London, where he was connecting to Moscow."

"I'm trying to piece together why the guy was in a hurry to leave so fast."

"Are you in the same ball park as me?" was the enigmatic response.

"Could be, if you reckon it's linked to what happened to Guiscard."

"I'd be lying if I said it hadn't crossed my mind."

The FS supremo sipped his wine. "When you consider the other possible scenarios, it's a struggle to make any of them stick – there's an obvious credibility problem. But that doesn't apply when you put Makarov in the frame."

"I can see where you're coming from but I guess there's a danger in rushing to judgment."

"I'm conscious of that but I reckon his prints are all over this crime and he would be top of my shortlist of suspects."

"So he'd want to make sure his alibi was water-tight."

"Exactly. I'm sure he can prove that at the time of the murder he was either about to board his plane or was in South African airspace."

"You must have considered a motive," said Wyatt.

"Of course. I believe the Russian saw Guiscard as an upcoming threat to his leading driver and that was all the justification he needed."

The Californian had a sharp intake of breath. "Where does that leave Stallard and Rodriguez?"

"Exposed – and constantly looking over their shoulders."

"You'll have to warn them."

"I've already had a discreet word with the two team owners and they know the score. But while they can and will take certain precautions, they don't want to alarm their drivers unduly, and I understand that."

"Have you run your theory past the cops?"

"What's the point? Makarov will have ensured he's untouchable."

"The police chief sounded like he meant business."

"Oh, Steyn made all the right noises at the press conference and I'm sure he'll work his balls off, but I'm not hopeful we're going to find the answer."

"With the world looking on, the authorities will want to nail this one. It won't look good if they don't."

"I know, image and all that. But, frankly, I'm not

expecting a lot." Wyatt refilled their glasses. "Meantime, the circus moves on and everyone gets back to work."

Tait nodded. "It's better that way. It doesn't make it any easier but at least the teams can focus on the next race."

"It was one helluva crime and it's sure gonna raise the profile of FS for the rest of the season."

"Don't need that sort of publicity, Jack. Never did. But you're right, it'll put us under the spotlight even more." The motor sport impresario looked hard at his companion. "And we need that like a hole in the head whilst we await…" he paused, searching for the right phrase, "project delivery."

He was about to continue when the waiter returned and deposited two plates of eggs Benedict and two coffees on the table. When the man had gone, Tait returned to his theme. "On that subject, you need to update me on where you're at."

Wyatt swallowed his first mouthful. "I figured it was time for a progress report. As you know, I have a well-established modus operandi – no phone calls, no emails, no texts, no form of communication that can go astray or be intercepted. I report face to face. It works for me and it's secure that way."

"It means there's nothing in writing and I like that. It benefits both of us."

"The Greeks had a word for it – symbiosis." Wyatt glimpsed a smile playing on Tait's face. "You seem to be amused."

"I hadn't realised you were a student of the classics."

"Just goes to show my college education wasn't a complete waste of time."

"That's good to know. Anyway, at least the ground rules are in place. So what's the current state of play?"

The Californian looked circumspectly around him, ensuring he couldn't be overheard. "I spent some time in Moscow and familiarised myself with the layout of the place. I had been there years before but things change. Still, I was able to access sources who knew the target and they came up with some useful background material."

"I'm not going to ask who your informants were – I guess you wouldn't tell me anyway – but it's good to know your research was productive."

"Oh yes, especially in one case." A smile crossed Wyatt's face. "It came from an unexpected quarter but was no less important for that. You know something, Lucas," he said in his West Coast accent, "I'm a firm believer in getting up close and personal when called for in the line of duty and I find it usually pays off."

"You can spare me the details. The need-to-know principle doesn't apply in this instance."

Wyatt laughed. "Just as well. It also helped that I have a useful contact in Moscow and was able to call in a long-standing favour."

"Is your contact reliable?"

"Totally. He's in the kinda business that keeps him well informed on such matters and was able to give me a rundown on Makarov's activities."

"What did he tell you?"

"As I recall, at our meeting on the yacht you indicated the Russian had links to organised crime."

"That was my view then and nothing since has made me want to change it."

"Well, you did him an injustice."

"How come?"

"It seems you were on the right track but you still

had some way to go. It turns out our mutual friend is the undisputed head of the Russian mafia."

Tait emitted a low whistling sound. "Let's be sure what we're talking about here. You mean, *the* Mr Big?"

"That's precisely what I mean."

"And you're convinced your guy's got it right on this one?"

"He'd have done his homework."

"Yeah, it's not something he'd want to screw up."

"I don't think he's in the habit of making bad calls at this level."

"I guess it makes for a more interesting ball-game."

"You could say that."

"No point in telling the other team owners. I don't want to worsen tensions in the paddock."

"Agreed. They could start asking awkward questions."

Tait studied his companion closely. "I trust this doesn't indicate a change in the rules of engagement."

"You've lost me."

"Perhaps you're about to tell me you want to renegotiate your contract."

For a second or two, Wyatt's penetrating blue eyes burned with resentment. "Let's get one thing straight, Tait. Don't ever underestimate me – others have and regretted it. But in my book, a contract's a contract and once I take on an assignment I always close the deal."

"OK, maybe I jumped the gun on that one," said the FS boss with a hint of contrition in his voice. "No offence intended."

"Let's move on." Wyatt looked south towards the coast, the sun's rays shimmering constantly on the waters off Hermanus. "At least now I have a fuller picture and know what I'm up against. It's gonna make it tougher and I might have to rethink part of my strategy."

"That's your realm of operation and I'm not about to trespass on your turf."

"Sure." Both men were quiet for a while, enjoying the view. Then Wyatt broke the silence. "It's gonna impact the location of the hit. Moscow is his home patch and it goes without saying he's most secure there."

Tait tensed and tightened the grip on his glass. "I told you before – it has to be after the race in Russia, and preferably someplace else. I had to oil a few palms to clinch the venue and I want to secure it for the future."

"If this is gonna work it'll have to be elsewhere."

"That's got to be your call. But there's one thing you have to remember. When this is over I don't want anyone pointing the finger in my direction."

"You need to chill out. I'm a pro – and don't forget it!"

"I know you're the best at what you do. That's why I hired you. But if anything goes wrong, you're on your own."

"You're just like the rest," came the scornful reply. "The guy who calls the shots always wants to save his own skin. I'm used to it."

Tait banged his fist on the table. "I don't need any lectures on morality from you, Wyatt. And just remember who's picking up the tab on this one – I reckon that entitles me to express a point of view."

"Sure, you can have your say, but at the end of the day there's only one guy who's putting his neck on the block, so I guess that gives me some rights, too."

"We both know the deal. The terms haven't changed."

"You're damn right, they haven't!" The Californian finished his coffee, wiped his mouth with a napkin and stood up. "There's something else that ain't changed, Tait. I think I told you once before – there's only one person I trust in this business and you're looking at him."

THIRTEEN

The early evening taxi turned off Ulitsa Ostozhenka and eased to a halt outside the luxury apartment block southwest of the Kremlin in central Moscow. "That's 670 roubles," grunted the driver of the yellow-coloured cab, relieved his shift was almost at an end. His elegantly dressed passenger handed over two 500-rouble notes, told him to keep the change and stepped onto the pavement. A dozen strides took her to the entrance of the building where she tapped in the four-digit security code on a wall-mounted screen. A reinforced plate glass panel slid silently open and revolving doors ushered her inside.

The foyer was dominated by four round white marble columns that stretched from the gleaming parquet floor to the high ceiling above. A four-seater settee covered in plush fabrics sat in one corner whilst two comfortable armchairs similarly upholstered were directly opposite. A single chandelier cast an unobtrusive light on a desk in the centre of the room where the concierge, a dumpy, grey-haired woman who looked older than her fifty-seven years, was seated. She glanced up from a well-thumbed copy of the romantic paperback she was reading and adjusted her spectacles to peer over them in another ritual, perfunctory inspection. Satisfied the new arrival was a resident, but concealing any trace of recognition or acknowledgment, she turned back to her book, inwardly resenting the fleeting disruption.

Inured to the brusqueness of the concierge, the tall blonde ignored her and walked towards the lift. Half a minute later she exited at the third floor and headed down the carpeted corridor, passing reproduction prints of still life hanging at intervals on the walls. Reaching her apartment, she inserted a plastic keycard in the lock and entered, turning on the light in the hall. Slipping off her lightweight jacket and dropping it on a chair, she caught sight of her face in a mirror and wondered if the long hours she was working were starting to take their toll. But such thoughts were quickly dispelled by the realisation that few other jobs open to her would provide the income and fringe benefits she currently enjoyed.

Moving to the kitchen, she poured herself a generous measure of dry martini, added some ice and a slice of lemon, and made her way towards the lounge. She opened the door, reached for the light switch and stepped into the room. She had taken barely two paces when she froze in her tracks.

"Hello, Valya."

Tightening her grip on the glass she was holding, she stared with incredulity at the man sitting in her leather-covered rocking chair. There was a trace of smugness in the voice. "I hope it's not too much of a shock for you."

"What are you doing here?"

"I felt it was time we talked."

"You might have called me. We could have met at the office."

"That wasn't necessary. You know I don't like formality.

Anyway, it's better we have this discussion in more private surroundings."

Her mind racing, Valya struggled to comprehend the situation confronting her. "Would you like a drink?"

"No," he responded curtly. "You need to understand this is not a social visit."

"So why are you here?"

"You do surprise me. Have you no idea?"

She swallowed hard but tried not to betray the nascent anxiety she felt. "I don't understand."

He motioned towards a sofa. "You really should make yourself comfortable. This could take some time."

Once his mistress had settled, Viktor Makarov pulled a sheaf of creased papers from inside his jacket. "I suggest we start by looking at these."

"What are they?"

"It's a record of financial transactions in your section over the last six months. And it doesn't make for good reading, Valya."

"What d'you mean?"

"I ordered a detailed inspection of the accounts and, compared to the same period last year, profits in the division are below what was forecast. That's not what I run this business for. Client numbers are up and charges were increased, so I would have expected that to be reflected in the figures."

"What are you implying?"

"I've had my suspicions for a while and these figures tell me something is wrong. And I want to know what it is."

Valya took a swig of her drink. "I always submit my accounts each year and there's never been a problem."

"This time it's different. This time they've been audited and some irregularities discovered."

"Don't you trust me, Viktor?"

"I thought I could, but…" His voice tailed away.

"But what?"

"Don't play games with me, Valya." Makarov's tone became more strident and he waved the papers in her direction. "Do I have to spell it out for you? Your profits are down when all the indicators suggested the opposite. I want to know why."

"There's probably a straightforward explanation and once I check the books I'm sure I'll find it. I was planning to be in the office early in the morning and—"

"I don't think you're listening to me. I'm not prepared to wait till tomorrow – I want an answer now."

"That's impossible. You have to give me time."

The Russian mafia boss rocked slowly forwards and backwards, staring coldly at the blonde. "That's the one thing you don't have. But I think you're right – the explanation is straightforward, as you put it. And we both know what it is, don't we, Valya?"

"I've told you, I wasn't aware there was a problem but I'll do everything I can to find out what's gone wrong."

"Why don't you just admit it?"

"Admit what?"

"You've been syphoning cash out of the system."

"For God's sake, Viktor, what are you talking about?"

"You've been stealing from me, taking money behind my back. I trusted you and that's how you repaid me."

Valya rose to her feet. "This has gone on long enough. I come home to find you in my apartment when you're not expected and then I'm treated like a criminal suspect and given the third degree."

"I'm not aware I need an official invite to come here. I

installed you in this place when I put you on the payroll, that was part of the deal. As you know, there were certain conditions attached but I don't recall any objections at the time."

"I don't think I had an option." She took a couple of steps towards the door. "I'm going to get another drink."

"Sit down!" The command was as unexpected as it was uncompromising. Valya, stunned by the instruction, stared disbelievingly at Makarov.

"What did you say?"

"I told you to sit down. I haven't finished."

Visibly shocked, she sank slowly, silently, on to the sofa. Her knuckles whitened as she clenched her empty glass ever more tightly.

Her accuser leant forward menacingly in his chair. "We need to be honest with each other. It would be better for you that way."

"I've told you the truth. I can't help it if you won't believe me."

"I've seen the evidence and it's all pointing in one direction. But we both know there's another can of worms that needs opening."

"I don't know what you're talking about."

"It's not working, Valya. Act innocent if you like but I know you've been cheating on me."

"How?"

"You've had sex with clients, haven't you?"

"That's not true. You're mistaken."

"No, you're the one who's made the mistake. There's a golden rule for every mistress – and you broke it!"

"I haven't, Viktor, I haven't! You must believe me."

"It's about time you stopped this pretence," barked

Makarov. "This is not a game we're playing. You've nothing to gain and everything to lose."

Valya's face began to betray the sense of desperation she was beginning to feel. "It doesn't matter what I say, I can't convince you."

"Nothing you say can do that," he smirked. "They say confession is good for the soul, so do yourself a favour."

The blonde leant forward and placed her glass on a coffee table, on which were scattered a number of fashion and property magazines. She looked her interrogator in the eye and sighed. "I can't win, can I?"

"I'm glad you're being sensible at last. You see, you can co-operate when you put your mind to it. I like that. It will make our situation a little easier."

"What do you want from me, Viktor?" she asked, trying to discern any hint of intention from his facial expression.

"We need to settle accounts," he said, rising from the rocker. "You still have some unpaid debts and the interest rate's just gone up."

Valya instinctively moved back on the sofa as Makarov stood over her, his brown eyes voracious as he studied her svelte figure. He stroked her hair then moved to her chin, pulling her head up until it was just inches from his. "I think you need to make amends in the only way you can," he said smugly. "Don't you think so, Valya?" She winced at the implication and stayed silent, considering the alternatives. But her questioner was showing signs of impatience. "Do you have a problem with that?"

After a while she shook her head and forced a glimmer of a smile. "You know me better than that, Viktor. Of course I don't."

Convinced that trying to placate the mafia boss was her

only shrewd option, the blonde stood up and held his right hand, running two of her fingers lightly along the faded two-inch scar on the back. "I think we both need to chill out. It's been a while."

"I'm glad you see it that way." Makarov pulled her closer. "But there is something else – I have a special request." He smiled thinly. "I think you know what it is."

Valya knew exactly what he had in mind. She had consented to it a number of times previously and although it wasn't a practice she wanted to participate in, let alone enjoyed, she had learnt to tolerate it as a trade-off to gain other benefits in the relationship. "I do, although you know how I feel about it. I will this time but I must have a drink."

"Sure, and get me one at the same time – make mine a vodka."

Two minutes later Valya entered the bedroom carrying the drinks and placed them on one of two art deco bedside cabinets. The spacious room exuded the style of decorative art with its linear symmetry characteristic of the early decades of the twentieth century. A flamed walnut veneer dressing table with curved ends and a full-length cheval mirror sat opposite a stool with ribbed edges and covered in light-blue cotton velvet. A pair of bedroom chairs, upholstered in cream-coloured silk, stood either side of a four-door wardrobe decorated with Grecian marquetry figures. But the centrepiece, by contrast, was a super king-size studded black leather bed, its metal headboard finished in antique brass, which dominated the room. Makarov had thrown his sand-coloured suede jacket onto a chair and removed his shoes and was sitting on the side of the bed. Valya kicked her high heels on to the thick pile carpet and joined him. She gulped down nearly half the contents of her glass then rested the container on her knees and smiled nervously at her companion. "I needed that. It's been a long day."

Makarov looked at her with indifference. "It's heartening to see such devotion to duty." He started to undress. "I expect you to show me the same commitment."

She finished her drink and put the glass on the cabinet. "I'm not aware I've failed to satisfy you in the past. At least, you've never complained!" The muttered response of her boss was inaudible as he continued to strip. Valya, in a mechanical, almost robotic, manner, unbuttoned and took off her white chiffon blouse and close-fitting grey skirt then removed her tights, bra and panties. Almost as an afterthought, she unstrapped her gold and diamond-encrusted Swiss-made wristwatch, with its mother-of-pearl dial, and laid it carefully on top of one of the cabinets.

From a drawer in the other cabinet, Makarov pulled out a large cloth pouch that he placed on the bed next to Valya, who was lying on her back on silver-coloured silk sheets. She grimaced as he untied the drawstring. "I'm uneasy, Viktor. I wasn't into this before I met you."

"I want you to relax. This will be the last time, I promise."

"Are you sure?"

"Oh yes, believe me." He tried to conceal the scorn in his voice as his hand emerged from the pouch with a pair of padded, purple-coloured handcuffs made from soft neoprene and linked to a four-foot length of nickel-plated chain. Valya raised both arms and forced them back over her head onto the pillow, the movement forcing a deep inward breath and driving her bulbous breasts upwards. Makarov cuffed each of her wrists then looped the chain around one of two transverse bars in the headboard frame and secured both ends by ramming shut the bolt in a small padlock.

"You're a voluptuous woman," said the Russian as he climbed on the bed, "but when you're shackled you're even more seductive. It excites me and I like that." Valya said nothing and closed her eyes. He was on all fours, straddling her. His head, moving with metronomic precision, swung like a pendulum above her bosom, his mouth hungry for and alternating between her nipples. He sucked ferociously, like a starving lost cub reunited with its mother. His slavering lips spiralled downwards, tracing a helter-skelter path to below her belly, his hands pressed flat against her hips, his licking tongue seeking her moistened core. Perversely, despite the bondage and her aversion to it, Valya found her body was responding, albeit involuntarily, to the oral stimulation and hated herself for it. She clung to the one consolation that the man forcing her into sexual submission had indicated, much to her surprise, that he would not persist in the practice in future.

Bestride the tethered woman, Makarov was breathing faster now, his lust intensified by a growing tumescence in his groin. But her lack of animation was starting to be a source of irritation. "Open your eyes," he snapped. "I want to see you enjoying this."

Valya obeyed but not through any inclination to co-operate. "You put restraints on me then complain when I'm not responsive. What d'you expect? You can't have it both ways."

Makarov's eyes narrowed in anger. "I'll have it whatever way I want, bitch!" She saw his raised hand and turned her face to the side to try to minimise the impact, but a stinging slap on her cheek left a reddening weal. It wasn't the first time Valya had suffered violence during sex with the Russian and previous experience had taught her that remonstrating with her abuser only made the situation worse. As before, she resolved to endure this latest episode of coercion passively, but she had made it abundantly clear she was only participating under protest.

As if to confirm his grudging recognition of the situation, Makarov lost patience. He had reached an advanced state of arousal and now his actions became hurried and mechanical. Valya was forced to bear the weight of his burly frame as he slid inside her, his arms enfolding her. His pockmarked face was inches away and she felt his breath, with its tobacco odour she loathed, as his movements became more vigorous, his thrusting more urgent. A final, frenetic judder. Then it was over. He moaned quietly, relishing the physical gratification he had demanded. Valya had satisfied his craving for carnal domination but it left her feeling violated. All she wanted was for him to get off her and free her aching arms from the headboard. It seemed an eternity to Valya before the thirteen-stone Makarov finally rolled off her and on to his back.

Both lay on the stained, crumpled sheets, staring at the French art deco chandelier with its wrought-iron frame and six illuminated opalescent glass bowls. It had been an early present from the mafia boss to his mistress after she had seen an example of the genre at a Paris hotel during their first trip abroad.

Valya broke the silence. "Viktor, my hands are getting numb." The plea implicit in her words did not evoke an immediate response so she tried again. "Can you release me now?"

Makarov turned on his side, one elbow supporting his

weight, a smirk on his face. "I hope you enjoyed that. Was it good for you, Valya?"

The blonde looked puzzled as her lover did not usually enquire as to whether she derived any pleasure from their physical relationship. "Why d'you ask?"

"I think you should know that was the last time. We won't be having sex again."

Valya's immediate reaction was one of palpable relief at the prospect of freedom from bondage in the future but then her mind started racing to absorb the implications of Makarov's words. She struggled to unscramble their meaning. "I don't understand."

He leaned closer to her, his voice not much more than a whisper. "The roulette wheel's stopped spinning. Now the casino's calling in the chips."

Clearly perplexed, she tugged vainly at the chain that bound her, exacerbating the soreness in her arms. "Viktor, you're talking in riddles. Just unlock the handcuffs and then we can talk. Please!"

The owner of the Russian racing team that bore his name shook his head. "It's too late for that. There was a time, maybe, when the outcome could have been different but it's no longer an option." He swung his legs over the side of the bed, stood up and started to put his clothes on.

"What are you doing?" shouted Valya. "You can't leave me like this."

As Makarov tucked his shirt inside his trousers and fastened the belt, he turned to look at her. "I really don't think you're in a position to make any demands, my dear."

"For God's sake, Viktor, stop playing games. This has gone on long enough. My wrists and arms are hurting. Please, let me go now!"

He stood over her, a look of mock surprise playing on his face. "Games? Games? This is no game, Valya. I couldn't be more serious."

She stared at him intently, her blue eyes incandescent and displaying a combination of defiance and dread. "You can't do this to me. I don't deserve it."

He sniggered. "You still don't get it, do you?"

"What d'you mean?"

"When trust goes, it's gone. I've lost all confidence in you and I can't afford to have someone like that in my organisation."

"I can't believe this is happening. What are you going to do with me?"

"You'll find out soon enough." Makarov picked up his drink from the bedside cabinet and downed it with one swig then left the room. An anguished Valya kicked out her legs in utter frustration and began to weep.

"Match point!" shouted Stallard. He used a wristband to wipe the sweat off his forehead, glanced at his opponent across the other side of the net then bounced the ball twice on the red clay in a ritualistic prelude to his service action. A second later, knees flexed and with a snap of the wrist, he unleashed a yellow missile. The ball rocketed down the middle of the court, hitting the centre line and flying beyond the reach of the outstretched racket thrust vainly at it.

"Damn it, Nick, you didn't give me a chance to come back!"

"Too bad, Dave," smiled the driver as the two men

shook hands at the net. "I had to close it out when I could. I found some form today."

"Say that again," retorted his manager. "You served well throughout the match. And you showed the killer instinct when it mattered."

Stallard laughed. "I need a bit more of that when I'm in the car. It might just get me the title."

"It certainly won't hurt your chances. It's about time you won a championship – you've been close twice and deserve it."

"Hey, spare me the pep talk, I'm here to relax. Come on, let's get a cooling drink."

Dave Hampton had promoted the interests of his driver for a decade and the pair had also built up a firm friendship outside their professional association. But Stallard's continuing failure to land the most coveted prize in motor sport had hung over the relationship like a darkening cloud, and the one glaring omission in the racer's CV had been felt almost as keenly by his manager. They towelled down then headed for the hotel terrace, which overlooked the tranquil, sun-dappled waters of the Mediterranean off the Cote d'Azur. Yachts of varying sizes dotted the bay off Villefranche-sur-Mer, located on the winding coast road between Nice and Monaco. Both men opted for thirst-quenching non-alcoholic cocktails as they sank into one of a row of comfortable sofas bordering the edge of the terrace.

"Four races to go and you're heading the drivers' championship. This could be your year."

Stallard, his towel still draped around his neck, smiled ruefully. "You said that last season, and look what happened! It came down to the last bend on the last lap of the last race and I lost the title by a single point."

"That's in the past, Nick," said his manager, a wiry man in his early forties. "You need to focus on what's happening now and the stats don't lie – you're at the top of the standings."

"There's just one point between Raffa and me, and the Russian's only eight points behind. It's too close to call – anything can happen between now and the last race in Morocco."

Hampton was nothing if not persistent. "Look at it this way. If the season had ended in South Africa, you would be champion. You have to seize that mindset and carry it with you to the last chequered flag of the year. You've got to believe in yourself."

"I get your drift," said the driver as he sipped his apple-and-cinnamon-flavoured drink. "But there's something you haven't factored into the equation."

"What's that?"

"It seems I'm having to fight my own team as well as my other rivals. I'm not getting the support I'm due as the number one driver. It's obvious to me that Gorton is giving Lockhart preferential treatment and that's already cost me points – points that could prove crucial at the end of this campaign."

"Surely you're not suggesting Kate poses a serious threat to you? She's currently P6 in the table on eleven points – that's twenty-five behind you – and we're already two-thirds of the way through the race calendar."

"No," said Stallard emphatically, "I don't believe she can win the championship, but what she can do is screw up *my* chances of doing it. From her actions on the track, she's made it quite clear it's a fight between ourselves. She's not a team player but she seems to have the backing of the owner and, as you know, I've got my own theory about that."

"Yes, I've heard the whispers like everyone else. But it's not the first and won't be the last time people in our sport have an affair – they're human, too."

"I don't give a damn what they get up to in their spare time but when it's likely to have an adverse impact on my career prospects, I do object."

"I can imagine it's eating away at you but don't let yourself become obsessed by it, Nick. It's never good when a driver's relationship with an owner deteriorates. It creates extra problems when all you want to do is concentrate on getting the balance of the car right, putting in the best qualifying laps you can, and winning races."

Stallard nodded agreement. "You're damn right. I don't need the hassle."

His manager appeared thoughtful, watching two large yachts in line abreast leaving the sheltered waters of the bay and heading out to sea. "Your contract is up at the end of the season. Has Gorton talked about extending it?"

The driver shook his head. "Nothing's been said yet but I'm not even sure he wants me in his car next year."

"If you're the reigning world champion he'll want you, make no mistake. I negotiated your current three-year deal and as long as you're in agreement, I'll make an approach. We're at that point when decisions about team line-ups are being finalised so it's important to establish lines of communication."

"It wouldn't surprise me if Gorton tries to stall the process. I've heard rumours he's had a scout watching a young Mexican guy who's been making a name for himself in the junior ranks, and could bring him into the team as the number two driver for next season, with Lockhart replacing me."

"Sounds like the FS rumour mill has been working overtime again. There's always idle talk flying around the paddock about possible signings, you know that."

"But sometimes the gossip-mongers get it right – and this could be one of them."

"Frankly, Nick, I think you need to be more relaxed about your situation. You're in the box-seat at the moment and if you were to grab the title, no team owner would cut you loose. You would attract even more sponsorship to the Gorton brand and have the number one emblazoned on his car. He's not going to want to throw that away."

"Yeah, I guess you've got a point. It's up to me to make it happen."

Both men were silent for a time as they admired the outline of one of the crown jewels of the French Riviera, the peninsula of Cap Ferrat. Then Stallard turned towards his manager. "Of course, there is another side to the coin."

"What's that?"

"If I win the title I might just consider retirement and quit while I'm ahead."

Hampton laughed. "Are you joking? If you win the championship you'll practically be able to name your own fee – and get it! There would also be a big spike in your other earnings, from advertising and sponsors and the rest; I reckon that alone would gross you in the region of ten million. So if you do finish as top dog, I suggest you think carefully before deciding to call it a day."

Stallard chuckled. "If I didn't know you better, Dave, I might think you had a vested interest in me continuing my career."

"Yeah, the words fable, goose, golden and egg come to mind, so I can't argue that one. I'm just advising you to assess where you are after the last race and not make a hasty decision. But my job is to get the best terms I can for you and it would be a chance to cash in after all the blood, sweat and tears that made it possible."

"I'm aware the financial package would be attractive but there's also an argument for getting out at the top. I've had ten years in this game and it's not getting any easier."

"We've been together a long time, Nick, and we understand each other. It's your future and it's your call but I would urge you to—"

"And what would you be urging, Dave?"

Hampton wheeled around to see the tanned, lissom figure of Sophie Hurst, clad in a lemon-coloured T-shirt and pale blue shorts, standing behind them.

"I'm trying to persuade your man that retirement may not be the best option if he becomes world champion. Just some friendly advice, that's all." She placed her hands on her fiancé's shoulders and ran her lips lightly across his sun-streaked fair hair.

"You haven't told me you're thinking of hanging up your driving gloves, darling."

Stallard gently squeezed her arm. "Relax, sweetheart."

"I always thought rule number one in a relationship is 'thou shalt consult.'"

"And I believe rule number two says 'thou shalt not jump to conclusions.'"

She laughed in the infectious, endearing way that first caught his attention when he met the thirty-year-old advertising executive at a party hosted by a mutual friend. "It's hard to imagine you not hurtling around a track but I suppose there is life after racing."

"There better had be!" said Stallard in mock trepidation.

"Who knows, you might even persuade him to settle down and raise a family," said Hampton with a knowing wink in Sophie's direction.

"Hey, steady on, you're my manager, not controller of my destiny," butted in the driver.

"Anyway," she smiled, "I'm a professional woman. Who says I want to give up my career just yet?"

"Fair point," said her fiancé. "You might need to support me if I stop working!"

"That's an interesting prospect," said the winsome brunette as she came around to the front of the sofa. "D'you mind if I join you guys or are you still talking business?"

"Sure, come and sit down," said Stallard. "We're just about done. Any decision about my future can be taken at the end of the season."

"Hold it, Nick," said his manager, "we can't wait that long. You don't have to sign a new contract just yet but I think we need to sound out Gorton to gauge his likely plans for next year."

"Go ahead, I don't have a problem with that. But I want to see how the championship pans out before I put pen to paper."

The driver turned to face his fiancée. "It's not something we've discussed in any detail. How would you feel if I continued racing?"

She looked affectionately into his eyes. "It's got to be your decision. No one else can make it for you. But whatever you decide I'll go along with."

Stallard gave a wry smile. "That's what I expected you to say."

"It doesn't mean it's not true."

"I know that but tell me, how do you *really* feel?"

Sophie sighed and clasped his hand. "I guess if you were to ask that question of the women in the paddock, most would give you the same answer. When their man is constantly driving close to the edge, and sometimes on it, they're bound to be fearful, and I suppose I'm no different."

"But it's something I've always done. It's been my life."

"I understand that and it's why I would never ask you to stop."

"We know the dangers. They stare us in the face every time we get in the car. But we do it because it's in our blood."

"I know, and that's why it would be unfair of me to try to influence you. One day you'll wake up and you'll know it's time to finish." She fingered a lock of his hair. "Until then, you really don't have a choice."

Hampton stood up. "She's got a point, Nick. I couldn't have put it better myself."

"Maybe that day isn't so far away," said the driver.

"Who knows?" retorted his manager. "Anyway, I need to change as I'm leaving for Nice airport shortly – I'm booked on a London flight tonight. I'll make contact with Gorton in the next couple of days to set up a preliminary meeting with him and I'll report back to you."

"Alright, Dave, but don't forget, I'm not signing anything in a hurry."

"I know that, but he doesn't need to." He kissed Sophie on the cheek. "I'll see you both in Paris next week. You were P2 in last year's race, Nick – I've got a feeling you'll go one better this time."

"Thanks for the vote of confidence," said Stallard as he and his fiancée watched Hampton walk towards the hotel reception area.

"I'm sure he just wants to do the best for you, darling," she said.

"He's been with me a long time. He's loyal and I trust him. And he's desperate for me to win the title."

"He's not the only one."

"I know that."

"You have to let him do his job. He's aware you can veto anything you're not happy with."

"I'm not sure he realises that winning the title might just be the spur I need to retire from the sport."

Sophie looked at him intently, her brown eyes conveying a scintilla of surprise. "Are you serious?"

He nodded. "It started to gnaw at me after what's been happening this season. I guess it adds to the pressure but it's something I have to cope with."

"You should have confided in me."

"I didn't want to put you in a position where you're counting down the races to the last one. This sport is not exactly risk-free and it would be unfair to saddle you with more anxiety."

"I appreciate your concern but I am aware of the dangers. I sometimes feel you're too protective of me."

"Maybe it's because you mean a lot to me."

She smiled. "That's the nicest thing you've said to me all day, Nick." Sophie took his hand in hers. "There's something I want to share with you."

"Oh," he said, patently curious. "I wasn't going to say anything for a while as I didn't want to distract you, but perhaps I'm trying to set a good example in the confession stakes."

He looked mildly amused but said nothing.

"I had my test results today and…" She paused.

"And?" He was impatient now. "Come on, don't keep me in suspense!"

"You're going to be a father next year." A huge grin appeared on Stallard's face. "Well, I'll be…"

"And there's something else you should know," continued Sophie. "There could be two!"

The driver's eyes widened as he grasped the implications of her words. "Twins? You're expecting twins?"

She hugged her fiancé, tears running down her cheeks. "It seems likely. I couldn't believe it when they told me but that's what the ultrasound scan indicated. And twins run in my family, as you know. I'm so happy, darling. Tell me you are, too."

"Of course I am, sweetheart. It's great news."

"I was going to keep it to myself until the season ended as I thought it might affect your concentration on the track but I couldn't do it. You have a right to know."

"I'm so glad you told me. I can't wait." He pulled her tenderly into his arms. "You know what? You've just given me another two very good reasons to go all out for the title. God knows I wasn't short of motivation before, but this," he placed his hand gently on her abdomen, "is different. I now have all the incentive I could ever need." Their lips touched, fleetingly at first, then converged again as if in a passionate validation of their future parenthood.

FOURTEEN

Sleep was never going to be possible. It beckoned with all the enticement offered by fatigue but fear kept her awake. Valya shivered although the room was well heated. She stared repeatedly at the ornate chandelier – a gift that had once symbolised the beginning of what she hoped would be a stable relationship but now merely appeared to taunt her. There wasn't much else to look at. The lighting fixture suspended from the ceiling was an enforced focal point as she lay on her back. The numbness in her wrists and arms had worsened and her restricted efforts to move them to try to increase the blood flow only added to the tidal wave of frustration that was beginning to overwhelm her.

Valya was also losing track of time. Mentally exhausted and enervated by her enforced captivity, seconds seemed like minutes and minutes passed like hours. Her luxury watch – another offering that had promised so much – lay agonisingly out of reach on the bedside cabinet. She turned her head and raised her shoulders as far as she could, striving to see the watch glass. But the handcuffs and chain were unyielding and after several futile attempts she slumped back onto the pillow, her distress compounded by the impotence of her plight and the uncertainty of what lay ahead.

At first she couldn't be sure if she had imagined it because she was desperate to hear anything. She listened hard, her ears straining to recapture whatever sound might have permeated her consciousness. Then it came again, distant and indistinct, but this time there was no mistaking the audibility of voices beyond the open bedroom door. It took a while for them to come closer. Valya, whose overriding instinct was to shout for help, instead found herself paralysed by fear and stayed silent. One voice was instantly recognisable but the other took longer to identify. Disoriented as she was, the blonde tried to comprehend why the men were cursing. From the sound of their exertions it seemed they were carrying a heavy object and struggling to manoeuvre it. Powerless to act, she could do nothing but wait.

Sweating and straining, and tipping what appeared to be a large storage crate on its side, the handlers succeeded in forcing it through the doorway. A few short strides took them to the side of the bed where, breathing heavily, they lowered the plastic container on to the carpet. Valya turned her head to look at Makarov and his chief henchman. They stared back with sullen eyes that betrayed nothing of their intentions. The pinioned woman then focused on the container. It appeared to be a nondescript rectangular box secured by two leather straps, but the small holes punched at intervals across its side puzzled her.

The mafia chief pulled a handkerchief from his pocket and wiped away the beads of perspiration glistening on his forehead. "That was one hell of a lift, Vuk. Awkward bloody thing!"

The Serb nodded his agreement. "You're right, boss. You couldn't have done it on your own."

"What's in there?" asked Valya, mustering as much authority in her voice as her predicament would allow.

"All in good time, my dear," said Makarov in a condescending tone.

"What's in that box?" she shrieked.

"It's no use shouting at me. You have to be patient for a bit longer."

"I want to know now!" she demanded. "Listen to me! Tell me what's in there!" He ignored her and bent down to release the straps encompassing the container. "You can't do this to me, Viktor. You're treating me worse than an animal." She started sobbing. "I hate you! I hate you!"

Unfastened, the straps fell back on to the carpet and Makarov started to ease the lid off. It slowly came away in his hand and he looked warily through the opening. He stared intently for over a minute. "Come and have a look, Vuk." The man hesitated for a moment then shuffled forward. He peered inside but quickly drew back and said nothing. "What d'you reckon?"

"Looks about the same," was the noncommittal reply.

The Russian glanced across at the woman whose facial expression captured in equal measure the contempt for those holding her and the consternation she felt. "I think it's about time we satisfied the lady's curiosity, don't you?"

"Sure thing, boss. Let's get on with it and put her out of her misery."

Valya instinctively tugged at the restraints that bound her, knowing it would be unavailing but persisting until the chafing of her skin became unbearable and further dragged her down into the maelstrom of despair she was helpless to resist. An object of downright humiliation and now certain her tormentors would show no sympathy, she was resigned to whatever additional indignities they decided to inflict on her.

She watched as they sat down, somewhat incongruously, on the pair of cream-coloured silk-upholstered chairs either side of the wardrobe. Neither man uttered a word but stared straight ahead in an apparent mood of expectancy. Valya's gaze was drawn compulsively to the top of the container standing just a few feet away at the side of the bed. Occasionally, but only for a second or two, she would flash a glance at the men who were subjecting her to such an ordeal. Their faces displayed not the slightest flicker of emotion but appeared cast in stone, such was their preoccupation. Five minutes passed. Ten. Fifteen. By now Valya's focus was wholly on the crate and its aperture, her craving to discover its contents matched only by a visceral fear of the repercussions for her.

Then she saw it, barely visible at first and seeming to vanish almost immediately. Visible. Vanishing. Visible. Vanishing. The blonde began to wonder if she was hallucinating. Extorting the last ounce of concentration she could summon in her fatigued state, she watched, fixated. Then it came again – but this time she knew there was nothing delusional in what was now in her line of sight. It chilled her to the core. The forked tongue flicked in and out of its mouth like a fencer's foil, thrusting forward then drawing back, the creature sensing its new surroundings. Then its head came fully into view, its unblinking eyes encapsulating a covert menace. Slowly the reptile exposed more of itself, its patterned skin with brown blotches bordered in black down its back emerging from the opening as if an unseen hand was orchestrating its movement.

Valya screamed. And screamed again. Neither man reacted. Both sat motionless, said nothing and continued to stare straight ahead. More than six feet of the Burmese python was now in view and still it was uncoiling from its temporary home. Rigid with fear, the hapless woman could only watch as the elongation process followed its course. She glanced again at those causing her such torment but their features showed no trace of mercy. When she looked back the snake had fully unwound itself and the bulk of its twelve-foot length was under the bed. No longer able to see it, she was completely unnerved. Her head jerked from side to side, like a boxer taking a beating on the ropes, desperate to locate the creature.

For Valya the suspense was unbearable. She knew it would appear again but exactly when and where, she could only agonise over. The Serb coughed and she looked in his direction. His face was expressionless. So too was that of Makarov. Both displayed an intensity of focus in stark contrast to the absence of any emotion. They waited. She waited. But what seemed an eternity to her was merely a brief hiatus. Valya felt it before she saw it. The faintest of touches, featherlike, against the heel of her left foot. Forcing her head off the pillow, she looked down at the bottom of the bed – and her blood ran cold. The reptile had stopped in its tracks as if suddenly aware of the presence of something alien. The only movement came from its head, its bifurcated tongue almost mechanical in its repetitive toing and froing. She screamed again and instinctively pulled both legs towards her, arching her knees.

The impasse was only ever going to be temporary, as Valya was fully aware. The snake continued its sinuous progress, slithering inch by inch across the silken sheets. Its cold skin brushed her right leg and thigh and then it paused again. Traumatised to virtual breaking point, the blonde's overwhelming impulse was to cry out for help but, terrified by the proximity of the python, she found herself unable to utter a sound. Struggling to retain a vestige of rational thought, she persuaded herself that if she could only lie still and stay silent the nightmare staring her in the face might somehow move away. As depressing and forlorn as her situation was, she clung fervently to the notion, however fanciful. It was the only thing she had left.

Her pulse racing but hardly daring to breathe, Valya froze every muscle as insanely, outrageously, she convinced herself she could hypnotise the constrictor. And for a minute – one long, nerve-racking minute – it seemed to work. Human and reptile, as still as sculpted stone, stared at each other. One terrified, the other impassive. From a deep and lonely recess of Valya's mind came a recurring yet tantalising thought that provided a glimmer of hope. Could she, against all the odds, somehow subdue the threat before her? It was the sudden and momentary illumination from the firing of the flashbulb in Makarov's camera that signalled the end of the stand-off – and destroyed the one scintilla of hope remaining to the shackled woman.

At that instant, coincidence or not, the python resumed its forward movement. It was also the moment Valya gave vent to the torrent of fear coursing through her body. The stark terror erupted, volcanic-like, in a sustained bout of shrieking. Energised by the creeping menace now approaching her upper body, she pulled repeatedly at the nickel-plated chain that bound her to the headboard frame. Despite the numbness in her arms and wrists from their prolonged restraint, her limbs worked like pistons in a frenzied attempt to break free but the metal was unyielding. Heart pounding, she felt as if a pendulum was swinging inside her chest and it was about to burst with the pressure.

"Viktor, you've got to stop this! I'll do anything you want, anything – just let me go!" There was no response. She implored him. "Please, Viktor, please… don't do this to me!" Again there was no reaction. Utterly distraught, Valya pleaded with Makarov's henchman, knowing she was begging for her life. "Vuk, you can't let him do this to me. I've done nothing to deserve it. Please help me, for God's sake!" The screaming began again and this time it was even more piercing and protracted.

It ended abruptly when the mafia boss stuffed Valya's lace panties into her mouth. "That's enough, bitch!" he snarled. "You're giving me a headache." Ensuring he was standing at a safe distance from his pet, Makarov looked down at his mistress but his eyes were devoid of the slightest glimmer of compassion. "You'll be glad to know this baby was fed recently so it's not hungry." He paused then smiled sardonically. "But – and it's a big but – it does like company and tends to show its affection by squeezing."

Gasping for air, Valya instinctively lashed out and one foot struck the snake mid-way along its body. Its open mouth, with sharp backward-pointing teeth clearly visible, was now less than twelve inches away. It fixed the tethered woman in its gaze. She rolled her eyes in terror, the colour draining from her cheeks as the python, perceiving a threat, drew back its neck in an S-shape and started to hiss. The warning was short-lived and ominous. The reptile's head lunged forward in the direction of the petrified victim's right arm, its teeth penetrating the smooth flesh above her elbow. The blonde felt an excruciating pain as blood spurted onto the sheets but her cries were muffled by the gag that was half-choking her.

The constrictor, with its grip secure, started to coil itself around Valya's torso and steadily tightened its hold. Soon she was fighting for every breath, her face beginning to display the blue tinge of someone who's being asphyxiated. Each time she exhaled the powerful animal exerted further pressure on her neck and chest as methodically, inexorably, it squeezed the life out of her. The last thing she saw before losing consciousness was the outline of the man who had used and abused and finally betrayed her with sickening depravity. Then Valya's blue eyes, bulging and staring, could see no more. The two onlookers to the gruesome scene of suffocation maintained their implacable focus; one slavering and lusting at what he was seeing, the other displaying a hesitancy stemming from an earlier confrontation that still haunted him.

Then the unequal struggle was over. The voyeurs watched, engrossed, as the python's jaw came away from its victim's upper arm, now studded with bite marks and heavily bloodstained, and it slowly started to unwind itself from her lifeless body. Valya's arms, still tethered, arced backwards over her head as if frozen in some macabre dance of death. The two men continued to gape awhile as the snake slowly moved away from the corpse and coiled itself contentedly at the foot of the bed.

Once he was certain his pet was not a threat to him, Makarov leant across and removed the panties from

Valya's mouth. Pulling a key from his pocket, he unlocked the padlock, releasing the chain, and uncuffed her badly bruised wrists. In stark contrast for a man whose brutality and lack of remorse were hard-wired into his DNA, he gently placed her arms on either side of her body. Then, belatedly, the woman who had routinely returned home after a day's work only to be subjected to an horrific ordeal that finally claimed her life was at last given some semblance of dignity.

Makarov turned towards his chief henchman, who had taken a couple of paces back from the bed. "I've seen the snake kill its prey at feeding time but that was something else."

Jovanovic was still staring at the reptile, astounded by what he had just witnessed. "It was," he muttered eventually.

"You look as though you could do with a drink, Vuk. Help yourself and bring me one, too."

"Sure."

"Then call Ivan and Mikhail and get them over here. We need to move her and the snake out of this place and get it cleaned up." As the Serbian headed towards the door the Russian added. "There's one more thing – make sure you seize the tapes from the video surveillance cameras inside and outside this building. Then destroy them!"

"I know what to do. Leave it with me, boss."

The racing car, in its distinctive black and green livery, turned into the pit lane after completing only three laps of the circuit located on a former military airfield 30 miles north of Moscow. The electronic limiter was activated to ensure compliance with the 55 miles per hour speed limit on entry and the vehicle slowed, finally coming to a stop outside the garage of Gorton Racing. The driver cut the engine and three mechanics pushed the vehicle backwards and wheeled it inside. Minutes later the debriefing was underway as Nick Stallard and his race engineer, in an improvised office, scrutinised telemetry printouts from the truncated session in first practice for the Russian race to be held three days later.

"There was no point staying out any longer, Jim. The balance of the car just wasn't right."

"If we wanted any confirmation it's in here," said Crowley, waving sheets of downloaded data. "This tells us everything we need to know."

"We've got to find the optimum set-up before qualifying."

"We haven't raced here before so there's no track history, no benchmark to make comparisons – that's the problem."

"That's something all the teams have to deal with."

"True enough, but we've got to get it right twice – once for the limited laps of qualifying, and then the race will require a different set-up due to other factors such as tyre wear and fuel loads."

Stallard nodded. "Of course, that's where you guys earn your corn. But you still need driver input and I can tell you, I was getting some understeer. There's a couple of tight corners out there and I had to fight the car, which wanted to go straight on instead of turning in."

"I could see you grappling with it from the monitor on the pit wall but we can make adjustments to improve the balance."

"I must have more grip in the corners. It just wasn't there today."

"We can improve downforce by increasing the amount of rear wing but that creates more drag and slows the car on the straights. There's no perfect solution, Nick, as you know. It's a question of finding the best compromise we can."

"You must have run computer simulations back at base before coming out here. What did they show?"

"Whenever we race at a new circuit we feed all the data we can get hold of into the computers and analyse the results. This track is 4.5 miles long and judging by the layout, it's going to be very challenging for tyres. The big test for us and everyone else in the pit lane is tyre degradation – and that's key where the race distance is over 200 miles. Whichever team handles it best is likely to win."

The driver nodded his agreement as he put down one of the printouts he had been examining. "Not much doubt about that, but there are also other factors at play here. We know the circuit owners have been under pressure to get it ready in time for the inaugural race but I'm wondering if the project has been signed off too soon. The track surface is very uneven in places, particularly on the section that was extended to run through the wooded area. There's a safety issue, too; there's no fencing or tyre barriers along that stretch, which is a bit worrying. And the track is badly off-camber at the entry points to several corners."

Crowley looked slightly amused. "Let's put it this way. It's at circuits like this that you and the other guys justify your money. See it as just another challenge."

"You're a hard taskmaster," chuckled Stallard. "But I'm trying to make a serious point – it looks to me as if the contractors have taken shortcuts in some areas and they've been allowed to get away with it."

"I suppose it's possible but we can't get involved in the politics of it. There's a job to be done and we have to get on with it."

"You're damn right. There's a championship to be won!" The driver strolled over to a chart pinned to the wall. "Look at this, Jim. Ten races completed, two more to go, and it's still too close to call."

"I know it's tight but there's one consolation: at least you're top of the pile."

"Sure, by just one point from Raffa. But no one's calling it a comfortable lead – anything but!"

"No, but however you look at it you've got the psychological edge. You're the guy in front, the rest of the pack are chasing and they have to try to take it away from you."

"That's where I want them to stay – in my rear-view mirrors."

"Your main rival is the Spaniard. The only other driver who can catch you and win the title is Petrenko, who's nine points off your total. Everyone else is out of the running."

"I know Raffa's the biggest threat. We've both won three races so far and there's barely any daylight between us. But it would be foolish to discount the Russian."

The race engineer joined Stallard at the wall and pointed at the chart. "Consistency is crucial and you've shown it this season. Although you didn't win either of the last two races in Paris and Caracas, you finished P2 in both, and that's important as it keeps up the pressure on the other two."

"But I have to win here in Russia to be certain of going to the last race in Tangier still heading the championship – and I need the car to do it."

"No need to worry on that score. The boys will pull out

all the stops to provide a winning car for you, even if we have to work through the night. We all want to see you lift the title after being runner-up twice. You've been in this game a long time and you deserve it."

The driver placed his hand on Crowley's shoulder. "Thanks, Jim. I appreciate that. I only wish I could bank on getting the same degree of loyalty from my number two."

The Gorton engineer sighed. "There are times, Nick, when you have to accept that things aren't the way you want them to be and you have to rise above it."

"I know you're right but it's difficult when your teammate decides she doesn't want to be a team player. And worse still, she seems to have the backing of the owner."

"You don't need to spell it out. I think most of us are aware of the background. What you must do is concentrate on the task in hand and stay focused. Aim for pole then go flat out for the win. And if you do that, it won't matter what Kate does."

"Sounds good in theory, Jim, but you know as well as I do that in this business it only takes one moment of madness or greed to derail everything. She can't win the championship so she should be riding shotgun for me but I can't rely on her."

"You've got to look at it from her point of view. She was given her chance after Corazza failed to deliver and she's determined to prove herself in her first season in FS. She missed the first three races and then when she made her debut she got on the podium. She's currently P6 in the standings and could end up in P5 if Pavani makes a mistake. Not bad for a rookie!"

Stallard wore the look of a man who understood the argument but had difficulty accepting it. "I hear what you say but I'm not convinced. I've put myself in a position to win the title but it's plain from Lockhart's actions on the track that she's prepared to fight me instead of putting the team first. And all I hear from the owner is a deafening silence!"

"I'm sorry, Nick, but I can't worry about the other driver in this team – that's not in my job description. I'm paid to put on track the most balanced and effective racing car I can produce so you can perform to the best of your ability every time you line up on the grid. That's all I can do."

"Point taken. You take care of your job and I'll look after mine."

"Let's go for it and with any luck, after the final race in Tangier, you'll be able to call yourself world champion."

Stallard smiled. "I like the sound of that. I think I could get used to it!"

Crowley moved towards his desk and picked up the sheets of data. "But first there's some serious work to be done. Come over here and I'll run through how I plan to improve the balance of the car."

"Sure."

"I mentioned earlier that this track is likely to be tough on tyres so it's important we find a set-up that's going to be less demanding of them. I think we should—" At that moment the race engineer's mobile phone jingled into action. He pulled the device from its leather case attached to his belt and saw the call was from England. "Excuse me, Nick, it's my wife on the line."

The driver gestured to carry on. "Go ahead, Jim."

"Hi Sarah, good to hear from you."

"Hi darling. How are you?"

"I'm fine. Busy, of course, with the race coming up. But I'm OK. And you?"

"Yes, I'm OK too. Been hard at it in work and there's always something to do around the cottage, as you know."

"You're a great homemaker, sweetheart. That's why it's always so good to get back."

She laughed. "You flatterer, you always say that."

"It's true and you know it!"

Sarah paused for a moment. "Jim, I know you haven't a lot of time to chat but there is something on my mind. Can you spare a minute?"

"Sure. What is it?"

"I don't know how to put it. I expect I'm worrying unnecessarily because I'm on my own but…"

"Come on, tell me."

"It's probably nothing but the other night I saw a car parked in the road at the end of our driveway. I hadn't seen it before and it was there for a while with its lights turned off. Then the same thing happened last night – the same car parked in the same place."

"Did you see anybody in the vehicle?"

"It was hard to make anyone out because it was dark. Racer was barking but he stopped eventually. I don't know why I'm telling you all this because—"

"I'm glad you did," Crowley butted in. "If you're ever uneasy about something you must always talk to me." He thought fast. He doubted anything could be amiss and was anxious not to alarm his young wife unduly, yet he would never forgive himself if there was a genuine cause for concern.

"Sarah, there's no need to be alarmed. It was probably just a couple looking for somewhere quiet to have a kiss and a cuddle; maybe they're having an affair. I know it's meant to be a private road leading to the cottage but the fact it's a bit secluded is an attraction."

"I suppose it's possible."

"That's the likely explanation. Really, I'm sure there's no need to worry."

"I hope so. I had thought I would get used to you being away so much but I don't like being here on my own even though the dog is with me."

"Look sweetheart, if it will reassure you why don't you ring the police and ask if one of their patrol cars could check it out? That would set your mind at rest."

"Oh Jim, I don't want to make a fuss. I'll be alright. I shouldn't have said anything – it will only distract you before the race."

"Don't fret about that. I would much rather you confide in me. I'll try to catch an evening flight from Domodedovo International after we've finished here on Sunday."

"That'll be nice. I'm so looking forward to seeing you again."

"I'll be home for a few days before the final race this season. Then afterwards we'll go away and have some quality time together. How does that sound?"

"I can't wait, darling. Come home soon."

"I will. Now you take care and try not to worry. Promise me?"

"I promise."

"That's my girl. Bye sweetheart."

"Bye darling. I love you."

"Love you too. Bye." Crowley ended the call then continued to stare at his mobile.

"Nothing wrong is there, Jim?" said Stallard.

The engineer looked up. "I'm not sure. I hope not."

"But something's bothering her."

"Seems to be. I expect there's nothing in it – a car parked

at night in the road leading to our place. Probably a young couple larking about, you know what it's like."

The driver laughed. "These things happen. Found myself in that situation years ago. It's all part of what they call growing up, isn't it?"

Crowley allowed himself a half-smile. "I've been there, too." But then he appeared deep in thought. "Sarah has never liked being there on her own. We've only been married eighteen months and I hate leaving her every time there's a race. She puts on a brave face whenever I have to go but I know it's hard for her." He replaced his mobile. "Anyway, it's time to deal with more immediate business."

Stallard gave him a sympathetic glance. Whilst he felt certain the engineer would buckle down to the job in hand at a pivotal time in the motor racing calendar, he also knew the man's thoughts would occasionally, inevitably, stray to a distant location and the woman he loved. It was as if Crowley had read his mind.

"Don't worry, Nick, I know what's at stake for you this weekend. I won't let it affect my judgment – I'm too much of a pro for that."

"Never doubted you," said Stallard. "Never would."

As the championship leader and his race engineer continued their debriefing session, an equally crucial meeting was getting underway in the team owner's motor home nearby. After weeks of sporadic communication, Joe Gorton had finally agreed to see Stallard's manager to discuss the leading driver's contract. An earlier meeting between the two, planned to coincide with the French race, had been postponed at the last minute by the owner, who declared there were a number of 'outstanding issues' still to be clarified. No further explanation had been forthcoming despite repeated requests by the driver's representative who, although determined not to be sidetracked, was beginning to fear the worst for his client.

"There's something stronger in the cabinet if you'd prefer it," said Gorton, handing a team-branded mug of coffee to Hampton, who was sitting in one of two armchairs in a corner of the room.

"No, this is fine. I try to stay off the booze when I'm working."

"Need to have your wits about you, eh?"

"It does help."

"I suppose you make an exception when your guy gets on the podium."

"I guess I can justify that."

"You don't need to. The champagne starts flying around here when one of our drivers gets a top-three finish." The team owner settled into the second chair, took a sip from his mug and faced his visitor. "I've got to hand it to your guy. He's having another outstanding season."

"There's no question about it. Nick's proving yet again he can deliver for you. He's done it in the past and he's doing it now."

"He has the talent, that's not in doubt. But to be up there in the very top league he has to win the drivers' championship."

"He knows that. He doesn't need you or me to tell him."

"But if I'm honest with you, Dave, time is running out for him. He's had a long career and come close but it's not getting any easier. And frankly, although he's heading the standings with two races remaining, I'm not sure he's got the killer instinct to do it."

Hampton uncrossed his legs and leant forward. "Joe, if that's the way you see it, I have to say I think you're wrong, but if we're going to be honest in our dealings then I hope you won't mind if I'm equally candid."

"Not a problem. As a Yorkshireman I've never shied away from plain speaking."

"The one thing that motivates Stallard every time he lines up his car on the grid is the desire to be the best. It's what he dreams about, it's why he gets up in the morning. But what's not helping is the uncertainty surrounding his future with Gorton Racing. It's taken me several weeks to re-arrange this meeting and I can only assume there's a reluctance on your part to discuss a new contract."

"I know we were due to meet in Paris and I had to call it off without much warning but there was never any intention to unsettle Nick."

"With respect, it seemed to me you were stalling on the negotiations."

"I'm sorry you gained that impression but there were other more pressing issues that required my attention at the time and I had to focus on those."

Hampton's brow creased slightly. "But what can be more important than the future of your number one driver?"

The owner stared frostily at his visitor before speaking. "Are you questioning my ability to run this team?"

"Of course not. How you run it is your business."

"Precisely," came the rejoinder. "I suggest you remember that."

"You don't need to spell it out for me." Stallard's manager sighed in frustration. "Look, Joe, your leading driver could soon be the next world champion and his contract runs out at the end of the season. But I haven't seen any indication yet that you want to sign him for the new term, and I find that surprising. It would be useful to have some kind of steer from you."

"I understand where you're coming from. Naturally, you want to secure the best deal you can for your man, but you've been in this business long enough to know I have to take into account various factors when deciding the team line-up. And it has to be my call."

"No one's disputing that but what I find difficult to stomach is why you should have a problem about renewing his contract. Surely you must recognise that if Nick takes the title, he'll boost the profile of your brand and bring in more sponsorship. And he'll put the number one on the front of a Gorton car – that's priceless!"

"I don't think you need to remind me. But there's just one question mark over your analysis – it hinges on the word *if*. In my opinion, it's a big if, and as I explained earlier, I've got my doubts as to whether he can deliver the championship."

The racer's manager stirred uncomfortably in his chair. "Joe, I'll come to the point. Can you assure me, as the team owner, that Nick has your full backing?"

"You do surprise me. Why d'you ask?"

"Well, I think he feels he doesn't always get the support that a driver of his standing is entitled to."

"Would you care to expand?" said Gorton coldly.

"I'm sure you can recall a number of races this season where Nick felt he was disadvantaged by his teammate and deprived of points that could prove crucial in deciding the title. That still rankles with him and it then becomes a distraction when he should be totally focused on his job."

"If he thinks I'm favouring Kate he's totally out of order. I made it clear from the start there are no team orders. That's the way it should be – it encourages competition. They're racing drivers, for Pete's sake, that's what they do. And if it means racing each other, so what?"

"Nick's a pro, he knows the rules. What he finds difficult to swallow is that Lockhart is not a team player and he can't rely on her to ride shotgun when he's better placed to score points. But if the situation was reversed, he wouldn't hesitate to help her."

"Maybe that's his problem," said Gorton with a hint of contempt in his voice.

"What d'you mean?"

"He's not ruthless enough. To use a boxing analogy, he lacks what it takes to put an opponent away when he's got him on the ropes. It's not something you can teach someone – you've either got it or you haven't." He paused. "But I think Kate has it."

"Petrenko's got it but I'm not sure I'd want to use him as a role model."

"I would never condone what happened to Maitland, no one could, but I have some regard for the Russian's approach to the sport. Perhaps it's the freedom of youth, but he drives that car with a passion and an arrogance that will make him a champion one day. You mark my words."

"Can't say I'm ecstatic at the prospect," said Hampton drily. "I'd prefer my man to win it with his integrity intact or not at all."

"Don't hold your breath. His best years are behind him and it may not happen." Gorton looked at his watch. "I've got to be out of here in ten minutes. It's a meeting to discuss a possible change to one of the technical regulations so I can't be late."

"There is something else, Joe. There's been some speculation in the media recently about a young Mexican driver. It seems he's the leading guy in the junior formula this season and his name's been linked with a seat in your outfit next year. Is there any substance to those reports?"

The owner emitted a boisterous laugh. "Been reading the sports pages again, eh Dave? You shouldn't believe everything you read in the papers, you know."

"Are you saying the reports are wrong?"

Gorton was unable to conceal a fleeting look of irritation. "You know what reporters are like when they've got an editor kicking their arse. They have to come up with a story and a speculative piece is the result. That's what happens. You get used to it."

Hampton still wasn't satisfied. "So there's nothing in it?"

The boss of Gorton Racing was starting to lose patience. "OK, so I may have had the Mexican watched, but what the hell? Teams are constantly on the look-out for new talent; that's what keeps this circus alive."

"So there was something in those reports after all."

"Nothing has changed. We might have a vacancy for a test driver next season and I'm just keeping my options open."

"Where does that leave Nick?"

"There are a number of permutations. I could extend his contract by another year – let's see how the season pans out. He could be talking to other teams or thinking of retirement, for all I know."

"Look, Joe, I need an answer. Is Stallard on the way out?"

Gorton stood up and scowled. "There's no point continuing this conversation. I've made my position clear. What I don't need is this kind of interrogation. I'm sorry, Dave, but I have to go."

FIFTEEN

A strengthening autumnal breeze rustled the copper-brown wavy-edged leaves of the common beech tree, nudging those at the periphery onto the unlit upper windows of the secluded cottage. The silence of the night was disrupted periodically by a passenger jet passing overhead in a moonless sky inbound for Gatwick Airport. Downstairs, Sarah Crowley watched the late news headlines then switched off the television. The slim, pretty brunette, in her early thirties, moved from the lounge to the farmhouse-style kitchen with her devoted boxer at her heels. "Come on, boy, time for some fresh air." She unlocked an outer door and the animal bounded through the brick porch leading to the garden outside.

Sarah tidied up, put her supper plate and mug in the dishwasher and wiped the granite top of the unit running either side of the sink. Moving to a chair next to the table, she jotted down on a notepad a list of jobs for the coming weekend and resolved to keep herself occupied whilst her husband was away. Hearing the dog barking, she moved towards the back door, which was ajar, and pulled it open. "Racer. Racer." Peering into the darkness, she waited for the dog to come to her but there was no movement and the barking had stopped. She repeated the call but there was still no sign of the boxer. Feeling tired and starting to become impatient, she picked up a torch hanging from its hook on the wall and stepped outside, shivering slightly in the late-night air.

The race engineer's wife walked slowly along the footpath that zig-zagged gently to the lawn, directing the beam of light from side to side. "Racer, where are you? Come on, boy, come inside now." The hooting cry of an owl pierced the stillness, momentarily startling her. Gripping the torch tightly she moved onto the grass, already damp with dew, and looked expectantly in the direction of a cluster of shrubs screening the six-foot-high wooden fence that bordered the property. Any second now, she told herself, Racer would emerge from the darkness at the bottom of the garden and run to her in his customary display of canine affection. Another call to the dog found her voice reduced to little more than a whisper, her mouth suddenly dry. The owl hooted again and for the first time she felt a tangible sense of unease.

Sarah quickened her stride as if to demonstrate an inner confidence she knew she didn't possess. She shone the torch haphazardly in the hope it would elicit a response. "Racer, where are you?" There was now a trace of desperation in her intonation. "I know you're out here. Stop messing about and come…"

A gloved hand pressed tightly against her mouth cut off the rest of her words. Unable to scream and with her arms held behind her back, she was half-dragged, half-pushed along the lawn and onto the footpath. The slender brunette struggled to free herself but she was no match for the two men who propelled her through the open door leading to the kitchen.

As one of them locked it, the other released his grip on her mouth and forced her down onto a chair. "Don't move! Don't say anything!" he told the traumatised woman as he leant against the side of the table.

"Where's my dog? What have you done with it?" Sarah winced as he inflicted a stinging slap to the side of her face.

"I told you – be quiet!"

"What d'you want?" she persisted. "What are you going to do with me?"

A second, harder blow was the immediate response. A big man, well over six feet, he bent forward, a scar on his right cheek clearly visible. "Shut up! If you don't, I'll kill you! I'm only going to tell you once – so listen!"

Frightened as she was, Sarah tried to fathom his accent. Eastern European, she wondered?

"We have to be out of here in five minutes. You need to pack an overnight bag because you're coming with us. But first I want your mobile. Where is it?" he demanded.

Reluctantly, she delved into a side pocket of her jeans and pulled out the phone. He took it from her and switched the device off.

"You won't be needing this for a while." He looked at his accomplice, also wearing gloves, who was standing by the door. "Ivan, go with her and make sure she doesn't cause any trouble."

"There's no chance of that," said the surly-looking man who appeared to Sarah as equally intimidating. She braced herself as he approached. "You heard what he said. On your way and don't try anything stupid or you'll regret it!" He grabbed the woman by the arm and hauled her out of the chair.

Cowed by fear and in deep shock, she made her way upstairs to the main bedroom. Under the watchful and suspicious eye of one of the intruders, Sarah packed some essentials for a journey she knew nothing about but that filled her with dread.

"I need to use the bathroom," she said with as much self-control as she could muster.

"No time for that," was the unfeeling reply. "We need to move."

"But I have to use the toilet," she protested. "It's urgent."

Ivan hesitated for a moment, looking at his watch. "Alright, but make it quick." But as Sarah reached the bathroom and tried to close the door, it was kicked violently and flew open. "You must think I'm stupid," snarled Ivan. "I'm not going to let you out of my sight."

"You can't do this to me. I need some privacy."

"You've got a choice – you can relieve yourself with me at the doorway or you don't bother. What's it to be?"

Close to tears, Sarah knew there was no point in arguing and resigned herself to the indignity imposed upon her.

"What kept you?" enquired the shaven-headed man as his accomplice and a tearful captive returned to the kitchen.

"The bitch had to use the toilet," said Ivan. "But I kept an eye on her in case she tried anything," he smirked.

The other man laughed sardonically. "I always thought you were a pervert. But you were right not to take any chances. Bring her over here." He fished out a piece of dark-coloured cloth from his jacket pocket, carefully folded the material over to double its thickness and pulled the ends apart. Sarah was now standing directly in front of him. "Turn around," he ordered.

"Why? What are you going to do to me?" she asked nervously.

"You ask too many questions. Now turn around!" he barked. Fearfully, she did as she was instructed. As Ivan gripped her arms, the second man placed the cloth over Sarah's eyes and tugged it tight before knotting the ends securely behind her head.

"Why are you blindfolding me?"

"You'll find out soon enough."

"Where are you taking me?" she pleaded. "I want to know."

"Shut up, bitch! You don't need to know anything. We're going outside and if you make a sound, you're as good as dead. Ivan, bring her bag."

The two men manoeuvred the terrified woman out of the back door, along the footpath and into the garden. Once on the grass they moved towards the area of shrubs that concealed the fence marking the outer limits of the property. Another 5 yards and the trio stopped. "Bend down on your knees and go forward," snapped the man with the scar.

Sarah obeyed and found herself crawling on the damp earth, her fingers sinking into the soil. Bizarrely, considering her plight, her immediate thought was one of annoyance at the likely adverse effects on her carefully tended scarlet-painted fingernails. Her right shoulder nudged something solid and she was pulled to the left.

"Now, go straight and you're through the fence," was the command. She crawled some more and her hands came into contact with concrete, and she knew she was on the driveway that ran alongside the cottage. She heard the sounds of her abductors scrambling through the hole and sensed an urgency in their movements. "You can get up now," came a voice from above as one of the men hoisted her unceremoniously to her feet. Sarah found herself walking swiftly along the driveway with one man keeping a tight grip on her arm. "Stop now!" he said and she heard the sound of car doors opening. "Get inside!" She was forced into the rear of the vehicle. One of the men climbed in after her and the other sat behind the wheel. "Let's get out of here, Ivan, but watch your speed – we don't want the traffic cops on our backs."

The driver grunted a response before firing the engine into life and easing the 4×4 along the driveway. It passed through the open gates, the steel padlock that once secured the entrance dangling impotently from a severed chain, and rattled over the spaced bars of a cattle grid just beyond. The vehicle picked up pace down the quiet lane and away from the cottage, the long reddish-brown tail of a fox vanishing into the hedgerow momentarily caught in the headlights. The nocturnal activities of the vulpine went unnoticed by the woman on the back seat. Her focus was on trying to visualise the route her captors were following, a relatively straightforward task at first as she was familiar with access to the main road. A short while later Sarah guessed they were on a dual carriageway heading south from Crawley but as the minutes passed and various junctions and roundabouts were negotiated, she became increasingly disoriented. Her initial optimism about pinpointing the direction of travel gave way to frustration and a growing sense of foreboding about what lay ahead.

The prisoner's isolation was intensified by the silence. Neither the driver nor the man sitting next to her said a word. But Sarah's lack of vision had the effect of heightening her other faculties and soon her mind was racing. The car with no lights. Parked near the cottage.

Late in the evening. Two nights running. Her suspicions. Such was her anxiety she had felt impelled to confide in her husband, hating herself for disrupting his preparations for a crucial race. She calculated the abduction had been carefully planned and could certainly vouch for the efficacy of its execution. But why? Why had she been targeted? It was a question that continued to gnaw at her but to which she could find no rational answer as she was driven into the night.

With less than a minute remaining on the clock, Stallard knew he had to make this lap count. His previous effort in qualifying had set the pace through the first and second sectors but pressing too hard at the final chicane resulted in his car clipping the kerb and spinning twice. The driver managed to prevent the engine stalling but the incident cost him precious seconds and ruined his attempt to seize pole position. Now time was literally running out and when told his main rival, Rodriguez, had gone quickest, the Englishman knew he had to drag the last ounce of performance from the Gorton if he was to prevail.

He crossed the start line with less than ten seconds before the clock ran down. Cursing himself for making a mistake when the car was responding so well, he was confident the engineers had found the set-up to maximise its potential around the Russian circuit. A short sprint led to the first corner, a slow left-hander, which gradually unwound onto a quick section, followed by a sweeping left and right leading to a hairpin, through the tight left then a long straight opened up and at the end the track veered to the right and through a lengthy wooded area with trees on either side. Travelling at 170 miles per hour and still accelerating, Stallard braced himself for the surface undulations and the occasional bumps in the road that were a feature of the forested section and that gave the unwary driver a severe jolt. He exited the woods and downshifted for a wide right-hander followed by a much tighter turn in the same direction, then it was up through the gears again for a spurt along a short stretch. The Gorton slowed to take the first of two chicanes then rapidly built up speed on another straight.

The voice of the race engineer came over the in-car radio. "Your sector times so far are quickest – keep it up and you'll be on pole." Stallard did not reply and Crowley was not expecting him to. With the end of the straight approaching, the driver hit the brakes at the one hundred-metre board and moved to a lower gear to take a slow right-hander, then tried to exit as cleanly as possible to get on the power as soon as he could for a short burst before the final chicane. Mindful of his earlier mistake at the same spot, the Englishman selected his line and slowed the Gorton to 80 miles per hour before jinking left then right, jumping the bumps and kissing the kerbs as he finessed the car through the obstacle. On the pit wall Jim Crowley watched the monitor in admiration as his driver gave a classic demonstration of how to hustle a racing car through a chicane under the intense pressure of qualifying. "Good man, now go for it!" urged the engineer to himself, not wishing to distract Stallard in any way.

Now the start-finish straight beckoned. The driver upshifted and floored the throttle, thrusting the Gorton towards the line that marked the end of the lap. Its V10 engine screaming, it thundered past the grandstand packed with enthusiastic Muscovites who were witnessing the thrills of an FS qualifying session at close quarters for the first time. A blur of black and green streaked over the line and Stallard's qualifying time flashed up on the screens, confirming he would start the race from the front of the grid. Crowley leapt up from his seat on the pit wall, both fists punching the air before establishing radio contact with the pole setter. "Superb job, Nick. You were three-tenths quicker than Rodriguez. Fantastic effort!"

The driver's response was typically modest. "Thanks, Jim. That was for you and the rest of the team for giving me this beauty. Let's see if we can put on a show again tomorrow."

The Englishman cut the speed of the Gorton and acknowledged the exuberant spectators, waving to them as he completed another tour of the circuit. When he eventually parked the car, he jumped out, hastily removed his helmet, flame-proof balaclava and earplugs, and was immediately surrounded by joyous engineers and mechanics. "Hey, guys, you were brilliant today. You gave me the tools to do the job – and on a new track, too. I couldn't have asked for more."

Crowley stepped forward to embrace his driver. "That was some drive, Nick. You showed the others how it should be done."

"Thanks again, Jim. I reckon I owe you guys. The car was great – it was one of those days when it felt like it was part of me; it did everything I wanted."

"You've done the first part – now you've got to finish the job. And I know you can do it."

Stallard gulped from a bottle of water handed to him by

one of the mechanics then laughed. "Yeah, I know what's required. Make a good start and stay in front. I know the theory, just got to put it into practice!"

At that moment the driver saw his fiancée approaching. "Hey, guys, make room for Sophie."

She ran the last few yards, thrusting her arms around his back and hugged him amid the jostling throng. "Oh, darling, you were wonderful today. I saw your time – that was something special."

"Thanks, sweetheart. It all came together for that lap – and it's the one that counts."

"It was amazing! I'm so glad I flew over to watch you this weekend."

"Me too. It's good to know you're here, it's given me a real boost. And I know it will tomorrow."

"Don't forget, darling," whispered the brunette, "you've got two other little people on your side. They're here as well and they want you to win."

"I haven't forgotten," he smiled. "I know I've got a great support team behind me – all three of you!"

Crowley moved towards the couple. "I'm sorry to butt in, Nick, but you're wanted at the press conference. It's starting soon."

"Yeah, I know. I'm on my way."

The race engineer winked at Stallard. "Tell the world how you got pole – but don't tell them too much!"

"I think I'm familiar with the routine by now, Jim," the driver chuckled. "I won't divulge too many secrets." He turned to Sophie and kissed her on the cheek. "I've got to dash now, sweetheart. I'll catch up with you later."

He hurried away and was about to climb the steps to the makeshift media centre when he was approached by his teammate. "Just wanted to say well done, Nick. That was quite a lap."

His steely pale blue eyes fixed her with a look that was as uncompromising as it was dismissive. "That's not something I expected to hear from you, Kate."

"I know we're rivals, but on the day, you qualified fastest and you deserve pole."

"That's the problem. You see us as rivals but we're also teammates – and you seem to forget that."

"Look, I know you're the number one driver but when I replaced Luigi, I was told there are no team orders and we both have to fight for all the points we can get."

"That's fine in theory but I've been a serious challenger for the title all season and, in my book, when one guy is in a position to win it, he's entitled to more support from his teammate than I've been getting. There were times this year when you would willingly have put me out of a race if it meant you could pass me."

"Nick, you know the score. If you feel so badly about it maybe you should talk to Joe."

Stallard laughed contemptuously. "Sure, and we both know what response I'd get!"

"What d'you mean?"

"Come on, Kate, stop playing games. There's only one driver in this team that Gorton has any interest in – and it's not me!"

Lockhart's cheeks reddened slightly. "I resent that remark."

"I expect you do but it doesn't alter the fact – it's still true. I don't care if you're his mistress but when your affair has a bearing on my chances of winning the championship, I don't like it!"

The American tossed her raven hair over her shoulders and her nostrils flared. "What I do in my own time is my business, and not yours! You need to remember that."

"I don't require any lectures from you but if you're so keen to dish out advice, try this for size: don't even think about screwing up my race tomorrow! I'm not expecting any help from you – that's a given – but what I don't want is you fouling up my prospects for the championship."

Lockhart gave him a withering stare. "I'm not your problem. Frankly, I don't think you've got the balls to win the title!" Then she swung around on her heels and stormed off.

The pole-setter glared at her before heading up the steps to join fellow drivers, Rodriguez and Petrenko – who qualified P2 and P3 respectively – and the waiting media pack at the news conference.

Jim Crowley watched the driver interviews on one of the monitors in the Gorton garage. There was a certain inevitability about the proceedings, he mused, as the teams fulfilled their broadcast obligations under the terms of their FS contracts. The drivers were generally in a positive frame of mind, having just posted the quickest lap times in qualifying to secure the top three slots on the race grid. The journalists, meanwhile, had their role. Whilst they specialised in a sport where statistics were paramount, they sought to look beyond them and instead focus on any human interest angle they could unearth in an attempt to bring some colour to their reports. Sometimes they succeeded in winkling out facts relating to strategy or rivalry or potential team signings that owners might have preferred to remain hidden.

But the longer Crowley observed the question and answer session, he thought his driver appeared increasingly uncomfortable in the verbal exchanges. Stallard seemed tetchy and his body language also indicated he was on edge. The race engineer pondered why the man on pole looked uneasy in a setting that was so familiar to him. He was acutely aware the driver was under growing pressure as he strove to achieve the ultimate prize in his chosen sport, one that had eluded him for so long and that would undoubtedly crown an impressive career. The Englishman had been in this situation before but perhaps previous failures to land the coveted championship had simply intensified the burden of fulfilment. Even so, thought Crowley, it was an unexpected and somewhat unsettling development and maybe something he ought to raise with the driver afterwards.

As he continued to mull over how he could best broach the subject, his mobile burst into life. Reaching for the case attached to his belt, he yanked out the phone and was relieved to see it was his wife calling. "Hi, sweetheart. Good to hear from you."

"Shut up, Crowley!" snarled the voice at the other end. "Just listen to what I've got to say."

The race engineer's mouth went dry.

"I'm only going to tell you once so make sure you listen."

Chest pounding, the Gorton race tactician tried to gather his thoughts as he swung himself off the stool and got to his feet. Why was this stranger using his wife's mobile? Who was he? And what accent was that? He walked in the direction of the garage entrance. "Who the hell are you? Where's my wife?"

"Shut up! I told you to listen. We've taken your wife hostage and we'll kill her unless you co-operate. D'you understand?"

Crowley's heart missed a beat. "Oh my God, what's happening?"

"Your wife is safe at the moment but if you don't obey our instructions she will die."

"Oh Sarah, my lovely Sarah. Don't do anything to hurt her."

"It's your call. If you want to see your wife alive again you must do as I tell you."

The engineer was breathing hard now, his mind struggling to comprehend the assault on his senses.

"Are you there, Crowley?"

"Yes, yes," he murmured.

"Right, listen closely. You must make sure your man, Stallard, does not finish the race tomorrow. You'll have to find a way to sabotage his car. I don't care how you do it but he has to be forced to retire. Is that clear?"

The engineer was outside the Gorton garage now. He glanced anxiously around him but no one seemed to be looking in his direction.

"Is that clear, Crowley?" A nascent impatience was evident in the questioner's tone.

"Yes, I heard what you said."

"Then you know what you have to do."

"There's something I need to know. What evidence have I got that you're holding my wife?"

"Here it is!" was the instant retort. The line went silent for a few seconds as Crowley clenched his handset expectantly.

"Oh darling, it's me, Sarah." The stress in her voice was

palpable. "Please help me, darling. I'm so scared. I don't know what's happening. Oh, Jim, please…"

"That's enough, bitch!" The engineer was horrified when he heard the sound of a slap and his wife started screaming hysterically. "Is that enough evidence for you, Crowley?" sniggered the kidnapper. "D'you need to hear any more or are you going to do what you're told?"

"Don't lay a finger on my wife, d'you hear me?" shouted the engineer, suddenly aware he might inadvertently draw attention to himself. "Don't hurt her – she's done nothing to deserve this," he said tersely.

"Well, that depends on you, Crowley. Do your job and you'll see your wife again. If you screw up…" The caller paused as if to underline the menace of the alternative. "I think you know we mean business. Don't forget – we'll be watching the race tomorrow. And one final thing, Crowley – don't call the police!" Then the line went dead.

The engineer stared in disbelief at his mobile. Feeling crushed and disconsolate, he needed to confide in someone but knew it was out of the question. The conversation with his wife's abductor played over and over again in his head as if mocking his sanity. A myriad of thoughts raced through the rollercoaster that was his mind, questions to which there were as yet no answers, and any attempt to rationalise the situation proved self-defeating. Although mentally battered, his instincts told him to try to regain some element of composure and then focus on the specific issue confronting him. Crowley reminded himself he had spent his entire career as an engineer applying problem-solving techniques and, whilst conceding this was a totally different and an intensely personal scenario, he still recognised the need for logical thinking.

A colleague heading for the garage found the engineer deep in thought and clutching his mobile, his face ashen. "Are you alright, Jim?" Crowley didn't respond immediately, still absorbed in his own thoughts. "Jim, are you OK? You look as though you've seen a ghost."

Slowly the engineer pulled himself together and his eyes met those of the chief mechanic. "I'm OK, Frank."

"You don't look it. Are you sure?"

"Yes, really. Everything's OK. No need to worry."

"Glad to hear it. I expect you'll be at the marketing reception later."

Crowley looked blankly at his colleague then nodded. "Sure, see you there."

"Your side of the garage has a lot to celebrate, what with your guy starting on pole."

"I guess we have, Frank, but we need to stay sober ahead of the race. I don't have to remind you, there are no points for pole, it's what happens tomorrow that counts."

"But at least Nick's got a head start – he's where he wants to be."

Crowley nodded but didn't say anything. He carefully slotted the phone back into its case attached to his belt and began to walk along the pit lane in the direction of the paddock.

"Now we'll find out how much your husband loves you," sneered the big man.

"I know that already," said the hostage defiantly, sitting uneasily on the floor on a section of carpet that looked old and grimy.

"But we don't, do we Ivan? He needs to show us the proof."

"We don't have long to wait," laughed the accomplice. "This time tomorrow we'll have the answer."

"You can't expect my husband to deliberately interfere with a car to prevent it finishing the race. It's illegal and he wouldn't do it. I know him – he's not like that."

The shaven-headed kidnapper stood over the woman. "Let me tell you something, lady. If he doesn't obey instructions then you," he paused ominously, "are dead meat."

She started sobbing. "Oh, I hate you! Why are you doing this to us? We don't deserve it."

"Shut up, bitch. You're starting to get on my nerves. Come on, Ivan, I've had enough." And both men left the room.

Sarah shivered and pulled her denim jacket tighter, recounting in her mind the sequence of nightmarish events that had befallen her. She had no idea where she was and her estimation of the journey duration was hazy as her watch had been removed. Eventually the vehicle had come to a stop and she heard the driver get out, followed by the sound of what she assumed was a creaking gate with hinges that badly needed oiling. The driver returned and the 4×4 moved forward slowly. Soon after, the kidnapped woman became aware of a pronounced rolling movement and she detected they were travelling on what felt like an uneven track. After several minutes the ride became softer, as though the wheels were negotiating grassland, before returning to a gravel-type surface.

The vehicle had finally came to a halt and, still blindfolded, she was led across what felt like paving stones and into a building. She was immediately conscious of a mustiness assaulting her from all sides as one of the abductors grabbed her arm and told her to lower her head as they made their way inside. "Ivan, take off the blindfold," ordered the big man. His accomplice complied and Sarah gradually opened her eyes, blinking rapidly as she acclimatised to the new environment, the only source of light a heavy-duty torch wielded by the leader of the kidnappers. Sarah's heart had sunk as she studied her surroundings. The room felt damp with crumbling plaster on the thick stone walls; the ceiling appeared to be overgrown with mould and the lintel over the doorway was clearly rotting. A strip of dirty hessian cloth was hanging from a wall over what she suspected was a broken window, such was the draught. The evidence of long and crippling neglect was all around her.

Sarah's knowledge of the building's interior was restricted to the one room where she had been imprisoned for the last two days but from that limited evidence, she was in no doubt that she was being held at a derelict farmhouse in some remote location. Scraps of patterned linoleum littered the stone floor and her bed consisted of the threadbare carpet that lay on a piece of matting. The abductors' only concession to their hostage was a shabby blanket to combat the falling temperatures at night. Barely adequate supplies of food and water were provided by her captors at varying intervals but it was the lack of sanitation that had proved the most distressing aspect of her confinement. When she needed to relieve herself, she was told to call out and one of the men guarding her would escort her along a dingy stone-walled corridor to another damp, musty room that had been designated as a toilet. Sarah was handed a torch and, in a warped concession to her privacy, left alone. The first time she used the facility a rat scurried past and disappeared into the gloom on the far side of the room.

She laid down fully clothed in the dark on the makeshift bed and pulled the blanket around her. Scared, lonely and tormented by what the next day might bring, she tried to blot out the degradations inflicted on her. Images of her beloved boxer and what fate might have befallen the animal came back to haunt her. Sarah's only sustaining thought was of the man who meant everything to her but who was so out of reach when she needed him most. Eventually, the comely, doe-eyed brunette cried herself to a fitful sleep, as she had the night before.

SIXTEEN

He moved quickly in the near darkness. Although time was against him he knew precisely what he had to do. The beam from the torch, standing upright on the painted floor where he worked, pointed directly at the overhead panels housing the electrical and compressed air ducts, but it provided just enough light for his purpose. Globules of sweat rolled down his temple but despite the pressure and the furtive nature of the task, he resisted the temptation to hurry. *Above all,* he told himself, *stay calm.* Occasionally he paused to glance in the direction of the window that ran high up along one side of the workshop, although he knew it could not be accessed from outside. It was as if he was seeking reassurance that he wouldn't be disturbed but paradoxically the frisson he was experiencing, stemming from the element of uncertainty, was a spur.

He had put in an appearance at the reception hosted by the team's marketing division but after an hour had managed to slip away unnoticed, the event providing the diversion he needed. The function was one of several organised during the season at which senior executives of companies with global brands were invited to a race weekend to enjoy lavish hospitality and experience at first-hand the excitement of top-level motor racing. But they were also left in no doubt as to the potent advertising force of an FS car displaying a sponsor's logo, seen by hundreds of millions via the worldwide television audience. The quest for backers wasn't confined to just one outfit; all those camped in the paddock were competing to attract substantial finances, some to fund ongoing development, others to ensure their survival in the sport.

Joe Gorton had spent much of the evening in animated discussion with a potential big-name sponsor who indicated a sizeable amount of cash might be made available for the following season. But the prospective backer, no mean negotiator himself, was seeking contractual guarantees as to the precise positioning and size of the company's logo on the car. The owner, well versed in such matters of fine detail, was convinced an agreement was not far off. The two men agreed to meet again the next morning, the day of the race, to see if they could hammer out a deal acceptable to both. The team boss was also keen to meet other guests, some of whom had been identified as possible sponsors and had already visited the Gorton Racing headquarters in Yorkshire, where they toured the design and engineering departments and viewed a scaled-down model of next season's car being put through its paces in the wind tunnel.

Eventually the owner left the reception, held in the largest of his team's three motor homes, and headed to his office to make a phone call. A few minutes later he decided he wanted some fresh air and wandered outside. A moonlit sky illuminated a now-deserted pit lane and he walked slowly along it, contrasting the silence with the disciplined but sometimes frenetic activity seen there on race days. He knew tomorrow would be no different. Gorton Racing's mission statement was simple – *Compete to win* – and efforts both on and off the track were aimed at underpinning that philosophy. The team's mechanics had been trained to a high standard and subjected to repeated drills so when the black and green cars were called in for refuelling and a tyre change, stopping inches from the front jack man, the much-practised pit stop routine swung smoothly into action. Although the procedure had generally gone to plan in the previous ten races, there had been a couple of instances when reliability of the fuel rig and speed of tyre-changing had been an issue, and Gorton hoped there would be no repetition tomorrow.

He strolled past the El Oro and Drogan units and continued along the pit lane towards the garage housing his own team. It was late and there was no reason to stop. But as he drew level with the door that guarded the entrance he paused in his tracks. Looking up, the owner detected a faint illumination emanating from the window above. He stood there for a while pondering the source of the light. Sometimes, when a gearbox needed replacing or there was a seemingly intractable hydraulics problem, the engineers would work late. Occasionally, when a car was badly damaged in a crash in qualifying and had to be virtually rebuilt, they would work through the night until the job was completed. But Gorton was puzzled. He knew Stallard was on pole with Lockhart qualifying in P6 and both cars had been cleared for racing the next day.

It was possible the last person to leave had forgotten to turn the light off and it wouldn't matter much if it stayed that way until the morning, mused the Yorkshireman, but that ran counter to the strict disciplinary code he imposed at every level throughout the organisation that bore his name. And he liked to think he was not exempt from such standards. Moving forward a couple of paces, he noticed the sliding garage door was unlocked and ajar. Grabbing the handle he pulled it slowly towards him, caressing the door on its runners to minimise any sound that could alert an intruder. Gorton stepped inside but it took a few seconds to adjust to the dimness before his finger found the switch on the wall.

Instantly the garage was flooded with light. A figure at the far end standing beside the championship leader's car spun around.

"What the hell's going on, Jim?" rasped the owner. "What are you doing here at this time of night?"

The colour drained from Crowley's face and for a moment he said nothing as both men stared at each other. Eventually he broke the silence. "Just giving the car a final check before tomorrow. Don't want any problems during the race, do we?"

Gorton's eyes narrowed. "I was told both cars were given the all-clear late this afternoon."

"They were but you know me, Joe, I always like to double-check everything."

"But you were here in the gloom. Why didn't you put the lights on?" The race engineer shifted uneasily from side to side, glancing at a pneumatic wheel gun on a bench nearby. "No need, really. Didn't seem much point. I had the torch – that was enough."

Gorton ran a hand through his thick light-brown hair and stepped forward. "That surprises me. This place is rigged up with every conceivable device to service a racing team but you choose to work in near darkness. It doesn't make sense."

Crowley shrugged his shoulders. "I guess that's up to me."

The team boss glowered. "Not if I'm running this outfit." He was now close to Stallard's car. "What exactly were you checking?"

"I told you. I just wanted to make sure we hadn't missed anything."

"That's not good enough, Jim. I want to know what you've been doing." Gorton bent down to get a better view of the cockpit. There was no answer. "Did you hear what I said? I want—"

The sentence remained unfinished as the wheel gun crashed against the back of the owner's head. He slumped to the ground, blood starting to seep from beneath matted hair and onto his shirt collar. Crowley stood transfixed, staring at the motionless frame of his boss and then at the improvised weapon he was clutching. A chill ran down his spine but he suddenly became aware that he was also sweating profusely. He stood there, seemingly immobilised for more than a minute, agonising over the consequences of his action before the reality of the situation hit home. The engineer picked up a large piece of cloth lying on top of a tool cabinet and methodically wiped the wheel gun before putting it back on the bench. Then he walked swiftly across the garage to extinguish the main lights. Returning to Stallard's car, he glanced down at the prostrate Gorton then picked up the torch, switched it off and hurriedly left the premises.

Stallard stirred slightly but the sound continued to permeate his semi-conscious state. He turned over in an attempt to muffle the noise but the ringing was insistent. Cursing silently, he slowly roused himself and reached out to the phone on the bedside table. "Who is it?" he said drowsily.

"Nick, I'm really sorry to disturb you at this time of the morning but it's Adam here from PR."

It took the driver a moment or two to assimilate the identity of the caller. "It's race day and you've woken me up early. I hope you've got a good excuse!"

"I do apologise again but I've been instructed to call you."

"What's up, Adam?"

There was a pause at the other end of the line. "Nick, I've got bad news I'm afraid."

"What is it?"

"It's Joe. He's on his way to hospital in Moscow. Doc Manvers examined him and it looks like he's in a coma."

Stallard levered himself up to rest against the pillow, aware that his fiancée was now beginning to stir. "What happened?"

"It seems Joe was found in the garage this morning with a bad head wound. God knows how long he'd been there."

"Who found him?"

"A couple of the mechanics who were making an early start. They said the door to the garage, which is always locked overnight, was open. But Joe never carried a key – he had no need to."

"Strange," murmured Stallard. "And why would he be there at night? It doesn't make sense."

"You're right, it doesn't."

"Let's get this straight, Adam. Is it possible Joe blacked out and fell then banged his head," the driver paused, "or is there something more sinister going on here?"

"I guess you were bound to ask. It's not looking good, to be honest. The doc was called to the scene immediately and found Joe stretched out. He had a pulse but a weak one. Manvers confirmed the boss had taken a blow to the back of his head from some kind of blunt instrument."

The driver pursed his lips. "But who would want to try to kill the guy? I guess the police have been notified."

"Yes, they're due at the circuit shortly. They'll probably want to seal off the garage and take statements. I know it's got to be done but it's the last thing we need on the morning of the race."

"Say that again," said Stallard, trying to assess the implications for the team. "That's assuming Gorton Racing is still competing after what's happened. It might be in doubt now."

"I've already asked the question. I've had a word with the operations director, who's working on a press release as we speak. He feels Joe would want us to carry on regardless and not be intimidated by this incident."

"That gets my vote, too."

"You're leading the championship and the team has a good chance of winning the constructors' title, so there's a lot still to play for."

"I guess the sponsors wouldn't be too happy if we pulled out of today's race – or am I just being cynical?"

"I couldn't possibly comment. Anyway, I've got more calls to make and I expect you'll want to get moving."

"Yeah, it looks like a difficult day ahead. I'll see you at the track later."

"Sure thing, Nick. If I don't see you before, have a good race."

"Thanks, Adam." Stallard replaced the phone and

turned to look at his fiancée, who was now wide awake. "Someone tried to kill Joe last night. It sounds incredible but that's what seems to have happened."

"Oh, Nick, that's dreadful. The poor man."

"He's on his way to hospital and Manvers believes he's in a coma."

"But who would do such a thing?"

The driver shook his head. "I've no idea, Sophie. I don't understand it either."

"He was in good spirits at the reception. I know we had to leave before the end to get an early night before the race, but Joe seemed his usual self."

"He was. He was doing the rounds, pressing the flesh of potential backers. There were no signs anything was amiss."

The brunette stretched out her arms, her breasts arching upwards. "Who could possibly want to kill him?"

"That's a question we're all going to be asking. I know this can be a dog-eat-dog circus at times, but attempted murder… that's something else! And the possibility it could be someone within the team doesn't bear thinking about."

"Oh darling, it's going to be so hard for you this afternoon. Try not to let it distract you."

"Come on, girl, you know me better than that. I know I have to stay focused. I'll just have to blank it out for the duration of the race."

"But can you?"

"Don't worry. Once I'm behind the wheel of a racing car lined up on the grid, everything else fades into the background and I can concentrate on what really matters." Then his brow furrowed. "But there's likely to be a difficult few hours before that with the police crawling all over the place."

"That's inevitable, I suppose. If a crime's been committed, they've got to investigate."

"Sure, but it doesn't help during the countdown to the race."

Sophie studied his face. "I know. There's so much at stake today and this will just add to the pressure on you." She leaned towards him and ran her fingers tenderly through the hairs on his chest. "I think you need to switch off for a while and unwind. We've got time; we don't have to leave the hotel for an hour or so."

Stallard smiled at his fiancée and put an arm around her. "I think that's what I found most attractive about you when we met. You're such a caring woman and you're always there for me."

"It's important to have someone in your life you know you can rely on."

"They don't come any better than you, sweetheart. And it can't be easy for you when I'm sticking my neck on the block every two or three weeks."

"When I bought into you I knew I was buying the entire package, warts and all. You can't take all the good stuff and not the bad. I know you never want to talk about it but we both know you risk your life every time you race."

The driver looked tenderly into Sophie's eyes. "I somehow agree with the philosopher who said that to live life to the full, one has to confront one's own mortality. I know I operate in a high-risk profession but testing myself gives me fulfilment." He paused. "I'm aware the longer I'm in the car without a serious accident, the odds of having one start to shorten. But life's not just about longevity – it's about achievement as well. You've got to remember that."

She sighed. "I do, but it doesn't ease the anxiety I have when I'm watching you on the track. There's always that feeling in the pit of my stomach that doesn't disappear until the race is over."

"I realise it takes a special type of character to cope with it all. I'm a lucky guy – I made the right choice."

Sophie nestled up to the driver. "You know something? So did I." She squeezed his hand and kissed him on the side of his face. "Come on, let me help you relax, darling."

Stallard looked at his watch and sighed. "I'm sorry, Sophie, but…"

"But what?"

"I imagine all hell is breaking out in the paddock after this incident with Joe. It'll be hard enough for the team anyway without me turning up late on race day."

"Oh Nick, I was hoping we could have a little time together this morning."

"I'm really sorry but I'll make it up to you later, I promise."

"I was only thinking of you."

"You do that in spades, sweetheart. And that's why I love you and always will." He kissed her on the lips then lifted the duvet and got out of bed. Sophie watched his naked figure disappear into the bathroom then lay back on the pillow and closed her eyes.

The light drizzle that had been falling since daybreak had turned to steady rain by the time the FS championship leader reached the circuit. He counted three cars, all marked *Politsiya*, one parked next to the track opposite the main grandstand and the others in the pit lane close to the Gorton Racing garage. A police officer, standing in front of a strip of thick white tape flapping in the breeze, guarded the entrance. As Stallard drew closer, a waved hand directed him further down the pit lane, but he ignored the signal and made to duck under the tape. "Nyet! Nyet!" bellowed the policeman and the uncompromising look on his face told the driver it would be unwise to attempt to enter. The Englishman pointed at the official security pass dangling from his neck but it made no difference.

"Nick, you can't get in." He turned around on hearing a familiar voice. "The police have sealed off the garage while they investigate." The team's number two driver was walking towards him. "It's terrible what's happened to Joe," said Lockhart. "I can't believe it." Stallard could see her hazel eyes were moist and her face drawn.

"Me too. It's a hell of a shock."

"Why would anyone want to hurt him?"

"I don't know. I think everyone in the team is asking that question. D'you have the latest on his condition?"

"One of our guys phoned the hospital ten minutes ago and he's still in a coma. They wouldn't say any more than that."

"Don't suppose they're allowed to."

"It sounds bad. I just hope he pulls through."

"When was the last time time you saw him?"

"At the reception but I left before the end. He was still there then and he seemed fine."

"That was the impression I had. He was on top of his game and everything appeared to be normal."

"That's what makes it so baffling. It just doesn't make any sense, and that's what I told the police."

"So you've been interviewed already."

"Yes, when I got here this morning. They had already set up a temporary office in one of the motor homes and are questioning members of the Gorton team."

"What did they want to know?"

"Oh, the usual stuff. Where was I last night? When was the last time I saw Joe? Did I see anything suspicious? But I wasn't able to help much."

"I guess they'll be wanting to talk to me at some point."

"I'm sure they will."

Stallard gestured impatiently towards the garage. "We don't need this. If we can't get our cars out of there soon it'll badly disrupt our race preparations."

"I know that but you've got to remember Joe seems to have been the victim of a violent attack and is unconscious in hospital."

"But the decision's been taken – it's felt the owner would want us to continue as normal so we're going to race."

"I disagree. I understand the argument but I don't think we should be racing today, I feel it shows a lack of respect after what's happened."

"No, I don't think so. Besides, you have to look at the wider picture. There are drivers' and constructors' titles up for grabs and our team is in with a good chance of both. And if we can do it that would be quite a feather in the Gorton Racing cap."

A look of cynicism passed across Lockhart's face. "I hope you're not saying that because you're leading the drivers' standings."

"Come on, Kate, that's hitting below the belt. You've no grounds to say that."

"Haven't I? You've been runner-up in the championship

twice and this could be your last season with a top team. With only two races to go, you must be feeling time is running out and you can't afford to watch this one from the pit wall."

"That's a cheap shot and you know it!"

"I realise it's stating the obvious, but if you don't compete today your chances of winning the title will probably disappear – and you're not likely to be in such a strong position again."

"Well, I'm sorry to disappoint you but we're going racing and you need to get used to the idea."

"Hey, Nick!" Stallard swung around to see the team's chief mechanic approaching. "You're wanted."

"Hang on, Frank. Give me a minute." He turned to face the American, who had not been distracted by the intervention.

"Joe could be dying for all we know and yet you want to race as if nothing has happened. I don't get it."

"Look, it wasn't my decision that we compete in today's race but that's what's going to happen – and we have to get on with it."

"It's easy for you to say that but it's no secret in the paddock that you and Joe have had your disagreements this year and there's a tension between you."

"I don't deny my relationship with the owner has been strained at times but have you ever asked yourself why? It might just have something to do with the fact you're having an affair with him."

"What's it got to do with you anyway?"

"When it affects the way the team is run and my prospects for the title, it's got everything to do with me! You've cost me vital points this season but the boss always backs you – and that's no way to run an outfit like ours."

"That's ridiculous. You're being paranoid."

The Englishman glared at her. "Frankly, I don't give a damn what you think! All you need to remember is that I'll be going flat out for a win today. I know I can't count on your support but don't even think of doing anything that'll make life difficult for me. You can't say I haven't warned you!" Stallard left his colleague fuming and walked towards the chief mechanic. "What d'you want, Frank?"

"It's the police. They want to talk to you."

"Which motor home are they in?"

"The one nearest the pit lane. There's a senior officer who seems to be running the show."

The driver nodded. "Been expecting it. I'm on my way."

It took him less than a minute to reach the makeshift office housing the crime investigation team and he just caught sight of his race engineer leaving. He called out but the hurrying Crowley appeared not to hear. As Stallard entered he found two officers seated behind a large desk on which rested a number of what he assumed to be handwritten statements. Standing to one side was the stocky figure of a man in a creased and slightly soiled grey, unbuttoned raincoat.

"Mr Stallard, thank you for attending for interview. I'm Captain Nikolai Sorokin of the Investigative Directorate for the Moscow Northern Administrative District. I know this is a busy day for you and I hope I don't have to detain you for too long."

"I would appreciate it if we can finish this as quickly as possible."

"I understand, but you must be aware the owner of your team has been the victim of a brutal attack and is now gravely ill in hospital." The senior detective, a man in his late forties with receding dark hair and a moustache, stared intently at the driver. "That is attempted murder and I have a duty to investigate." He gestured the Englishman towards a chair in front of the desk. "Perhaps you can tell me where you were last night."

"I was at a reception organised by our marketing division, which was attended by a number of potential sponsors. Most of our team, including Joe, were there."

"When was the last time you saw Mr Gorton?"

"At the reception. I suppose I was there for about an hour or so but left early because I needed a decent night's rest before today's race."

"Did he seem to be acting normally?"

"Yes."

"There was nothing to indicate he might be concerned about anything, as far as you could tell?"

"No, he appeared to be his usual self." Stallard noticed one of the policemen was taking a shorthand note of his answers.

Sorokin moved closer and perched on the end of the desk. "And you didn't see him again?"

"That's right."

"Are you quite sure?"

"Of course I'm sure! Do you have any reason to doubt me?"

The detective thrust his hands deeper into his raincoat pockets and fixed the driver with an unblinking gaze. "Mr Stallard, in a case like this I doubt everyone. Now tell me, how long have you known the owner?"

"I've raced for him for the last three years but our paths crossed long before that as we've both been involved in FS for some time."

"How would you describe your relationship?"

"It's had its ups and downs but that's only to be expected as we work in a high-pressure environment that's driven by results."

"But sometimes relationships turn sour."

"They can do but I wouldn't use that word to describe it."

"No? Maybe you've got a better one."

Stallard shifted on his chair. "Look, we've had some differences of opinion from time to time but that happens in any activity, and motor racing is no exception. People in our sport often hold opposing views but it doesn't mean we can't work together."

The detective raised his thickset frame from the desk and looked directly at the Englishman. "I suggest there's more to it than that."

"I'm not sure what you're driving at."

"Aren't you? Let's be honest with each other, Mr Stallard. This has not been an easy year for you and the owner. There were arguments over team strategy after Miss Lockhart was given a racing seat. I believe you consider Mr Gorton has favoured her at your expense and there's a big question mark over your contract renewal. That's some difference of opinion, wouldn't you agree?"

The driver stood up, anger burning in his eyes. "Are you seriously suggesting I would want to kill Joe Gorton?"

"I'm not suggesting anything. I'm just stating the facts as I know them. Are you saying they're not true?"

"I don't think I need to deny anything. I've come here to assist your investigation only to find I'm accused of having motives for killing my boss. It's ludicrous!"

"I'm simply doing my job and you have to recognise that."

"Let me put you straight, Captain – if you think I'm responsible for what's happened, you're very wide of the mark. Anyway, these so-called facts about me – I'd like to know who you've been talking to."

"I'm seeing a number of people in connection with this inquiry and all interviews are conducted in confidence. Just like this one."

"If Kate Lockhart has been dishing the dirt on me then I urge you to ignore her. There's something you should know: that woman is Gorton's mistress and she has an axe to grind. We don't get on. End of story!"

The detective shrugged his shoulders in a gesture of indifference. "If people have affairs that's not my business, Mr Stallard. I have only one objective and that's to find the person responsible for the vicious assault on Mr Gorton."

"If you're looking in my direction, you're wasting your time."

"Perhaps you ought to let me be the judge of that." The Russian pointed at several files on the desk. "As you can see, this investigation is still in its early stages and could last some time. I've asked other members of the Gorton team to make themselves available for possible further questioning in the next day or two and I would appreciate it if you would do the same."

"I had planned to return to the UK after the race. The flight from Domodedovo is booked for tonight."

"I think it would be better for all concerned if you cancelled your flight and stayed in the Moscow area until such time as—"

"Until when?" butted in Stallard. "How long have you got in mind?"

"We have to assimilate all the evidence so I can't give

you a definitive answer, but I can assure you this case has priority."

"It sounds like I don't have much choice."

"It depends how you look at it, I suppose." Sorokin took three or four steps away from the desk then turned around to face the driver. "But before you go, there is something you might be able to help me with."

The driver eyed the officer with suspicion. "What's that?"

"Did you see Mr Crowley at the reception last night?"

"Yes, of course he was there."

"Do you recall when he left the event?"

"Frankly, I don't, but that's not surprising as there were lots of people milling around. Why d'you ask?"

"That's my job, Mr Stallard, to ask questions. Thank you for your time. You can go now."

SEVENTEEN

The Russian's grip on the printed email tightened as he read it. He started to shake his head and his brown eyes blazed in contempt. Then he swore and screwed up the piece of paper, the faded two-inch scar on the back of his right hand becoming raised and more prominent for an instant, and hurled the mangled printout across his desk and onto the floor of the motor home. "The guy's a clown!" Makarov glanced up at Igor Smirnov, Petrenko's race engineer, who was standing on the other side of the desk. "Tait wants to waste his own time and everyone else's, including mine."

The engineer appeared puzzled and asked the obvious question.

"He's decided to conduct his own inquiry into Guiscard's murder. It seems our dear leader thinks the police investigation in South Africa has stalled. He's instructed his bootlicker, Wyatt, to talk to all the team owners and expects full co-operation from everyone."

"What does he expect to gain by that?"

"That's what I'm beginning to ask myself." The team boss lifted his feet somewhat ponderously from the top of the desk where they had been lounging and tucked them under his chair. "Let the police get on with their job and leave us to do ours. There's no need for him to get involved."

"It's been a while since it happened," said Smirnov. "If there was a breakthrough in the case they would have announced it by now."

"That's the point. The police have access to all the evidence and forensic stuff and if they can't solve it, how the hell does Tait think taking statements from the owners is going to help?"

"I suppose he's frustrated that no one's been charged with the killing and after all the adverse publicity for the sport he wants to be seen to be doing something."

"It sounds like you have some sympathy for the guy."

The engineer shifted uneasily from one foot to the other. "No, boss, I was just trying to be open-minded. We've been getting a bad press this season after all that's happened so I suppose Tait is trying to show FS in a better light."

The owner stared darkly at his employee. "You don't need to trouble yourself with the wider picture – that's not in your job description. I want you to concentrate all your efforts on making sure your man wins the drivers' title in his rookie year. Nothing more, nothing less!"

The engineer nodded but said nothing.

"I don't need to remind you, Smirnov, that your future with this team depends on it."

"I get the message."

"Good." Makarov picked up a paperweight lying on the desk and idly turned it over in his hand. "Now, the race starts in less than three hours. I trust there are no last-minute issues with Petrenko's car."

"No, we've done all the checks and everything is in order."

"It's a shame he's not on pole, especially at his home circuit."

"I agree, but you've got to hand it to the Englishman – he produced an amazing lap at the end of qualifying and there was no time for Yuri to go out again. But he's starting from P3 so is well placed to attack the leaders."

The owner looked out of the motor home window and saw it was still raining. "It looks like the weather is going to be a factor today. We've got to make sure we get our strategy right. I don't want any problems."

"The latest forecast we've had indicates it's likely to stay wet for most of the race but it could ease off towards the latter stages."

"We must stay alert for any change in conditions and react quickly. We can't afford to be caught off guard. There's too much at stake."

"The guys know the score. They won't let you down. And Yuri has shown he can drive in the wet – he's got the skills to do it."

"Why d'you think I wanted him to race for me?" asked the owner smugly. "Petrenko's young but it was obvious from the start he had great potential. It's hard to believe this is still his rookie season but he's demonstrated an all-round ability on any kind of track. He's developed beyond—" He faltered mid-sentence as the phone on the desk burst into life then leant forward. "Makarov."

Smirnov watched and thought he detected his boss tensing.

"What d'you want?" he snapped as his free hand rolled the paperweight to and fro in an agitated manner. "You're not giving me much notice. You must realise it's race day and I'm busy."

The team owner exchanged glances with the engineer and his facial expression told Smirnov all he needed to know. "OK, I'll spare you twenty minutes but, frankly, I think it's a pointless exercise and won't lead anywhere." Makarov slammed the phone down and repeatedly tossed the paperweight between both hands. "Wyatt!" The Russian spat the name contemptuously. "The guy who's doing Tait's dirty work. He's insisting on seeing me now – today of all days! If he reckons he's going to get anything useful out of me he can think again." He stood up and motioned to Smirnov. "He's on his way. You get back to the garage and prepare for the race. I'll join you as soon as I've dealt with Wyatt."

The mastermind of Russia's most competitive motor racing outfit paced his office with a symmetry of step and the rhythmic regularity of a big cat confined to its cage. In other spheres of his life Viktor Makarov yielded to no one yet, paradoxically, participation in the ego-strutting world of FS involved the need for compliance with a system of regulation imposed from above. At first it was something he found irritating but as the season wore on, a smouldering resentment had turned to downright embitterment. Now, the man who governed the sport – and the target of the Russian's ire – was acting like a dictator in issuing a decree that all team owners would be questioned about a murder that was already the subject of a police investigation. Makarov looked at his watch and cursed, his vexation worsening as Tait's intermediary appeared to be keeping him waiting. Just five more minutes, he vowed, and then

Wyatt would have to grovel for an appointment another time.

As the Russian stared bleakly out of the window the phone rang. "Yes." As he listened to the caller, he checked his watch again. "Show him in." He replaced the receiver and sat down behind the desk.

The door opened and one of the owner's assistants entered, muttered, "Mr Wyatt is here," and left the room. Makarov said nothing and stayed in his seat as the tall American walked slowly towards him. The Russian ignored the outstretched hand and instead gestured his visitor to a nearby chair.

"I appreciate you taking the time to see me, Mr Makarov."

"Let's get one thing straight, Wyatt. I didn't ask you to come and I don't want you here. I think Tait should have better things to do."

"Maybe I should outline what I've been asked to do and then we can move on from there."

"You don't need to explain. I know why you're here. You've been hired to do another grubby job for your employer."

Wyatt ignored the taunt. "I'm sure I don't need to remind you that all team owners have been asked to co-operate with this inquiry and it would be appreciated if you would assist us."

"It's a farce! Why is Tait meddling like this? He's got no authority to run a criminal investigation and should stay out of it."

"He's got every authority. Lucas is the head of FS and the commercial rights holder. So when one of the world's best drivers is murdered soon after winning a race and the police fail to make an arrest, I think he's entitled to ask a few questions."

"You can say what you like but I still think he's got no right to interfere."

The Californian struggled to conceal a burgeoning impatience. "I'm only gonna say this once, Mr Makarov, and you need to listen. After you signed your FS contract you probably put it away someplace safe and forgot about it. Now, there was a clause in it that your lawyer would have drawn your attention to but you're a busy man and since then you've probably not given it much thought."

"What are you talking about?"

"Clause number twelve, section one A, to be precise."

The Russian looked blankly at Wyatt, who was unfolding a piece of paper pulled from inside his jacket.

"You know what those legal eagles are like once they start drawing up contracts – it's gobbledygook to most of us, but for your benefit let me summarise that particular section. And I'll put it in plain language so there's no room for doubt. In any dispute between a team owner and FS, where agreement between the parties is not possible and the dispute has lasted more than twenty-eight days, the commercial rights holder is deemed to be the ultimate arbiter." Wyatt, a half-smile on his lips, glanced up at the man opposite him. "In any language, I reckon that means you don't have a leg to stand on."

Makarov's face darkened, a fluttering vein at the side of his temple suddenly obtrusive. "You wouldn't be trying to blackmail me by any chance?"

"The thought never crossed my mind."

"Let me give you some advice, Wyatt – don't even think about it!"

"You know something, Viktor – if I can call you Viktor? – I'm only pointing out that contracts can sometimes come back to bite people when they least expect it."

"And there's something you should know: I don't usually deal in contracts. I find them – how shall I put it? – unnecessary most of the time. The only reason I signed this one was to gain access to FS and to everything that came with it. I saw it as joining an exclusive club and if it meant putting my signature on a few forms, what the hell!"

Wyatt eased his muscular frame into the chair. "I think you just put your finger on it. You joined a club that provides many benefits but it also has certain rules. It's a two-way process – members enjoy the one but they have to abide by the other. The commercial rights holder feels he's justified in calling on the owners to state their views and provide any information they might have that could help the police solve a murder of one of our own."

"I'm not convinced. I think it's just a distraction and won't lead anywhere."

"But it may throw up something that sheds new light on the circumstances surrounding the death."

"It's still not going to bring Guiscard back to life."

"But it could nail his killer and that would give the family some measure of justice." Wyatt produced an envelope and placed it on the desk, his eyes engaging the Russian. "Lucas has drawn up a questionnaire, which I'm going to leave with you. It's straightforward and you shouldn't have any problem completing it."

Makarov fingered his pockmarked face and stared sullenly at the American. "There's something about you, Wyatt, that's been bugging me."

"And what would that be?"

"I don't know – and that's what bothers me. You turned up one day out of the blue and then Tait announces you've been hired but I'm not sure what it is you do."

"I thought he made it clear what my role is."

"Something about being a troubleshooter, but that can mean anything."

"You sound suspicious."

"Maybe I am."

"Are you questioning my appointment?"

"It wasn't something we were expecting."

Wyatt got to his feet. "Life can be full of surprises, Viktor."

The Russian was not amused. "Some are worse than others."

"Don't leave that questionnaire for too long – we're interested in your response. I'll see myself out."

"Before you go, Wyatt, there's something that intrigues me. Now you're on the FS payroll, what is Tait expecting from you in return?"

"All you need to know is that a contract's a contract." As he reached the door, the American turned to face the owner. "By the way, I signed mine and intend to honour it."

Nick Stallard pulled his visor down and gave the thumbs-up to the mechanics gathered around his car at the front of the grid. The sign was intended as much to boost their morale as indicate all was well in the cockpit in a week that had left the team's owner fighting for his life and police searching for his attacker. Despite the ensuing turmoil and the burden of accusations directed at him by the investigating detective, the driver was determined to blank it out and focus entirely on a race that was potentially the most challenging on the FS circuit. Forty-five laps of an untried track measuring 4.5 miles lay ahead at a total distance of over 200 miles.

The Gorton garage had opted to start their drivers on wet-weather tyres as the rain continued to fall, although not as intensely as before. The latest forecast indicated drier weather was on the way although estimates about timings varied, and contingency plans had been drawn up for an early pit stop to switch to intermediates when conditions improved. The unpredictability of the climate was a factor the teams – despite all the high-precision technology at their disposal – were unable to control, but for the lower-ranked entries it sometimes levelled the playing field and provided opportunities to surprise their more illustrious opponents.

As the mechanics wheeled away the grid trolleys, the Englishman looked across and slightly behind him and saw the P2 car in the gold and blue colours of El Oro Racing. Rodriguez, his main rival for the championship and just a single point adrift in the rankings, was looking straight ahead. A glance in his rear-view mirror confirmed Petrenko, trailing the leader by nine points and the only other driver with a chance of taking the title, was lined up directly behind in the P3 slot. The Gorton driver's thoughts turned briefly to the plight of his boss, the same man who had accused him of lacking the passion needed to win the sport's ultimate prize when finishing runner-up at the end of the previous season. He would dearly love to prove the owner and other critics wrong and this could be his last realistic chance to do so.

Seconds later came the signal to begin the warm-up lap and Stallard led a procession of cars off the grid, their throaty, high-revving V10 racing engines sending a cacophony of sound swirling over the thousands of spectators sitting in the main grandstand. As he swerved the Gorton from side to side in an attempt to put some heat into the tyres to increase traction, he observed small pools of water accumulating on various parts of the track, despite previous efforts to clear them. Minutes later and all twelve cars were lined up in their qualifying positions, with their drivers staring intently at the big starting light suspended above them. They included the Russian Alexandr Orlovsky, who was returning to competition after being badly injured in the fourth race of the season in Kowloon. Few were surprised that after such a lengthy absence he had been the slowest in qualifying and was starting in P12.

Light rain was still falling from a leaden sky as red turned to green, engines began to shriek and tyres struggled for grip on the wet surface. Stallard made a smooth start and maintained his lead during the short sprint to the first corner, a slow left-hander that gradually unwound onto a quick section, followed by a sweeping left and right leading to a hairpin. At the end of three laps the Englishman had pulled out a half-second lead on his two main rivals, who were paying the price for starting the race on intermediates. The first signs of consternation were becoming evident amongst the El Oro and Makarov team officials on the pit wall as they alternated between monitoring printouts on the updated weather predictions and looking skywards for any changes.

Next in line were the Indian driver, Pavani, in the second El Oro car, followed by the Chinese driver, Wang, in one of the Setons – both on intermediates – and they were coming under increasing pressure from Kate Lockhart in P6 in the other Gorton, who, like Stallard, had the advantage of wet-weather tyres. The remaining six cars in the race had also opted for the full wets. All drivers, with the exception of the leader, were having to deal with a visibility problem from the tidal wave of spray created by the cars in front, as well as struggling to maintain control in the wet.

Inevitably, it was Stallard, with a clear track ahead of him, who had the first indication the rain had stopped. By this time, on lap 7, he had extended his lead to almost two seconds as he exploited his early race advantage. But as the track started to dry out, aided by a strengthening breeze, his nearest pursuers, both on inters, started to reel in the Gorton driver. The gap lessened dramatically as Rodriguez and Petrenko, spurred on by the changing track conditions, saw their chance to hit back. But the pair had to exercise a degree of caution; as the racing line dried out and their grip improved, the road on either side was still wet and they knew any misjudgment in overtaking could send them spinning off the track.

By lap 11 the Spaniard was crawling all over the back of the Gorton and just waiting to choose his moment to attack. It came after Stallard exited the hairpin and a long straight beckoned. Rodriguez had picked his spot a couple of laps earlier but now he was close enough to make the manoeuvre stick. Upshifting through the gears and at a speed approaching 155 miles per hour, he pulled out and drew alongside him, placing his car as close to Stallard's as he dared. The Englishman saw him coming but was powerless to do anything about it. Raffa went past, followed almost immediately by the Russian. By now the

Englishman's tyres were shot and he had to use the wet side of the track to try to cool them. It was no surprise that Pavani and Wang, also on tyres better suited to the rapidly changing circumstances, overtook the Gorton soon after.

"I'm coming in this lap. My tyres have gone," Stallard radioed his garage. "What's the latest forecast?"

"Staying overcast but the rain seems to be dying out," replied Crowley. "We'll put the inters on."

"It's stopped already," snapped the driver. "I think we ought to go with the dry-weather slicks."

"It's probably too soon for that. Let's try the inters and we can change again when the track's fully dried out."

"But that'll mean another pit stop and more lost time. I want the slicks on when I come in."

"It's a gamble," warned the engineer.

"You can blame me if it goes wrong but if we do the unexpected it could give us the upper hand. And I'll take on some fuel at the same time."

A minute later the Gorton driver turned into the pit lane and activated the electronic limiter, cutting his speed to 55 miles per hour at the entry point before slowing as the chief mechanic waved him in with the lollipop sign to the marked line outside his garage. The front and rear jack men lifted the car off the ground and the pit crew leapt into action. Three mechanics were at each wheel, one operating the air gun whilst another took the old wheel off and a third put the new one on. Then the air gun went in again to complete the process. A spare man cleared out the radiator ducts and cleaned Stallard's visor as the refueller pulled the delivery nozzle out of the fuel tank without incident.

The driver was poised to go, awaiting the signal from the chief mechanic – but it didn't come. The Englishman must have been stationary for at least five seconds and they still wouldn't release him. Then a glance in his mirror told him there was a problem with the offside rear wheel. He saw the air gun had jammed and a mechanic hurl it to the ground. A replacement was quickly in place and the wheel secured but the glitch had cost Stallard precious time. When the lollipop man finally waved the frustrated driver away, the pit stop had lasted over ten seconds – more than twice as long as that routinely taken in practice. Despite his anger at the delay, Stallard told himself he had to stay focused and not exceed the speed limit as he drove down the pit lane – the last thing he needed was a drive-through penalty. Crossing the exit line, he released the speed-limiter button and the Gorton devoured the remaining 100 yards before re-joining the track in P6.

The Spaniard was leading the race, closely followed by the Russian, with the Indian next and the Chinese driver in P4. All four were still racing on inters and not expected to pit for a change of tyre for several more laps. Lockhart, still struggling on wet-weather tyres, was called into pit on the next lap and was equipped with inters as her team was not yet convinced conditions demanded slicks. Knowing he was now on dry-weather tyres, Stallard knew he had to proceed cautiously at first to see how the car reacted to the changed rubber underneath him, but as the track continued to dry, he felt confident the pendulum would swing in his direction as the race wore on.

The Gorton's early lap times were not fast enough to make an impact on the leaders but by lap 15 there was a discernible improvement as the racing line widened and the slicks started to grip the rapidly drying road. Conversely, those drivers on inters found they were unable to maintain their earlier pace; it was a marginal drop-off at first but soon becoming more pronounced. As Stallard emerged from the final chicane and onto the start-finish straight he closed right up on the back of the car in the all-green colours of Seton Racing. Wang saw him in his mirror at the last moment and although he moved across slightly to try to deter the Gorton driver, it was only delaying the inevitable. Stallard, now with much better grip and his car well balanced, sped past the Chinese in front of the main grandstand and by the end of the straight had also caught and overtaken Pavani.

Fired up by the relative ease with which he had gained two places and put in a fastest lap, the Englishman targeted the next man in his path, Petrenko. The Russian had stayed close to Rodriguez from the start and had never trailed him by more than half a second. Both drivers had been warned over the garage-to-car radio of Stallard's impending arrival but their teams had yet to decide when to bring them in to put on tyres better suited to the changing conditions. On lap 18, at the approach to the sweeping right-hander that led to the hairpin, he had closed the gap to the rookie to less than a car's length. The Gorton driver attempted to dive down the inside but the Russian squeezed him to the side of the track, which was still damp. Stallard's car twitched and started to spin but he regained control, although was forced to yield position through the corner. Exiting the right-hander in close formation, the pair headed towards the hairpin with Rodriguez leading them by three-tenths of a second. The Englishman needed no reminder of Petrenko's reputation for ruthlessness when under pressure and was content to follow him through the corner and wait for the long straight that lay ahead. As he stalked the car in the glaring purple and orange colours of Makarov Racing, downshifting to first gear and braking to around 45 miles per hour for the tight left turn, he could see the deteriorating state of the Russian's rear tyres and knew he was vulnerable to a pass. Once through the corner, both men accelerated hard as the straight opened up. Stallard had noted on the two previous laps that one side of the racing line appeared to be drying faster than the other and that was the one he would aim for.

Now in sixth gear and travelling at 160 miles per hour, the Gorton driver feigned to go left and Petrenko reacted swiftly by trying to block the move. Prepared for such a response, Stallard immediately swung right and drew alongside with his two outer wheels almost touching the verge that lined the track. But as he fought to stay on the road, knowing that if his tyres ran over the wet grass it would hurl the car into a violent spin, he suddenly felt a vibration in the Gorton's steering. It was the faintest of movements and fleeting, but it surprised him. Instantly, he re-focused on passing Petrenko, expecting another attempt to push the Gorton off the track, but it didn't happen and Stallard pulled clear of the rookie.

Now the current championship leader had the El Oro car clearly in his sights as he slipped into seventh gear at 175 miles per hour and the rev counter continued to climb. The Englishman, who had been haunted for years by claims he lacked a killer instinct and was aware he had to take more risks to win the title, swore this time he would prove his critics wrong. He slipstreamed Rodriguez for 200 metres before darting to the right. The Spaniard moved across to cut off the manoeuvre and Stallard was forced to go even closer to the grass to draw level. They reached the end of the straight where the track veered to the right and the cars, with Stallard slightly ahead, entered a forested area. But Rodriguez knew his tyres were no match for that of his rival and having made one blocking attempt, he saw Stallard pull clear and accelerate into the tree-lined section of the circuit.

Flooring the throttle and almost at full revs, the Gorton driver steadied himself for the uneven patches of track that were a feature of the ride through the woods. He was surprised to feel another vibration in the steering but assumed it was due to the road surface. He was unnerved when it happened again a few seconds later, but this time it was more marked. The race leader took a tighter grip on the wheel as it began to judder violently. A loud cracking sound followed, audible despite the noise in the cockpit, and he feared the worst. Piloting a car at over 190 miles per hour, Stallard was horrified to discover he was just a passenger with no control over its direction of travel. He braked hard ahead of a right-hand curve that was looming and had cut his speed to close to 140 when the Gorton went straight on, hurtling across a muddy area of woodland before ploughing head-on into a tree and slamming sideways into another. The violent impact crushed the nose of the car and tore off both front wheels, one of them flying through the air and striking Stallard's helmet before rolling into the undergrowth. The chassis was split by the force of the crash and the steering wheel, with a severed length of the column attached, dangled forlornly over the side of the car. As the wreckage rebounded and came to a halt, a shower of spray was dislodged from the rain-sodden branches above and cascaded onto the driver, who was not moving.

From his vantage point close behind, Rodriguez witnessed a black and green blur leave the track at speed but lost sight of it as he negotiated the corner that was soon upon him. He assumed from what he had seen that a major mechanical failure had sent the Gorton careering into the woods and radioed his garage to report the incident. Thirty seconds later, double-waved yellow flags were shown to drivers approaching the forested area, telling them to slow down and be ready to take evasive action, including stopping if necessary. It took the nearest marshals a couple of minutes to reach the crash scene, which was located at a remote part of the circuit, and they immediately called for the safety car to be scrambled.

Another ninety seconds elapsed before the FS medical director and two paramedics reached the lump of mangled metal – all that remained of the Gorton. Stallard was motionless in the wrecked cockpit with his head slumped to one side. As the paramedics supported the driver's back, Rick Manvers removed the helmet and fireproof balaclava. Stallard's eyes were closed and blood and other matter was oozing from his nose. The doctor felt for a pulse but there was none. He raised the Englishman's eyelids but the pupils did not react and there was no response to any kind of stimulation. Manvers knew immediately that the driver had suffered a massive brain injury but also suspected a broken neck had killed him instantly.

The medical team released the lap and shoulder belts and slowly lifted the driver out of the car and laid him gently on the ground before summoning an ambulance to transport the body back to the paddock. Whilst he waited by the wrecked car, Manvers spoke to Lucas Tait. "I'm afraid we've lost another one. It's Stallard this time."

"Oh my God! Are you certain?"

"Absolutely. There was nothing we could do for him. Looks like a broken neck but he also suffered major brain damage, which would probably have been fatal."

"How did it happen?"

"The car left the track in the forested section and smashed into a couple of trees, judging by the signs of impact. But what caused it to veer off the road is a mystery at this point."

"Shit. And there's no catch fencing or any type of tyre barrier along that stretch. I should have insisted on putting something there but the organisers were already way behind schedule."

"I reckon that's your department, Lucas, but it's too late for Stallard. I know his fiancée is at the race today and someone will have to break the news to her."

Tait sighed dejectedly. "I guess that's down to me now that Joe's not around to do it but it ain't gonna be easy."

"Never is."

As he talked, the FS supremo's mind was already moving up a gear and focusing on the immediate implications of the fatal crash. "They're all in position behind the safety car at the moment but we've got to get Stallard back here – that takes priority."

"The ambulance should be here soon."

"Good. I'll stop the race so there's no problem with traffic. Then once he's back at the medical centre we can make the re-start."

"I expect his fiancée will want to see him as he is."

"Yeah, I know. It's gonna be tough for her."

"Is there anyone who can look after her?"

"I don't know but there are a couple of drivers' wives

hanging around the paddock – I'm sure they'll do their best to comfort her. Then we'll have to make plans to get her back to England."

"It would make sense to get her away from the circuit as soon as possible. Anyway, the ambulance has just arrived. I'll see you later."

"Sure."

Twenty-seven minutes after the crash that claimed the life of the current championship leader, the race re-started. Reacting to the fast-changing conditions, all the teams opted for dry-weather tyres for a contest that had been reduced to twenty-five laps. The drivers, who had to concentrate anew and try to insulate their minds from the fatality, lined up on the grid according to their positions when the race was stopped, with the Spanish aristocrat at the head of the field. The dash to the first corner, a slow left turn, passed without incident and Rodriguez emerged from it with Petrenko hard on his heels, followed by Pavani, Wang, Lockhart and Seton.

As the race developed the front-runners put some space between themselves and the next four cars, which struggled to stay in touch. The Spaniard, setting a blistering place, registered a new lap record only to create another one soon after and gradually pulled away from his Russian rival. Every time he passed the spot where he had seen Stallard's Gorton spear off the track and into the woods, Rodriguez mentally blotted out the stark image and stayed totally focused. He didn't know it at the time, but the grim mental picture would come back to haunt him in the early hours as he sought in vain to find the solace of sleep. A glance in the mirrors confirmed the radio message from his team on the pit wall that Petrenko was trailing by half a second, although he knew the Russian still posed a major threat and would take advantage of the slightest mistake. As the race wore on Rodriguez noticed his front tyres were wearing badly and knew he would have to pit for replacements earlier than planned. Gambling that his rivals would also need to put on fresh rubber before the end of the race, the El Oro driver radioed his team to say he would be coming in on the next lap. The stop was not as well executed as normal and he lost vital seconds before rejoining the track in P7, but steadily gained places as other drivers diverted into the pit lane.

The Spaniard regained his earlier lightning pace and, moving to P2, found himself twenty-one seconds behind Petrenko, who had yet to pit. Both teams were well aware that the level of competence displayed by the Russian's mechanics during the pit stop could be critical to the result. Raffa's audio receiver burst into life and he got the message he was waiting for. His race engineer was suitably laconic. "He's coming in this lap. Now go!"

Rodriguez had been driving at nine-tenths – almost on the limit of the ability of the car and himself – for most of the time but now he sought to squeeze the last ounce of power from the three-litre V10 engine howling behind him. Makarov Racing had calculated its driver had built up a sufficient lead to ensure they could bring him in for a tyre change and get him out again still in front of the pack. The young rookie duly came to a halt in an inch-perfect demonstration of pit stop parking and the mechanics swooped on his car. They worked as one, proficiently and silently, in a display they hoped would impress their demanding team owner, watching from his elevated perch on the pit wall. In a tad under four seconds, the driver was heading down the pit lane as many eyes focused on the monitors to determine the precise location of the Spaniard.

Exiting the final chicane and emerging onto the start-finish straight, Rodriguez floored the throttle, knowing his chief adversary had just completed his pit stop. The Spaniard found sixth gear and his gold and blue machine flashed past the main grandstand at 165 miles per hour, still accelerating. Petrenko de-activated the electronic limiter as he crossed the white line marking the pit lane exit and thrust his car towards the track entry point 200 metres away, a strident voice over the garage-to-car radio warning him of the fast-approaching El Oro. The Russian re-joined the track from the right at over 130 miles per hour as Rodriguez, now just 150 metres behind and on the racing line, was starting to brake hard for the first corner, a slow left-hander. The car in the purple and orange livery of Makarov Racing started to move across from the side to the centre of the track, forcing the Spaniard to take evasive action and point his car to the left. Both men neared the bend having cut their speed to under 70 miles per hour, but Petrenko had the better line and nosed ahead, although clipping the kerb on the apex and running slightly wide. As he tried to recover, Rodriguez dived down the inside channel and edged ahead, maintaining his advantage as they exited the turn.

Despite the best efforts of his pit crew, the Russian found himself once more in P2 and staring at the exhaust pipe of the Spanish car with seven laps to go. Two seconds adrift of the leaders and locked in their own battle were

Pavani, Wang and Lockhart, with the American swarming all over the back of the Chinese driver in a fight for P4. At the front Rodriguez pressed on, foot hard to the floor, in an attempt to put some daylight between himself and his arch-rival, but Petrenko clung to him like a shadow in the sun.

Meanwhile, the Spaniard's punishing pace was setting off alarm bells in the El Oro camp. The engineers monitoring the stream of data from the telemetry readouts started to voice their concern about oil pressure levels and signs the engine might be overheating. "Raffa, you need to short-shift and lower the revs," was the radioed instruction. "Go easy on the engine – you've got to make it last."

The driver uttered a curt acknowledgment but sacrificing performance in a bid to get his car to the finish line was not a prospect he relished with the Russian looming large in his mirrors. With just three laps remaining, he vowed to press on and take his chances on engine reliability.

Unaware of the unfolding drama ahead of him, Petrenko was relentless in pursuit, hoping that constant harassment would produce an error from the Spaniard. As both drivers emerged from the wooded section on the penultimate lap, the rookie had his first indication the leader was in trouble. A wispy trail of smoke from the rear of the El Oro engine was followed by a plume escaping from the left-hand side of the V10 power unit. Within seconds, the Russian was forced to brake hard and swing his car wide as a blanket of smoke leapt into the air. Rodriguez could only curse his luck as he pulled over to the side of the track, flames shooting from the blown engine, and came to a halt. He quickly freed himself from the cockpit and two race marshals were soon on the scene to extinguish the fire whilst their colleagues waved yellow flags to warn drivers to slow down and be prepared to stop if needed. But the Spaniard's evasive action had minimised the effects of oil leaking onto the track and Race Control decided not to activate the safety car.

With victory in his sights and comfortably ahead of Pavani in P2, Petrenko was urged by his race engineer not to take any risks on the last lap and the rookie brought his car home to take the chequered flag in an unexpected win for Makarov Racing. The battle for the final place on the podium was won by Lockhart in the Gorton after a race-long duel with Wang of Seton Racing, but the American left it late to establish supremacy. She nosed ahead of the Chinese driver, whose tyres had degraded badly, as the pair emerged from the last chicane and stayed there until the start-finish line. Dan Seton, in the other Seton car, claimed P5 and the Brazilian, Ricardo Gonzalez, in the Akron, took the last scoring position in P6.

Later, as the eleven FS drivers pondered the seismic event that had cruelly ended the life of one of their own, they reflected with some irony that their former rival was still heading the championship table, albeit posthumously. After eleven races and with just the Moroccan event remaining, Stallard had accumulated forty-six points, one more than Rodriguez. Petrenko, in his rookie season, had forty-three, with the murdered Frenchman, Guiscard, fourth in the standings on twenty-eight. Pavani was next on twenty-four with Lockhart in sixth position on seventeen.

EIGHTEEN

It was a sombre-looking FS boss who sat in his motor home, the fingers of his left hand drumming the desk in a staccato rhythm. He had thought about heading down the pit lane to the Gorton garage to talk to Stallard's fiancée but, on reflection, realised she would need privacy in the minutes after being told the grim news. As he waited for a Gorton Racing official to bring her to his office, he recalled the previous times he had had to perform the onerous duty. Experience had taught him it never got any easier. Whatever the circumstances of a fatality, trying to explain it to a loved one of a dead driver demanded tact and sensitivity and he always found such episodes emotionally draining, as if, by the nature of the business he controlled, he was in some way responsible.

Tait's train of thought was cut short by a knock on the door. He leapt to his feet and as he hurried to open it, an agitated Sophie Hurst rushed into the room. "Where's Nick? What's happened to him? They say he's had an accident but they won't tell me anything."

The FS impresario took one of her hands in his and squeezed it gently. "Sophie, let me try to help you."

"Please, just tell me what's happened – that's all I want to know."

"I'm afraid the incident was a bad one." He paused, detecting a sudden susceptibility in her deep brown eyes.

"But Nick's alright though, surely? Tell me he's not seriously hurt, tell me!"

"It was a big crash and—"

"What d'you mean?"

"I'm sorry, Sophie, but he didn't make it. No one could have survived it."

"Oh my God! Say it's not true! It can't be!"

The brunette, weeping and utterly distraught, slumped into Tait's arms. He held her close and stayed silent as Sophie's body convulsed with her sobbing. Eventually, the emotional spasms grew less frequent and she was able to catch her breath. She looked appealingly into Tait's eyes, seeking the assurance she craved. "Did he suffer?"

"No, he wouldn't have felt anything. It was that sort of accident."

"Are you sure?"

Tait nodded benignly. "Yes, I'm sure."

"I couldn't bear it if…" She stopped as the tears came again.

"Don't upset yourself, Sophie. From what I've been told, it would have been over in an instant. There would have been no pain."

"I hate myself for saying this," she sobbed, "but if it was going to happen, it was better this way."

Tait hugged her reassuringly and nodded but said nothing.

"I know he wouldn't have wanted to be in a wheelchair for the rest of his life. For him that would have been a fate worse than death." Sophie pulled away from the American, the tears coursing down her face. "Nick would never talk about it but he knew the risks. Every time he got in the car, he was aware he was putting his life on the line."

"I guess all drivers think about it at some time but they can't dwell on it or they would never do their job."

"It's strange but this morning, almost the last thing he said to me, he quoted Sartre and that to live life to the full, one has to face up to one's own mortality. Nick also said life wasn't just about its span but what you can achieve in the time you have. It's odd when I think about it now but it seems almost prophetic."

Tait swallowed hard. "It must look that way to you. What I do know is that Nick not only achieved a hell of a lot in his chosen career but he was also a nice guy, and they tend to be in short supply in this business."

For the first time the grief-stricken advertising executive allowed herself a glimmer of a smile. "Nice of you to say so, Lucas. He was so kind and caring to me and I know he would have been…" She faltered and he looked at her with compassion.

"Yes, Sophie?"

Her eyes filled again. "He would have been a loving father, too."

For a moment Tait appeared puzzled then grasped the inference. "Did he know?"

"Yes, I told him a while ago and I'm glad now that I did – it was the least he deserved. But it's so sad he won't be around to…" Her voice fell away again.

"I'm really sorry, it makes it that much harder for you."

"It does but it also means I'll have a part of Nick that's always going to be with me – and that's special."

The two looked at each other, no words needed. The silence was broken by the ringing of the phone. Tait walked across to the desk. "Who is it?" He listened then his brow furrowed and his body began to tense. "When did it happen?" Another pause. "This is going to put the cat among the pigeons." The American realised an explanation was required. "It's just a phrase we use when something is likely to stir up a pile of trouble." He listened again. "Don't worry. I'll make sure you have access to those on your list." Tait put the phone down and turned back to Sophie. "A bad day just got a whole lot worse. That was the Russian cop investigating the attack on the boss of Gorton Racing. It seems Joe died an hour ago. He never regained consciousness."

The sky had looked threatening for much of the morning and shortly after midday the dark clouds finally unleashed their watery contents over a substantial area of the South Downs in southern England. Undeterred, the two ramblers, more than adequately equipped for the conditions, reached into their rucksacks, donned their waterproofs and resumed their hike. They had made steady progress and were nearing the halfway point of their planned ten-mile route across the rolling chalk downland, encountering a solitary horse rider on one of the bridleways that crossed their path. The Lingards, both in their late sixties, were retired but a lifetime of rambling had helped maintain a good level of fitness and they were confident they'd complete the trek before dusk. But as the rain intensified they decided to seek shelter. A study of their map with its laminated cover indicated a farm located about a mile and a half away and the couple set off towards it. Despite the increasingly wet conditions, they boosted their spirits with the knowledge a packed lunch and a hot drink would be the reward on reaching their destination.

The range of chalk hills, an area of outstanding beauty, was starting to become enveloped in patches of mist and John Lingard consulted his compass to confirm they were still heading in the right direction. The couple pressed on and an hour later, peering through his binoculars, the former naval officer spotted their target. Drawing near, they could see a farmhouse and a number of outbuildings that appeared to be derelict. Evidence of neglect was palpable with rotting timber, missing roof tiles and the rusted skeleton of a tractor in a yard overgrown with weeds. But the ramblers were relieved to have found a temporary refuge from the driving rain. Lingard pushed at a partly opened door with faded green paint peeling off it, which groaned under duress as he stepped inside what he presumed had once been the focal point of farmhouse living, the large kitchen. His wife, Paula, followed a couple of steps behind, glancing nervously about her as though they were somehow intruding on private property, although the building displayed every sign of being abandoned long ago. The room, reeking of damp, was devoid of furniture and the stone floor was cracked and cold.

"John, let's have lunch in here," she said, placing her walking poles against a wall and taking the rucksack off her back. "There's not much chance of getting silver service treatment at this establishment but we'll cope," she chuckled.

Her husband smiled. "It's not the first time we've had our sandwiches leaning against a wall. I'm just glad to get out of this weather for a while."

"Say that again. I know we're used to whatever the British climate throws at us but we weren't expecting it to be this bad."

"We could stay for a while in the hope the rain eases but there's no sign of that at the moment. I think we ought to be out of here as soon as we've finished our meal, and making tracks for home."

"I agree," said his wife, pouring two mugs of steaming coffee from her flask. "This place is giving me the creeps."

Twenty minutes later they repacked their rucksacks, taking care not to leave any evidence of their brief visit. John Lingard peered out of the opening in the wall above the sink, which had once contained a slab of glass, and shrugged his shoulders. "We would normally look for a makeshift toilet outside but I think we can be excused in these conditions." He turned to his wife and pointed towards an inner doorway that led from the kitchen. "I'll check out where that goes, see if I can find somewhere suitable."

"I think I'd rather wait until later. Do be careful, dear."

Pulling a torch from a side pocket in his rucksack, he walked towards the open doorway with the upright bearing of a man who had spent his professional life in the military. "It's obvious this place is not habitable so I don't have any qualms about using it."

His wife watched him enter the murky stone-walled hallway then reached inside her jacket for her mobile phone to check for any incoming texts. She found one missed call but it wasn't from any of her contacts and she didn't recognise the number. *If it's important,* she thought, *the caller will ring again.* Whilst she waited, she started to look at some of the photos taken on her mobile earlier in the day but was startled by a distant shout from her husband.

She took a couple of steps towards the doorway when she saw the light from his torch swinging from side to side along a dimly-lit corridor and he rushed into the kitchen, his face ashen. "What is it, John? You look as though you've seen a ghost!"

He stared at his wife, his mind disbelieving of what he had just seen. "There's a body in one of the rooms."

"What? There can't be! You must be mistaken!"

"I wish I was. It's a woman. Looks like she's been shot in the head."

"Oh, that's terrible." She crossed her arms tightly in a dual reaction of shock and trepidation at the implications of the grim discovery. "What on earth have we stumbled across? We'll have to call the police."

Her husband nodded. "I was just about to. And we'll have to wait here until they come – we can't disappear into thin air once we've raised the alarm."

Aghast, Paula Lingard slumped against a wall and put a hand to her head. "Oh, John. Why us?"

It had taken Jim Crowley some time to adjust to the harsh lighting that flooded the small, sparsely furnished office. A square-shaped table and unyielding wooden chairs in the centre of the room took up much of the space and two filing cabinets stood like inanimate sentries either side of the door. A venetian blind covered the only window and the plain grey-painted walls added to the functional ambience. The race engineer sat on one side of the table facing the two men who had been questioning him for more than an hour on the fourth floor of the police station located near Leningradskiy Prospekt in northern Moscow. A digital voice recorder placed between them was a silent witness logging the verbal exchanges, the allegations and denials, criss-crossing the table.

The senior investigating officer and leading interrogator, Captain Nikolai Sorokin, occasionally referred to an A4-size notebook on the table in front of him whilst his colleague, Lieutenant Vladislav Lavrov, periodically leant forward to check the voice levels on the recorder. The Englishman appeared tense and nervous, fidgeting with the sides of his chair and rolling a pencil aimlessly back and forth on a single sheet of blank paper provided for him. He had witnessed members of the Gorton Racing family wrestling with their grief amidst the trauma of losing their owner and the team's number one driver, but they were unaware of the nightmare scenario tormenting the engineer. He had been on tenterhooks waiting for the one phone call that would end his personal agony when police arrived at the circuit early on the day after the race to arrest him. They wanted to question him for a second time and promptly confiscated the one lifeline to restoring his sanity – his mobile – to scrutinise recent call activity on the device.

The stockily built Sorokin had acquired a reputation as a formidable interrogator and had been put in charge of investigating a murder that cast a significant shadow over the inaugural FS race in Russia, with doubts already surfacing about its future staging in the country. He had already scented the first whiffs of political pressure from above and suspected his superiors were being swayed by a higher authority wanting the crime solved swiftly for reasons other than judicial. But the Muscovite prided himself on being his own man and had always resisted external attempts to exert undue influence.

"I have to ask you again, Mr Crowley. Where exactly were you at the time Mr Gorton was attacked?"

"I've told you. I was at the marketing reception for potential sponsors."

"We know you were seen there during the early part of the evening but according to several of your colleagues, who made written statements, you appear to have left some time before Mr Gorton. I want to know where you went after leaving the function."

"I returned to my quarters in one of the motor homes. I was tired after a busy day and read for a while before going to bed."

"And you didn't go out again that night, even for just a few minutes?"

"No."

"Did you at any time after you left the reception see Mr Gorton again?"

"No, I did not. I keep telling you that but you don't seem to believe me."

The officer ran two fingers lightly across his moustache. "I get told many things in my job but I get used to it," he said enigmatically. "How would you describe your relationship with the owner?"

"I didn't have a problem with it. Joe was an easygoing sort of guy you could approach if you had something on your mind. He didn't interfere much and let me get on with my job."

"Would you say he was hands-off in his dealings with the workforce?"

"Yes, definitely."

Sorokin glanced at Lavrov before turning back to the suspect. "It's interesting you should say that because you appear to be at odds with other members of your team. The picture we're getting is that Mr Gorton ran his company with an iron fist and kept an eye on each aspect of the business. It seems he was a man who paid close attention to detail. That doesn't square with what you've told us."

Crowley shifted uncomfortably in his seat. "Of course, he would want to know what was going on – anyone who ploughed millions into the team like he did would do the same – but I'm telling you that I found him alright as a boss."

"Are you saying you never came into conflict with him?"

"Yes, I am saying that."

"You never argued with him?"

"Look, Captain, no one's pretending we're all saints in this business, but you can have a difference of opinion with someone without becoming enemies."

"It doesn't look that way to us. Mr Gorton clearly had one enemy who wanted him dead."

"Well, it seems that way but if you think I had anything to do with it, you're way off-beam. You're both wasting your time, frankly."

"I think that's for us to decide, Mr Crowley, and not you!" The senior detective glanced down at his notebook then looked up. "It appears from your mobile phone records that the last call you received was from your wife. What was the nature of that call?"

A pained expression passed fleetingly over the engineer's face as he mentally relived the traumatic conversation. "She wanted to check I was OK. We keep in touch on a regular basis whenever I'm away from home."

"So, just a routine call from your wife?"

Crowley swallowed hard. "Yes. It was an important race coming up and she was keen to know how I was coping."

"And what did you tell her?"

"I said…" He faltered. "I said everything was fine and there was no need to worry." The engineer leant forward in his seat, his hands clasped together on the table. "How much longer are you going to keep me here? I've answered all your questions and told you all I know. There's nothing more I can do to assist your investigation."

"I suggest that is for others to decide," said Sorokin, barely able to conceal a growing irritation. The officer referred to his notebook again. "I want to turn now to another related aspect of this inquiry – the death of the Gorton driver, Nick Stallard. We've been handed the preliminary findings of the technical team investigating the cause of the crash that killed him. It makes for interesting reading, Mr Crowley."

The engineer stared stolidly ahead but said nothing.

"The investigators made a disturbing discovery when they examined the wrecked car."

"And what was that?"

"It appears the steering column had fractured so the driver was unable to keep the car on the track. It doesn't take a genius to work out that from then on, Mr Stallard was merely a passenger in a high-speed car in a wooded area of the circuit. There was some evidence of braking but the velocity and forces involved were so great he had no chance."

"That is surprising."

"Is it, Mr Crowley?"

"Yes, it is. All the mechanical parts are stress-tested and undergo a rigorous inspection before every race. I've not known anything like it happening before. I suppose there's always the chance of metal fatigue but that would be unusual."

Sorokin stretched both arms to relieve a growing tension in his back. "I don't think this was due to fatigue. Further tests are being carried out but the initial inspection of the column indicated it had been weakened, probably deliberately. We should have conclusive proof in a day or two but if Stallard's death was due to sabotage," he paused to give added weight to his words, "we will be investigating a double murder. And then we have to determine if there's a link between them."

The engineer sipped from a glass of water. "That's impossible. Sounds like you're jumping the gun, Captain. I think your theory is flawed. Why would anyone want to kill the team's top driver? It doesn't make sense."

"I couldn't agree more. It doesn't make sense, but in my experience, Mr Crowley, these cases seldom do. Motive can be an odd creature at times. I believe you have a saying in your homeland – *without rhyme or reason*. I think that sums it up very well."

The Englishman shook his head. "Let me quote you another saying we have in my country –*barking up the wrong tree* – and that's what you're doing with me. You're making a big mistake by treating me as a suspect and should let me go."

"That's how you see it but you need to understand we have to approach this investigation from a different angle."

"I don't care what angle you take. I'm telling you I shouldn't be here and I want a lawyer."

"You will be assigned a lawyer in due course but first you have to answer more questions."

The engineer could not disguise the agitation in his voice. "I don't know how you operate in this country but I'm a UK citizen and have a right to contact the British Embassy in Moscow. You can't deny me that!"

"You're in no position to make any demands, Mr Crowley. The sooner you realise you have to co-operate with us, the better." Sorokin glanced at his watch. "Another twenty minutes and we'll stop to have a break. I know my colleague has some questions for you. Vlad."

Lieutenant Lavrov, a tall rake of a man with a mop of unruly reddish hair, satisfied himself that the voice recorder was still functioning properly then looked up at Crowley. "How long had you worked with Mr Stallard?"

"Three years. I became his race engineer when he joined Gorton Racing."

"You must have been close to him. Can you think of anyone who might want to cause him harm?"

"No, I can't."

"Maybe a rival team? Stallard was leading the drivers' championship when he died and we've heard reports of infighting at FS. Did he have any enemies?"

"Not that I know of. Motor racing can be a tough place at times but I can't imagine anyone would want to have him killed. It's an absurd idea!"

"You might think so but stranger things have happened. We have to deal with the evidence we find but we also have to consider the most unlikely scenarios – and sometimes that points us in the right direction. It's lateral thinking; sometimes we have to move sideways to go forwards."

The engineer looked distinctly unimpressed.

"You had easy access to Stallard's car. If you wanted to tamper with it, you had every opportunity, didn't you?"

"But why would I? I had no reason to."

"The fact remains, you could get close to the car unobserved."

"But so could others. I wasn't—"

The engineer stopped mid-sentence as the phone suspended on the far wall came to life. Sorokin pushed his chair back and walked across the room to pick up the device from its cradle. "Yes?" An enquiry was implicit in his tone of voice.

As his senior colleague took the call, Lavrov paused briefly then resumed the interrogation. "You were saying, Mr Crowley?"

"I was about to tell you I wasn't the only one who had access to Nick's car. Other members of the team could do the same."

"I'm not talking about other people," snapped the Russian. "For the purpose of this interview, let us concentrate on you. I repeat, you could at any time get close to that car and no one would ask any questions. That's right, isn't it?"

"Yes, but it was part of my job description. It was expected of me. Can't you see that?"

"I don't think it's advisable to start asking me questions. You should remember you're here to answer ours. Now, I want to know, when was the last time you worked on Stallard's car and were you alone?"

The engineer was about to answer when he became

aware of Sorokin's thickset frame standing over him. He glanced up and noted the detective appeared to be uneasy. The two men looked at each other, then the Russian spoke.

"Mr Crowley, that call was from the British Embassy. They've asked me to pass on some bad news to you."

The Englishman's grip on the pencil he was holding tightened and he swallowed nervously. "What is it?"

"It's your wife. I'm afraid she's dead."

"Oh my God!" The engineer hurled the pencil to the floor and clenched the desk with both hands. "What happened?"

"It appears she was murdered. Her body was found yesterday."

Crowley buried his head in his hands and began sobbing, the emotional trauma too much to suppress.

Sorokin tried to sound sympathetic. "I'm sorry, but I have to ask – did you know she was missing?"

There was no response from the engineer, his body convulsing from the stress of many hours in custody, made worse by the ravaging grief that now engulfed him. The police officers exchanged glances and the senior man spoke again. "It's time you had a break, Mr Crowley." The engineer was helped to his feet and led into an adjoining room. "Wait here and we'll bring you some strong coffee," said Sorokin, closing the door behind him.

The Englishman used the back of a hand to wipe his eyes then looked around him. A portrait of the Russian president gazed austerely down from one of the walls. The only furniture consisted of two hardbacked chairs standing side by side on the opposite side of the dimly lit room, which was smaller than the one he had just vacated. The only light came from a rectangular window about five feet above the thinly-carpeted floor.

Crowley looked at the door to reassure himself it was shut then walked quickly towards the window. His fingers reached for the metal bar resting at its base, pulling upwards to release its grip on the protruding pyramid-shaped struts that secured it. He tugged again and again but couldn't dislodge it. He cursed. It was stuck solid from lack of use, he reckoned. Sweating now, he hurried across the room and picked up one of the chairs. Wielding it like a weapon, he slammed it into the window, shattering the pane of glass. As he climbed onto the chair he heard the door opening, followed by Sorokin shouting. The detective sprinted across the room but Crowley had clambered onto the window ledge outside. The officer made a desperate lunge but his outstretched hand flailed in vain as the Englishman jumped. Breathing hard, the Russian leant out of the window and stared down at Crowley's body, prostrate on the concrete in the central courtyard forty feet below.

NINETEEN

A fierce North African sun shone out of a cloudless sky and glinted on the octagonal minaret of the Kasbah Mosque as the muezzin, the appointed Muslim religious official, called the faithful to midday prayer. The tower dominated the white-walled, compact houses of the medina, which seemed welded to the hillside that sloped down to the port. The Moroccan national flag, with its green five-pointed star in the centre of a deep-red background, hung limply in the windless air from its pole atop a nearby rampart. Television aerials climbed from rooftops like skeletal steeples, interspersed with the occasional satellite dish, and washing of contrasting hues dangled from lines stretched across sun-kissed balconies. A car and passenger ferry from Algeciras in southern Spain had almost completed its journey across the Strait of Gibraltar and the vessel cut its speed as it approached its berth in Tangier. Nearby, the fishing harbour was dotted with numerous small boats in assorted colours, their owners unloading the morning's freshly caught catch. Moulded by its geographical location – straddling Africa and Europe, with the Atlantic Ocean to the west and the Mediterranean Sea to the east – the traditional homes of the medina were in stark contrast to the high-rise blocks and wide avenues to the east of the city.

Suddenly, from the long sweep of the Bay of Tangier came audible evidence that the Moroccan port with a romantic, exotic past had embraced the modern world. The whine of high-powered engines shattered the air as first practice for the final race of the FS calendar got underway. The circuit, lying between the port and Cap Malabata, was close to the sea and consisted partly of blocked-off public roads together with specially built stretches of track. Several thousand onlookers, made up of enthusiasts and the downright curious, had assembled at various vantage points to watch with a growing fascination a procession of supercharged cars as the world's fastest drivers acclimatised to their new surroundings. The inaugural race in the Maghreb had taken more than a year to set up, involving secret negotiations between Lucas Tait and senior representatives of the Moroccan government seeking to invigorate the country's economy. The FS supremo had sought to exploit his chief bargaining chip – the knowledge that those sitting across the table were desperate to attract a major sporting event to their region – and set his financial demands accordingly. But the high-ranking officials were keenly aware that FS wanted a presence in North Africa to extend motor racing's global exposure. In the event, the talks ended amicably, with both sides feeling they had managed to wring a concession from the other.

The following day, Saturday, the qualifying session was dominated by the gold and blue-coloured cars of the Spanish team, El Oro Racing. The twenty-six-year-old nobleman,

Rodriguez, seized pole position two-tenths of a second ahead of his teammate, the Indian, Pavani. The Russian, Petrenko, was on the next row of the grid, half a second slower than the leader. The American, Kate Lockhart, put the Gorton alongside in P4. The surprise package was the Brazilian driver, Ricardo Gonzalez of Akron Racing, who reversed a series of lacklustre performances by qualifying in P5, closely followed by the Englishman, Dan Seton, in P6.

A cooling north-westerly breeze rippled the curtains at the open window and sent its reviving current of air across the room, still warm in the October evening. It came as a relief to the two occupants of the king-size bed, naked and panting. Finally, she came off him and rolled to one side, admiring his tall, muscular frame. Arm outstretched, her fingers impishly, gently, pulled the hairs on his chest. The Spaniard turned towards her and she gave him the same alluring smile that had so enticed him earlier in the day. "I needed that," he said. "You know how to satisfy a man."

His companion, whose long dark hair almost reached her firm, petite breasts, laughed. "It was good for me, too. You're an attractive guy. You made it easy for me."

Rodriguez smiled and reflected on their chance meeting in the paddock after the qualifying session ended. After fulfilling his duties at the press conference, followed by a debriefing session with his engineering team, he was walking to one of the El Oro motor homes when he was intercepted by a reporter and cameraman working for Teledeporte, the Spanish sports channel. The pole-sitter was happy to accommodate his fellow countrymen and answered a few questions, knowing the interview would be screened in a prime-time slot. Inevitably, a number of bystanders soon gathered and one, a young woman of striking appearance, caught the driver's eye as he was talking.

After he had finished with the sports crew, the flamboyant Spaniard signed several autograph books thrust towards him. But as the crowd began to disperse he noticed the woman, who was displaying official accreditation, lingering nearby. Twirling a strand of hair, she flashed a captivating smile as he approached.

"You must be the famous Raffa I've heard so much about," she said in a marked Andalusian accent.

He chuckled. "I suppose it's better than being infamous." His pulse quickened as he studied her willowy figure. "And who are you?"

"I'm Maria."

"And what brings you to this madhouse?"

"I know what you mean but I love the atmosphere – it's so exciting." She fingered the amulet that dangled from a slender gold-plated chain around her neck. "One of my friends has a contact in FS so when I was asked if I wanted to see the race, I jumped at it."

"Let's hope we don't disappoint you."

Her dark eyes lit up. "I'm sure you won't."

Rodriguez gazed amicably at her. "I guess you're from around these parts."

"You could say that. Not too far away, just over the water in southern Spain."

"And how do you occupy your time when you're not watching motor races?"

"I do some modelling work and I'm also a professional flamenco dancer."

The driver smiled. "Ah, I thought you looked a little feisty."

"It must be something to do with my Latin temperament," she laughed. "But you must know a thing or two about that."

"Just a bit," he winked.

"I expect it helps in your job."

"Probably. Some people accuse me of being aggressive on the race track but I'm not the only one. We operate in a business that's driven by results. End of story." The racer lifted his cap and ran a hand through his dark, wavy hair. "I'm heading to the motor home to get a cooling drink. Would you like to join me?"

She nodded. "Thanks, I'd like that."

Five minutes later the pair were parked on a sofa in one of the El Oro hospitality units, each clasping a glass of freshly squeezed orange juice.

"You went for the healthy option," remarked Maria. "I don't suppose you're allowed anything stronger the day before a race."

Rodriguez looked at her quizzically. "I wouldn't bet on it if I were you."

"I didn't think you were the type to obey all the rules."

"You might be surprised what I get up to the night before a race."

"That sounds promising," she smiled. "Perhaps I'll find out some time."

The aristocrat leant across and she found herself staring into his deep brown eyes. "Maybe you will."

Several hours later Maria had joined the Spaniard for

their clandestine rendezvous in a luxury hotel located close to the circuit. El Oro Racing had booked the entire fifth-floor for its drivers, engineers, senior managers and VIP guests and she had taken care not to be observed. Rodriguez had given her a spare plastic keycard for swift entry to his room and to minimise any chance of her being spotted by a team member in the corridor outside. Recently showered and clad only in boxer shorts, he was lying on the bed flicking through the pages of a sports magazine when she entered. Neither said a word as she dropped her handbag on the floor and threw herself on top of him, her lips urgently seeking his as he helped her undress.

The soft evening light of autumn had darkened by the time the couple stirred. Maria glanced at the illuminated clock on the bedside table then ran her fingers through her lover's tousled hair. He opened his eyes and grinned at her. "You didn't have to wait long to find out about my pre-race preparations, did you?"

She smiled and adopted a tone of mock rebuke. "You're a naughty boy, Raffa. I'm sure your boss thinks you're tucked up in bed – on your own!"

He laughed. "I think I'm old enough to know what gets me through the night."

"I might reduce you to a state of exhaustion by the morning."

"Have you noticed me complaining? I'll take my chances."

"That's good to know. I need a drink. Can I get you one?"

He gazed at her lissom frame as she gracefully eased herself off the bed and bent down to pick up her handbag. "Sure. There are some beers in the mini-bar."

Maria had her back to the driver as she poured the drinks. A small tablet dropped silently from her fingers into one of the glasses. She handed it to the Spaniard then rejoined him on the bed. "I think we've earned this. Salud!"

"Salud!" retorted Rodriguez, gulping about a third of the glass. "Tastes good. Sex always makes me thirsty."

"I had noticed," she smiled. "You must be excited about the race tomorrow."

"The day I'm not, it'll be time to quit and do something else."

"You must have a good chance of winning."

"I'm on pole so that helps but nothing is certain in this game. Too many factors outside my control can go wrong – but at least I've got the best starting slot on the grid."

"And there's a world championship at stake."

"That's impressive – you've done your research." He downed more beer. "You're right, now that Stallard's gone it's a battle between me and Petrenko." He raised his hand to stifle a yawn. "And I want it badly. I was runner-up one year but it's not the same as having the title."

Maria brushed his hand with hers. "I think you're being hard on yourself. It's still a great achievement."

"Coming second just means you're the first of the losers. That's the reality." He yawned again and looked at her. "I must be more tired than I thought."

"You've had a busy day and you were no slouch in bed tonight – I can vouch for that!"

Rodriguez managed a half-smile. "It's a good job I had something left in the tank but I do feel a bit drowsy now." He emptied his glass and leant back against the velvet-covered headboard, struggling to keep his eyes open. "I'm sorry, Maria, but I can't..." His words tailed away as he slumped sideways onto the pillow.

She waited a couple of minutes and calmly finished her own drink before removing the glass from the driver's hand and thoroughly washing the container in the ensuite bathroom. With a reassuring glance in the mirror, the model picked up her underclothes, blouse and skirt and dressed quickly. She walked to the side of the bed and looked down at the unconscious driver.

"I'm sorry, Raffa," she whispered, "I really like you."

Clutching her handbag, Maria walked to the door and opened it. Checking the corridor was clear, she secured the room and hurried towards the elevator.

Eduardo Lopez Santos liked the reassurance of routine. Order and method were key in his approach to work, qualities forged by his chosen career. A university education was followed by a spell in the aviation industry before his passion for engines led to an opening with a leading car manufacturer and he quickly made his mark in its aerodynamics division. Such was his reputation that the Spanish motor racing team, El Oro, head-hunted the thirty-six-year-old and he leapt at the chance to apply his skills in the high-octane world of FS. The recruitment paid off and there was a notable improvement in the team's competitive record, although both the drivers' and constructors' titles had so far eluded them. But this morning there was an uncharacteristic edginess about the race engineer as he paced up and down the garage. An early start was vital ahead of the afternoon race but there was no sign of his driver. Santos was tolerant of the nobleman's playboy lifestyle and his propensity for escorting attractive women, but he knew the racer took his profession seriously and was always striving to improve the car's performance. Rodriguez was seldom late for appointments but his failure to appear on the day that he could clinch the drivers' championship left the engineer baffled and somewhat irritated. Calls to the racer's mobile went unanswered so Santos phoned a colleague staying at the team hotel and asked him to investigate.

The shock discovery, when it came, was a bombshell to El Oro Racing. Within minutes the team doctor had been summoned to examine Rodriguez, who was lying in bed, conscious but groggy. The physician's initial diagnosis was that the driver had been drugged and was suffering from dizziness and blurred vision, and was not fit to race. He added that tests were needed to establish the specific narcotic that had been administered but the process would take time. Despite his condition, the racer said he wanted to be on the starting grid and pleaded with the team owner to back him. Ramon Lorenzo Torres, who was quickly on the scene after being told his leading driver was unwell, carefully considered the ramifications of letting Rodriguez drive. As a media tycoon, he needed no reminder of the torrent of adverse publicity that would be unleashed if he allowed him to race and the Spaniard sustained a serious injury or posed a threat to other drivers due to impaired judgment. But a countervailing argument also weighed heavily on his mind. His number one driver was within touching distance of winning the championship for the first time and apart from the personal glory, the team would benefit from the substantial commercial spin-offs that would follow. When the owner asked if the intervening five hours before the race would give the driver sufficient recovery time, the doctor shook his head.

Torres turned to his driver, who was now sitting up in bed. "Raffa, have you any idea what happened?"

"All I remember is having a drink and the next thing I'm waking up with a hell of a headache."

"Nothing else?"

"No."

"Were you alone last night?"

The driver smiled ruefully. "No. I invited someone for a drink. She's never been to a race before."

"Who was she?"

"I don't know. She had official accreditation so she wasn't a gatecrasher."

The owner sighed. "Raffa, you should know better." The magnate appeared deep in thought. "We need to think about this in a logical manner. The evidence points to someone wanting you out of the race. So we have to consider who that might be."

"There's only one other guy who could take the title," said Rodriguez, "and that's Petrenko."

"That's the direction I'm heading, too."

"But surely Makarov Racing wouldn't…" His words trailed away.

"We can't go throwing accusations around without proof but someone spiked your drink last night and I'm entitled to have an opinion about who may be behind it." The owner eyed his driver. "There's still some time to go before the race. I want you to stay in bed for a couple of hours and then see how you are. If you decide not to compete, that's your call and I'll accept it. But – and it's a big but – if you feel you can last the race I'll let you go ahead. But you have to be totally honest with me."

"That's fair enough, Ramon. I'll settle for that."

Torres turned to the doctor and other colleagues. "It's best not to say anything at this stage. We must give the impression that everything is normal. If Raffa doesn't race we'll have to give some explanation but if he does, we'll stay silent. There'll be a time and a place to raise this incident with the head of FS afterwards. In the meantime, I'll instruct the hotel to keep this under wraps. Is that understood by everyone?"

The Russian's pockmarked face registered incredulity. He wasn't sure he believed what he was seeing on his monitor in the pit lane. Two hours earlier Viktor Makarov had told his drivers that a reliable source had informed him that Rodriguez had been taken ill and was out of the race. The owner had derived considerable satisfaction in telling the twenty-one-year-old Petrenko that if he finished P3 or better he would be world champion in his rookie season in what would be classed as a phenomenal achievement. But now the television coverage clearly showed the Spaniard being strapped into the car bearing the gold and blue colours of El Oro Racing and drinking from a water bottle prior to the warm-up lap of the circuit.

The presence of Rodriguez in pole position was beginning to unsettle Petrenko, whose car was behind the Spaniard's in P3 on the grid. The Russian had assumed the slot in front of him would be vacant and he would have an unimpeded run to the first corner but now he was staring at the exhaust pipes of the pole-sitter. The rookie was pondering the unexpected turn of events when his radio burst into life.

"I don't know how Rodriguez has made it to the start line but he can't be fully fit," rapped Makarov. "Pressure him whenever you can. Climb all over him."

"He'll know I'm here. If he makes a mistake I'll have him," retorted the driver.

"There's a title at stake here. Don't forget it!"

"No chance of that," said Petrenko, easing his machine off the line and following the two cars ahead of him at the start of the warm-up lap.

As he led the field, swerving his car from side to side to force some heat into the tyres to improve grip, Rodriguez reflected on his decision to race. If, as his team suspected, there had been a sordid attempt to prevent his participation in the final round of the championship, the move had backfired. The Spaniard's resolve to compete had been strengthened, even though he was still feeling the after-effects of what the doctor had diagnosed as a sleep-inducing drug. The air temperature had climbed to the low-twenties degrees Celsius and the driver knew that completing forty-two laps of the four-point-seven-mile circuit – the longest on the FS tour – would be a gruelling test of both his physical and mental stamina. Suddenly, there was an extra hazard: a stiffening breeze was blowing sand across parts of the track and creating uncertainty about grip levels.

Rodriguez positioned his car at the front of the grid and the eleven other drivers lined up in their allotted places behind him. The nobleman engaged the clutch, selected first gear then raised his eyes to focus on the two-foot square light suspended thirty feet above the track. From his elevated vantage point on the rostrum, the official starter satisfied himself that all the racers were ready. A second later his finger hit the button that activated the computer-controlled process. The big overhead light glowed bright red. The Spaniard swallowed hard and tried to ignore his twitchy fingers. Chest thumping, he attempted to normalise his breathing but knew this was no time for meditation. His right foot rested gently on the accelerator, poised to unleash the might of the three-litre V10 engine. Engulfed by a wave of intense concentration, his mind screamed for the light to change. Then, in an instant, brilliant red became glowing green.

Rodriguez did not have the optimum start. As his car sped off the line, the front wheels spun and he lost some of the advantage of pole position. One consolation was that team strategy required his colleague, Pavani – who had qualified in P2 – to ride shotgun in an effort to protect the race leader from attack by title rival Petrenko. The Indian driver pulled alongside his teammate on the run to the first corner and had the chance to take the lead, but was under strict orders to stay behind the Spaniard. As Rodriguez struggled to build up speed, Pavani duly held back and slotted into P2. The Russian cursed as El Oro Racing's number two driver moved across in front of him and took the racing line for the first corner, a fast right-hander leading to a section of track that wound uphill and inland. Although still a rookie, he had matured sufficiently to realise there was a long way to go and overtaking opportunities would occur. By any standards, his debut season in the top flight of motor racing had been impressive. Seven podium finishes out of eleven races, including three victories and three runner-up spots, had put him third in the championship standings. But Petrenko had few friends in the paddock. Widely held to be responsible for causing the death of another driver in his first race, the young man from St Petersburg had failed to show any remorse and only succeeded in antagonising his rivals even more.

The leading trio were followed into the corner by the American, Lockhart, in the Gorton; the Brazilian, Gonzalez, driving an Akron; and the Englishman, Seton. The Chinese driver, Wang, in the second Seton, was in P7; the South African, Phil Scolton, in the Drogan, was next; and he was tailed by his teammate, the Hungarian, Yanos Varady. The final three places were taken by the Russian, Alexandr Orlovsky, of Makarov Racing; the American, Al Boyd, in the second Akron; and an Australian, Tony Faulkner, making his FS debut in the other Gorton as replacement for Nick Stallard, killed in the previous race. All twelve cars swept through the bend without incident and accelerated up the slope, twisting left and right before the track levelled out; then hard on the throttle followed by heavy braking to take a tight right that led onto the fast back-straight. A left-right kink in the road forced a slight loss of pace then rev counters soared again as engines shrieked and cars reached 195 miles per hour. Then down through the gears to negotiate a vicious right-hander before the drivers picked up speed as the track went downhill. A series of tight bends followed by a fast left and right brought the cars back onto the start-finish straight, watched by a packed grandstand. At the end of lap 1, Faulkner, who was at the rear of the pack, was already four seconds behind the race leader.

Pavani knew exactly what his race plan was, and he was executing it well. As the early laps unfolded, he was letting his teammate build a gap by keeping the other drivers at bay. The Indian transmitted a radio message that he was spending almost as much time looking in his wing mirrors to assess the threat from behind as focusing on the track ahead. Petrenko and his team on the pit wall were becoming increasingly frustrated by his inability to overtake, aware that Rodriguez was extending his lead and not coming under pressure. The impasse continued until lap 12, when the Russian's race engineer, after conferring with the owner, told his driver of a change in race strategy.

"Yuri, we want you to pit on the next lap. You're getting blocked so we need to get you out into clean air," said Smirnov. "We're going for a three-stopper instead of a two."

"Not before time," was the terse response. An efficient pit stop put the rookie back into the race in P10 and on fresh tyres he progressed through the middle of the pack. By lap 19 he had gained more places and was in P4 behind Rodriguez, Pavani and Lockhart, who had yet to pit. El Oro Racing was operating a two-stop strategy and, according to plan, brought the leader in to refuel and change tyres at the halfway point, followed a lap later by Pavani. Lockhart stopped at the same time as the Indian, who just managed to stay ahead as they drove down the pit lane and rejoined the race. Petrenko was now leading from Wang, who was running a long first stint and had yet to pit, and Gonzalez in P3, who was being chased by Rodriguez.

The young Russian was extracting every ounce of performance from his car in an effort to put distance between himself and his pursuers. As he neared the end of the back-straight he had the tail-ender, Faulkner, in his sights and prepared to lap him on the downhill stretch that followed. As both drivers started to brake for a sharp right turn, Petrenko had closed the gap to two metres when the Gorton failed to take the bend and ploughed through several rows of straw bales at 80 miles per hour. It careered along a strip of wasteland and eventually came to rest against some fencing, its driver barely moving. The safety car was called out as the emergency medical team sped to the aid of the Australian, who was found to be suffering from concussion. It was only later, while recovering, that he revealed a bird strike on his helmet had made him lose control of the car, an incident verified by the Gorton's onboard camera.

As the drivers toured around the track behind the safety car, Makarov Racing seized the opportunity to bring Petrenko in for his second pit stop. When he rejoined the circuit the cars were racing again, but he swore as he slotted in to P3 behind Rodriguez and Pavani and realised the Indian would repeat his earlier blocking tactics. With his team owner's order to overtake ringing in his ears, the Russian threw caution to the wind and closed on the Drogan. Driving aggressively and with his tyres in better condition, the rookie began to put Pavani under extreme pressure. On lap 30, as they exited the first corner and roared up the hill, Petrenko feinted to pass on one side then coolly flicked his car the opposite way and edged in front. For the first time in the race the Russian now had an unobstructed view of the Spaniard, who held a three-second lead.

In the cockpit of the El Oro machine the nobleman was sweating badly, his energy increasingly sapped by the mystery narcotic substance swallowed the previous evening. With a dozen laps remaining, his team on the pit wall viewed the change in race order with growing pessimism. Both drivers still had to make a final pit stop but the Russian was recording faster sector times and gaining on the leader by over half a second a lap. The rookie hunted down the Spaniard relentlessly and by lap 37 the gap between them was down to two-tenths of a second. The pair braked hard for the sharp right that led onto the fast back-straight, the El Oro car clipping the verge and throwing up a cloud of sand, which temporarily blinded the Russian and forced him to lose ground. But halfway down the straight, Petrenko had regained position and was close enough to slipstream the race leader at 185 miles per hour. The car in the gaudy purple and orange colours of Makarov Racing filled the wing mirrors of the ailing Spaniard as both men sought to pull the last atom of power out of their machines... 190... 195... 200. Both three-litre engines screamed at maximum revs as the Russian drew alongside his rival. The eyes of the engineers and team principals on the pit wall were glued to the enthralling duel playing out on their monitors, as were those of the thousands of fans watching on the big screens located around the circuit, together with the vast worldwide audience.

Telegraph poles and palm trees dotted on land adjoining the track flashed by in a headlong haze. The braking point for the sharp right-hand bend with a troublesome camber, leading to the downhill section, was looming and the racers downshifted a couple of gears as they cut their speed to 155 miles per hour. Both men were not yet on the brakes, hoping to leave it as late as possible to gain the slightest advantage as they fought to take the racing line. Rodriguez, convinced that Makarov had tried to put him out of the race, was in no mood to allow his driver and championship rival to exploit the situation. The 300-metre marker board came and went, followed swiftly by the 200. Observers could detect no sign of braking. Neither driver was prepared to give an inch on the approach to the corner, which posed an additional hazard as the track surface fell away after the apex. The cars raced neck and neck as they passed the one hundred-metre board. Only then did each man hit the brakes, telemetry analysis later revealing the Spaniard had applied retardation pressure marginally later. That gave him a slight edge as the cars headed towards the tight turn.

Rodriguez, whose deteriorating physical condition was made worse by a headache that seemed to be intensifying with every lap, was aware that if his rival exited the corner in the lead, the odds were against overhauling him in the remaining five laps. But the aristocrat also knew that if he finished in P2, he would still be champion by one point, even if Petrenko won the race. This scenario had not been lost on the Makarov Racing pit wall and had been communicated to their leading racer. The young Russian was fully aware of the various permutations and knew that to take the title in his rookie year, he would have to win the Moroccan event and Rodriguez must finish in P4 or worse. Compromise is not a concept that comes easily to racing drivers in the heat of battle and for the two men striving to achieve the sport's ultimate accolade, it was never an option. Side by side, braking hard and just inches apart, they turned into the bend, each knowing the laws of physics were weighted against them. The Russian, knowing his every move would be scrutinised due to his previous conduct on the track, gambled that a crash would be adjudged a racing accident and he would escape disciplinary action. Both men dived for the apex, their front wheels banging. The violent collision sent both cars hurtling off the track, ripping a front wheel off Petrenko's machine and splitting the nose cone. The Spaniard's front wing and suspension were damaged beyond repair and his race, too, was over.

The cars ploughed across a stretch of gravel before bouncing off a wall of tyres and coming to rest about eighty metres from the point of impact. The Russian unfastened his safety harness, clambered out of the wrecked machine and, shaking his fist, walked towards Rodriguez, who appeared dazed and was still strapped in the cockpit. Removing his helmet and fireproof balaclava, Petrenko swore at the Spaniard but two track marshals were quickly on the scene and led the rookie away as a third marshal went to help the other driver out of his car.

With the two major contenders out of the race, another fight for supremacy was being played out under the North African sun. Pavani was in P1 but his slender lead over Lockhart was being whittled away as she pressed him hard. Both had made their final pit stops and were on fresh tyres for the last stint. Nearing the end of the penultimate lap, the American forced her way past the Indian at the fast left-hander but ran wide at the exit and the El Oro driver regained first place. By the time the cars streaked past the main grandstand for the final time, the Gorton was within a metre of the leader.

The gap was maintained through the first corner and as the cars sped uphill and inland. A potent motivating factor for each driver was that neither had won a race in the current season, although both had one runner-up finish to their credit. But now they were totally focused on the immediate battle as each scented victory. V10 engines howling, the cars thundered along the back-straight in seventh gear at speeds approaching 200 miles per hour, Pavani just managing to keep some daylight between himself and the Gorton. Then both downshifted and braked hard for the sharp right at the end of the straight before plunging downhill and negotiating a series of tight bends. Lockhart had narrowed the gap by the time the pair reached the penultimate corner, a fast left-hander where she had overtaken on the previous lap but run wide. This time she exited better and had drawn level as they approached the fast right-hander. The American feigned to pass on the outside but cut back to take the inside line in a move of individual daring and brilliance. The cars touched as she went past but both drivers retained control. Out of the last bend and a 300-metre sprint to the finish. Pavani strained every sinew to thwart his rival as the pair rocketed towards the line, but Lockhart held on and took the chequered flag by inches as thousands of cheering Moroccans in the grandstand leapt to their feet.

Her triumph was witnessed by the two men whose crash had destroyed their hopes of lifting the drivers' title. A frustrated Rodriguez and an embittered Petrenko, watching from their garages, were all too aware that the FS world championship had been won posthumously by Gorton Racing's Nick Stallard, killed during the previous race near Moscow. The Englishman's total of forty-six points was one more than the Spaniard, and the Russian ended the season on forty-three. Pavani was fourth in the standings on twenty-nine points; the murdered Frenchman, Philippe Guiscard, was next on twenty-eight; and Lockhart had twenty-three.

Despite her achievement – being the first woman to win a motor race at the highest level – it was a subdued Kate Lockhart who stood on top of the podium for the trophy presentation ceremony, flanked by Pavani and the Chinese driver, Wang, who finished in P3. Tears flowed down the American's cheeks as the Stars and Stripes was hoisted on the flagpole and a band played *The Star-Spangled Banner*. She spurned the traditional champagne-spraying after receiving the victor's silver cup and as she was interviewed on the podium, it was clear she had mixed emotions.

"It's been an unbelievable afternoon for me but I want to dedicate my win to Joe Gorton. He did so much to encourage me and he would have been proud to see me standing here today." Clutching the cup, Lockhart, her voice faltering, raised her eyes to the sky. "This… this is for you, Joe."

As the drivers posed for the cameras, the head of FS stepped onto the podium and was handed a microphone. Looking down, Lucas Tait addressed the large crowd gathered below. "Ladies and gentlemen, this has been a remarkable day in the history of FS. For the first time we have seen a woman driver win a round of the championship, and do it in the most exciting way. All credit to you, Kate. But we're also conscious that this has been a sad year with the loss of four drivers, three on the track and one in tragic circumstances off it – Pete Maitland, Otto Werner, Philippe Guiscard, and the posthumous world champion, Nick Stallard. We also lost in the most brutal way another member of the FS family – Joe Gorton, founder of the British racing team that bears his name. I think it's appropriate today to call for a minute's silence in their memory."

Hundreds of people took their cue from Lucas Tait and stood still with heads bowed. But one man in the crowd ignored the request. Limping slightly, a thickset figure with a pockmarked face hurried away. He had no time for such civilities. His dream was in tatters.

TWENTY

The Spanish flag, with its three horizontal stripes of red, yellow, red, and featuring the national coat of arms, flapped with a fickleness generated by a gusting breeze above the presidential box. The sand-covered ring, more than seventy metres in diameter and surrounded by a wooden, red-painted fence over a metre high, was still in the full glare of the early evening sun but the walls on the west side of the amphitheatre had cast a shadow over some of the concrete terraces. Young men in sweat-stained T-shirts and shorts, with ice buckets hanging over each shoulder, climbed the mountain of steps between the raised circular tiers selling chilled beer and mineral water, almonds and salted peanuts. An air of expectancy rippled through the thousands of spectators, many perched on their rented plastic cushions to mollify the effects of sitting for hours on unforgiving stone seats.

The president took his place and waved a white handkerchief. From high above the arena, the trumpets of the brass band sounded and the ceremonial procession got underway. Three matadors, dressed in their gold brocaded and jewelled capes, paraded across the sand, each followed in single file by their retinue of assistants, three banderilleros and two mounted picadors. The matadors came to a halt beneath the presidential box, doffed their flat-topped, two-cornered black hats and bowed low to the man who would later judge their individual performance in terms of mastery of the bull and swiftness of the kill; a man whom by tradition would also be subject to attempts by the crowd, if sufficiently impressed by what they had seen, to influence him in the awarding of one bull's ear, or both, or its tail.

After the other participants in the procession had acknowledged the president and were leaving the arena, bullring attendants using wide, long-handled brushes smoothed the surface of the sand that had been churned up by the hooves of the horses. The matadors – each contracted to fight two bulls – removed their heavy parade capes, laying them across the wooden fence, and two of them settled in the narrow corridor running between the fence and the first row of seats. The senior man was handed a large fighting cape then positioned himself behind one of the shelters – at chest height and made of timber with steel supports at either side, standing close to the edge of the ring – in which he or his assistants could evade the bull if pursued. Two of the three banderilleros were standing at opposite ends of the arena, tight against the perimeter. The crowd, sensing the beginning of the drama was imminent, quietened. At a signal from the president, the trumpeters sounded another fanfare and the heavy steel door leading to the bull pens was slowly pulled open.

Amongst the aficionados, the habitual fans seeking their weekly fix of gore-spattered thrills, and the merely inquisitive eagerly awaiting the start of proceedings, two men surveyed the arena with more than a passing interest. Neither had witnessed a bullfight before but the prospect of a violent struggle resulting in certain death for the animal and the possibility of serious injury or worse to its caped tormentor, appealed to their baser instincts. The spectacle of a matador exhibiting his finely honed skills in what critics claimed to be a somewhat unequal struggle between man and beast was not uppermost in the thoughts of these onlookers – far from it. Their minds were still spinning from events across the water earlier that day.

The Russian's anger and frustration had shown little sign of subsiding during the short helicopter flight across the Strait of Gibraltar to southern Spain. As ever, his chief henchman had borne the brunt of the ranting but Viktor Makarov was only going through the motions. Deep down he knew the game was over, at least for another year. The previously unattainable holy grail – a rookie winning the title – had been snatched away when seemingly within his team's grasp. Even more insufferable, a dead driver had been crowned world champion. And efforts to extract improved financial terms from the FS commercial rights holder had proved futile, with a lack of support from the other team owners a major factor. For a man ruthless in obtaining his objectives, the stench of failure was overpowering. But such was his overweening nature that even as he looked down on the sun-clad sand that would soon be stained crimson, his focus was already on seeking retribution in the following season.

The hefty door leading to the pens where the bulls are kept before their turn to enter the ring had swung open to reveal a stone-lined passageway a little over a metre wide. The eyes of the thousands of paying customers in the rows of seats exposed to the sun, those partly in the shade and those in the covered balconies, were fixed as one on the open doorway. They didn't have long to wait. Half-walking, half-running, a black titan of a bull emerged into the sunlight. Weighing over 600 kilogrammes and packed with testosterone, its primary outlet for violence was channelled through two large, curved horns with points as sharp as needles. It came to a halt and stared at the mounted men, then turned to look back at the open door through which it had made its entry before refocusing on the other occupants of the arena. One of the banderilleros, trailing a large pink and yellow cape, moved away from the fence and ran towards the centre of the ring to catch the eye of the bull. The animal watched the flurry of movement closely before bellowing and then, ears pointing, it lowered its horns and charged. The assistant zig-zagged the cape across the sand as the matador, from his viewpoint behind the shelter, looked on. He watched with studious concentration to assess the quality of the bull – the way it charged, whether running straight or changing its angle of attack; testing its vision, whether favouring its left or right horn when striking at the cape. The banderillero ran the bull several times until it ceased charging and came to a standstill, with its back to the fence and a short distance from it.

Another authorising gesture from the presidential box and the two picadors, each clutching a lance more than two metres long with a triangular metal-spiked tip at one end, entered the arena on horseback. The horses' chests and bellies were protected with a heavy mattress-type padding and both animals were blindfolded on one side to prevent them seeing when the bull charged. The picadors, wearing wide low-crowned hats with a tassel on the side and dressed in close-fitting jackets and silk breeches, reached the middle of the ring then diverged. As they rode across the sand in opposite directions, both men raised their pikes to acknowledge the crowd but maintained an unwavering gaze on the big beast pawing the ground at the edge of the arena. At a signal from the matador, a banderillero standing near one of the picadors slowly approached the bull. Spreading his cape wide in a series of exaggerated movements, the assistant instantly gained the bull's attention and used the cloth as a lure in an attempt to draw the animal in the direction of the picador. Recognising it was about to charge, the banderillero ran towards the rider, whose mount was positioned at such an angle that it couldn't see the bull, and took cover behind them. The picador gripped the lance firmly with his right hand, tightened his hold on the rein strap with the other, and braced himself for the onslaught he knew was coming. Hard experience had taught him that over a short distance, a bull, despite its weight, can unleash an explosive burst of speed – and if it gets close enough, its horns, driven by powerful neck muscles, can lift a horse off its legs and unseat its rider.

    The crowd, seized by the moment, held its collective breath. The horse's head strained against the bit and the animal moved nervously from side to side. It couldn't see the bull but could smell it and the memory of previous encounters in the ring put it on edge. The picador tried to calm his mount, briefly releasing his grip on the rein strap to stroke its mane. At that instant the bull began its charge. From a standing start with head down and tail lifted, it swiftly gathered momentum, its scurrying hooves sending a cloud of sand flying into the air behind it. The horseman steadied himself and turned his mount side-on to the advancing threat, just yards away. As the bull's horns embedded themselves in the wall of mattress, the force of the impact lifted the horse's forelegs six inches off the ground – but the picador now had his target well within range. Firmly seated in the saddle and looking down on the bull, he thrust the metal-spiked tip of the lance into the hump of muscle rising from its neck. He withdrew the weapon and for a second time drove the pike into the same area nearest the shoulders. Blood started to seep from the double wound across its back and down its flanks. The process of sapping the strength of the bull had begun.

From their vantage point high above, the Serb took a couple of swigs from a bottle and handed the water to his boss. "Maybe there won't be much of a bull left to fight by the time the matador gets to him."

"We'll find out," was the terse and insouciant response of a man with other things on his mind.

"If they weaken the bull too much, where's the contest?"

"I suppose they know what they're doing."

"I want some real action. Those horns can do serious damage and I'd like to see that."

"Steady, Vuk, you're sounding bloodthirsty."

The irony of the comment was not lost on either man as they waited for the next phase of the drama playing out below them. Viktor Makarov frowned as the discordant ringtone of his mobile came to life. His mood was not improved when a glance at the cell phone revealed the caller's identity. For a moment he considered ending the call.

"Yes."

"Is that you, Makarov?"

The Russian mumbled confirmation.

"It's Lucas Tait here. I need to have a word with you." The team owner said nothing and the FS boss continued. "The race stewards are investigating an incident involving the Spanish driver, Rodriguez. An allegation has been made by the El Oro team that he was the victim of an attempt to drug him before today's race."

"Why tell me?"

"The stewards have a duty to consider all the circumstances surrounding the allegation and to establish what happened as far as they can. They're holding a special session in Tangier tomorrow to take evidence and want you to appear before them."

"I have no idea what you're talking about and it would be a waste of time."

Tait ignored the comment. "But before the stewards convene they require a preliminary statement, so I've sent Jack Wyatt to take one from you."

Makarov bristled at the prospect. "Listen, Tait. I've no intention of appearing before the stewards or giving a statement to Wyatt. Whatever happened to the Spaniard had nothing to do with me or my team."

"I suggest you listen to me, Makarov. The stewards have a right to summon anyone they think can assist them in their inquiries and they've decided they want to question a number of people, including you."

"I've told you – I've nothing to say. As far as I'm concerned, we've had the last race and the championship is over. My focus now is on next season."

Tait tried to control the rising anger in his voice. "I'm just going to say this once, and once only. If you don't co-operate you won't have a next season – your team won't be on the grid. End of story!"

Makarov gripped his mobile tightly, the faded two-inch scar on the back of his right hand suddenly more prominent. "You can't do that. I've got a contract in black and white – you can't just tear it up."

"You're forgetting something. You signed up to a code of regulations and if there's a major breach, your contract is worthless – and that's no idle threat. So I want you to give a statement to Wyatt. He's at the bullring and waiting for you in the basement below the entrance to Bloque G. It's the block before the pens. Be there in five minutes!"

Makarov stared sullenly at his mobile after Tait finished the call abruptly, then turned to his chief henchman. "Vuk, I've got a job for you. Tait has sent his bootlicker to see me to do his dirty work. I want you to handle it. I think it's about time you introduced yourself to Mr Wyatt."

The Serb grinned sardonically. "I think our meeting is long overdue. Leave it with me, boss."

Both men looked out into the arena as the trumpets sounded again and the crowd roared as two of the banderilleros, each carrying two thin wooden shafts measuring less than a metre with steel barbs at one end, strode across the sand. Amid the hubbub, the Russian leant close to his right-hand man to pass on the details of Wyatt's location. Jovanovic nodded, eased his frame to its full height and set off in the direction of the concrete steps that led down past the rows of serried seats to the bullring entrance.

In the ring, one of the banderilleros, with a shaft in each hand, walked to within twenty feet of the bull and waved his wooden poles, decorated with coloured paper, to attract its attention. As the animal stared at him, the man broke into a run and, swerving from side to side, ran towards the bull, which began its charge. Closing fast, it dropped its head to hook but the banderillero, with an adroit side-step, evaded the horns. With both feet together and arms raised high, he jumped in the air and thrust the two shafts into the hump on the lowered neck of the passing bull, the barbs catching under its skin. The shafts, positioned away from the wounds made by the picador, hung down the flanks of the animal. The bull ran on, unable to turn in a distance less than its own length. When it stopped and started to pivot to pursue the man who had just inflicted additional muscle-weakening injury, it was distracted by the second banderillero wielding a big pink and yellow cape. The bull took the lure and charged a new tantalising target across the ring. But the man holding the cape, experienced and adept at his trade, swung the cloth away from his body at the last moment and the bull hurtled harmlessly past him, coming to a halt near the fence. The scene was set for a third banderillero, armed with two shafts, to emulate the handiwork of his colleague. Watching the activity with a practised eye was the official in the presidential box, whose role was to judge the matador's assistants on their command of the bull and the degree of artistry displayed in tiring the animal.

    The big Serb pushed his way through a group of latecomers clutching their tickets under the stone archway in the entrance hall of the circular building, his coal-black eyes scanning the overhead signage. He found what he was looking for and, hurrying past a food stand with the piquant aroma of chorizos hanging in the air, headed along a deserted stone-walled corridor, his echoing footsteps the only sound. He followed the gradual curve of the passageway, a staleness bordering on mustiness exuding from its walls. The corridor opened up on the left but a sign indicated he had further to go so he pressed on, quickening his pace. Thirty seconds later the passageway widened again and, looking up, Jovanovic saw the sign that told him he had reached Bloque G. A flight of stairs led up to the packed amphitheatre, from where the distant sounds of the crowd undulated in response to the action in the ring. Adjacent was a stairway leading to the basement and the Serb, after glancing behind him, began to move warily downwards.

Descending with all the furtiveness of a feline, he reached the bottom step and paused, his eyes adjusting to the dimness while he strained to detect the slightest sound that would help pinpoint the location of the man waiting for him. A pillar just inside the entrance to the basement partly obscured the Serb's vision but peering around it, he could see two wooden benches against the walls at either side of the room with what appeared to be a large unit of storage lockers in the centre. Some metal crates were stacked to head-height at the far end of the basement and a door was nearby.

"Where are you, Wyatt?"

"I'm over here," replied the American, stepping silently out from behind the lockers.

"That's better. I don't like dealing with shadows."

"You surprise me. I thought that's where you operated."

"What would you know?"

"Maybe more than you think."

The Serb's mouth tightened and there was an edginess in his voice as he took a couple of steps forward. "What d'you want, Wyatt?"

"I wouldn't want you to take this the wrong way, Jovanovic, but you ain't got an invite to the party."

"What d'you mean?"

"I reckon the message must have got lost in translation. It's your boss I want to see."

"He's busy, so you'll have to deal with me."

"Now that's a real shame. I was looking forward to having a one-on-one with Mr Makarov."

"I can't say he feels the same way. But whatever's on your mind, you can tell me."

"You know something?" said the American. "You're starting to bug me and I don't need the hassle."

The shaven-headed Slav moved closer until the two men were just a few feet apart. "You could say the feeling's mutual."

"You ain't listening. You're wasting my time and I don't like it. Go back to Makarov and tell him to get his arse down here – and I won't be putting in another request."

"You might as well save your breath. My boss has no intention of meeting you now – or any time."

"You're gonna make it hard on yourself, Jovanovic."

"That's where you're wrong, Wyatt." The Serb slipped a hand inside his lightweight jacket and emerged with a black-handled fixed-blade knife that had been nestling in its leather sheath. "You really shouldn't meddle where you're not wanted. It could be bad for your health."

Wyatt merely shrugged and looked stolidly ahead when he saw the weapon. "Easy, now. You could do yourself some serious damage if you're not careful."

"I don't think it's me you need to be worried about."

"I reckon we might have to differ on that one."

"It's not going to change anything. You're about to regret doing Tait's dirty work for him."

"I wouldn't bet on it."

"I think the odds are stacked in my favour, Wyatt." The Serb waved the knife, comprising a six-inch blade with a curving edge and straight back, from side to side. "You may have noticed we're alone. No one will hear your screams down here." He moved forward, his mouth twisted malevolently, and lunged at the American, who adeptly avoided the thrust and backed away.

All the instincts of a man whose career was steeped in the dark arts of intelligence gathering and covert operations kicked in as Wyatt reached for the shoulder holster concealed inside his shirt and emerged with his finger around the trigger of a Glock 19 pistol. Jovanovic had his right hand above his shoulder with the knife poised to strike when a quizzical expression crossed his face. An instant later, a nine-millimetre bullet slammed into his head just above the right eye. The Serb fell lifelessly to the ground, his weapon clattering on the stone surface. The American holstered his gun then bent down and dragged the body to one side of the room towards a large metallic rubbish container. Removing the lid, he struggled to lift the corpse before manoeuvring it head first into the storage bin. Wyatt threw the knife inside and replaced the lid before checking his watch, then waited in the shadows.

Outside in the ring, the third and final act of the bullfight was about to get underway. The senior matador, holding his sword and the *muleta* – a small, scarlet-coloured, cape-like cloth – stood looking up at the presidential box. Hat in hand, he saluted and formally asked for authorisation to kill the first bull. His request granted, the matador focused on a section of the crowd below the box and dedicated the bull to his current female companion, a raven-haired beauty in a striking red dress. He threw his hat in her direction and when it reached her, via the hands of spectators eager to help, she smiled radiantly and blew him a kiss as the crowd cheered. He smiled back and ran a hand across his oily, slicked-down hair before turning inwards to the ring. At the far side of the enclosure stood the fighting bull that he would try to dominate in as stylish, yet spectacular, a manner as possible. The creature had lost much of its speed and parts of its thick black hide, once smooth and shining, were now stained red from the work of the picador and banderilleros. But whilst it no longer carried its head high, it still posed a mortal threat to the man committed to killing it. With an arrogance of stride, the matador approached the bull, stopping about a dozen feet away. Holding the *muleta* in his left hand and the sword in the right, he faced his adversary. Responding to a sudden movement of the cloth, the bull charged. The matador swung the *muleta* across his body and the animal followed, its horns flailing in the air as it went away from the man.

The bullfighter turned swiftly, in readiness for a second charge. The focus of his attention had come to a halt about six metres away and was staring at him through sullen black eyes. Then, ears twitching and raising its clump of neck muscle in a display of anger, the beast put its head down and charged. When it was almost upon him, the matador, with a skilful movement of the wrist, thrust the *muleta* to one side and swayed out of range of the nearest horn. The bull hurtled past him and thundered across the sand for a short distance before crashing into the inch-thick timber of the fence and toppling over it. The crowd gasped as the animal found its feet and ran the full length of the narrow circular corridor separating the barrier and the first row of seats. A photographer and a police officer threw themselves over the fence into the sanded ring to escape the fast approaching four-legged juggernaut. The drama ended when a quick-thinking bullring attendant pulled open a heavy wooden door, which blocked the animal's progress and forced it back into the arena. The three banderilleros, waving their sizeable pink and yellow capes, lured the bull away as the two men who had sought safety in the ring clambered back over the fence and out of danger.

As he watched the unexpected action from his position overlooking the arena, the mafia boss was becoming restive. He stamped on a half-smoked cigarette and pulled another from the pack of Sobranie Black Russian cigarettes. The soles of his shoes bobbed up and down in a rhythmic revelation of angst as he looked at his watch again. His chief henchman had been gone a while and calls to his mobile phone went unanswered. Makarov knew the action in the ring would be approaching a climax in the next ten minutes or so and, like the thousands of others in the amphitheatre, he wanted to be a witness to the ritual denouement. The man whom he relied on to carry out his orders, most of a criminal nature, who shared sordid secrets, was an efficient operator who had never failed him. But somehow the Russian felt a burgeoning sense of unease despite trying to convince himself otherwise. He waited a couple more minutes, dumped his unfinished cigarette with its black paper and gold foil filter on the ground, and made another attempt to contact the Serb. The response, as before, was an answerphone recording asking the caller to leave a message.

Makarov ended the call and left his seat. He hurried down the seemingly endless plunge of concrete steps leading to the bullring entrance then followed the signs to *Bloque G*. He reached the top of the stairway to the basement and paused before easing his burly frame down the steps and taking cover behind the pillar at the bottom. A Beretta pistol appeared in the Russian's hand, then he waited, listening intently for any sound. But there was nothing. Just silence. A perplexing, suspenseful silence.

"Are you there, Wyatt?"

Out of the dimness came the distinctive tone of an American accent. "What kept you, Makarov? I thought you'd never make it."

"Maybe I get a kick out of keeping you waiting."

"Wouldn't surprise me."

"Where's the Serb?" There was a discernible irritation and urgency in the inquiry.

"You know something, Viktor, that's a good question. Let's just say our old friend Jovanovic is in a better place."

"What have you done to him, Wyatt?"

"You could say he's having an extended time-out from the game."

The mafia boss cursed under his breath, bemused by whatever fate had befallen his right-hand man but now fully aware he would have to deal with Tait's troubleshooter on his own. He moved his head gingerly to one side of the pillar in an attempt to glimpse his foe. The interior of the basement was poorly lit and there was no sign of the American, but he tried to establish the layout of the room.

"Where are you, Wyatt? We need to talk."

"I reckon you finally got the message, Viktor."

"Stop calling me Viktor!" snapped the other man.

"Gee, that's a shame. Just when I thought we were making real progress."

"You can cut the funny stuff, Wyatt."

"Come to think of it, Viktor, I always reckoned you lacked a sense of humour."

The Russian's grip on his pistol tightened. "Why don't you show your face, Wyatt? You're not scared, are you?"

"Are you gonna place a bet on it?" The American, who was standing behind the unit of storage lockers in the centre of the room, drew his weapon.

"I'm told you want a statement from me so what are you waiting for?"

"Yeah, that's right, but first there's some personal business I have to take care of. I need to know how Valya's making out these days."

The question took the Russian by surprise and it showed in his voice. "What the hell has she got to do with you?"

"She was a real nice woman who seemed to have a problem with her boss. I'd like to know she's OK."

"Now I know why I could never trust her." Makarov gave a hollow laugh. "You could say one of my pets had a crush on her. It's a shame no one told you about the funeral."

"You bastard! You're gonna pay for that."

"Talk is cheap, Wyatt. It's time you came out of the shadows."

"Look, I'm over here, behind the lockers." As he spoke, the American exposed a white handkerchief beyond the end locker. Immediately two shots rang out, the bullets pinging past him and into the wall at the far end of the basement.

"Now I think we're getting somewhere," said Makarov, who was about to venture out from behind the pillar when a bullet from the Glock 19 ripped into the other side of the concrete column.

"Just so you know, Viktor, you ain't been dealt all the best cards."

The sound of gunfire was amplified in the confined space but went unheard by the thousands absorbed in the contest taking place in the arena. Their attention was firmly on the senior matador, who was demonstrating his skills with the *muleta*. He had gained a reputation for flamboyant use of the cape but his ability and bravery were unquestioned. For the crowd, the bull had been a good one – hostile and unpredictable in its charging – but a series of ineffectual sorties aimed at the man with the cloth had worn the animal down to such an extent it had become increasingly reluctant to attack. The bullfighter advanced circumspectly and with short steps, but the creature, increasingly leaden and lumbering, remained motionless. The matador moved closer, thrusting the cape to within several feet of the bull, and with a series of jerks dragged the cloth along the ground. Despite the enticement there was barely a flicker of reaction and certainly no sign the animal was interested in charging. The man with the sword looked at the crowd, a scornful expression on his face. He knew the time had come. And judging by the reaction of the spectators, they knew it too. The matador turned to face the bull again.

After the initial exchange of fire, a stand-off had ensued between the two men in the basement, where the clammy conditions were becoming oppressive. Each was pinned down by the other but the Russian was now acutely aware of the rules of the game, whilst having to adapt to the mystifying disappearance of his Serbian heavy. For his part, Wyatt knew the element of surprise had gone but was determined to try to retain the initiative. He moved stealthily to the opposite end of the lockers then threw a coin onto the floor where he had previously been standing. Before the piece of metal stopped spinning more shots rang out, the bullets ricocheting harmlessly off the back wall. Makarov lowered the gun and with his other hand wiped away the sweat that was starting to trickle down his temple. He hadn't budged from his position behind the pillar but knew he needed to change his location if he was to outflank the American.

Slowly, very slowly, he peered out from behind the column and noticed the big storage bin standing close to a wall. Inhaling deeply, the Russian bent down as low as his thickset figure would allow and tiptoed the dozen feet or so towards it. There was just enough of a gap between the wall and the container for him to crouch down between them. Although the manoeuvre wasn't physically demanding, he was startled to find his heart pounding and struggled to control his breathing. Concealed behind the bin, Makarov had an unobstructed view of one side of the lockers that dominated the centre of the room but there was no sign of Wyatt. The mafia boss, squatting on his haunches, listened and waited, his trigger finger poised.

The silence was broken by a creaking sound from an unoiled hinge as one of the locker doors swung open. The Russian fired two shots, the bullets piercing the metallic door, which then swayed eerily back and forth until losing momentum. The American, standing on a bench to lever himself up the back of the ten-foot-high locker unit, had slipped and set the door in motion. He returned fire from behind the unit then, regaining his footing, furtively resumed the climb and clambered on to the top where, lying face-down, he inched his body forward. Makarov, uncertain of Wyatt's exact location but suspecting he might be seeking an aerial advantage, fired a couple of shots into the ceiling to force the American to keep his head down then, with his limping gait, made it to the far end of the basement and took cover behind the wall of crates. Alerted by the movement, Wyatt looked up to see his adversary disappearing behind the barrier and fired a couple of rounds. More shots were traded in an intense exchange, bullets whistling past the heads of both men. After a short lull the Russian pulled the trigger of his semi-automatic but, to his horror, merely heard a chilling click that told him the fifteen-round magazine was empty. He flung the Beretta to the ground and looked around him. Nearby was a wooden door but he had no idea if it was locked. For a moment he froze, paralysed by indecision, but he knew he couldn't stay where he was. He reached the door and forced the handle sharply downwards and a huge sense of relief coursed through him as an escape route opened up.

Outside in the early evening sun, the senior matador's focus was wholly on the animal standing a dozen feet from him. *Muleta* held low in his left hand and the sword in his right, he stood with his left side facing the bull and slowly drew the weapon from behind the cape, raising it until it was level with his head. Body pulled taut, the man with the sword looked along the blade at his target, sighted the intended area of attack and moved towards it. As if somehow sensing that danger was imminent, the creature roused itself and charged its tormentor. The matador swung the *muleta* low across his body out to the right and the bull, head down, followed the cape. The man adeptly leant over the horns and buried the sword between the animal's shoulder blades, almost up to the hilt. The bull stumbled, its front legs started to buckle and it slowly sank to the ground as the cheers of the crowd rang out.

Although mortally wounded, the single sword thrust had missed the animal's aorta. One of the banderilleros ran towards the stricken creature with a dagger and administered the death blow by severing its spinal chord. Impressed by the performance, a tidal wave of white handkerchiefs raced across the spectators as they demanded the bullfighter's skill be rewarded. Acknowledging the gallery, the president signalled an award of both ears and they were duly cut off the dead animal and handed to the matador. Smiling broadly and clutching his spoils, he strutted a lap of honour around the ring, waving to the crowd, as the body of the bull was tied to a harness and dragged from the arena by two horses, leaving a bloody trail in its wake. As the animated onlookers watched the bullring attendants wielding their long-handled brushes, getting to work on smoothing the surface of the sand, an air of expectancy permeated the amphitheatre. The president would shortly authorise the entry of the second bull and all eyes would turn to the heavy steel door that led to the pens.

Wyatt heard the door slam shut and swore. Pistol in hand, he crawled along the top of the lockers to the rear then dropped several feet to the bench and on to the ground. He ran to the back of the basement and saw Makarov had abandoned his weapon. Tracking his target, the American found himself in a narrow corridor lit by a couple of overhead tubular fluorescent lamps twenty feet apart. In the distance he could see another door and hurried towards it. This one was different from the first, hanging heavy and sturdy, and needed a strenuous effort from Wyatt's muscular frame to push it open. With the

Glock raised and cocked, he went through the opening and pushed the door flat against the wall, the agency training drilled into him at Langley long ago as imperative now as then. The instructor's barked commands were ringing in his ears. *"Check left! Check right! Check overhead!"*

The American forced his eyes to adjust to the gloom. Above him was a roof supported by criss-crossing beams of timber and the only light came from four narrow windows just below the rafters. In front was a wall about twelve feet high with a metal ladder clamped to it. There was no sign of Makarov. Wyatt stepped onto the ladder and eased himself silently up the rungs. Three-quarters of the way up he extended his right hand, clutching the pistol, and reached for the iron grip protruding from the top of the wall. He had barely touched the ferrous handhold when an intense pain ripped through his fingers as the Glock was kicked from his grasp and sent spinning to the ground below. He looked up and saw Makarov's smirking face as the Russian aimed another kick, this time at his head. Clinging to the ladder with his left hand, Wyatt dodged the blow and grabbed his adversary's leg. But Makarov managed to stay on his feet and his fist found the American's jaw. Momentarily stunned, Wyatt was forced to release his grip. When the Russian saw Wyatt pull out a twelve-inch-long stiletto knife he turned and fled.

The Californian pulled himself up the remaining rungs, clambered onto the top of the wall and set off in pursuit along a central concrete strip a metre wide that ran parallel to footways on the two outer walls. Makarov was hampered by his limp, dragging one leg behind him like a hunted, weakened animal, and his breathing was laboured. The American, a noted athlete in his college days, was just yards away and gaining on his quarry. To his dismay, the mafia boss found his path blocked by a waist-high safety barrier consisting of two horizontal iron bars. Beyond was a four-foot gap over a high-walled corridor. Panting heavily, he looked over his shoulder to find his pursuer almost upon him. For the Russian there was only one option. He climbed over the obstacle and flung himself across the chasm, arms outstretched, hands aiming at one of the iron bars of the barrier on the opposite side.

Makarov willed himself to make the leap but a lack of momentum from a standing start pulled him down. The fingers of one hand grazed the wall inches below the lower bar but there was nothing to grip. The Russian dropped like a stone to the concrete floor, cursing as pain surged through his left knee after the twelve-foot fall. Disoriented and badly winded, he struggled to stand up. He had almost got to his feet when he heard it. The unmistakable sound was close by and behind him and sent a torrent of fear coursing through his body. Makarov had begun to turn to face the nightmare but didn't complete the movement. A razor-sharp horn penetrated his thigh and he was tossed several feet in the air, blood spurting from a severed femoral artery. Before he landed, the bull caught him again with its other horn, this time deep in the chest, and tossed him once more. His screams lasted only seconds as 650 kilogrammes of pent-up ferocity repeatedly gored the Russian as he lay on the ground, his life-blood draining away.

Wyatt wasn't the only observer of the horror. Also looking on from above was the bull pen supervisor who, by operating a pulley system involving heavy-duty ropes, had just released the animal from its stall into the passageway that divided the pens. As the creature unleashed its savagery, the dimness of the corridor was pervaded by shafts of bright sunlight as the steel door leading to the arena was pulled open. Outside, the second matador adjusted his black hat for the final time, tightened his grip on the cape, placed himself behind a shelter close to the perimeter of the ring and took a deep breath. His trusted aides had warned him the next bull, like the first, came from fighting stock specially bred for size and strength, and was armed with horns as thick as a man's wrist. The matador's eyes, and those of every spectator, focused on the open doorway. The sense of anticipation was palpable.

Then, in an instant, the mood was shattered. The trumpeters of the brass band, previously vibrant and harmonious, ceased playing in dissonant disarray and the crowd, hugely expectant, was stunned into silence as the lifeless, brutalised body of Viktor Makarov was thrust into the ring like a rag-doll by horns soaked in blood. The creature, whose shiny black hide was spattered with gore, seemed to have tired of its frenzied onslaught. Its big dark eyes stared at the corpse lying at its feet, then the animal lifted its head to look around the arena. As if at an unseen signal, the massed observers of the horrifying spectacle started to react. Many were traumatised. Only one man in the amphitheatre had any cause for satisfaction. As he headed swiftly for the exit, he took consolation in avenging the death of a spirited young woman whom fate had dealt an accursed hand. She had deserved better.

The distant drone of an engine alerted Lucas Tait to the imminent arrival of his visitor. By the time the motor racing supremo had climbed the circular teak stairs to the main deck, the seaplane was within a couple of hundred metres of the yacht 5 miles off Puerto Banús in southern Spain. Approaching from the starboard side, the single-engine aircraft descended and skimmed the tranquil waves of the Mediterranean before coming to rest, the floats mounted under the fuselage keeping it buoyant. A motorised dinghy was despatched from the Nassau-registered vessel to collect the only passenger on the four-seater craft, which was bobbing gently on the water twenty metres away. The tall, lithe figure was quickly transferred to the yacht and the two men made their way to the privacy of the main saloon.

"Well, Jack, you old son of a gun, you did it!" said the beaming FS owner, filling two crystal champagne flutes from a chilled bottle of vintage Dom Perignon and handing one to the man who had just boarded. "This is a time for celebration."

Wyatt took the glass and nodded. "I guess so. You got what you wanted."

"And paid for!" retorted Tait. He looked closely at the other man. "You don't sound like a guy who's come out the right side of a tough assignment."

"It was another contract and it's mission completed. That's all that matters."

"You're right there." He motioned to Wyatt to sit on one of two black leather sofas while he settled on the other. "So it turned out to be something of a blood-bath."

"Yeah. Makarov was never going quietly but he could not have imagined it would end that way."

"Poetic justice, I call it."

"You could say that."

"Few will shed a tear over him."

A wistful expression crossed Wyatt's face. "I also had a private score to settle. I got payback for one of his victims, someone who helped me. But it doesn't change anything – she still lost out big-time."

"And the Serb?"

"I had to take him out. It was him or me."

Tait's mood changed and there was an urgency in his voice. "You won't be surprised to know the Spanish police have launched a major investigation and it's put an unwelcome spotlight on FS again after an already tragic season."

"That was bound to happen."

"Jack, we need to get you outta here, pronto. I've arranged your escape route – the seaplane will take you close to the southern coast of Portugal, where a speedboat will put you ashore at a secluded beach. A driver will be waiting to transport you to a remote airfield where you'll board a small aircraft that will fly you across the Channel to an isolated airstrip in Kent. From there you'll be driven to London, where you can lie low for a while before catching a flight back to the States. We've used both runways before; they're off the beaten track and it means you'll avoid immigration controls. Got it?"

Wyatt nodded and Tait continued. "That just leaves one outstanding matter." Putting his flute on a glass-topped coffee table, he stood up and, reaching behind the sofa, pulled out a large black-leather briefcase. "Inside is half a million bucks, the second tranche of payment." The FS owner opened it to reveal its tightly packed contents. "You've earned it!"

The Californian gave a cursory glance at the notes. "This is sure gonna take some laundering."

"You could have been paid through staged bank transfers to various offshore accounts as happened before, but this time you wanted cash."

"You know something, Lucas, in a troubled world perhaps I just need the reassurance of seeing and touching Uncle Sam's currency."

"Well, you've made enough dough this time to take it easy for a while."

Wyatt frowned. "It's not about the money – never was. It was always more than that." He got to his feet and moved across the room, staring out of a porthole before turning to face Tait. "I'm not sure I want to stay in this game any longer."

"Don't tell me your conscience is giving you a hard time."

"It's possible, but maybe I've just had enough. My line of work takes its toll in other ways – on a personal level."

"How d'you mean?"

"There's no one to confide in. How could I share my life with someone and keep dark secrets?"

"Sounds like you've become a lone wolf."

"I've had to, it comes with the territory. Don't get me wrong – I've made a good living out of what I do but it's got a hell of a downside and I'm not sure I've still got the motivation."

"Only you can figure that out."

"Yeah, it's my call. I know that." Wyatt downed the remnants of his champagne then eyed his compatriot. "When death stares you in the face, blinks, then moves on, you change."

Tait nodded. "I guess if you get that close it's gonna leave a mark." He glanced at his watch. "You need to be outta here. The sooner you're on your way, the better." He closed the briefcase and handed it to his fellow countryman. "Remember, Jack, this is our secret, and ours alone. No one must ever know. We still have to trust each other."

Wyatt allowed himself a wry smile. "Lucas, I told you once that in this business I only trust myself. I'm not sure I can do that anymore." They shook hands and three minutes later, Wyatt was strapping himself into the front passenger seat of the seaplane as the pilot turned over the 220-horsepower engine. The aircraft began to move, slowly at first then picking up speed, leaving a trail of white foaming water in its wake. On the main deck of the yacht, Lucas Tait raised his binoculars and watched as the seaplane's floats lifted from the Mediterranean. Once it had gained sufficient height, the pilot gradually turned the fixed-wing craft around and headed westwards, passing within a hundred metres of the ship.

Looking down as dusk descended, Wyatt could still make out the figure of the vessel's owner. Placing the briefcase on his lap, he squeezed the two metal studs at either end of the container and it snapped open. A glance at the pilot confirmed he was preoccupied with the instrument panel as he put the seaplane on course for the Portuguese coast. The American unfastened his seatbelt and reached for the hydraulically operated passenger door opener.

"What the hell are you doing?" barked the man at the controls.

Wyatt ignored him and hurled the briefcase and its contents through the opening, then rapidly activated the door-closure system.

Tait was still focused on the plane. He swallowed hard and his fingers clenched the binoculars as the briefcase plummeted towards the sea, followed by a cascade of 5000 one-hundred-dollar notes drifting through the air. "What's the guy playing at?" he muttered.

Wyatt secured his restraining belt again then looked across at the pilot. "I guess I raised your blood pressure back there."

"Say that again."

"Don't ask me why. It was something I had to do."

The yacht was out of sight now. The American leant back in the contoured beige leather seat, closed his eyes and felt an overpowering sense of relief. The short lives and gruesome deaths of two women still haunted him. Poignant memories were all he had and his anger at their early loss would never dim. And the violent events of the day stayed with him, too. But as he pondered the futility of the past, he sensed a different future beckoned. And maybe, just maybe, it would be a better one.

FS Championship – Final Driver Standings

Position	Name	Team	Points
1	Nick Stallard*	Gorton Racing	46
2	Raffa Rodriguez	El Oro Racing	45
3	Yuri Petrenko	Makarov Racing	43
4	Dev Pavani	El Oro Racing	29
5	Philippe Guiscard*	Drogan Racing	28
6	Kate Lockhart	Gorton Racing	23
7	Dan Seton	Seton Racing	13
8	Wang Hu	Seton Racing	11
9	Ricardo Gonzalez	Akron Racing	6
10	Alex Orlovsky	Makarov Racing	3
10	Otto Werner*	Drogan Racing	3
12	Phil Scolton	Drogan Racing	2
	Pete Maitland*	Akron Racing	0
	Luigi Corazza	Gorton Racing	0
	Al Boyd	Akron Racing	0
	Dmitry Baikov	Makarov Racing	0
	Janos Varady	Drogan Racing	0
	Tony Faulkner	Gorton Racing	0

*Posthumous

FS Championship – Final Constructor Standings

Position	Team	Points
1	El Oro Racing	74
2	Gorton Racing	69
3	Makarov Racing	46
4	Drogan Racing	33
5	Seton Racing	24
6	Akron Racing	6

Acknowledgements

My research for this book was extensive. It involved travel to numerous countries across the globe to ensure authenticity in description of far-flung locations. For their hospitality, and giving generously of their time to drive me around the Western Cape in South Africa, I am very much indebted to Peggy and Jeremy Wynne, of Kleinmond.

I am equally grateful to Mary Evans, now residing in Australia, but formerly of Nelson on New Zealand's South Island. She, too, gave freely of her time and home as I explored that part of the Antipodes bordering Tasman Bay as part of my fact-finding quest.

My thanks, also, to Dave Maree, formerly of the South African Police Service, who was Commander of Detectives at Kleinmond in the Western Cape. His willingness to give me the benefit of his many years of duty in the Service, and sharing his thoughts on crime in the region together with his expertise on handguns, is much appreciated.

I must also express my gratitude to Lynn Jones, Emeritus Professor of Pathology at the University of Birmingham, for sound advice on all matters pathological. Venturing into a branch of medical science as a lay person is fraught with difficulty so I am extremely grateful for professional guidance in this sphere.

Many thanks, also, to my son, Nick – no mean writer and a published author himself – for constructive suggestions made during the early stages of this project.

Finally, or should it be firstly, I am hugely appreciative of the steadfast support of my Dutch partner, Rony. Her unstinting encouragement and belief in my book made the writing process – which has its own demands and can be arduous and exasperating at times – so much more tolerable. Ontzettend bedankt, liefje.

About the Author

David Setchfield lives in Cardiff and had a long career as a journalist. He worked as a newspaper reporter at the Cardiff-based *Western Mail* and *South Wales Echo*, and then joined BBC Wales, where he undertook various editorial and broadcasting roles. *Redlining* is his first novel.